The Cross and the Arrow

Other books by ALBERT MALTZ

The Cross and the Arrow

Albert Maltz

Introduction by Patrick Chura

CALDER

CALDER PUBLICATIONS
an imprint of

ALMA BOOKS LTD
Thornton House
Thornton Road
Wimbledon Village
London SW19 4NG
United Kingdom
www.calderpublications.com

The Cross and the Arrow first published by Little, Brown in 1944
This edition first published by Calder Publications in 2024

© The Estate of Albert Maltz, 1944, 2024

Introduction © Patrick Chura

Front cover: David Wardle

ISBN: 978-0-7145-5078-7

Contents

The Cross and the Arrow
  Introduction   VII

  The Cross and the Arrow   I

  Prologue   7
    Part One: *The Investigation*   II
    Part Two: *The Wrath of Jehovah*   179
    Part Three: *The Vision of Jakob Frisch*   295

  Notes   383

Introduction

Literature wasn't Albert Maltz's first love – nor even his second. Before the writing of novels came boxing and philosophy.

Both of Maltz's parents were Jewish immigrants. His mother, Lena, was born in Poland and brought to New York as an infant in 1876. As a girl she dreamt of becoming a teacher, but was forced to quit school in her early teens to work in a clothing factory, where she contracted a debilitating eye infection. Maltz's father Bernard arrived from Lithuania at the age of fourteen in the 1890s. He worked as a street pedlar, grocer's boy and house painter before becoming in mid-life a prosperous building contractor.

Albert was the youngest of three brothers, all born in Brooklyn. At the age of three he witnessed anti-Semitism when his father borrowed $1,000 to move the family out of a Williamsburg slum into the middle-class Flatbush neighbourhood. As his father and siblings unloaded belongings, they were attacked by a gang of boys shouting anti-Jewish slurs and throwing stones, one of which broke through a window and cut Albert's lip. He never forgot the episode, and said it made him sensitive to injustice.

In childhood he was inspired by real and imaginary family stories about brave outsiders who fought back against bigotry. In adolescence he became passionate about boxing because of his father's advice that "a Jew must learn to fight".

As a teenager Maltz was more of an athlete than a scholar. His mother's eye ailment led her to assume that her sons also had weak eyesight and should avoid reading. There were few books in the Maltz household, and Albert was even forbidden to have a library card. But his fear of failure made him a good student.

He showed enough promise at Brooklyn's Erasmus High School to be admitted to Columbia University, where he majored in philosophy. He made the tennis and swimming teams and trained as a Golden Gloves pugilist, but the first time he got a B on a philosophy exam, he quit all sports. With a professor he worshipped, he studied Plato, Aristotle and Santayana, taking course after course, searching for the truths of life. He felt as though he'd come to a well and was thirsty, and all he had to do was drink.

As a boy Maltz had been introduced to the New York Yiddish theatre. In his free time at Columbia he attended the best modern plays and dabbled in the art of the short story. Gradually a goal dawned on him: a writing career that would enable him to apply what he'd learnt about philosophy – logic, ethics, epistemology – as a tool to fight evil and celebrate mankind's search for meaning through moral action.

The Cross and the Arrow is Albert Maltz's masterpiece and the fulfilment of that ambition.

Set in a village in Nazi Germany, the book explores the psychology of Willi Wegler, a humble forty-two-year-old industrial labourer whose wife and son have been killed in Hitler's war. Though Wegler is decorated with a German Service Cross, he is inwardly sickened by both Hitler's genocide and the complicity of his fellow citizens in Third Reich brutalities. Wracked with guilt, Wegler suddenly betrays his country in a stunning gesture of protest and self-sacrifice: while an air raid is in progress, he fashions an enormous arrow out of hay in an open field, then ignites it as a flaming signal to direct British bombers to the site of the camouflaged tank factory where he works.

The novel opens at the precise moment of the protagonist's act of heroism. At 11 p.m. on an August night in 1942, with British bombers thundering overhead, Wegler, "a German citizen of German parents", touches match to hay and justifies his existence. By 1 a.m. the saboteur lies in the factory hospital, near death from a gory abdomen wound inflicted when his seditious act was interrupted by an armed SS patrol. There is no possibility of his recovery.

"Action from principle, the perception and the performance of right, changes things and relations," wrote the transcendentalist philosopher Henry David Thoreau, "it is essentially revolutionary. It not only divides states and churches, it divides families – ay, it divides the *individual*, separating the diabolical in him from the divine."

Having dissociated himself from the diabolical, Wegler is ready to die: he struggles to live only long enough to know whether his signal to the British bombers has produced its intended result: "Had the British pilots seen the arrow? And would they return?... He *wanted to know*!"

The book's action takes place over the next twelve hours, during which Wegler drifts in and out of consciousness, pretending he is comatose to thwart his would-be interrogators. While his life passes before him in vivid flashbacks, the world is frantic with an investigation into his treason and with hurried preparations for the renewed bombing raid that must now be anticipated.

Maltz is deeply interested in the motives of Wegler's civil disobedience, its long foreground in factors personal and political. What is the breaking point of a conscience? Whence the willpower to turn against one's country?

The view of Germans as inherently wicked – which in the novel is espoused by Hermann Zoder, the slightly unpredictable and mentally fragile doctor who looks after Willi as he lies unconscious in the hospital – represents an ethical controversy that fascinated Albert Maltz. In the 1940s, the fact that the German nation accepted the crimes of the Nazi war machine gave rise to an international debate. Baron Robert Vansittart, a British diplomat, famously embraced a theory (which became known as "Vansittartism") that Germany was addicted to war and predisposed to follow murderous authoritarians. Vansittart proposed forcing the German people to comply with a programme that would re-educate them. If this plan failed, their extermination as a race would be warranted.

Among the many messages of *The Cross and the Arrow* is a refutation of the deterministic beliefs of the English baron – an assertion that Vansittartism is not a theory about race, but a racist theory. "As a matter of principle," Maltz explained late in his life in interviews with biographer Jack Salzman, "I could not accept a racist judgement about any people."

Maltz also told Salzman that he wanted the novel to send messages about the racist history of the United States. He hoped the emphasis given to Third Reich chattel slaves in Wegler's awakening would prompt readers at home to compare the Nazi system with America's own apartheid. Progressives like Maltz were keenly aware, for example, that Hitler studied American lynching and admired the racial terrors of the Jim Crow South, and that in significant ways it was Birmingham that taught Berlin.

Abjuring simple formulae and instead dealing profoundly with central issues of humanity, Albert Maltz produced an absorbing, intensely dramatic philosophical novel about the soul of man – its ghastly corruption and its capacity for redemption. The "motor power" of the story, Maltz asserted, "is supplied by a moral quest."

Upon its release in 1944 critics universally praised *The Cross and the Arrow*, citing Willi Wegler as evidence of man's capacity for good. In *New Masses*, Samuel Sillen called the book "one of the truly outstanding literary achievements of the war period", a work that gave Maltz "new stature" as an artist.

Another endorsement came from The Council on Books in Wartime, an organization that promoted the use of novels to educate the American people and clarify war aims in the fight against world fascism. The Council speedily issued *The Cross and the Arrow* in a pocket-sized Armed Forces edition of 140,000 copies for distribution to GIs in Europe and the Pacific.

With the end of the World War and the beginning of Cold-War anti-Communist hysteria, Maltz's "stature" was quickly forgotten. In 1947 the US House Un-American Activities Committee came knocking at his door, armed with a subpoena. For refusing to cooperate with the congressional investigation into alleged Communist subversion, Maltz was sentenced to a year in prison and blacklisted.

At the height of McCarthyism in 1953, the United States Information Service issued an internal directive stating that "all Communist authors" were henceforth banned from public libraries and USIS information centres. Among the books that were removed from library shelves both overseas and in the US was *The Cross and the Arrow.*

This new edition restores the novel to its rightful place.

Patrick Chura, University of Akron

The Cross and the Arrow

To
DOCTOR BERNARD ROBBINS*

Many mistakes have been made in the world which now one would hardly think a child could make. How many crooked, narrow, impassable blind alleys, leading far off the track, has mankind chosen in the effort to reach the eternal verity!... And how many times, even when guided by understanding that has been given them from Heaven, they have managed even then to halt and go astray, have managed in the light of day to get into the impassable jungle, have managed to throw a blinding fog again over one another's eyes and, lured by will-o'-the-wisps, have succeeded in reaching the brink of the abyss, only to ask one another with horror: "Where is the way out? Where is the road?"*

— NIKOLAI GOGOL

Roaming in thought over the Universe, I saw the little that is Good steadily hastening towards immortality,
And the vast all that is called Evil I saw hastening to merge itself and become lost and dead.*

— WALT WHITMAN

Prologue

On a night in August 1942, the sky was dark above a small village in Germany. There was no moon, and a dry, hot wind stirred the field grasses. Although the hour was late and the countryside itself was serene and still, many in the community were awake. Men, women and children lay in their beds, most of them at ease, but some incorrigibly nervous, listening and waiting. A harsh metallic warning had just sounded, as it did almost nightly in this vicinity. These sleepless ones knew that the decent night quiet would be soon violated by a familiar hornets' drone – of British bombers, passing fast and high overhead, passing with fury to a savage destination.

Exactly then, in a field a few miles from the village, a catastrophe occurred to which there were few witnesses – an arrow of burning hay flared towards the sky. It did not burn very long. The burst of flame was accompanied by a woman's high scream; it was followed by hoarse cries, and then by rifle shots... but by the time the planes had passed, the hot silence of the August night was supreme again, and the field crickets and night insects held normal sway.

It was of no shattering importance, this affair: a minor hen track in the record of a people. Nevertheless, despite its obscurity, it involved the personal histories of a number of men and women, and the bitter history of the world for quite a number of years...

BOOK ONE

THE INVESTIGATION
An August night in the year 1942, from 11 p.m. until 6 a.m.

Chapter 1

There was the village, which we may call the village of X, and there were the surrounding farms, and so it had been for as far back as there was memory. Into this pastoral German community, seemingly overnight, came a factory. A few miles from the village there were a good many acres of wooded land. As a housewife disembowels a chicken, stuffs it with alien victuals and yet succeeds in serving it up so that the outward appearance of the bird betrays nothing of the transformation within, so, in the space of two months, an army of workmen had disembowelled the copse, stuffed it with two dozen factory buildings and more than a hundred bunkhouses – and yet preserved the aspect of a wood. The hawks from Britain, who flew over it regularly, regarded it without suspicion. The German War Ministry had photographed the wood before the transformation began; when it was completed – when from its quiet heart an unending phalanx of tanks clattered over a camouflaged road to a railhead thirty miles away – the wood appeared as it always had to the eye of a bomber.

At first the presence of the factory had frightened the local residents. With the arrival of the workers a secret had come out: that the plant had been formerly in Düsseldorf. Factories are not rolling stones: where man builds them, they stay – everyone knows that. This factory had moved because Düsseldorf had ceased to be a manufacturing city: it had become an embattled front-line trench. Such being the case, the villagers enquired uneasily how long it would be until their own little community had its guts blown out by the damned Stirlings.*

They enquired, but of course only in whispers, and amongst themselves. It was the most idle of enquiries, since the factory was there whether they approved or no. Only the British could make this German factory move a second time.

The British had not made it move. In the seven months since the plant had begun to operate, the villagers, the farmers and the workers within the compound had learnt to their satisfaction that they were thoroughly secure. At night the only inconvenience was the rigid blackout. Several times a week, depending upon the weather and the inscrutable plans of London, they would hear the air-raid warning and rouse out of sleep for a moment; they would be snoring again with complacency before the drone of the last bomber had passed out of hearing. And so the factory came to be regarded as a good thing, not an evil. For every backward mother who complained because her daughter's belly had swollen under the attentions of an SS guard, there were two tradespeople or farmers who had received work or a crumb of benefit from the alien presence. That, in any society, is a fair percentage.

But on this night in August, all things hovered on the brink of incalculable disaster. The planes were heard at 11 p.m. At thirty seconds before the hour, Willi Wegler, drop-forge man, German citizen of German parents, held an ersatz match to an arrow of hay pointed towards the factory.

2

1 a.m.

In the factory hospital a blurred shadow appeared behind the glass partition of the door that led to the operating room. Julius Baumer, Labour Front Leader of the plant, coughed slightly to relieve the tension in his throat and dropped his cigarette butt to the floor. The door opened, a stretcher table appeared. It moved towards him, for a moment ghost-driven, as though in a Surrealist painting. In fascination, but with a painful foreboding in his heart, he fixed his eyes upon its inert burden. The nurse appeared. Quietly, evenly, she propelled the table towards the unpainted pine doors at the opposite end of the corridor.

From the outside, even though the nearest building was several hundred yards away, came the pound and roar, the crackle and clang, of the plant at work. But here the clinical hush was so intense that Baumer tiptoed forwards.

In automatic deference to his position, although it went against the grain of her training, the middle-aged nurse stopped. Baumer peered down at the swathed mummy on the table, seeking the face. Only the shut eyes, the big, fleshy nose, were visible. A drop of sweat hung idiotically to the tip of the nose, but there was no sound of breathing.

"Alive?" he asked hoarsely.

The nurse, Sister Wollweber, nodded.

"How long before—"

Deferentially she interrupted. "Would you speak to the doctor, please? It's necessary to…" She nodded towards the ward by way of explanation, and at the same time commenced propelling the table forward again.

Baumer walked quietly down the corridor to the open door of the operating room. He called softly. "Zoder?"

"Yes?"

"Baumer."

"Come in, come in." A slight, absurd laugh. "I'm very curious about this."

Baumer stepped inside, smiling faintly. Invariably Zoder climaxed his sentences with a foolish cackle, as though it were a form of punctuation.

"Where are you, doctor?" He stopped, uttering an involuntary gasp. His stomach rolled. The room stank horribly of ether, blood, faeces.

"In here. Second door to your left. The dressing room." The doctor laughed again, to no purpose. "How did that lad get shot, hey?"

Lean and hairy, Zoder was standing over a sink rubbing his chest with a washcloth. He was wearing only his patched underwear pants. His seamed, ugly face greeted Baumer with a foolish grin, as usual. "Excuse my dishabille." He jerked his head towards his operating gown, which hung like a wilted rag from a wall hook. "When a butcher performs, he sweats. When he sweats, he becomes odorous. When he becomes odorous, the girls don't fancy him even for a smuggled pound of Black Market coffee. Or have you heard that stale one before?… And what's the matter? You catch a bullet, too?"

Baumer shut the door. "That God-awful stink in here." He was holding a handkerchief over his nose.

Zoder guffawed. "Why, Baumer… my dear man… my dear sir… you are a positive lily. I grant you that according to the best medical procedure the scrubbing-up should already have begun. In wartime, of course, we make sacrifices. But meanwhile, speaking as a friend, as one blood comrade to another, you amaze me. Not like this smell – this juicy flavour of the lower bowel? You should stick your nose near a ripe cancer of the feminine mammary. That would—"

"Shut up!" said Baumer with marked irritation. "Just shut up." He kicked the door closed.

The grin vanished from Zoder's face. "I didn't mean—"

"It's all right. Only skip your jabber tonight, please. I'm very tired, and I have no time to waste."

"Of course. Beg pardon," said Zoder. He laughed lightly, to no purpose.

Baumer put his handkerchief back into his pocket and pulled out a cigarette. His face remained severe, but he was grinning inwardly. He was fond of Zoder. Zoder was an original, an eccentric with scrambled eggs in his head. But Zoder was also the jewel of his heart. At a time when most surgeons were at the front, to have someone who could handle the daily sick calls and factory accidents with competence was to be unspeakably blessed. Even if he was a madcap.

"Well, doctor," he began, "some questions... No, don't stop dressing. I want to get out of this smell."

"I sympathize. At Heidelberg... my first anatomy—"

"Wegler..." the other interrupted. "What about *him*?"

"I'm really proud. Modestly speaking, I was superb. A penetrating abdominal wound. The bullet cut part of the colon – three inches from the appendix, to be precise. Peritoneum torn – colon ruptured, as we of the butcher's profession say. Would you like the bullet? I kept it for you. You can wear it on your watch chain. By the way, how did he get plugged?"

"How soon can I talk to him?"

"Talk? My dear Baumer! Let me explain. You appreciate the nature of the peritoneum?"

"No."

"Briefly, a sac holding the stomach, intestines and other titbits. To pierce the peritoneum is in all cases to violate Nature at her most delicate. Result? Acute shock. Inevitably. The patient is a powerful man, great physical development, musculature, et cetera. Yet a transfusion was necessary even to perform the operation. Another may be called for. I have already ordered a drip infusion of gl—"

"When can I talk to him?"

"I simply don't know."

"When will he be out of the anaesthetic?"

"Two or three hours."

"I'll be back then."

"Impossible."

"Why? Don't you understand? I must talk to him. *Must!* Never mind your shirt. Throw on your coat and come outside."

Zoder nodded, and for a moment gazed intently at the Party Leader. The doctor's eyes were curious. They were a lustreless grey; they didn't seem right for his eternally grinning face, his babbling and his laughter. He picked up his jacket. "I'll admit it," he exclaimed with a burst of glee as they crossed to the corridor, "there's no doubt of it: my sanitary operating room is definitely pervaded by an essence of cat vomit." He shut the door behind them.

Baumer drew a deep breath. "Why *can't* I talk to him?"

"In cases like these it's two or three days at least before the physician knows if the patient will even live. There's a considerable danger of sepsis. I've left a drainage tube. At best Wegler can't be seen by anyone for a week. Not even you."

Baumer smiled. He was a handsome man – blond, fair-skinned, with clean, strong, chiselled features. He stood very erect in his well-tailored, blue serge suit, slim and fit, and ordinarily one would not have guessed him to be close to forty. But the smile compounded his years. Of a sudden, with that small, unhappy smile, he changed from a handsome youth to a worn, driven man – to the Nazi functionary he was, with bitter lines cut fine around his mouth, to a man with a hard mouth and even harder eyes.

"You don't understand," he exclaimed in a low, furious tone. "Do you think I care if this patient of yours" – he spat the word out as though it were dirty phlegm – "gets well?"

"No?"

"There's a People's Court waiting for him. His goddamned head is going to be separated from his goddamned neck. With a rusty butcher knife, I hope, so it won't be quick."

Astonishment turned the doctor's ugly face into a comic mask. He stared down at Baumer with his mouth gaping open.

Baumer grinned at him, but without amusement. "Yes," he said, "*exactly*." Then, irrelevantly, "By God, for six months I've been wondering where I saw you before, Zoder. Now I know. When I was a student, in a medieval woodcut. A court jester to some king or other. That's just what your ugly mug is like, do you know that?"

"But why?" asked Zoder. "What did Wegler do? Man, just yesterday… He's the one you gave a—"

"Yes," Baumer interrupted bitterly, "a War Service Cross! It had to be him. I've been a functionary in the Labour Front off and on since '33, and I never made a blunder to equal it. This Wegler, this 'exemplary German worker', if I remember my own speech correctly, lit a fire tonight."

"What do you mean?"

"And succeeded very nicely, thank you. In a field just the other side of the foundry. Like the exemplary German worker he is, he very carefully fashioned an enormous arrow out of hay – and then poured on kerosene. When the British bastards came over, he touched it off. How do you like it? Pointing towards the factory, of course."

Zoder didn't answer. He stared, speechless.

"Why do I want to talk to him? Now you know."

"So!" the doctor exclaimed softly. "The honeymoon is over! Now the bombings begin."

"Maybe not," Baumer replied. "We got to the fire before it reached its full height. Maybe the Britishers didn't see it."

"Him!" said Zoder. "Why *him*? What sort of man—"

"Exactly! Is he operating for British Intelligence? Or with some Red scum in the factory? *What?* You understand?"

"I see," said Zoder, with his silly laugh. "The question now becomes, '*Who is Wegler, what is he?*'"

"What can you do to bring him around? You realize how much depends on you, Zoder? If he's part of an organized group in the factory, who knows what they'll do next? I tell you frankly: in the calculations of the War Ministry the continued security of factories like ours... Damn it, you know how they're beginning to bomb the Ruhr and the Rhineland. From now on half of our national production may depend on these camouflaged plants. We don't have the time to build into the hills any more. That was peacetime luxury."

"But please," said Zoder, "you mustn't put the security of the factory on me. It depends on the patient's condition."

"You can give him some drug to wake him up, can't you? A stimulant?"

"I'll have to wait until the ether wears off. I can tell nothing until then."

"All right... Now look: it's already after one. If the British saw the fire, the damage is done. Either they'll do reconnaissance and bomb us when they're ready... or they may come back tomorrow night for a quick raid. But if they didn't see the fire, then someone else – working with Wegler – may try this again. That's what I want to stop. And that's where you come in. We have about twenty hours until tomorrow night. This situation has got to be under control by then."

"I understand. I won't budge from Wegler's cot. As soon as he becomes conscious, I'll call you."

Baumer turned as an SS man in the black, skull-and-crossbones uniform of the Elite Guard came in from the outside. He was a brute of a lad, with the jaw and jowl of a finely bred English bull.

"Yes?" Baumer asked curtly.

"Gestapo Commissar Kehr has come. In your office, sir."

"No one else? You mean they only sent one man?"

"That's all, sir."

Baumer frowned. "Does he look intelligent, at least?"

The SS man gargled a little and remained silent. The question involved a judgement about a superior he was not accustomed to make. Also, he was afraid. Either way such judgements could lead to trouble.

"Never mind," said Baumer with bland scorn. To Zoder: "One reminder... Keep your eyes open and your trap shut. If there are consequences tomorrow night, everything is finished. If not..."

"The morale of the workers... I understand," said Zoder, nodding energetically. He waited until Baumer and his aide had left. Then he hurried down the corridor to the ward.

3

As Baumer made his way along the rough path that led from the hospital to the Administration Building, he did something quite extraordinary. In the middle of a stride he stopped walking, so that Latzelburger, the SS man, had to spring to one side in order to avoid stepping on him. At the same moment he exclaimed half aloud, in a thoroughly astonished voice, "I'm an exhausted man."

"Sir?"

Baumer kept silent. Latzelburger, positive he had heard incorrectly, not certain whether Baumer had been speaking to him or not, fidgeted uneasily for a moment and then repeated again, "Sir? You said something?"

"Get along to the commissar. Tell him I'm coming."

"Yes, sir."

Baumer watched until the black uniform had disappeared, then he took out a handkerchief and wiped his forehead. His involuntary exclamation had surprised him quite as much as it had Latzelburger. More than that, it had left him a bit frightened. It was true: at this moment he was a thoroughly exhausted man, who wanted to crawl off into a hole somewhere and be left alone.

For a moment he remained where he was, thinking. Finally, as though he were making an impersonal, organizational decision, he said to himself, "Julius, sit down calmly and think things over a minute. Kehr can wait."

He fumbled for a match. He held it carefully in the cup of his hand and searched out a tree stump a yard away. Then he lit a cigarette and sat down. "Now, what the hell's the matter with you, man?" he asked himself sharply. "Look at it straight. No dodging."

What worried Baumer was the knowledge that his exhaustion was not physical. The week before, feeling ill, he had gone to Zoder for a check-up. Zoder, grinning his usual, silly grin, and getting off his usual silly joke, had pronounced that he was in fine shape – so fine he must be eating off the Black Market. Zoder was a fool, but Baumer trusted him as a doctor. Yet if he were physically well, what was the matter with him? At the time Zoder had suggested that his fatigue might come from worry: "Psychological exhaustion induced by anxiety." Baumer had dismissed the idea. Yet now, as he reflected on his behaviour over *l'affaire* Wegler, he was not so sure.

Why had Wegler's sabotage upset him so profoundly? It was too simple to answer that Wegler was the last man in the factory he would have suspected of treason. That might surprise him – why should it disorganize him? When he had been standing over Wegler, watching the man tear at his blood-soaked overalls and roll around on the earth, he had been possessed by a ghastly urge to leap on him with both boots and stamp his brains out. The desire to kill with brutishness had been almost overwhelming! But still... it was more normal than what had followed. Why had he done that? The British planes were at fifteen thousand feet at least. Yet he had raised both fists over his head, yelling at the top of his voice: "You filth! If you think you can count on traitors, you're mistaken. For every bomb, we'll give you back a thousand. Before we get through with you, you'll wish you'd never been born!" He had shouted it in a blur of fury, and very absurd it all was, too. But why?

Baumer flicked away his cigarette in a gesture of impatience. He was becoming more and more annoyed with himself the closer he came to realizing what was really wrong. (Zoder, the fool, had been very keen that time.) He had not yelled at the British planes because he was under the illusion that they could hear him – nor had he done so for the edification of the SS men. It was clear that he had been roaring in the dark like a small, quite terrified boy who hopes to frighten away his fears. This piece of sabotage was the climax to a series of disturbing events, and now that he faced the question honestly, he knew exactly what they were. He was a worried man, and he had become so increasingly in these last months, and that was the core of it.

Baumer spat and reached for another cigarette. He was very thought-ful now, and angry with himself. Either he was psychologically fit for his job or he wasn't. If nothing else, he'd be honest. There were too many hangers-on in the Party already. If he was slipping, he'd be off to the front with a gun in his hand.

He had it there, of course, in thinking of the front. The resistance of the Russians had been the first of the events to shake him. The earlier campaigns had brought quick victory and the expectation of peace. But from the beginning the damn Russian war had been like a fever: one could see the drain on the body politic from month to month. For the first time in two years of war, rations had been cut, and morale – the key to everything – had begun to drop perceptibly. He had felt it in his marrow: a chill, a pall amongst the workers that no victories seemed to counteract.

And now, finally, the Wegler sabotage. Ever since the factory had moved from Düsseldorf, there had been little things – increased scrap from the production line, tools breaking, a clogged water pipe – little things one couldn't pin down. He had kept his judgement in reserve, but he remem-bered that in Düsseldorf such things had not happened. Now, with the Wegler business, it was too clear that there were active enemies amongst the workers.

"Exhaustion induced by anxiety..." Of course he was anxious. Who wouldn't be? He wasn't one of those naive fanatics the Party pro-duced nowadays amongst youngsters. Events had their logic, and no government could rule for long unless it satisfied its people. To ask for sacrifice was all very well – but there was a limit to it. Even he was getting tired of sacrifices. Where was his idealism of 1929? Where was the promise that had been in his heart when he joined the Party as a young architect?

Baumer rose suddenly from the stump. He kicked viciously at the earth with the point of his shoe. "All right, my lad," he told himself angrily, "no more of this crap! You have doubts, you face problems, you feel tired. Meanwhile, the British may be mapping out a party for tomorrow night, and that bastard Wegler may have a whole under-ground organization you know nothing about. Baumer, you're scum, you're a whining little toad. Pull yourself together – stop complaining, go do your job!"

He walked quickly out onto the path.

4

1:40 a.m.

The pretty, sleepy-eyed girl at the switchboard, who had been routed out of her bed in town by an SS man in a Party car, sat up energetically as Baumer entered the office.

"No information as yet from District Command, sir."

Baumer nodded without pausing. "Call again in fifteen minutes. Ask for Major Deterle this time." He strode quickly into the inner room.

The Labour Front and Party offices, occupying a wing of the long, one-storey administration building, reflected the primitive level of existence at which everyone connected with the factory had to live. The buildings had been erected hastily, the office furnishings were odds and ends. Baumer, who took pleasure in moderately aesthetic surroundings, never entered his office without wincing. A desk, salvaged from the Düsseldorf bombings, a wooden table from the local school, a few bent files, a picture of Hitler – how different they were from the pre-war appointments! In many ways it gave him the feeling of the early days of the movement – and that was not pleasant. To operate on a hand-to-mouth basis when a party is on the way up – that's natural and even exciting. But to face the same thing ten years later, after a flush period in between, makes for anxiety.

Gestapo Commissar Kehr, occupying the lone easy chair in the room, jumped to his feet with a smile and an outstretched hand. Since the top half of his skull was narrower than his firm, florid jowls, Baumer received the instant impression of a small ham on display in a butcher shop. Even more depressing to him was the neat Adolf Hitler moustache, which was clearly of the 1933 bumper crop. He knew Kehr's type thoroughly, and it made him wince with irritation. He had hoped for at least two first-class Gestapo men – instead, they had shipped him a lone wheelhorse, who would have only the limited shrewdness of his kind.

"Commissar Kehr?"

"*Heil Hitler!*"

"I'm Julius Baumer – Labour Front Leader, also Party Section Leader." With a weary grin: "Take your choice."

They shook hands. "No, he is not even intelligent," Baumer decided. He sat down with an audible sigh and gazed resignedly at the commissar's good-humoured, porcine face. Kehr was about fifty, a burly man with dark, neatly parted hair and handsome brown eyes. His tweed suit was rumpled, baggy at the knees and clearly a pre-war item. "How he must long for a uniform!" Baumer thought disparagingly. "His kind always does."

If Baumer was not impressed by Commissar Kehr, neither was Kehr with Baumer. "Aha... a Party fanatic," Kehr had already decided. "His sort you can tell by the smell. One of those long-haired idealists who have to be buttered with slogans. Very well... to smear butter is easy."

"I'm rather surprised to see you alone," Baumer said quietly, in as affable a tone as he could command. "We're facing a serious business here. I asked for two men at least."

Kehr spread his hands with an easy smile. "Do you know what Gestapo Headquarters is like these days? A madhouse. We're bombarded with thousands of calls a day, half of them without foundation. Suspicion is at a premium, you might say. Besides, we're short-handed. Where the army advances, the Gestapo must follow."

"Yes, I know," Baumer replied. "You see – my brother-in-law is on Himmler's staff."*

"Indeed," Kehr exclaimed softly. He blinked a little, but his face remained bland.

"SS Leader Raabe," said Baumer. "Do you know him?"

Kehr shook his head. "The fact is I've been in the Gestapo for only two months. Before that I was a Senior Police Commissar."

"I see," said Baumer politely. "May I ask when you joined the Party?"

Kehr's reply was stiff. "May 1933."

Baumer nodded. "Sit down, won't you? Be comfortable. We have a lot to go over."

Kehr resumed his seat in the easy chair, spread his legs and opened his briefcase. His face remained amiable, but he was furious. He knew exactly what Baumer had been up to: the question about his Party membership was designed to reveal whether or not he was an old Party fighter. His reply automatically placed him in an inferior category – that of a government employee who had been granted special permission to join the Party after the National Socialists took power... And the information about Baumer's brother-in-law – that was merely prestige boasting of the cheapest variety, calculated to let Kehr know which of them had the higher connections.

Very well, he decided now, if Baumer had a brother-in-law on Himmler's staff, then he would tread softly, of course. He could afford to be philosophic about it. The Baumers came and the Baumers went – but it was men like himself who survived in the long run. In thirty years of police work he had served under more chiefs than he could recall, and he had watched official heads roll under political winds while his own remained nicely cushioned on its sturdy neck, thank you. It made him laugh to think of it. The truth was that he – Adolf Kehr – *was* the State. The State wasn't the Kaiser – because the Kaiser was gone. Noske wasn't the State, nor was Ebert or Rathenau.* Everybody knew their names, and nobody had heard of Kehr. But where were they today? A simple question, yet when he put it that way, all things became clear. Yes… He could afford to let a Party radical look down his nose at him. The radicals had their day, and then they invariably vanished. It was men like him who continued right on, providing the State with its backbone.

With these thoughts safely hidden behind a placid face, Kehr unbuttoned his vest and prepared for business. He took a fountain pen from his vest pocket and a large, black notebook from his briefcase. Lastly, he bit off the end of an Italian twist. Chuckling a little, he said, "The only thing I hate worse than these Latin rope ends is not smoking at all. I smoke with an irritated throat and a grieving heart. Some day we'll have to annex Cuba." He stopped laughing and became serious, folding his hands over his modestly corpulent belly. "Well, Baumer, what's the business? They said something about sabotage."

Baumer nodded. He grimaced a little, in the nervous, aimless manner of a tired man, and answered, "A worker here tried to signal the British tonight."

"Signal? How?" Kehr's voice was solid, unperturbed. He might have been a businessman enquiring about a shipment of olives. Since he had cultivated that precise manner over the years, the impression was not accidental. He regarded himself as being in the business of law and order; dramatics were out of place in any business.

"Let me give you the whole thing," said Baumer wearily.

"Good."

"We make medium tanks here, and recondition motors. Turn 'em out like rolls. We used to be in Düsseldorf, but the bombings got too hot. We were moved seven months ago."

"Exactly when?" Kehr interrupted.

Baumer shrugged. "What's the difference?"

"Please…" said Kehr genially, but with an edge of professional pedantry. "I have to be thorough – it's my way."

"Production started the last days of December."

"December '41," Kehr repeated, making a note.

"As you'll see tomorrow, we're situated in a wood. All around us is farming community. Our camouflage people have done a first-rate job. In eight months there've been British planes over here on the average of once or twice a week, lately much more often, but always after another objective. We black out every night, and we sleep snug as you'd like."

Kehr sighed enviously. "Getting to be hell where I am."

Baumer's voice turned a bit hoarse, as it always did when he was angry. "Tonight a worker here tried to signal the planes."

"How?"

"My dear Commissar Kehr, I have no intention of keeping it a secret from you. Do you have to interrupt?"

"Excuse me. Force of habit." Kehr reddened a bit. He was aware that Baumer was getting back at him for his condescension of a moment ago. (One corner of his mind asked: "But why do I feel like fighting him at a time like this? After all, we're both Germans…") "A police officer's way, you know."

Baumer nodded. He had no desire to put the commissar's back up, but on the other hand his nerves were too frayed for him to accept this type of schoolmaster's badgering.

"On the east edge of the factory there's a farm. The owner is a widow, Berthe Lingg. Her hay has recently been cut – that's why it was still in the field, damn it. The saboteur, named Wegler, piled the hay in an arrow about fifty feet long – pointing towards the factory. When the planes came over, he touched it off."

Kehr pursed his lips in a silent whistle; his handsome eyes rolled a little, very thoughtfully. Then he said, "Fresh-cut hay doesn't burn by itself."

Baumer nodded. "He had some kerosene all right. Also, a wind to help him." He paused, frowning. Kehr waited quietly.

"It so happens our SS men were close by on patrol. Last night we had another bit of subversive activity, you see. The woman – Lingg – she yelled. We got there in time to douse the fire before it burned too long… Well, that's it. Now let's have questions."

Kehr was silent for a moment. "I suppose…" he began.

The telephone was buzzing sharply. Baumer jumped up.

"Hello. Yes. Who is this?" His voice became intense and loud: "Listen, Major Deterle, you know what's happened? We've got to have some anti-aircraft set up here by tomorrow night. And plane protection. As much as you can spare." He was silent for a moment, listening. "I'm no expert, major. If you say it's enough, I accept it. But remember what's here. Why can't we have the same number of guns as before?"

Again he was silent. His teeth bit nervously at the flesh of his lower lip.

"All right. You'll rush them?... All right." He hung up, swearing. He turned to Kehr, and his tone was suddenly forlorn. "You'll see, we'll have to move again." For a moment he seemed like a despairing youth who wanted nothing more than to pour out his troubles to an elder. "But how often can we move? And where? Soon there won't be a spot they can't reach. And the time that's lost – the production! When we started here we had more guns around than you could count. After two months, when it was plain we were a secret, the guns were shipped elsewhere – all except one battery, little good that'll do. Now, when we need them again, Deterle tells me we can have only a third as much."

"I sympathize," said Kehr. "But you put it yourself, they're needed elsewhere. I've done some travelling. Believe me, the need is real."

Baumer lit a cigarette with a hand that trembled slightly from fatigue and rage. "You don't know what I've put into this factory to keep morale high these six months, Kehr. My heart's blood, believe me."

Kehr nodded. He was surprised to find himself experiencing a touch of warmth for Baumer. He liked earnestness in a man, devotion to duty. Too many of these Party Leaders were just clever windbags. For the moment, at least, the German in Baumer was predominant, not the doctrine-spouter. He said slowly, "Do you think the British planes spotted the fire?"

"I don't know. We have to act on that possibility. Naturally we'll take all protective measures. But meanwhile, if they didn't spot it, there's the danger that the scum working with Wegler will try again. That's why you're here. Maybe you can find out something and prevent a repetition." He added to himself, wearily, "I hope."

"Do you know for a fact that the saboteur is part of a group?"

"No. I assume it."

"Was there anyone with him tonight?"

"Not that we know."

"You've examined him?"

"He's in the hospital with a bullet in his gut," Baumer replied bitterly. "One of our prize SS men – sharpshooter, great devotion to the fatherland – only slightly handicapped by having the brains of a chimpanzee. He couldn't have shot him in the leg. Wegler's just been operated on. Who knows if we'll ever be able to talk to him."

"Bad," said Kehr. "Well, I'll want Wegler's record and the record of every friend of his in the factory. I want to see the woman, of course, first thing. By the way – how much investigation of witnesses has been done already?"

"None. We have an anti-sabotage unit here, of course, but I ordered them to keep out of this. I didn't want the waters muddied up, or people put on their guard, before you came."

"Very good, thank you," said Kehr with pleasure. "Too often, when a case calls for special investigation—"

Baumer interrupted a little brusquely. "Wegler's record is right there, on the desk. I've been studying it myself – much use it is. I'll put SS Leader Zimmel at your disposal. He can make anyone talk who needs help. You can use these offices. The Party Cell Leader in Wegler's bunk is Fritz Keller. Call for him when you want. And phone me at any time, please. The switchboard will know where I am."

"Good," said Kehr, busy with his pen. "Do you have any clue to offer about Wegler? Anything at all?"

Baumer's face became crimson. "You might as well have your laugh now. Only yesterday morning, on my recommendation, a War Service Cross was awarded to a factory worker for exemplary devotion."

"Not to Wegler?"

"Yes."

Kehr sighed. "In that case, this won't be a simple affair, that's clear... Let's see, you mentioned some other sabotage."

"We have slightly over four thousand Poles in our happy community. War prisoners – recent arrivals. Some have been earmarked for farm labour gangs, the rest are being trained in the factory. We've had an army call, y'see: all moderately able-bodied men between thirty-seven and forty-six – except unusual skills."

"And?"

Baumer's voice became sharp with contempt. "A bit of underground activity – slogan-painting. You know the sort – 'German workers – if you enslave others, you will yourselves be enslaved.' That sort of crap."

Kehr thought it over, smiling a little. "Marxist, eh?"

"Definitely."

"What records have you got of former concentration-camp inmates?"

"Complete, naturally. About four per cent. Personnel is fifteen thousand."

"How many 'reformed' Communists?"

"Not one – that's it. I made some telephone calls and saw to it that no one of that breed got in here."

"The others?"

"A miscellaneous assortment – trade unionists, oppositionist Catholics, Social Democrats, complainers, sluggards, listening to foreign radio, Black Market lads… You know the stripe. All reformed, presumably, if we're to believe their dossiers."

"Have they been watched?"

"Carefully. I might explain: our barrack houses contain seventy-five to a hundred men. But for purposes of morale – and partially to make surveillance easier – I've had partitions built inside. Gives them less of a feeling of military life, y'understand? So we have eight or ten men in each bunk – and at least one trusted Party man as Cell Leader. All leaders report to me regularly, and there's only one man with a police record allowed in each bunk."

Kehr thought this over for a moment. His thumb played with the Gestapo button under his lapel.

"I might add," said Baumer, "that the men work twelve-hour shifts. To leave the factory grounds, a pass is required from my office. Day-shift men must be in their bunks by eleven at night – except on Saturday."

"Have you been liberal with passes?"

"Yes. I try to make life as congenial as possible. Regulations are merely the minimum required for handling fifteen thousand workers in an artificial community."

"I see… Have there been any other recent signs of underground activity?"

"No. At least nothing certain."

"What do you mean?"

"I mean that even our engineers can't always tell if a machine breaks down because it's worn out or because…" Baumer stopped talking. The same look came over his face that Zoder had observed a half-hour earlier. His features seemed suddenly years older, his eyes hard, harassed. "But damn it, if you ask me, I say there's a bubbling here, and I don't know why. You know what I think? I think half of those bastard workers are brown outside and full of dynamite in their hearts. Yet if you look them over on paper, they're all Party members, Party candidates or reliable elements."

"Like Wegler, eh?" said Kehr smiling.

Baumer bit his lip. Then he burst out hoarsely, "Will you tell me why, Kehr? Have we made Germany whole, or haven't we? Have we become strong? What do they want – the stinking, corrupt Republic again – the unemployment, the inflation? It's enough to break a man's heart." He caught hold of himself and grimaced sourly. "Excuse me. It's my sore spot.

I came into the Party because I was unemployed, y'see. I haven't forgotten those times. I think back to the agony of having to live on the edge of life, like I did, and… Damn it, you'd think every German would remember those days, too. Sometimes now – when I struggle with the new problems we have… such as trying to run an industry with foreign prisoners… it gets me down. I'd like to be able to count on my blood brothers at least. It's such a personal defeat when I can't. You understand me, Kehr?"

Kehr smiled a bit. Indeed, he did understand. This was the over-passionate Party idealist he had come to know so well. No balance… one extreme to the other. "You're an overworked man, Party Comrade Baumer, if you'll permit me. You have a lot on your shoulders. A matter like this upsets you, naturally. But if I may point out: workers, and the sons of workers, make up a large part of our army. What about that army?" A measure of pride entered Kehr's voice. "Is it treasonous? Bad morale? Hah – ask the Poles or the French. Look where we are in Russia… At the gates of Stalingrad!* This new draft you mentioned… it's to replace the summer casualties, no doubt. That means we're coming to the core of the old trade-union working class! So? Do you doubt that they'll drive ahead just the same?"

"Yes, I know. I tell myself those things, too. But believe me, I want the war to end. I don't want it to drag on. Our casualties must be so heavy now, Kehr. Forty-six-year-old men are being taken… Anything, but don't let it drag on."

"You've heard the Führer. Russia is finished. And when Russia collapses, what can England do?"

"With America—" Baumer interrupted himself. "The devil with this chatter. Man, we're working against time. It's one forty-five."

"I have another question. This farm woman…"

"I forgot. That's complicated too. She and Wegler were going to be married. That's how Wegler came to be on her farm in the first place."

"The woman who betrayed him?"

"Yes."

"Hm!… What reason?"

"I haven't talked to her. I've been too busy with other things. Besides, she was hysterical. She ought to be ready for questioning now. Wegler was let off from work yesterday, but whether he spent the day with the woman I don't know."

"I see."

"If there's anything else, phone me, please."

"I will. Get some sleep."

"Sleep? Man, I've got to see every factory foreman, I need a meeting with the plant director... I... sleep! Tomorrow night we'll see who can sleep – and when."

Kehr smiled. He had been waiting for this opportunity from the moment Baumer told him about his brother-in-law. Now it had presented itself nicely. "Baumer... we're in a hurry, but let me take another minute. Years ago I learnt something. You know who taught it to me? Horst Wessel.* Ever meet him?"

Baumer's response was no less excited than Kehr had expected. "You actually knew him?"

"For about ten years. Used to do a lot of drinking together." It was said modestly, with an easy shrug that indicated they had been blood brothers.

"What was he like? Personally, I mean. Did he—"

"An amazing man – but I'm afraid that'll have to wait. Anyway, Horst came to me one day in a hell of a jam. Personal, you know – I can't go into it, even now. But I can tell you this: any average man would have been talking suicide. And Horst? Serious, yes. But despondent? Not a bit. Even laughed. 'Man,' I said, 'where did you get this kind of courage about life?' Do you know what he answered? 'I believe in the Führer. So long as he leads, nothing evil can happen to the fatherland. And if the fatherland is sound, my personal troubles are only a flea bite...' Baumer, that's my advice to you right now: believe in the Führer."

Baumer sat down. He was deeply moved. He asked slowly, "Horst Wessel said that?"

Kehr stroked his firm, plump chin in silence, a smile on his lips.

"It's so true, too," Baumer murmured softly. "Oddly enough – I wouldn't have expressed it that way – but at times in the past, when I've been worried... when things seemed to be going wrong – big things, too... I've said to myself, 'The Führer... remember him. Others may make mistakes, may be corrupt, even – but never the Führer.'"

Kehr nodded. "A healthy attitude in trying times."

Baumer looked up with a little smile. He knew now that in at least one respect he had misjudged the commissar. A wheelhorse, yes. But any man who had been that close to Horst Wessel was no mere opportunist: he could be relied on to do his best. "Well, thanks," he said quietly. "I'll send Zimmel to you. You can begin." He stood up smartly. "*Heil Hitler!*"

"*Heil Hitler!*"

Kehr watched him go out. The smile on his lips broadened. He couldn't recall when it had first occurred to him to invent this story about Horst Wessel, but it had been a happy moment. Herr Wessel was safely dead, and it did no harm. An inspiring piece of invention, when one came down to it, and it had greased the wheels for him in many little ways. He never told it to the Party cynics. But the Party idealists rolled it on their tongues like a Catholic accepting a wafer – right before Kehr's eyes they became one with the Body of the Lord. It was touching. Sometimes Kehr wished he had known Horst Wessel. Their contact had been so brief. With another detective he had gone looking for the man on a morals charge. He was always glad he had not been down as the arresting officer. The other man – Sergeant Scheuermann, was it? – had had his head chopped off a month after the National Socialists took power. Who was to know that a pimp would become such a hero?

Scratching his chin, Kehr settled down comfortably at the desk and opened the file marked "WEGLER, WILLI".

Chapter 2

Doctor Zoder sat hunched forward by the side of Wegler's cot, his bony elbows on his spiny knees, his long hands cupping his thin, long, dark face. If Baumer had caught a glimpse of him, he would have burst out laughing: in that posture the doctor appeared doubly the court jester; every line of his ugly figure had been designed by a caricaturist. Sister Wollweber, however, who had twice appealed to him to go to bed, regarded this vigil over their patient in a different light: to her motherly heart, it was a most moving example of the solicitude and enduring humanity of a good physician. And even though Zoder had partially taken her into his confidence, she knew that neither Baumer's orders nor patriotism required him to go to these lengths. It would take several hours at least for the patient to come out of the anaesthetic. There was little that any doctor could do until then.

The truth was that Doctor Zoder was not keeping his vigil for either medical or patriotic reasons. Hermann Zoder, the man, had nothing in common with what Baumer thought of him, or what a nurse thought of him. It was true of Zoder, as it is to a lesser degree of all men, that he led two lives – one with his fellow men and one eternally alone. So it was that he could appear a patriotic German, a self-sacrificing doctor and a mirthful fool – and be none of them. The outer shell of the man conducted itself as might a well-trained robot in a vaudeville show: it ate, laughed, gabbled and worked with its fellows. But within the shell was a soul squeezed dry, a heart no longer capable of emotion, a bitter bleakness in which love, pity, vanity were no more than pellets of dung from a life past and forgotten. He knew one emotion, this man: hatred. And only in the prick of it did he know he was alive.

Doctor Zoder, in his robot's role, was an experienced physician. To provide his patient with the maximum opportunity for recovery, he had decided to spare him the noise and disturbance of the common ward. One of the several examination rooms had been cleared, a bed installed, and a sign marked NO ADMITTANCE hung on the door. Before the operation the patient had been given a blood transfusion; now, to maintain the level of his body fluid, he was receiving a drip infusion of salt and glucose. On the alert for infection, the ever-vigilant robot peered frequently at the bandages for any sign of seepage, and to the same purpose had gently palpated the abdomen more often than diagnostic procedure demanded. And always, under the force of thirty years of training and habit, the robot studied the fever chart as a prisoner ponders his future in a square of legal paper.

	PULSE	TEMPERATURE	RESPIRATION
11:25 p.m. (*pre-operation*):	40	96	30

The doctor's mind added mechanically: "*Appearance of face:* ashen grey, cold sweat... deep shock."

	PULSE	TEMPERATURE	RESPIRATION
1:10 a.m. (*post-operation*):	96	99.5	30

So far so good! Thirty years before he had written it in a notebook with the delicate gold fountain pen given to him by his mother:

Let the temperature remain constant, gentlemen, and the pulse moderate, and there God and the physician have the patient well in hand. Let the temperature rise to a hundred and three, the pulse to a hundred and sixty, and you will know that septicaemia is at work, gentlemen, and neither God nor the physician has yet learnt control of that devil. I bid you, remember the drain!

The robot had remembered. The other man, whom we might call Hermann Zoder, was not concerned. The mind of that man was concentrated upon a single question. He had spoken it aloud to Baumer half an hour before, and from then on it had not left him. "Who is Wegler, what is he?" In fascination, like a small bird sitting transfixed before the eye of a snake, Zoder sat staring at his patient's face. *Who was Wegler; what was he?*

Wegler worked in the foundry – other than that, Zoder knew nothing about him. Although he had seen Wegler for a few moments in Baumer's office the day before, he had paid no attention to him. Now, regrettably, he could only speculate on the basis of the man's appearance – and that told little. The patient appeared to be in his early forties. He was over six feet in height, thick-bodied, huge-muscled in arm and shoulder, yet strangely and cruelly sparse of flesh. Zoder had been told that he was a drop-forge man. He knew what that meant. The drop forge was the iron brute of the foundry that few men cared to fight. Something of the machine seemed stamped on this man, and like the face of the machine itself, Wegler's face was stony, inexpressive. It was a face that was neither handsome nor ugly, distinguished nor common: the ordinary face of an ordinary working man. The features were large, heavy in their bone structure, of a blond, Teutonic cast; the eye sockets were deep, the jawline hard, the chin wide. It was a strong face, even in mortal sickness, but that was all. In the thin grooves around the wide mouth, in the fine, serried lines on the forehead, were written only the years of grinding work at a machine. There was no delicacy to it, no fine quiver of sensitivity, no brooding and no poetry. One had passed this man on the streets for thirty years, and now daily in the factory compound, and one gave him no thought. Except that he was a bigger man than average, he was in no way different from his million anonymous fellows.

Who was Wegler, what was he? Zoder's brain pounded the question.

There was a mumble from the bed. Sweat, like a film of grease, was on Wegler's forehead; his face was flushed. At the side of the bed was a metal tripod supporting a rubber bag. A tube descended from the bag to the bed and then to the patient's arm. There it became a long needle, and the needle vanished beneath a bandage which held it in place. Drop by drop the fluid descended into the bloodstream, so many drops an hour. So science decreed, but not even science could know for certain the ultimate chemistry, or what the fever chart would reveal by noon. And Zoder knew that these shut eyes might never open, nor the mouth give answer to his question.

The large head rolled a bit on the damp pillow. It dropped to one side, hanging at a sick angle to the trunk. The muscular, corded neck was limp, a weak reed to sustain so heavy a burden. The mumble now had become a long, drawn-out sigh – it faded to nothingness.

Cynically Zoder thought: "This man is an individual. Yet how meaningless his individuality becomes in the extremity of illness. The ether will wear off presently, as it does with all men. And then Nature will stoke the fire in his bowels. It will be the same fire for him as for a Nazi or a Jew, for a soldier or an architect. He will become thirsty. And I will say 'no water'. He will burn with thirst, go mad with thirst, and for forty-eight hours I will say 'no water', and it will be all the same to science and to Nature what he is."

The doctor sat motionless, an ugly man of fifty-five, with a face that once had been gentle and sensitive, but was now as transformed by his secret bitterness as though a pox had physically marred it. He sat staring with lustreless eyes at the inscrutable face on the bed. His mind said again, "Who is Wegler? I must know…"

* * *

Gertrude, Zoder's wife, always used to think of him, "Not a very pretty man, but so beautiful." The observation hadn't meant that Zoder was one of those characters who are universally loved. It was merely the personal reflection of a sentimental wife. They were both middle-class people out of decent homes who had made a decent, comfortable life together. Zoder specialized in internal medicine as a diagnostician and surgeon. He did well. In the decade after the World War they bought a home in a suburb of Stuttgart and acquired a modest summer cottage by a lake in the Black Forest. And if Gertrude thought of her husband as a man who was beautiful, it was not that he was beyond others in deeds or perfection of soul, but that he was so fitted to her as a mate. They were both of a quiet temperament, content with each other and their growing daughter, without great need to devote their energies to changing the world. As a result, even though they were liberal in their social views, they confined their political activity to voting for the Republic at election time – and to professing in conversation that society was surely advancing.

In the latter half of the 1920s, however, the activities of the growing Hitler movement began to intrude into their sheltered life. Zoder read the leaflets mailed so regularly to his home; invariably he used them to light his stove. He didn't like the violence of the Nazi creed – he despised the absurdity of its racism, and he felt certain that no intelligent person would adhere for long to a movement so stupid. Even later, when the Nazis grew powerful, Zoder was still not frightened. If Hitler ever did become chancellor, he told his wife, Germany would nevertheless continue on its democratic way. No one could turn a society on its head. That was unthinkable.

So Zoder had reasoned. Then reality confounded his reasoning and smashed the foundations of his thinking – leaving him rudderless and utterly bewildered. In the period after the Reichstag fire,* when the Nazis really swung into their social programme, Zoder's faith in his fellow Germans turned to contempt. When he saw what was happening, and how the people accepted it, he relapsed into the only refuge for a disillusioned man of his kind: an attitude of profound cynicism. Out of self-protection he heiled when others heiled; he made no protest when the blow he had been expecting came, the purge in his own hospital, which removed both the Jewish and the radical doctors – made no protest because he saw no support and felt it would be useless – and in his heart all the while felt like scum. Like many another decent German, he became a cynical, frightened human being who threw up his hands and kept quiet, and who became over the years increasingly regimented, increasingly terrified, increasingly cynical.

Throughout this long, bitter nightmare, when it seemed as though all of the basic decencies of life had been forgotten by everyone, Zoder leant more and more heavily upon his family as a means of keeping his soul alive. At home, where things continued more or less as they had always, he felt secure. It was the working day he found unbearable – not because the outside world had changed so much, but precisely because the outside world was so bewilderingly the same. The Jewish doctors had been removed – but the hospital still functioned. The content of all newspapers had been changed – but newspapers were still published. And people had been arrested – no one knew how many, but the streets were still crowded. The old stones were still immaculately clean; Stuttgart was still as lovely as formerly; people laughed, planted flowers in their window-sill boxes, loved, grew ill, died as before. To the casual eye Germany was still Germany. This, above all, beat at Zoder's sensitive nerves, injected a steady, cold horror into the quick of his humane heart, confused and bewildered him. And Zoder's secret anguish, which he never admitted in its fullness to anyone, was made the more terrible by the fact that he himself still went to the hospital, saw patients, attended the concert on Friday night, laughed, petted his daughter, held in warm embrace the body of his handsome wife.

But then, a year before the Second World War, the frenzy that stalked the new Germany reached into his home. Ellie, their daughter, was nineteen when she bore her first child. She was a fine young woman, winsome-faced, slim, brown-haired, possessing the same calm grace of personality as her mother. The Zoders were passionately devoted to her, and were delighted when she fell in love with the son of their old friend Wolfgang Beck. They had been afraid that the ways of biology might bring one of the Nazi zealots into their home. Norbert Beck, like Ellie, had been exposed to the concentrated propaganda directed at all German youths. (Ellie had even spent six months in a labour camp.) But although both youngsters outwardly conformed to the new rules of behaviour, both had retained their sanity – Ellie, perhaps, because of the counter-influence of her home, Norbert because he was already in his middle twenties. Occasionally, it was true, they revealed a type of thinking that shocked Zoder. Ellie, particularly, tended towards the conventional hero worship of Hitler, whose purity of heart was being sold to the German people. Whenever his daughter reflected this, Zoder listened, suffered and kept silent. He was too intelligent not to realize that by sheer osmosis any young person would have to absorb at least part of the gigantic Nazi propaganda. But so long as they remained human beings who could say "Good morning" in the bosom of the home instead of "*Heil Hitler*" (the young couple had moved in with them), so long as Norbert could sigh upon discovering a copy of Heine in the attic of their summer home and read it over before thrusting it into the stove, Zoder rested comparatively content.

The blow fell in a manner that no one could have predicted. Gertrude had always been a member of the Confessionalist Church,* a small, proud sect within the Lutheran creed. Her calm piety, like most things with her, was temperamental rather than the product of any philosophy. And Ellie, early in childhood, acquired the same unreflecting relationship to her Church and her God. She was married in church, and her boy was baptized in church, and that was all there was to it. Some of her friends had sneered, but Ellie had not even the need to reply. *Her* God was quite beyond argument or pride. And He must have been deep within her indeed, because she bore a child on the first of January 1938, but for her creed she killed her child and herself not quite four months later.

The events which led to the tragedy began, as did everything else in their world, in Nazi headquarters. Once the trade unions and the opposition parties were smashed, the Nazis moved in for the kill on the only other form of people's organization left – the Churches. To those like Ellie, who were both pious and patriotic, the recognition of a widening breach between Church and State came only gradually. They felt certain that it was the result of a series of blunders, and that it would not continue. The arrest of Pastor Niemöller,* leader of the Confessionalists, was the first clear sign of naked cleavage. Yet until the trial no one knew what the final State attitude would be.

In March of the next year, however, Pastor Niemöller was brought to trial. Ellie, although busy now with an infant son, could talk of little else. With all of the *naïveté* of the pure in heart, who believe that the ways of a society are governed by truth, Ellie expounded the facts of the case to all who would listen. Pastor Niemöller, she pointed out, was the last man in Germany who could be charged correctly with treason. He was a World War hero, who had supported the National Socialists from the first – a Party member, in fact. As the pastor of the most elite congregation in Germany, Niemöller had preached in the pulpit that Hitler's movement was an instrument approved by God for the revival of the German soul. But – and at this point Ellie always became most indignant – there were Party radicals and atheists who were attempting now to control the free organization of the Church. This the pastor was resisting on the ancient ground that Caesar and God were separate, and must be kept separate. And what German Protestant, she asked, born and bred in a Lutheran creed, could deny the truth of Niemöller's position? But the trial… the trial would see God's cause vindicated. Of that she was certain.

To all of this her husband, Norbert, would only reply, "We'll see." He wanted no argument with his young wife, whom he dearly loved – but even less did he have the moral conviction to wage a conflict with the Party Juggernaut.

The court verdict in the Niemöller case was announced on an afternoon when Ellie, together with several other women, was at the railroad station to welcome a new pastor. Ordinarily her mother would have gone on such a mission. But Gertrude Zoder had been stricken a month before by a sudden, crippling attack of arthritis, and Ellie had taken her place.

The station was not the central one in Stuttgart, but the small one-platform affair in their own suburb. Ominously, they found another welcoming committee – from the Party – a silent clump of men who had come to look over the new pastor for their own purposes. The news burst upon both groups as the train was sliding to a stop. The court had sentenced Niemöller to a term no longer than he had already served – a victory for the Church – but he had been immediately rearrested by the Gestapo and taken for "protective custody" to the concentration camp at Sachsenhausen. And this, the papers announced, was on the personal order of the Führer himself.

To Ellie the news was unbelievable. While she was aware that others in the Party leadership were open pagans, she had always been certain that Hitler himself gave simple fealty to a Higher Being. Together with the other women she begged the new pastor for guidance. He, it turned out, was even more stunned than they. Stammering, he insisted that he would have to think it over… that they must all await further news. And with confused, frightened hearts the women went home. They were being forced to choose between their Church and their country, their God and their Führer – and how could they choose?

That night Zoder, too, became frightened. Something about the quality of Ellie's indignation warned him that the matter would not end with mere conversation. When Norbert explained that he had some office work to take care of on Sunday (he was in the legal department of a large factory), Zoder said he would accompany Ellie to church. Even at the time he wondered why Norbert's work could not be postponed for the two hours of a service. Later, with a sick heart, he was to understand that Norbert, too, had sensed the gathering storm.

That Sunday the church was more crowded than it had been in months. To a tense flock Pastor Frisch revealed himself disappointingly as a short, frail, colourlessly blond young man of twenty-nine, with a reedy voice and frightened eyes. The Party Leaders, having seen him at the station, expected no trouble. Nevertheless, out of routine, they had delegated several representatives to listen to his sermon.

The young pastor conducted the service with not a few stumblings. But his flock took to him, notwithstanding. His manner was simple and earnest, and he was obviously a man of deep piety. When the time for the sermon came, the pastor mounted the pulpit, opened the huge Bible which had rested there for a century and read from the twenty-third psalm.* His voice had begun to shake now, and his face was the colour of weak milk:

The Lord is my shepherd; I shall not want.
He maketh me to lie down in green pastures: he leadeth me beside the still waters...
He restoreth my soul...

The pastor paused, swallowed. Then slowly, with unmistakable deliberateness, he turned towards the row of Storm Troopers. Gazing directly at them, his eyes burning feverishly, he spoke from memory:

...he leadeth me in the paths of righteousness for his name's sake.
Yea, though I walk through the valley of the shadow of death, I will fear no evil: for thou art with me; thy rod and thy staff, they comfort me...

Excitement swept through the church. The pastor intended to take a stand hostile to the Party, and everyone knew it. Faces became tense, eyes turned frightened – or angry, or quietly joyous. Zoder, in a pew near the pulpit, felt as though he had been thrust into a blazing furnace. Of a sudden his tongue became dry, his shirt clung to his back, his forehead burned. This startling, unexpected demonstration of courage from a human being so unspectacular rendered him both exalted... and panic-stricken.

Thou preparest a table before me in the presence of mine enemies: thou anointest my head with oil; my cup runneth over.

Surely goodness and mercy shall follow me all the days of my life; and I will dwell in the house of the Lord for ever.

With his eyes fixed upon the Storm Troopers, the pastor began to speak. He looked ghastly, half a corpse already. He knew perfectly the fate that lay in store for an obscure cleric who criticized the government. But this moment of terror was even more his life's triumph. It was the moment he had imagined a thousand times in the still of the night when he was a student of theology – the walk to Golgotha, when for one reason or another he might have to choose between his God and all else. He had not known beforehand whether he would have had the courage to choose as he knew he ought. He had not known at the railroad station or in the dreadful intervening days, when, like the biblical Fathers, he had wrestled with his soul in his own humble fashion. It would have been so easy to preach safely – and to quote Scripture at himself for so doing. Most others had done that, and would. Even on that Sunday morning he had not decided what course he would take. The Party Leaders would never come to know it, but it was they who had made the decision for him. The row of Storm Troopers grinning in the House of the Lord, they were the ones. Where love of God had not been strong enough, hatred of the pagans had put iron into his heart.

He began his sermon in a high-pitched, quavering voice. The righteous, he told his congregation, had faced the persecutions of the wicked more than once before in history. So it was in Germany today. New and pagan doctrines, that would make citizens choose between their Führer and their God, were being broadcast by men of alleged responsibility.

A dangerous muttering began amongst the SA men.* Ignoring it, the pastor put a question to the whole congregation: "What does a German citizen owe his State?" He answered loudly, almost oratorically, "Absolute obedience, for the ruler is ordained by God!"* The muttering stopped. Pastor Frisch turned back to the Troopers, fixing them with his feverish glance. "But what," he continued, "ought Christians to say of the following?" He quoted from Dr Ley, leader of the German Labour Front,* mentioning him by name:

> The Party claims the totality of the soul of the German people. It can and will not suffer that another Party or point of view shall dominate in Germany. We believe that the German people can become eternal only through National Socialism, and therefore we require the last German, whether Protestant or Catholic.*

Simply, reaching the bedrock of his emotion, Frisch spread his hands upon the huge old Bible.

"For this there is only one answer: it is a pagan error that will lead to Germany's destruction. Eternity comes from God – and from no Party of men. I say, with Pastor Niemöller: 'As a citizen I will serve the State unto my death. But as a Christian I will resist the interference of the State with my Church even unto the same death.'"

The Storm Troopers rose from their seats. Their faces were flushed and swollen with anger, and they could hardly restrain their choleric need to shout him down. Acting on previous orders from the Party, they marched in single file, heels clicking, out of the church. But the pastor and everyone else knew that it was not a mere demonstration: they had seen the police outside.

"In Jesus Christ alone is our salvation," the pastor said in a trembling voice to his congregation. "We know this as Christians, we believe it as Germans. God bless you."

A few minutes later, when the service was over, the congregation filed out. Frisch stood at the door. Those who were National Socialists of the orthodox variety, and there were more than a few, brushed past him in anger. Others, afraid of the Party bloodhounds who had assembled outside, looked the other way and moved out even more hastily. But some stopped to shake his hand in silence. These, dwindling into a handful, remained as the white-faced young pastor walked back into the empty church. They watched as a booted lieutenant of the police walked after him – until the lieutenant had shut the doors. Then, at the command of another officer, they went home with breaking hearts. Ellie and Zoder were among them.

All that day Ellie stormed, called neighbours on the telephone (most of them refused to discuss it), announced one minute that she would go to the Gestapo, planned the next to appeal directly to the Führer – actually to go to Berlin. Norbert, her husband, became more and more frightened with each passing hour, until by nightfall he was almost hysterical. If Ellie dared so much as protest, he shouted at her frantically, it would mean a concentration camp for her – perhaps for all of them. It would certainly cost his job and blight his future. Ellie, with the *naïveté* of those who have always felt secure, wouldn't even listen. She was a patriotic German. She wasn't a Jew or a Roman papist or a troublemaker. Everybody knew the Zoders and the Becks. Was she to stand by while a few Brown Shirt atheists ran riot? She'd be ashamed of herself for the rest of her life, and so would he. And whatever there was to do, she expected her husband's support!

Zoder, sitting in the next room with his sick wife, groaned as he listened to them, bit his knuckles and remained silent. He knew that Ellie was right – and he knew that Norbert was right. If in one moment he hungered to join his daughter in a protest, in the next he was overcome by panic, by the encrusted despair in his soul that told him it would be of no earthly use. He knew that this was no irresponsible deed by a few SA men: the arrest had been ordered from on high.

At nightfall a neighbour telephoned without giving her name. She told Ellie that the Brown Shirts were taking the pastor to the railroad station. Ellie ran out instantly, with both her husband and her father trailing miserably at her heels. Norbert knew the shame of what he was doing – and did not care. He was determined that Ellie must not compromise him. Zoder knew an even greater shame. In these five years he had been reduced from a human being to a terrified thing without honour – and now he admitted it. And yet his mind squirmed still, salving his shame, telling him that his wife would perish if he were taken from her – that he must not betray his wife for a hopeless cause.

The pastor was on the platform of the station. They had placed him under a light so everyone might view him. At first, to Zoder's frayed nerves, it was fantastically comical. He had a genuine urge to laugh. For a man to pretend he was a dog... to walk like a dog and bark like a dog... it was monstrously comical. But then he said to himself, "This is Pastor Frisch, this is a man!" – and he almost fainted.

They had shaved his head. They had smashed his eyeglasses so that the dignity of a last public walk would not be his, but he must falter like a drunkard while they hooted. And around his neck they had hung the sign of their contempt: I AM A SLAVE OF THE JEWS.

Thus they marched him to the station. There the men in brown uniform made a circle around him. They forced him to get down on his hands and knees. When he tried to get up, they kicked him down again – until, by the time the crowd gathered, he was ready to do as they said. He was not a strong man, the young pastor. He was not even a courageous man, built for the role he had assumed. He had pulled his own soul up to pulpit size that morning, he had given one moment and his full strength to his God, and now he was an empty sack.

So the crowd saw him, too broken even to weep, knowing only terror as he walked around and around in a circle on his hands and knees, his bony rump thrust comically into the air – barking like a dog.

There were perhaps thirty of the Brown Shirts in the circle, and a hundred or more citizens who were watching. Most of the citizens were silent, but some hooted and laughed. And as they watched, Ellie cried out in a husky, strangled voice. "Shame," she cried. "Shame! Shame!" A few others followed her, calling "Shame." The Storm Troop Leader ordered men to go into the crowd to stop the shouting, and to take the names of any who would dare utter a word more. He had not finished his command before Ellie's husky cry arose again, "Shame! Shame!" Her voice was silenced before the Brown Shirts could spy her out. Norbert had clapped his hand over her mouth. He held her, even though she struggled and bit at his flesh. Then he picked her up in his arms and ran with her into the security of the darkness.

They had been married two years, this boy and girl. They had loved each other well, joined their flesh, rejoiced together in the issue of their passion. Who will pass judgement upon Norbert – who not recognize that the human soul may be good yet meek, decent but easily intimidated, honest but subject to terror? Norbert was all of these things: good, decent and honest – and meek, easily intimidated, in terror for the unknown, for his wife, for himself. It is too much to ask that all of humankind be capable of accepting martyrdom. It is not written so in history – it has never been in life. In a happier society Norbert and Ellie Beck would have lived their lives in contentment and mutual reward. But a week later, feeling himself betrayed, hysterical and in terror, Norbert betrayed his wife.

After what happened at the railroad station, Norbert went home to his father. There had been a terrible quarrel, and Ellie had been like a demon towards him in her scorn. And nothing, nothing that he could summon up for argument prevailed upon her. As he was beyond shame, so she had passed far beyond reasonable behaviour. Finally, he left the house in despair.

They heard no word from him until he came to the door on the following Friday. It was apparent that he had waited deliberately until nightfall. He looked like a man who had been drunk for a week – but he had not been drinking. His handsome, good-natured face was puffed and blotchy, his eyes hysterical. Ellie was sitting at a table, mending a nightdress for their little one. Zoder was at the other end of the room, pretending to read. For Zoder the week had passed in a phantasmagoria of anxiety and confusion.

After the scene at the railroad station, Ellie had become stubbornly silent. Whenever he tried to speak to her, she put him off with a dull refusal even to discuss the matter. Now, as her husband entered, her face turned a terrible, chalky white, but she remained where she was, quietly sewing. Without even a "hello", Norbert walked over to her. In a low voice, already rotten with despair, he asked if what he had been told was true: that Ellie and a number of women were preparing a demonstration for Sunday.

For a long moment Ellie did not answer. Then she said slowly, as cruelly as she could: "Are you travelling with informers now?"

Norbert was beyond being hurt. He only muttered miserably, "Then it is true! A friend high up in the Party warned me. They know already, you see. I'd hoped it wasn't."

Ellie said nothing.

"Darling," he whispered pitifully, "don't you realize? Our child... me?..." He stopped, choked by her look of scorn. He retreated to the door, almost as though he were physically afraid of her. With sick eyes and a sick face, with a voice that he could scarcely make speak and a hand that twitched violently against his chest, he said mechanically, "Then – for my own pro-tection – I must ask for a divorce. I warn you – I'll demand it on political grounds. It's... necessary."

Ellie only looked at him. And so he left.

At noon the next day the police came to the door. Zoder was away at the hospital, Gertrude asleep. The lieutenant in charge had a court order. The order notified one Ellie Beck that she was under arrest. It was charged by Ernst Walters, Party Leader, and by Norbert Beck, her husband, and by Wolfgang Beck, her father-in-law, that Ellie Beck was not politically fit to educate a child. Until the trial should come about and the verdict was known, it was ordered that the child be taken to a state institution for safe keeping.

Ellie read the order, and then a second time, in silence. It may be surmised that not until then had she quite realized the world she was inhabiting, or what that world could do to human beings.

"I'll get the child ready," she said. Even at that moment there must still have been room in her heart for a grain of cunning, for she added, "Please sit down."

Then she went into the child's nursery and shut the door. Ten minutes later, when the lieutenant became restless, he went to the door and knocked. A trickle of blood had already seeped under the jamb and was soaking into the carpet at his feet...

* * *

Now, in the summer of 1942, Zoder could realize that from the time of his daughter's suicide until almost two years later, when an army medical board in Poland committed him to an institution, he had been more or less unbalanced. His wife followed their daughter to the grave. If her death had come ten years earlier, Zoder would have grieved as any man grieves – even more deeply, perhaps, because they had been so well mated. He did not grieve: his sick, stunned soul was beyond sorrow for another. Along every step of the way that had led to his daughter's death he had told himself that it was his first duty to care for his wife. That was true. It was also true that his wife was surely dying, and both of them knew it. In the last period, although he sat by her side without rest, he never once dared look into her eyes.

Zoder's body had gone on living after his wife died. His practised hands had performed operations. When his colleagues observed that he had begun to develop a peculiar manner that they could only describe as "foolish", they put it down to grief, and did not probe further.

In September of the following year, Zoder was called up by the army. He was sent to Poland. Since the victory was a quick one, there were no more surgical cases by winter. On Christmas Day 1939, he was assigned to be medical inspector of a number of soldiers' clubs in Warsaw – an easy berth. Three days later, his adjutant, coming to awaken him, found him paralyzed from the hips down. His colleagues discovered quickly that the paralysis had no physical origin. They wrote on his card, "Nervous Breakdown".

When a good man who has believed in the goodness of other men comes to experience – and to acknowledge fully to himself – the depths of depravity and cruelty, of viciousness and animalism of which corrupted men are capable, his revulsion is catastrophic. The soldiers' clubs turned out to be brothels, and Zoder's assignment required him to test the health of the girls. They were not prostitutes: they were decent Polish women held there by force – peasant girls ripped from homes, parents and husbands, locked in a room and compelled to serve two dozen men daily. There were women with madness in their eyes – women like dead lumps of flesh in a state of manic depression, girls who laughed uncontrollably when Zoder entered their rooms – and daily suicides. He tended them for two days. If he had not awakened then to paralysis, he would have destroyed himself.

Zoder had hated the Nazis, but his burden of self-guilt over the death of his daughter had clouded his mind. After Poland, this personal guilt became submerged before a gigantic, consuming hatred for all Germans. In the course of two years in a sanatorium it was this hatred that glued the pieces of his shattered being together. He became again a man quite capable of carrying on his medical work and of walking a path through society. His foolish manner and his foolish laugh were still with him, but now they were the devices of calculation: he played the fool both to disarm others and to express the malice he could not wholly contain. And when he asked himself why he continued to live, and why he continued to calculate and manoeuvre amongst these men he abominated, he had a ready answer. In the months of his recuperation a recurrent dream had come to him. The dream was his answer – and it was this. There would be a plague. Within the space of a day it would strike down every living German. And he, Zoder, would walk through streets and cities and villages piled with corpses. He would do so because he had been assigned a task by God: to count every last corpse until it was certain that every last German had died. And then he too would die, for he too was German.

It had begun as a dream, but now it was a waking fantasy. It came to his fevered mind a dozen times a day, sometimes as a brief image, sometimes in its entirety. And it was for this that he lived...

But now this man on the bed threatened Zoder's creed. Wegler had separated himself from other Germans. He had lit a fire and pointed the fire towards the factory. By this he challenged the principles of Zoder's existence... and Zoder recognized it. His confused soul sensed that this man could not be hated as he hated other Germans. But his mind, keener than his heart, warned that if he helped a German, he would destroy the basis by which he lived.

Zoder had been a good man with a good heart; he had understood life in terms of work, of the sound of his child's laughter, of the grace of music; he sat now, baffled and beaten by a world he no longer understood, wringing his hands in abject helplessness. His mind, like a cracked record, revolved on the turntable of its hate, and could come to no decision. This Wegler challenged him as he could not bear to be challenged. This half-dead, silent figure lay pleading with him: "Look at me. I am a German you may not hate!"

Zoder groaned. It was for him to decide whether Wegler would be made to speak. He could prevent it. If he did not, Baumer would come with knife and faggot in hand, and Baumer would be implacable. But why ought he to interfere? Wegler was a German. What right had any German to say to Hermann Zoder, "Have human feeling for me"?

Yet still he kept pleading, that one. The silent mouth was eloquent. "I have done something... you know what it is... help me, for in me you can believe."

No, Zoder could not believe. Once he had believed in the goodness of men. But not now. Least of all could he believe in another German.

The patient stirred. His big head rolled on the pillow, and a groan burst from his lips. Zoder thought suddenly: "What would Pastor Frisch want me to do? He'd want me to help Wegler. Dear God, whom must I help? I must not help Baumer. He is my enemy. But Wegler is a German. I have seen what these Germans do when they have the power, *all of them*, with no exception. Why must I help Wegler? Or anyone?"

Against his will, Zoder's mind returned to Pastor Frisch. Six months before, when the factory first began to operate, the pastor had risen like a ghost from the ashes of his dead life. Pastor Frisch had been two years in a concentration camp, and a year in a labour battalion after that. With the increased need for manpower, he had been sent into factory work. And then, one day, Zoder had come upon him, quietly sitting in his clinic waiting room.

Frisch had not recognized Zoder. Their only contact had been a moment's handshake at a time when the pastor was too frightened to mark anyone. But Zoder, confronted so suddenly by this near-sighted, unforgettable little man, had exclaimed "Pastor Frisch!..." and then had told him the story of his daughter.

Thereafter, until bluntly and violently rejected, the pastor had sought Zoder out. He had assumed, quite inaccurately, that Zoder was dedicated to what he called "the liberation of the German people". Zoder had told him in so many words to go to hell. He had no interest in "saving" the German people. The world had suffered enough from them already. By what ethics, he had asked, ought anyone to save a tainted race – a people destined always to murder their fellow men? This they had done, and this was their creed, and this they would always do. He wanted them exterminated, all... all... ground into the earth and forgotten.

But now, in his uncertainty, Zoder thought of Pastor Frisch again. They had not seen each other in months. For all he knew, the pastor and Wegler were linked in an underground cell. He wanted to forget the pastor – he wanted to run from the room and forget Wegler – but he could do neither. Instead he remained where he was, and his confused thoughts swung like a pendulum from one decision to another... and decided nothing. "I'll have a talk with Pastor Frisch," he thought. "He works on the night shift. I can see him at six in the morning. (*But why do I want to see him?...*) Yes, by six in the morning Wegler will surely be conscious. That means Baumer will be at him... unless I prevent it. I'm the physician in charge. There's no one to challenge what I do. (*DO I WANT TO PREVENT IT?*) Yes, I can keep Baumer off until I've spoken to the pastor. (*But why? What is Wegler to me? Or the pastor?*)"

With a trembling hand he wiped the perspiration from his forehead. He took out his thermometer, whipped it down and placed it under the patient's armpit.

Outside, the factory was at work. He could hear the distant clatter of a tank as it rolled off the assembly line. He could hear other noises, too... the multi-keyed clangour of the home front, the witch's kettle boiling as it spewed forth its trained, deadly metal. A German had tried to destroy this. A German!

Zoder's mind probed again, insatiably: "What must I do?"

He sat motionless, his eyes fixed upon Wegler's face.

Chapter 3

Gestapo Commissar Kehr grunted and looked up from the dossier on his desk. He plucked a wet half-inch cigar stub from between his teeth and bawled loudly, "Zimmel!"

There was an immediate stir in the adjacent office. The door opened smartly, and SS Leader Zimmel appeared – a short, extremely broad-shouldered young man of twenty-seven in the black uniform of the Elite Guard.

"Sir?"

"If you please, Zimmel..." Kehr believed in a decent tone with subordinates. The "If you please" had been arrived at after long experience. Properly enunciated it was polite – but a command. "I'm ready for the woman now, Berthe Lingg."

"In two minutes, commissar. She's been resting." Zimmel had a curiously thick way of speaking, as though his mouth were half full. "I gave her a cot that's a bit away from here."

Kehr nodded and put the cigar butt back between his teeth. A second later he jerked it out again. "Where have I seen you before, Zimmel?"

Zimmel turned in the doorway, his square, good-natured face wreathed in a smile. It would have been an attractive face but for the nose, which was squashed down almost flat. Zimmel had been wondering if the commissar would ask that question, and afraid he wouldn't. "At the six-day bike races? I used to ride a little." He looked hopefully at the commissar.

Kehr stared at him. "Why, of course... Otto Zimmel – 'Thunderbolt Zimmel'. I've put money on you many a time. Didn't recognize you for a moment."

Zimmel nodded, very pleased. "My nose. That's why I quit."

"An accident?"

Zimmel sidled closer to the desk. He said eagerly, "Pacing a motorcycle in an exhibition... riding behind, you understand? Front wheel broke at fifty-eight miles an hour."

Kehr whistled.

"Broke both arms, every one of my ribs, my jaw, and knocked all my teeth out."

Kehr shook his head.

"Look," said Zimmel. He opened his mouth wide, and in a quick movement pulled both his lower and upper dentures out of his mouth at once. "You see?" He waved the plates. "Complete set." He clicked them back into his mouth with a practised thrust and bite. "Cost me twelve hundred marks."

"A shame," said Kehr. "What a sprint you could uncork."

"Six months in the hospital. Day and night nurse. Two specialists."

"Well, well… so now you're an SS Leader," said Kehr, becoming a little bored.

"Old days are gone. The music and the shouting, as they say. Now I'm just another face in the Elite Guard. Although it's a privilege, you understand," he added hastily. "To serve the Führer, I mean."

"Tell me, a man like you, accustomed to his picture in the paper, to crowds… You must miss that, eh?"

"I'll tell you: half and half. The fact is" – Zimmel grinned good-naturedly – "I'm lazy. I never liked the training. A job like this…"

Kehr laughed. "Well, well… So now, if you please – the woman."

"Yes, sir." Zimmel went out smartly, his face glowing. Kehr grinned after him. "Thunderbolt Zimmel," he thought. "Ebert and Stresemann,* Hess and Zimmel…" Where were they? It was the sober, steady ones who counted in the long run. Five years ago he had sat in the gallery applauding Zimmel. Today Zimmel took orders from Commissar Kehr. How are the mighty fallen!

Kehr belched a little and turned back to Wegler's dossier, chewing his cigar stub. He ran his eye down the page and frowned. On the face of it he had never met anything more baffling.

Name:	WEGLER, WILLI
Birth Date:	7th July 1900
Birth Place:	Berlin
Residence:	Cologne, 1920–34; Düsseldorf, 1934–41. Evacuated to X after Düsseldorf bombings in December 1941
Racial Stock:	Aryan; Nordic
Parents:	Deceased
Wife:	Käthe (Rentschler). Killed in bombing, December 1941

That was the first thing: it seemed obvious that a German whose wife had been killed in a British bombing must hate the British. Yet Wegler had signalled to them.

Children: Son, Richard, born 12th Jan. 1919. Lance Corporal in Waffen SS. Killed at Narvik, 1940. Decorated posthumously, Iron Cross, Second Class

That was the second contradiction. For the son to have been a member of the SS meant that the father had been investigated by the Gestapo. Although the Party spoke incessantly of its ineffable regard for the working class (Kehr always grinned over that one), it acted otherwise when it came to selecting men for the SS. Anybody could get into the Brown Shirts – which was why that body had been reduced to a "Winter Help" group. But for its trusted corps of last-stand fighters, the Party always considered that the sons of farmers, bank clerks and their like were more desirable than the spawn of men who might once have been members of a Red Party. For Richard Wegler, son of a worker, to have gotten into the Elite Guard was a comment not only on the boy, but on the record of the father. Unless an error had been made somewhere! That he would have to investigate.

Religion: Lutheran. Non-churchgoer
Habits: Quiet; reads neither newspapers nor books
Morals: Seems to have formed attachment to Berthe Lingg, widow farmer, since coming to X; Lingg able to have children; should be visited

At least he would find out something from the woman. Wegler had courted her – probably they had been to bed. The woman must have learnt something about him, unless she was altogether a peasant cow. (That, too, was possible. Such things always happened to Kehr.)

Occupation   Plumber; occasional bricklayer. Since 1939 labourer in
(Skills):   foundry. As of date, drop-forge operator in foundry
Political History   Membership in Marxist parties: no record. Masonic
(Associations):   lodges: no record. Jewish associations: no. Catholic associations: casual. Trade unions: member of Building Trades Union till 1933. Held no offices. Anti-Party activity: no. Anti-Party expression: no

Kehr paused for a moment. Wegler had been a member of a trade union. Under the Republic, of course, all workers were in unions. Therefore it might mean something, it might not. His eye continued down the page.

General Comment: Politically inactive both before and after Third Reich. Did not respond to Party effort to involve him in activities. Vouched for as friendly by Block Leader and by son, Richard Wegler. World War record excellent. (See attached page)

Current Comment: May be considered definitely friendly. Cell Leader regards him as solid, patriotic German

Kehr chewed his cigar butt and closed the folder with a sigh. It couldn't be said that Wegler's record explained anything. But they would see – the twenty-four hours were still young.

The door opened. Zimmel thrust his head in, eyebrows lifted in question. Kehr nodded. As the woman entered, Zimmel barked in proper style: "Frau Lingg." He stepped back smartly and shut the door.

Kehr, like all detectives, had evolved a procedure for his interrogations. While in special instances he varied his attack to suit an unusual character, for the most part his method consisted of what he called "the fatherly approach". He was quiet, sympathetic and reassuring. He tried to maintain this even with hardened criminals. The man being investigated might understand the method perfectly, but that didn't reduce its effectiveness. Naturally, as Kehr himself put it, he played variations on his little piccolo. For instance, the "father", when confronted by lies, became indignant; his rage then was terrible to behold. Or, when faced by deceit, he looked long at the ungrateful one before him, shook his head, sighed and prolonged the silence until the poor fish was ready to jump out of his skin with anxiety. And so on. In the case of Berthe Lingg, the fatherly approach would not, if he could help it, take on the aspect of an investigation at all. Where a situation made that possible, the very best results were always to be obtained.

Frau Lingg, to his agreeable surprise, was not a bad-looking woman, although her appearance was marred at the moment by a dirty, tear-stained face. With the snobbishness of a city man Kehr had expected a thick-legged sow, wide at the beam, with manure on her shoes. Frau Lingg was obviously a farm wench, from her shawl to her blunt chapped hands, but she was one of those well-built peasant women who are of a good height, and who have supple figures that hard work keeps from corpulence. Very agreeable indeed, Kehr thought. He had a heart that melted over every attractive woman. At home was his spindly wife, who had won him with her brittle prettiness at twenty, and who had become a dried bone by thirty. It was the one misfortune in his otherwise pleasant life – especially hard, he always said, for a warm-hearted man like him. Although he never, never let it interfere with business, he was always on the lookout for a bit of relish.

"Frau Lingg," he began, coming around the desk to meet her, "you have my deepest admiration. What you did tonight earns the gratitude of every German."

A sigh, as though she had been holding her breath, came from the woman. She said nothing. Her eyes were averted from his gaze.

"Sit down, please. My name, by the way, is Commissar Kehr... No..." He touched her arm gently. "A better idea first." He pointed to a sink in the corner of the office. "A little water on your face. Please. It'll refresh you."

Obediently the woman crossed to the sink. Kehr opened the tap for her. Then he retired a few paces while she washed her face. Her tension bothered him, and he watched her thoughtfully. She straightened up, eyes shut, face dripping.

"Please, my handkerchief." He whipped it out. "There's no towel here. It's clean, absolutely."

"No," she muttered.

"I insist." He began to dry her face. She accepted the handkerchief quickly then, and, smiling, he stepped back. She was not a little pleasing, this woman, he decided – the sort who made no great impression at first glance, but whose femininity grew on one, as it were. No whipped cream and strawberries, he always said about such females, but a good pot roast. Now that the dirty tear marks were off, he judged her to be in her middle thirties. She had a pleasant face. It was not a pretty face – a short, blunt nose, a too-wide mouth – but it was round, white-skinned, with a bit of a saucy look. And with her shawl thrust back she displayed quite magnificent breasts under her burgundy sweater. Kehr felt rather in a glow.

"Well, my dear... Sit down, won't you?" He took his handkerchief from her, nodding at her muttered thanks. She sat down as he directed, on a straight-backed chair before the desk. Jovially, his eyes on her, he said, "If I may... a very attractive sweater you're wearing." He was surprised to see her face turn hot under his comment. He was curious about the sweater. Her shawl, skirt and shoes were shabby and patched, but the sweater was new and obviously expensive – a modish cashmere slipover. She was a bit too old to blush at a compliment over a sweater... or even at the inference that his eyes were on her breasts. A woman who wore a tight sweater like that wanted men to appreciate her.

"It's… it's from France, sir," she said in a low, strained tone. "My son, Rudi, in the army – he brought it to me."

Kehr nodded. Then he said, "You don't have to call me 'sir'. We're just going to have a friendly chat, eh? I'm an easy man to deal with, you'll see." He walked behind his desk and sat down, spreading his legs comfortably. "Now then, my dear, you've had a horrible experience, no sleep… I'll let you go home as soon as possible. But you understand… the safety of the factory… I must talk to you."

She nodded nervously.

Quietly, with a friendly smile, Kehr elaborated on the important role she might play, and on her duty towards the State. She was to hold back nothing, to provide all possible clues. "So, if you please, Frau Lingg… from the beginning – what happened tonight?"

She looked at him straight then, for the first time, as though trying to decide whether he was her friend (or, perhaps, he thought, how gullible he was). Her eyes bothered him. They combined meekness with a very definite craft. Meek eyes in a woman were fine, and Kehr approved – always very attractive. But the detective in him was bothered by the craft, as it had been by the blush and the tension. This woman had done a patriotic thing, yet she seemed more worried over it than normally jubilant. What was she hiding?

"Can you tell me…" Her voice was pitched very low. "What's with the man – Wegler?"

"He's in the hospital here."

"He's all right?"

"They operated. We don't know yet."

"If… What will happen if he gets well?"

Deliberately, his eyes on her face, he replied, "He'll be executed for treason."

Her face went a pasty white. "So?… Good. Very good."

"Still, it must be hard on you."

"On me? Why should I care?" Her voice became shrill.

"You were going to get married, weren't you?"

"I? No such thing. A complete mistake, sir. To him? What nonsense!"

"I thought—"

"Why, it's stupidity. I hardly knew him. I won't be mixed up with him, Herr Commissar."

"I see. Excuse me. He was only a friend, then?"

"Not even a friend."

"You didn't know him?"

"I knew him – but not as a friend." She was very emphatic. The colour had returned to her face, and the craft to her eyes.

She was not very practised in dissembling, Kehr decided. Simple people never were: lying came harder to them than almost anything else. "Just an acquaintance, then. I see. Well, tell me what happened tonight."

"Tonight?"

"You know, my dear, the fire in your field."

The woman wet her dry lips. "I was in bed. Something woke me up, I don't know what. Maybe the air-raid siren. Yes, it was the siren. Then I saw him through the window running in the field." She paused, eying Kehr. He nodded encouragingly. "So I yelled to him. The window was open. But he didn't stop. I could see he was doing something with the hay, but I didn't know what. I ran outside. He wouldn't talk to me. When I tried to stop him, because he was tearing up my haycocks, he… he knocked me down." Again she stopped.

"Please."

"Then, when he began to pour the kerosene on the hay, I understood what he was doing – I saw the way he had piled the hay, I mean. So I thought, 'Maybe he'll kill me, but it's my patriotic duty.' I ran towards the wire and yelled." Anger came into her flat voice for the first time. "He ran after me with a pitchfork. He wanted to kill me." Just as abruptly the anger subsided, and she slumped in her chair. "That's all."

Kehr stroked his chin and remained silent, gazing at her.

"That's all," she repeated. "I don't know anything else."

Kehr nodded, saying nothing.

"Can I go home, now, please?"

"Nothing more you can think of? Anything he ever said that would be a clue?"

"No."

Kehr stroked his chin. Frau Lingg stood up, gathering her shawl around her. She patted her thick braids. Her dark, handsome eyes were veiled.

"Better wait," he said gently. "Sit down a bit."

"But—"

"Please, my dear…"

She sat. Kehr eyed her and sighed a little. He would have liked things to go smoothly with her. He might have called on her before he left. A farm woman, she'd be impressed with a Gestapo commissar. Now she'd resent him for her own lies. People always resented a policeman, especially after they were found out.

"Excuse me." He crossed the room and went into the other office, closing the door behind him. Zimmel jumped to his feet, hastily buttoning his jacket. Kehr picked up the phone. "Gestapo Commissar Kehr... I want to speak to Labour Front Leader Baumer. Locate him, please."

"He's in the assembly plant, sir, at a meeting," the phone girl replied. "He'll be back in—"

"Never mind when he'll be back," Kehr interrupted. "Didn't he leave instructions? He's to be called whenever I want him. Locate him in the plant and get him to a telephone."

"Yes, sir."

Kehr turned to Zimmel. "What do you know about this woman and Wegler?"

"Nothing, sir."

"Have you cleaned Wegler's things out of his bunkhouse?"

"There they are." He pointed to a bundle in the corner.

"Any papers?"

"Not even a letter."

"Photographs?"

"No, sir."

"Is there a locker in the plant where he might have something?"

"Yes, there is."

"Send someone to clean it out."

"Yes, sir. Now?"

"It should have been done already. *You* should have thought of that, Thunderbolt Zimmel. Make believe you're back on the track, eh, lad? Think hard. You know this plant. I don't. You can help me. We don't have much time on this case."

"Yes, sir." Zimmel ran out.

Kehr smiled. How are the mighty fallen!

"Herr Commissar?" said the phone girl.

"Yes."

"Here he is, sir."

"Baumer?"

"Yes."

Kehr lowered his voice. "The woman, Lingg – she maintains Wegler was only an acquaintance. You said—"

"She's lying, the bitch," Baumer interrupted angrily. "Just two nights ago I had a visit from the Peasant Leader in this community, Rosenhart. He told me they were to be married. They had come to him for a work transfer – I mean, they wanted Wegler to live and work on her farm."

"Did you give him the transfer?"

"No. Wegler was already marked for the army."

"I see. Do you think your refusal had anything to do with his sabotage?"

"I don't know. Never even thought of it till now. Maybe you've got something there."

"Well... we'll see what the woman says. I suppose she lied to me about her relationship with Wegler for the obvious reasons – afraid to be tarred with the same brush, and so on."

"She's got nothing to be afraid of. What the hell's the matter with that cow? We've got to move ahead on this, Kehr. There's no time, damn it."

"I know."

"My man Zimmel will take some of the cleverness out of her, if that's what she needs."

"Don't worry," said Kehr. "I won't require that. Call you later." He hung up and returned to the inner office. The woman was in the chair, her hands folded in her lap, her eyes on the floor. She didn't look up. Kehr leant against the edge of the desk, which placed him only a few feet away from her. "Frau Lingg," he said sorrowfully, "you haven't been frank with me. I think I know why. To a simple, honest woman like you a Gestapo commissar seems a terrible man. The name itself makes you afraid. But believe me, we might have coffee together, or sit in a beer house, and you'd find me jolly and good-natured, because that's the way I am. Maybe we'll still do that, who knows? But right now, when I'm acting as an official, you mustn't be afraid of me."

"I'm—"

"One moment. You mustn't be afraid of the law, either. I know you country people. The word 'law' terrifies you. You're not being suspected of anything, Frau Lingg. I, the Gestapo commissar, am relying on *you* to help *me*. Truly. Without your help, I can't move. Now, you know Wegler, and you can tell me about him. You were going to be married to him—"

"No," she interrupted. "I told you before—"

"Please—"

"He was just an acquaintance, sir."

Kehr straightened up. His porcine face reddened, his burly body seemed to swell. "Very good!" he shouted. "You want me to consider you're linked with this traitor? Very good. I will! For some reason you're denying what everybody knows – that you knew Wegler, that you were lovers, that you intended to be married."

"It's a lie!"

Kehr slapped her mouth. The woman gasped, but he gave her no chance to speak. "Shame on you! Only two nights ago the local Peasant Leader came to the factory on your behalf. You think I don't know that? Stop lying to me now. You're acting like a child. I'll give you a spanking if you don't stop it." He bent over her. "I will now. So help me, I'll give you an old-fashioned spanking, right over my knees, Frau Lingg."

The woman burst into tears. Kehr looked down at her, his face still wrathful, his eyes amused. "Come, come… Now listen to me: you're afraid that if you admit the truth, I'll think you were mixed up in this with Wegler. I won't. You're no traitor. For goodness' sake, woman, it was you who called the guards and saved the factory, wasn't it?" He seized her arm suddenly. "Or are you hiding something serious? Maybe you were really mixed up in this, hey? Maybe it was just a lover's *quarrel* that made you betray him?"

She looked up in frantic protest. "Oh no, sir."

He continued without pity. "So maybe there'll have to be two customers for the axe, eh? An axe isn't particular, you know. A woman or a man, it makes no difference to the axe. The head rolls into the basket just the same."

She gave up then, as she had known she would be forced to in the end. From childhood on she had learnt too well that a woman was ultimately helpless in a world run by men. Sometimes guile helped a little, or a smile, but in the end it always came to this: they had their way with a woman. And she wept loudly for a moment, not only because Kehr was a man and she couldn't trust him, not only because she was afraid of what he might do or how his man's brain might involve her… but because in this moment she felt the indignity of her whole life, and knew that somehow it was involved in this ghastly betrayal of the man she loved. Yet even now in her surrender – since this, too, she had learnt in childhood – her brain fought to be cunning, to tell Kehr so much and no more, to yield now that she must, but to yield with craft. She raised her head from her hands. "I was so afraid. I didn't know what might happen to me."

"Nothing will happen to you, nothing!"

"I *was* going to marry him…"

He nodded sympathetically.

"He was at my house tonight. Then he left – I thought to go home, to the barracks. I went to my room. I undressed and got into bed. Then I saw him like I told you… The rest is just how I said. Truly."

"Why did he do it? That's what I want to know."

Her brow furrowed. Again he saw the crafty look in her eyes, and this time it genuinely angered him.

"I don't know."

He slapped the desk hard. "See here—"

"Please, sir, I'm just going to tell you. I don't know why, but—"

"Yes? I can't spend all night, woman!"

"He…" (Dare she say this? Would it persuade him of her cooperation, or involve her deeper?) "He told me he was going to do something."

"To burn the hay?"

"He didn't say. Just do something 'important', he said. I asked him what, but he wouldn't tell. He wanted me to say in advance that I'd do it with him."

"Do what?"

"A deed, he said."

"What sort of deed?"

"That's what I'm trying to tell you, Herr Commissar. He said we were both guilty because of the Pole."

"Guilty? What does that mean?"

"That's what he said. It sounded crazy to me. I still don't know what it means."

"Who's the Pole?"

"On my farm – a prisoner. He works for me now. I bought him." Kehr's face lit up with satisfaction. "Wegler was mixed up with the Pole, eh?"

"No."

"No? That doesn't make sense. And how do you know he wasn't?"

"I've only had the Pole since two nights ago. There was no time."

"Are you sure?"

"Positive, sir. Willi didn't even know him."

"In that case, why did he say he was guilty?"

"That's what I don't know. I've been thinking all night. I think he was crazy."

"Why do you think so?"

"To do a thing like that – he had no reason."

"How do you know he had no reason?"

"He was always so patriotic. His son—"

"*Was* he always patriotic?"

"Positively."

"You suspected nothing? He never said anything?"

"I?" Her heart began to pound. "You think I wouldn't have reported the slightest thing? What do you think I am, Herr Commissar? After all, I…"

To himself Kehr said: "You're a woman, and God knows what goes on in your mind." He leant back against the desk, frowning. "He must have meant something in saying he was guilty."

"I asked him. He just said, 'I'm guilty.' He talked real wild, Herr Commissar. And when I'd keep asking him to explain, he wouldn't say further."

Kehr frowned. Wegler's record suggested he might have acted out of insanity. He himself had put it down as a vague possibility after studying Wegler's record. Now the woman's testimony began to lend credence to it. Only, there was a suspicious method in such craziness. A man who goes crazy… just goes. He doesn't pile hay in the form of an arrow.

"Did Wegler have any friends?"

"Friends? In the factory, I guess. But with me he never talked about them."

"What did he talk about?"

"About maybe we could have a farm together… and a kid. He wasn't much of a talker."

"He talked about the war?"

"Oh… a little." She felt a tightness in her chest, and she wriggled a little in her chair, as though to get more comfortable.

"What did he say about the war?"

"Oh… nothing much. When… when our soldiers would take Stalingrad… things like that." A little hastily she added, "Farmers like me… we only talk about small things, mostly, like the potatoes, or our children."

"Did Wegler ever criticize the Party leaders?"

She kept her eyes on the floor, but her voice was firm as she answered, "Oh no, sir."

"You mean he didn't even criticize Labour Front Leader Baumer? Wegler wanted to work on the farm, didn't he? What did he say when he was refused permission?"

The woman shrugged. "He hardly even spoke of it. He just told me he was called for the army."

"He didn't want to go to the army, surely? He's no youngster."

Again she wriggled in her chair. "He only told me tonight. I don't know what he felt. He was just talking crazy, like I said. About the Pole."

Kehr was silent, thinking over her replies. "So far, very little," he decided with a sigh. Then he asked, "What kind of a Pole do you have?"

She sighed. "Just a Pole. A lazy one. Not good for anything. I got cheated."

"You've talked to him?"

"I tell him what to do, naturally. He's from near the border... speaks German, I'm all alone on the farm."

"Why is it reported that the Pole and you had intimacy with each other?"

"What?" She bolted up from her chair. "Who dares? With a Pole?"

"You know it's forbidden for a German woman and a—"

"Me? With a Pole?" She spat coarsely.

"Is that why Wegler spoke of being guilty?"

"This is crazy, absolutely crazy," she cried violently. "This I won't even let you say."

Kehr grinned. "All right, my dear, but sit down. Calm yourself. A policeman has to ask about everything... even what he doesn't believe himself." He knew that the stab was unfounded. "Now, what about you and Wegler? Did you have a fight last night?"

She shook her head. Her face was still flushed. "Except he was talking so crazy and I told him so."

"Did you ever quarrel over anything?"

"No, sir."

"How long was Wegler with you yesterday?"

"Oh... maybe half an hour... no more."

"At night?"

"Yes, sir. Just before he... did that."

"Wasn't he with you all day? He had a pass to leave the factory."

"No, sir. He only came at night, late. I was in bed already."

"Are you sure, Frau Lingg?"

"I can prove it. I was in the fields all day. The Pole was there."

Kehr sighed. He consulted his notebook. "This kerosene Wegler used to light the hay. How did he get it?"

Frau Lingg's eyes met his. "It was mine. My month's ration. He even took my lamp. Broke it, too. I'll have no light for a month."

"Why did you let him take it?"

Her voice became shrill again. "Let him? I didn't know. I was in the bedroom. I only saw it later."

Kehr was silent. Then he closed his notebook with an angry snap. So far he had no more real information than a gnat could digest.

"You... ah... loved Wegler very dearly, eh, Frau Lingg?"

She kept silent.

"You still love him, in fact."

"No such thing. The idea!" she exclaimed angrily. "Love a traitor?"

"It's been known... A woman's heart—"

"A lot of men know about a woman's heart. To do a thing like that... Why, the British might have killed *me* too." She pulled her shawl angrily. "Pure crazy, that's what it was."

"You hate him now?"

"I should say. Signalling to the Britishers. I'm German."

"Good riddance to him, eh?"

"I should say."

"If you like, my dear... I can arrange it... you can be present when they cut his head off."

She retched violently, leaning forward and clutching at her belly with both hands as though she had been struck. She was so white that he thought she was going to faint.

"You wouldn't like that? Why?"

She said nothing, but her eyes showed her sick bitterness at this male cruelty.

"Excuse me," he said, "but a policeman has to ask about everything." He stared at the closed dossier containing Wegler's record. He was inclined to feel that the woman was not hiding anything important from him – yet it seemed curious that she didn't have more to offer. Surely Wegler would have betrayed some previous signs of hostility to the government.

"You know, Frau Lingg, sometimes a man says things and we take no notice. Then, later, we go back in our minds and realize some of the things he said had a significant meaning. Can you think back to anything he ever told you that..."

"Nothing, Herr Commissar, believe me. I've been thinking and thinking since it happened. Nothing at all. You can judge for yourself: he was even given a War Service Cross by the factory."

Kehr sighed. Simple people found it hard to lie – but they also found it hard to think. If Wegler were a member of a Communist group and a really clever saboteur (the only logical presumption), a cow of this sort might be overlooking a dozen clues. Unless it *was* insanity, as she said.

"Well, my dear, I think you can go back to your farm now. I will likely want to see you again in a few hours."

"Thank you, Herr Commissar."

"You must forgive me if I said anything to hurt your feelings… I'm truly a kind man. If you knew me better…"

"Of course, Herr Commissar." She stood up.

He walked around the desk, chuckling. "No one likes a policeman. That's really hard on a bachelor like me." Their eyes met for the briefest instant, and he reflected with amusement that, simple or no, a woman always understood *that*.

He opened the door. "Zimmel."

"Sir?" Zimmel jumped up.

"Send a man home with Frau Lingg."

"That's not needed," she said. "I just live—"

"Please… it's late. You have someone, Zimmel?"

"Yes, sir."

"Tell him to bring back the Pole on her farm… Goodnight, Frau Lingg."

"You're taking my Pole?" she cried in alarm. "The hay will rot if it rains. There's been no one to store it in the barn. It has to be stacked again… *Please*."

"Just for a few questions. If I can't let him go back by morning I promise you there'll be someone else. Your hay won't rot."

"Thank you, thank you, Herr Commissar. You don't know what it means. My quota…"

"He was locked in the barn all night – the Pole?"

"Yes."

"Couldn't get out?"

"No, sir. I have the key."

"Well… get some rest, Frau Lingg."

"Thank you, Herr Commissar."

He watched her as she went out, taking pleasure in the sturdy walk, the full sweep of her flank. As the door closed, he reached for his last cigar, cursed the war rations and struck a match. Even with the opportunity given to one in his position for a little trading on the Black Market, he was still starved for tobacco. It was his single greatest discomfort. Sighing, he looked at his wristwatch. He always liked to conduct an investigation at a decent pace: time for thought, for rest, for a methodical gathering of evidence. What could be done on a basis like this? The excitement of starting a new assignment, and of a two-hour ride in a special airplane, had passed – now he was just plain sleepy.

He walked over to the corner and picked up the bundle of articles that had been taken from Wegler's barracks. He carried it into his office and spread the things out on his desk. There wasn't a great deal – a worn, blue serge suit, a white shirt somewhat torn at the armpits, a pair of faded overalls, four pairs of patched socks, a suit of dirty underwear, a towel, an inch of ersatz soap. He took a razor from a pocket in his briefcase and very carefully commenced to slit the lining of the suit. At the sound of Zimmel's footsteps, he called to him.

"Sir?"

"Get me Wegler's Cell Leader now. And the other men in his bunk, too."

"Yes, sir."

"Anything in the factory locker?"

"Just his work gloves, sir, and a rag."

"All right. Get busy, Thunderbolt."

Zimmel hopped to the phone, looking pleased.

"Ever have a try at that woman, Zimmel?"

"Frau Lingg?"

"Yes."

"Sure. Every SS man around here has tried. Nothing doing."

"Wegler cut you out?"

"Even before that she wouldn't let us get more than a smell. The bitch wants a husband."

"Why don't you marry her, Zimmel? Not a bad piece there."

"And work on a farm?" Zimmel laughed. "Not me. I enjoy life too much as it is."

"Thunderbolt Zimmel," said Kehr. "Well, well... such a sprint you had."

Chapter 4

Sister Wollweber, disobeying orders as usual, softly opened the door to Wegler's room. With blinking, near-sighted eyes she peered around. Instantly her plump face puckered up into a scowl, and she thrust the door back angrily. She strode inside, clucking her tongue to express violent disapproval.

Zoder always commented that it was fortunate for him that German nurses, whether Catholic or not, were called "Sister". Otherwise the Wollweber woman would have insisted upon his calling her "Mother", and would have taken to kissing him morning and night out of her overflowing, maternal spirit. Nurse Wollweber was in her late fifties. She was broad-shouldered, wide at the hips, and had a bosom like an eiderdown pillow at which some eight children had been suckled. Her fleshy, big-nosed face, at once simple and arrogantly determined, expressed both her competence and her colossal ignorance. She was strong as a horse and could lift a man from one bed to another without assistance. She was also as gentle as an angel with the most difficult case, and would scour a bedpan as though she were preparing a vase for roses. Doctor Zoder leant upon her as a shepherd upon his dog, was indebted to her, grateful to her, in constant admiration of her – and twice a day contemplated murder. Sister Wollweber had been trained in nursing some forty years before. After only a few years of hospital work, she had married a hotel porter and departed from the hospital for a happy career of *Kinder, Kirche, Küche*.* Now, with her husband dead, her two sons in the army and her six daughters raising their own children, she had volunteered as a nurse in this moment of crisis for the fatherland. There was nothing which had been taught her forty years before which she did not remember exactly; there was nothing taught since which secretly she did not resent. Worst of all, Zoder had to fight constantly for the right to button his own trousers. Sister Wollweber, for instance, worked the day shift. The only other nurse allotted the factory, Sister Scheithauer, was temporarily incapacitated by a gonorrhoeal infection. (Her fiancé, an Air Force officer, had been on furlough some weeks before.) Consequently, it had been necessary for Zoder to use Sister

Wollweber for Wegler's operation. After the operation his orders to her had been that she must, under no circumstances, lift a finger for any other patient before morning. Wegler's condition would need real attention during the next day, and unless she got some rest, she would be useless. Sister Wollweber had replied "Yes, sir" as she always did most dutifully, and then had spent the hour and a half until this moment in surveying the ward, in washing a nightgown for Sister Scheithauer, in writing short notes to each of her sons in the army. Now, as she contemplated Doctor Zoder in glowering disapproval, she told herself that she had been utterly correct in paying no attention to him. Zoder was leaning forward on Wegler's bed, his face pillowed on his arms, his mouth sagging open. He was quietly snoring. Sister Wollweber clucked her tongue loudly for the second time, partly out of an expression of her sentiment and partly to awaken him. Zoder's snoring stopped, but he remained asleep.

"*Well*, doctor!" she exclaimed loudly. Zoder snapped erect, gasping a little, his eyes startled. She had not meant to be quite so loud, but it was very difficult for her to whisper: her voice always issued from the great bellows of her chest as though it were bound on an errand of its own. When Zoder saw who it was, an expression of weary irritation crossed his face, and his eyes returned to their usual lacklustre state. Sister Wollweber, knowing what to expect, rushed ahead instantly in what Zoder called "her Panzer attack".

"Well, I like this! A fine thing. I told you the operation had exhausted you. Look at yourself. A wet rag. What will you be good for tomorrow if the patient develops infection? Eh? Go to bed now. I insist."

Prepared for his usual, sarcastic counter-attack, Sister Wollweber was thoroughly surprised to see Zoder grin at her with weary affection.

"Doctor, please," she continued eagerly, "a man like you, you have to *think* all the time. It tires you out. Look at you. I can see right into your head. Your brain's asleep and you don't know it. Go to sleep now, doctor. I can doze anywhere. I'll sit in the chair and be fresher than you tomorrow."

"Only, don't growl so, woman. You make me black and blue. Take his pulse."

Her face beaming in triumph, Sister Wollweber obeyed instantly. She held Wegler's wrist and watched the doctor fondly as he rubbed his eyes. "I was fine until a few minutes ago," he muttered half aloud.

He turned as the patient stirred and mumbled. The big head twisted on the pillow. Wegler's face was still flushed from the operation, his forehead greasy with sweat, his blond hair damply tousled.

"Ninety-nine," said the nurse.

"Hm! Up a few points."

"Now, doctor – it's no sign of anything for the pulse to go to ninety-nine. Even you should know that."

"Even I. Take his pulse every half-hour."

"Really, now, as though every hour weren't enough…"

"Damn it, woman, will you do as I say?"

"Yes, sir. It's not that I mind, only I don't like to see you lose your calm. A doctor always should be calm. What happens to a patient if the doctor isn't calm?"

"He dies, he dies," said Zoder. "He dies, he is buried, and the worms enjoy him. Soon it will happen to you, sister."

"In due time," she replied urbanely. "Now to bed, doctor."

"Every half-hour, remember. I want you to absolutely call me if his pulse goes higher than a hundred and one."

"Yes, sir."

"Absolutely," he repeated. "The drip infusion is to continue. You might begin putting some wet gauze on his lips."

"Yes, sir."

"If you're too tired to be any use tomorrow, I'll—"

"Rattle, rattle, rattle… you never stop talking, doctor."

"Sister," he said suddenly, "this Wegler here – you know anything about him?"

"Only what you told me. He must be a beast."

"Why?"

"To do what he did! I could strangle him myself." She said it with earnest venom. "The lowest thing on earth is a man who goes against his country. That's what my father always said, and he was a court clerk."

"I know your father was a court clerk, I know," he said.

"A decent man supports the government," Sister Wollweber continued earnestly. "It's the only way to live. The government's doing its best, isn't it?"

"Goodnight," said Zoder. "And goodnight to your father, the court clerk. The worms must be finding him full of wisdom."

"It's likely," she replied calmly. "Mind you, get altogether undressed, too. Put on your pyjamas. They're mended now."

Zoder stopped with his hand on the doorknob. "Sister, there's one thing I won't forgive you: if Baumer comes here, you must absolutely call me."

She nodded. "I will, sir."

"Baumer's so anxious to talk to the man, he'll kill him by trying it too early. I've absolutely decided that we must keep Wegler quiet until morning. At least until about eight or nine o'clock. If Wegler starts to awaken, you call me. I'll give him a hypo."

"But, sir—"

"Sister," he interrupted angrily, "I'll have no argument about this. I know about medicine, and Baumer doesn't. Wegler won't even be clear-headed by morning. If Baumer goes at him *before* then, all he'll get is a lot of rubbish. It's our duty to protect the fatherland. Are you a patriot or aren't you, sister?"

"Yes, sir. I am."

"Then do as I say. If Wegler comes to, call me instantly."

"Yes, sir."

"If you follow your usual bull-headedness in this, sister, I'll have you up on charges of immoral relations with the patients. Goodnight."

"Goodnight," she said. "Now remember, shoes off and underwear too." As the door closed on him, she added loudly, "I'm a chaste woman, I'd like you to know. I resent even the joke." She giggled suddenly, like an adolescent, blushed and sat down. She looked at Wegler and clucked her tongue. "What a beast!" she muttered aloud. "You wait. You'll get it good."

2

2:40 a.m.

The machine at which Jakob Frisch worked, a small stamping press, was so placed that he could peer into the adjacent locker room when someone went in or out. An hour before, he had caught a glimpse of a number of SS men rifling the wooden lockers. From that moment on he was certain he had been betrayed.

Although they had not come for him directly, Frisch thought he knew the reason for it. Men with power never had to hurry. With their methodical efficiency they were scouring around for further evidence. (They were always so thorough, these supermen.) When they were neatly ready, they would come. And they would come as he had pictured them in that dark corner of his mind that would always be frightened – with a smile, inevitably with a thin smile of triumph on their lips.

Frisch had known it was the end since that afternoon when Wegler had spoken to him. He had known it as do some old men who have lived beyond a normal span, and who guess with absolute clarity the approach of death. He was not old, but every moment of these last six months had been lived on the borrowed time of an old man. And during every day of it, beneath the surface of his life, he had known the odour, the living presence of the sadness which gripped him now.

How incurably naive was the human heart! It clung to hope without rhyme or reason. When he reviewed Wegler's manner, it was clear that the man had not been even expert in his hypocrisy... a clumsy provocateur attempting to trap him into self-betrayal. Yet there was a moment when he had been inclined almost to trust him.

He knew what would happen now. He would be led before an SS Leader – in some room in the administration building that had no windows. Quite pleasantly the man would say: "Ah... so you're the bedbug who's been writing those subversive slogans on the walls?" He would reply, "Why, no, sir. It's a mistake." Then the SS Leader would bark, "Mistake, is it? Blumel, call in Wegler." And Wegler would finish him off. "Yes, sir. I saw him last night in the woods. I watched him. He had a little bottle of paint. I saw it all." And the only grain of comfort he would have before they put the screws on him would be his six months of loneliness: that he had never been able to make contact with any group in the factory – and so need have no fear that he would betray a comrade.

Wegler, Willi Wegler. He had liked Wegler. A quiet man, seemingly decent towards others. He would have understood betrayal at the hands of Keller or Hoiseler. They were Party men, their brains already decayed under the layers of Nazi manure. But not Wegler. Betrayal at his hands did not even involve the dignity of perverted conviction. He would expect them to double his tobacco ration perhaps – that was all.

How profound it was, this stew of corruption into which so many of his people had been plunged – how deep and awful and unbelievable! There was no brain to encompass it, or tongue to speak it – and it was the saddest page in the ledger of humankind.

He remained calm in spite of his inward terror. He had been prepared too long for this moment for it to be otherwise. He continued to feed his machine, thrusting the little brass cylinders into the clamping jaws with his right hand, snatching the cylinders out, already moulded for war, with his left – twelve to the minute. All around him men and women were feeding machines which stamped and pounded and cut and ground, disgorging the metal parts which would become a tank. And as Frisch watched them, a wave of incommunicable pity welled up in his heart, for he knew that this was not what they wanted, that even for those who were poisoned with malice and utterly, irretrievably damned, this was not what they *really* wanted. And in the same moment that he saw the door open and SS Leader Zimmel enter from the locker room, he cursed these men about him, and blessed them, and wept for them – and bled in his heart for his land and for himself.

He watched covertly. Zimmel went up to Bednarick, the foreman. They whispered together for a moment. Then Bednarick, alone, walked hastily down the long aisle to the corner where he stood, continuing to work. He looked up at the foreman calmly.

"You're wanted in the Party office," Bednarick shouted. His mouth twisted and grimaced in the exaggerated articulation that men learn in a noisy shop. "Shut off your machine."

Frisch waited, his left hand automatically poised, until the operation was completed, then he plucked out the brass cylinder, dropped it in the box by his side and clicked off the power switch. He nodded to the foreman and wiped the sweat off his forehead with a dirty handkerchief.

"Been raping minors again, eh, pastor?" said Bednarick jovially. He was a Bavarian in his late sixties, much given to bawdy talk in his declining years. "Oh, you clergymen, you pure ones, I know you. Well, come along, lad. Let's hope you get off with a fine, whatever it is."

Frisch followed him down the aisle. He knew without turning his head that the others in the shop would be watching him every step of the way – the men who had been transported from different cities and the women from the surrounding villages. So, without appearing to be even interested, they always watched with inscrutable faces when someone was summoned by an SS man. And he knew, too, that some would say to themselves, "What's up with the pastor?" – because the word had gotten around that he had once been an ordained clergyman – and that others would shrink inside and whisper, "The pastor's in trouble... God help the pastor", but that there were some whose lips would curl and who would prejudge him, saying, "Pastor's done something, eh? Let him get it." Only the Polish prisoners, who were being trained at every third machine in his shop, would not watch. In the two days since they had come to work in the factory, it had become clear that they cared nothing for what happened to Germans.

A short, frail, colourlessly blond man of thirty-three, he walked up to SS Leader Zimmel and stood facing him, his right shoulder drooping a little, his head tilted. He looked more or less as Doctor Zoder had seen him four years before on the platform of a railroad station, except that now his face was both thinner and harder, and now his eyes were not frightened – behind his glasses they were, in fact, limpid, serene and as beautiful as the eyes of a girl. He nodded to Zimmel and received a nod in return. He thought to himself, wryly, "I was wrong about one thing. At least there's no smile on his mug."

He followed Zimmel out of the building – past the two SS guards with carbines and whips, who had become decorative features of their shop since the arrival of the Poles, past the two other guards at the door – and then into the darkness of the soft August night.

3

3:10 a.m.

Anna Mahnke, former grade-school teacher, now head of the National Socialist Welfare Organization for the village and the surrounding farm community, was suffering from an old-fashioned bellyache. In Republican Germany it used to be that cramps were cramps – nowadays, at least for an earnest Party member like Anna, cramps were a political matter too. One not only felt a responsibility towards the shortage of medicines, one also practised a spartan attitude towards life, as urged by the Party healers. Anna, for instance, took only ice-cold baths; she refused medication for ordinary ailments; and she exercised religiously, even though she had always abominated callisthenics. But tonight both her principles and her pride had come a cropper. She had awakened to her discomfiture at about midnight (the stinking piece of fish Peasant Leader Rosenhart had served her for supper...) and had tossed on her bed for more than an hour. She decided then that, principles or no principles, she couldn't accept such misery any longer. It was obvious that her bellyache was no ordinary ailment, and that it would not be relieved by studying a chapter in *Mein Kampf,** which she had been trying to do. Accordingly she banged on the wall until she awakened her thirteen-year-old, Otto, and then sent him down to rouse the druggist.

It was now past three in the morning. Although Anna was feeling more comfortable, she was still belching in several keys and had not yet succeeded in falling asleep. As a result, it was particularly irritating to her that an SS car should come roaring down the village street and stop before her door. Robert Latzelburger, her nephew, was a member of the Elite Guard and had awakened her more than once by his noisy homecomings. Among other things, the hulking nineteen-year-old lad had a deep, bass voice: his rumbling laugh, which he never muted, could shake a wall. Being both patriotic and modern, Anna was willing to allow that duty on the one hand, or normal male activities on the other, were sufficient excuse for a young man to come home at a late hour. She wouldn't allow, however, that his arrivals couldn't be managed more quietly. At the moment, to judge by the sound of their booming laughter, Robert and his friend were exchanging off-colour stories. They had left the motor of their car running ("What about the national oil supply, Party Comrades?") and altogether they were conducting themselves as though it were broad daylight and peacetime. Listening to them go on and on, Anna suddenly flew into a temper. She jumped out of bed and strode across to the window, her two black braids flopping around angrily behind her. She was a tall woman of thirty-three, lean and well built, with rather ugly features – something of a horse-face, in fact. She banged the casement window open, and her voice split the night air with the shrill thrust of a buzz saw. "I suppose this is the considerate German youth of today! You pigs, you're waking up the whole neighbourhood!"

Startled, the two young men looked up. They could see only a white nightgown and the shadowed outline of a face, but they knew who it was. Robert, with a sheepish grin, jumped hastily out of the car.

"You," Anna exclaimed in bitter reproach, "at least *you* ought to have better sense, Robert. But do you even think of your relatives? Not you. Drunk too, I suppose!"

"Who's drunk?" the driver demanded insolently. "Likely you, but not us. *You're* making all the noise around here."

"Peter Blumel, eh?" Anna shouted. "So help me, I'll report you, Blumel."

"So report!" he shouted back. Deliberately he backfired the car. "Report this too, Auntie." He backfired the motor again and shot off down the street.

Raging, with a splitting head, Anna pulled the blackout curtains and turned on the light. She crawled back into bed and waited for her nephew to come upstairs. She felt doubly furious now because of Blumel's impertinence. Blumel was mistaken if he thought she wouldn't report him. People were at least entitled to their sleep – in times like these his behaviour was conscious political sabotage, no more, no less.

"Robert!" She heard him trying to pass her door.

"Yes?"

"Come in!"

"I'm coming." He peered in at her diffidently, his bulldog face split by a sheepish grin. "Did you think I wasn't coming?"

"Don't try to be smart, Robert. Shut the door. Otto's asleep. As though I didn't hear you tiptoeing down the hall. You're a nice boy, but please don't try and be smart with me, Robert. Now, listen, Robert – once and for all, I want an end to this. Here I've been up half the night, sick as a dog—"

"You're sick? I'm sorry, Aunt Anna," he interrupted with genuine concern.

"Let me finish... I just won't have it any more, Robert. You can spend your nights the way you like. But this business must stop..."

As Anna had said, Robert was a rather stupid boy. Nevertheless, he had a canine appreciation of his aunt's weaknesses. To avoid the half-hour lecture he knew was coming, he decided to blurt out the news he had intended to save until morning.

"Excuse me, Anna, but just listen... I was on duty tonight—"

"Keep quiet until I finish!"

"I have news, Anna."

"It can wait. Once and for all, Robert—"

"Anna – sabotage at the factory!"

She sat up in bed, her eyes wide.

"I mean it. We're not supposed to tell. But I know *you* won't spread it."

"So tell me! What are you waiting for?"

Grinning a little, Robert sat down on the foot of the bed and told her about Wegler. As she listened, Anna's bony, mobile face mirrored a succession of emotions: apprehension, rage, indignation. But when Robert brought Berthe Lingg into the story, she suddenly jumped out of bed with a loud exclamation.

"What's the matter?" he asked, eyeing her with a bit of embarrassment.

"Berthe Lingg... So what do we do about that?" Anna muttered.

"You know something about the woman?" He gazed at her covertly, his face flushing.

"Eh?"

"Do you know something about the woman, Auntie?"

"Aha! Indeed I do," she exclaimed vivaciously. She shivered a little in the night cool of the room and crossed to a chair for her worn bathrobe. She patted his shoulder in passing. "I'm very grateful to you, Robert. This can avoid a nasty mess. For me too."

"Anna," he said eagerly, "if you tell me and I go to the Gestapo commissar or to Baumer, do you know what it can mean?" His blue eyes commenced to snap as he thought of it. "If you've only got something good on that woman—"

"It's nothing like that."

"You said—"

"Nonsense. You don't understand a thing about it, boy."

"So what is it?"

"My secret," Anna retorted triumphantly. She bent over him, laughing. "Never mind, Robert. You're a good lad. I'd tell you if I could, but it's out of the question." She patted his shoulder in the affectionate, patronizing way she had. "It relates to *my* work, not to any Gestapo commissar."

"All right, then." Robert could feel himself flushing at her nearness. Aunt or not aunt, he had not seen very much of her until he was assigned to this district. She was only thirty-three. Walking around in front of him in just a nightgown... he couldn't help his thoughts. The big question, which he had pondered over and over, was whether she really considered him a child, as she was always making out. An SS man, he was scarcely to be considered a child by any woman. His comrades, now, they took it as a matter of course that he was sleeping with Anna... her husband in the army and all that. Nor did he deny it, naturally – he had his pride. But how to take the first step, that was what always baffled him. If it turned out wrong... His uncle's wife!... He was frightened to think of it.

"Well, all right," he said again. "Just as you feel, Anna."

"Now listen, Robert!" She said it in a curious voice, rather loud and uneasy. "Look at me." He looked up and saw with astonishment that she had a finger to her lips. She turned towards the door. "Now listen, Robert!" Padding very softly she crossed to the door. "This is not a matter that..." In a quick movement she flung the door open. Robert, who had risen, stared over her shoulder at the dark hallway.

"What's the matter?"

She didn't answer, but walked into the hall, peering around. She returned, shutting the door softly. "I could swear I heard a board creak. That Otto! I don't know what to do with him. It was my imagination this time, but will you believe it, he's taken to spying on me?"

Robert grinned.

"Never mind, it's not funny. I caught him the other day reading a letter of mine. I gave his ears such a boxing I almost wore my hand out."

"A kid," said Robert.

"It's no excuse."

"Maybe his Youth Group is having spy exercises."

"Then let him not practise on his own mother, if he knows what's good for him... Anyway, listen, Robert – did you get that tyre fixed on your bicycle?"

"Yes."

"Let me borrow it."

"When?"

"Right now. I have to see Berthe Lingg. Is she on her farm?"

"We just drove her home."

"Good."

"But when can you be back, Anna?"

"When I'm back... how do I know? Maybe in a few hours, maybe longer. It's an important matter."

"But I have to report at seven. There's big doings at the factory over this."

"What a gentleman! You want me to walk when I feel like a dog – and a strong lad like you has to ride?" She gave him a playful shove. "For shame, Robert."

Robert caught her hand as though joining in her play. "If I do you the favour, will you return it?"

"Sure. What?"

He suddenly felt scared. He let her hand drop. "All right. Take the bike." He ran his hand nervously over his close-cropped head.

Anna sat down on the bed. "What time is it?"

"Three forty-three."

"Let me think a minute. Don't talk to me."

Watching her so near to him in her state of intimate dress, Robert didn't know what to think. Even though this woman bullied him with a maternal solicitude that his mother had never shown... still... if it made no difference to him that she was his aunt, it might be the same for her. There was no blood kinship, after all... in a way she wasn't even a relative.

Robert was nineteen. He was only shortly out of an adolescence in which his unhandsome bulldog face and his rather slow wits had made him the butt of his fellows. As a result, in spite of his hulking body, he was inwardly unsure of himself, especially with women. He had had a few experiences with prostitutes on visits to a city, but that was all. Since his arrival at the village, the local girls had uniformly rejected his blundering advances. (His SS status had not wrought the miracle he expected.) It was a sparsely settled farming community into which the factory had brought an abnormal concentration of men. Those girls who were of a mind to go walking at night could afford to be selective. As a result, Robert hungered after anything in skirts, and burned day and night with that special, frenetic desire peculiar to adolescents. Moreover his thwarted longings were not alleviated by the company he kept. His comrades in the Elite Guard regaled each other incessantly with accounts of their nocturnal achievements in haystack, meadow and barn (true and imaginary). One lad in particular, Schmidt, who had experienced the first months of the Russian campaign and who was home on invalid's furlough, was a vivid raconteur. His stories of unbridled male activity – hampered by no law, sense of guilt or moral restraint ("That sort of bitch is lucky to have a German push them over") – had a special effect in stimulating his fantasies about Anna. The taboos he would have felt ordinarily at lusting after a relative gave way before this intoxicating male world in which others lived. These days, in his imaginative conquests, Anna always yielded to force.

But now, as he peered at her out of the corner of his eye, the ease of his fantasy world was not at hand to help him. He shivered equally from desire and fright, and his mind trembled over the various possibilities. She was so close he could reach out easily and embrace her. But if she became insulted, he might get in trouble. She held a political post in the community, after all. And what if she chucked him out of her house? He would be obliged to live in the barracks then, where a man could never be alone and the food was vile… Perhaps there was another way – if he didn't commit himself, as it were? He might merely ask her if she were cold… hold a blanket around her. Then if she let him do that… Or perhaps he ought to say something clever. Some ingratiating approach…

But maybe all of these things were no good. His comrades always boasted of just grabbing a girl without any preliminaries. Women liked that, they said. They wanted a man to be aggressive. After all, why was she sitting there like that? Wasn't it a direct invitation?

Anna was leaning forward as she sat, one hand pulling concentratedly at her lower lip. The posture was such that her small, hard breasts were outlined against the thin robe. With hot eyes and a choking sensation in his throat Robert suddenly said, "Anna."

She turned to him immediately. "I've got it!" she exclaimed with a triumphant smile. "I was worried about something, but now I know just what to do. Very good. I'll get started."

"Anna," he said again, hoarsely.

"What?"

He wanted to say "You're very pretty, Anna", even though it was a lie, or something else that might start things for him. But he was utterly tongue-tied.

She looked at him with a teasing smile. "You want to ask me for that favour?"

It seemed to him then that she surely understood, that she could not but feel as he did, and that her question must only be designed to make him act. Roughly he embraced her, one arm around her shoulders, a hand instantly at her breast. "Anna, Anna."

She gasped, trying to stand up. "What are you doing?"

The blood rushed to Robert's head. Anna's breathless, bewildered voice told him that he had judged her wrongly, that she felt nothing of what he had hoped. The possible consequences terrified him. Through a sudden dizziness and a pounding in his ears he heard her voice, as though from far away, "Are you crazy? What have you got in your mind? Let me go."

She was struggling against his grip, tugging at his hands. Rage seized him, a fury compounded of fear and his injured male pride. He flung her back on the bed, violently, covering her with his heavy body. With sudden hysteria in her voice she cried, "Robert. God in Heaven. Stop, Robert!" He said nothing. His hands tore at her robe in a drunken clumsiness. "You'll wake Otto," she cried with absurd irrelevance. "Robert, you'll wake Otto." He tried to kiss her, more from an urgent, frightened need to still her speech than from desire. Anna's nails suddenly dug into the flesh of his face. She raked the skin open from temple to jaw, leaving a pattern of bloody streaks. The pain was intense, and Robert jerked away from her automatically. Instantly she rolled to one side in a sharp movement of her strong body. He fell over – and in the next moment, although he tried to seize her again, she was on her feet. With that he was finished – suddenly defeated and back to his senses. He stared at her enraged face for a moment, and then, with a gasp of dismay, buried his head in his hands.

"Oh!" Anna exploded, in a voice that was choked by fury. "Oh, you pig! Your own aunt! You must be crazy. Such a filth, you are. You belong in a concentration camp, that's where you belong!"

"I didn't mean it," Robert cried stupidly. "Honest, Anna, I don't know what happened to me."

"When I write your mother, what she'll say!" Anna continued savagely. "A fine SS man. You'll be out tomorrow, do you hear? What a beast!" She spat at his feet. "*Pfui!* A dirty little boy!"

In absolute despair Robert did the best thing he could have in the situation. He stopped trying to find excuses and blurted out the truth. "Anna, believe me... it wouldn't have happened – but I couldn't help myself. You were in your nightgown. I know it was wrong, but you don't know how attractive you are. And I'm so lonely, Anna!"

"I see!" Anna cried sarcastically. "Trying to blame me now? You pig – how should I know a child like you, a relative, would have such dirty thoughts in his head? A decent woman doesn't think of such things."

Anna was lying. There had been several occasions when the notion had come into her mind of going to Robert's bed at night. Her husband had been called up on the very first day of the war, and by now she was starved for a man's embrace. And on all sides she saw other women yielding to a similar need – a hunger that was far from being purely physical. Chaste mothers, whom she had known for years, were surreptitiously carrying on with strangers from the factory, or with SS youngsters. It was like a fever, infecting everyone, and on all sides one observed that rigid standards were breaking down, and that people no longer cared. There was only one thing the higher-ups couldn't ration, people whispered with a grin. And with a lad like Robert, who lived under the same roof, it could be managed so that word never reached one's husband. But until now Anna's mind had always rejected the temptation. In spite of her Party duties, which included the supervision of illegitimate births in the community, the idea of taking a lover – a relative at that – remained basically abhorrent to her. Nevertheless, she would have reacted with a bit less disgust to Robert's advance had she not been already so guilty in her thoughts.

Hearing his plea, however, she was touched by his confession of loneliness, and more than a little flattered by his insistence that she was irresistibly attractive. And although she knew that he couldn't be let off without a good calling down, she was already softening towards him in her heart. "Ah, you," she said, "the more I think of the insult, the more disgusted I become. If you want to practise rape – go off to war. Rape a Polack or a Russky – it won't make any difference to them. But a German woman you can't treat that way."

"I know, I know it was wrong," Robert whined. "I could die, I'm so sorry. But you don't know how attractive you looked." He was playing the piper's note deliberately now. Anna's mobile face, which could rarely conceal her feelings, had betrayed her. "I just couldn't help myself, Anna."

"I suppose you have to sleep here tonight," she said, "but tomorrow morning off you go to the barracks. Not another night in my house!"

"Please, Anna!" He fumbled for an argument. "Please don't—"

"It's my last word!"

"Anna," he cried suddenly, "you don't realize what happened to me earlier tonight. I shot a man! I was trembling all over when I came here."

She looked at him suspiciously. "You're lying. You shot someone? Who?"

"I was the one who shot Wegler!"

"You?" A different note came into her voice. "This is the truth you're telling? *You* saved the factory?"

"Yes."

The implication of the brilliant news became instantly clear to her. "Robert, this is wonderful. You'll get promoted. You scoundrel, why didn't you tell me before?"

"I just... you see... I thought I wouldn't!"

"Not tell your aunt a piece of news like that?"

Robert stood dumbly, a hand to his bleeding cheek, not knowing how to extricate himself from this new complication. It was true that he had shot Wegler – as a matter of fact, a perfect snap shot at fifty yards, with only a bonfire to illuminate his target. It was also true that Baumer had almost brained him with his own gun in the next moment for not aiming at Wegler's leg. If Anna were to spread the news now that he was a hero, he would be in a ghastly fix with his SS comrades, who knew better.

"Listen, Anna, you mustn't tell this to any outsider, you hear?" He spoke very firmly.

"Why not? My own nephew—"

"It's a secret."

"Why?"

"I don't know why – but Baumer made me swear. Nobody must know now that I was the one who shot him. Maybe later. I'll get in trouble if you tell, Anna. You will, too."

"I won't tell!" she said with a sigh. She stood regarding him with sour affection. "So! My nephew's a hero... but he's also a pig. What a business."

"I'm sorry, Anna."

"Oh, get out now. I have better things to do than listen to you say 'I'm sorry!' Next time be sorry in advance, please. Now get out. I have duties to attend to."

Sheepishly, Robert left the room. He heard the click of the door lock, and he grinned a little. It hadn't turned out so badly. Anna would keep her mouth shut. Likely she'd let him stay on in the house too. She wasn't so angry that he couldn't see she liked it when he told her she was attractive. She drank it down like a sweet syrup. In a way this evening might even break the ice. She would think of him differently from now on.

Content with himself, Robert swaggered into the bathroom and commenced to bathe his face.

Standing before the mirror, her nightgown in her hand, Anna looked at her naked body. Now that it was over and Robert was safely out of the room, she hungered after him. He was a stupid lout, and he had an ugly mug on him if ever a man did, but he had a rude male force that spoke to her in primitive terms. Yet it was evil – it was really evil to think of lying with him carnally. A lad of nineteen – a relative...

She wondered about the morning. Ought she to make him move? She didn't want to. It made a great deal of difference in preparing meals to have a third ration card in the house. And Robert brought home extra things from the factory canteen sometimes.

She decided against it. It was certainly best to forgive him – with an additional rebuke, of course. Anything else would be biting off her own nose – especially now, when he was in line for a promotion, the pig.

She rubbed her hand softly over her flat, smooth belly. She closed her eyes for a moment. It was really flattering: to be wanted so by a lad of nineteen. And it wasn't as though they were related by blood.

She burst out laughing, suddenly, and began to dress.

4

3:30 a.m.

Slowly, reluctantly, Willi Wegler was returning to consciousness. For quite some time now the dark murk within his veins had been receding before a life tide that was claiming him again.

Wegler had no reasonable basis for returning to life. He was doomed. Even in the pit of his unconsciousness his soul must have known that. There was no escape for him, no possible miracle, no door that man or God might suddenly disclose. A nation, a way of life, an army, a code of laws... and police and jailors and judges... all, all existed only to doom him... and he was indeed already doomed.

So there is no telling why he had not succumbed already to the steel pellet fired into the core of his belly by Robert Latzelburger. He had no reason for continuing his life, no hope and no future. And these things weigh high in the body's chemistry, as any doctor will testify. Perhaps it was that a single life force of a sort still remained to him – a curiosity. Wegler had left a deed undone, and his soul was curious. In the instant that he had fallen to the hot earth, with the whole world spinning insanely before his eyes, his mind had cried "What will…" The power loom of his brain stopped dead in that moment, but the thread only half spun dangled and sought completion. And now, as the dark tide ebbed from body and limb, as a dull pain marked the return of life after an armistice during which pain, thought, anger, desire had all been stilled, his mind spoke again: "What will…" – in a quickening surge.

He was dreaming now, reliving in delirium the last frenzied moment of his conscious life – but weakly, monotonously. It was all detached from himself, and incredibly far off in an opaque space – the shouting, the blazing fire, the high, thin scream of Berthe Lingg, the overall droning of the Stirlings. And so he lay, as though at one end of a giant funnel of darkness, with pain and memory, anguish and curiosity, slowly, slowly returning through endless space to give him life and consciousness again.

He stirred on the bed, groaning. Sister Wollweber, lying on a blanket at full length on the floor, opened her eyes momentarily and then drowsed again.

By this time the Stirlings had touched English soil. The crew members were giving their reports.

Chapter 5

It was all thoroughly bewildering, and Pastor Frisch scarcely knew what to make of the situation. An hour before he had left the machine shop at the side of SS Leader Zimmel. (The smell of the concentration camp was in his nostrils, the skin on his back was cold, already dancing.) He had walked in silence – resigned, stubborn and calm, thinking only that a man in extremity has one possession unalterably his own: the right to spit before he dies.

He found things not at all as he expected. Zimmel led him to an office in the administration building. There, dozing at their ease, he saw a group of his own bunkmates. And there, at his ease, Zimmel left him. Frisch knew instantly – with a sense of relief so keen it stabbed his breast – that somehow he had been granted reprieve. But even while his heart beat furiously and a hot sweat burst out on his palms, his brain grew cold.

There is a biology to the underground conspirator for freedom: he is twice a man and half a man, he is a hero and he is a ferret. And with a greed for any information that might be turned to his uses, Frisch's mind commenced to gnaw at the problem – but carefully, and with cunning. He sat down, nodding to the others, smiling the little twisted smile that came so often to his lips these days. The others nodded back, glad for his presence. He rolled a cigarette and commenced to smoke.

Frisch was popular with his bunkmates. They liked his quiet talk, the sense of genuine sympathy they felt in him, the lack of moralizing. It was known that he was a former pastor. At first some of the men were annoyed at the idea of a clergyman in their bunk. They were of no mind to have their conversation limited, or their activities subject to even silent disapproval. But shortly they found that he was what Hoiseler called "not a bad egg". He didn't get drunk like some of them on Saturday night, he didn't talk of women quite as they did – but a man could tell him a smutty joke and get another in exchange. Frisch had been a worker's son and a worker himself before he became a pastor; he knew how to get along with men of their sort. It was not known, however, that Frisch had been in a concentration camp. In their bunk only the Cell Leader, Fritz Keller, had been informed.

This was deliberate policy on the part of the higher-ups. The Kellers of the factory, whose main function was to report on the conduct of the workers, obviously had to know the history of everyone in their bunk. Beyond that, it was considered wise to maintain discretion about the record of men like Frisch. Wartime urgency made it essential to use all able hands, but there was no point in advising secret dissenters amongst the workers where they might find another of their stripe. Men like Frisch, who were considered "reformed" by their stay in a concentration camp, were under double surveillance, but were not otherwise singled out.

Sucking his cigarette, the wry little smile on his lips, Frisch tried to estimate the situation. There was one obvious fact at hand: none but his own bunkmates had been summoned. Beyond that, there were only a series of confusing possibilities.

The matter must be acutely important, however. This he knew. Two things revealed it to him: that Eggert, Weiner and himself, who were all on night shift, had been taken off the job at the same time, and that the others, who were day-shift men, had been plucked out of bed in the middle of the night. If it were a casual inquiry, they would have kept the night men at work instead of losing production time – besides, since the higher-ups knew that the hours of work and the low quality of food made the workers flop into their cots like exhausted field beasts at night, they were not carelessly robbing the day men of the sleep they needed. Therefore the inquiry under foot must be acute, and it must also involve a time factor. This was a first important conclusion.

Leaning his head back, Frisch surveyed his mates through half-closed eyelids. There were five of them – Hoiseler, Eggert, Pelz, Rufke, Weiner. Frisch thought suddenly that one understood a great deal about the Germany they were living in by merely knowing the ages of such men. Hoiseler, Eggert and Weiner were between forty and fifty-five. They represented, for the moment, the male worker in wartime Germany. The young men had departed from the factories as though a plague had carried them off. (And had it not!) Except for lads like Pelz! Pelz was a new phenomenon – very interesting, too. A lad of only twenty-one – tall, straight as a birch, handsome, with one arm off at the shoulder and a confused look in his eyes. Yes, Pelz was very interesting to Frisch. Ten years of Nazi education, from the time he was eleven – a farm boy with more manure thrust into his head than had ever been granted him for his land... but crippled at twenty-one in the campaign in France and wondering, always wondering where the glory had gone. Yes, Pelz, with his one arm and the hurt, questioning look in his eyes, Pelz had a past... but he also had a future. He was a farmer whose crops had suffered a sudden blight, as it were. He didn't like it, he was angry and bitter, he didn't know whom to blame... and he had possibilities, Frisch thought. He had an anger under the layers of manure, an unanswered question.

Then there was Rufke, one of the factory barbers. Rufke was a vigorous wart of a man who looked fifty-five and was approaching seventy. That was interesting, too, because Rufke had been five years in retirement when the war came. If they were beginning to use men of his age, it told something.

Yes, Frisch thought now, one could learn a great deal from a man's age these days. But what that same man was like in his heart – ah, that was quite a different matter. No one ever could completely know the heart of another. This had always been so, and it would always be so, too. But whereas in the past one could venture a guess about the soul of another, nowadays in Germany one could no longer even guess about the souls of most men. And that was the most interesting fact of all.

Pelz, now... you could guess about him to a degree: hurt, bewildered, angry. Hoiseler, you could guess a little about him too. Hoiseler was a surly, dark-faced man of forty-five, who had been a salesman for a hardware concern, and who disliked intensely his new proletarian status. Hoiseler was a Nazi by soul's choice. Somewhere in the dog-eat-dog of his salesman's life, somewhere between the innocence of his first day's life and the rapacious adult satisfaction with which he read aloud his brother's account of a furlough in Athens... somewhere along there he had become a human being for whom Adolf Hitler was spokesman, not corrupter. The Nazis had not been obliged to pervert and coerce the Hoiselers as they had others – they had merely to provide a coherent philosophy for them. Hoiseler was moderately clear: where there was dung, there one found flies – and Hoiselers.

But Eggert and Weiner (yes, and Wegler too, now that he knew Wegler had not betrayed him... where was Wegler, by the way?...), they were fascinating men to contemplate. Eggert and Weiner, who looked different, and who came from different towns, who had different religious backgrounds and completely separate personalities, were nevertheless as alike as twins: they were silent men, they were men who wore hard masks where a face should have been, they were men with a singular disinterest in conversation. They worked, ate, slept, got swinishly drunk on most Sunday nights – and were silent. And in this they were strangely, fascinatingly typical of a great many of the male workers in the factory between forty and fifty-five – hardbitten, taciturn workmen who ate, slept and got drunk on Sunday night if they could. And about no one of them could one be sure what secrets his heart held. One could only suspect and speculate, as Frisch did endlessly, probing whenever he could – as a ferret gnaws and probes, and will not give in when a hunger is upon him.

But there, at least, was the third important conclusion. They had summoned the men of his bunk, yet Wegler and Fritz Keller were absent. Why? This, perhaps, was a point on which he might begin to work.

Frisch pinched off his cigarette butt (thrusting the quarter-inch that remained into his pocket for a later shredding and reuse) and glanced around at the other men. The office was small, and they sat on benches along the wall – old Rufke and young Pelz on the bench with Frisch himself; Weiner, Eggert and Hoiseler sprawled out opposite. Except for Eggert, who was patiently cleaning his cold pipe with a wisp of straw (stolen surreptitiously from a factory broom), the others had their eyes closed. But he knew they were not really asleep.

"A pleasant good morning to all of you," said Frisch softly, with gentle irony. "The birds are singing sweetly, the Stirlings have gone home, and the rutabaga crop will be extra special this year." He waited a moment. One by one the men opened their heavy lids and gazed at him wearily, but with slight, expectant smiles. Frisch had a genuine gift of mimicry that they always enjoyed – and that he employed with measured cunning whenever possible. "I take it we're assembled here because we're off to" – his eyes opened wide in a sudden comedy stare – "Greece. Correct?"

The others grinned, tired as they were. This was a take-off on Hoiseler, and on the letters he read them from his brother in Greece.

"Dark-eyed virgins aside," Frisch continued with a wink, "what's up?"

"We haven't been told a thing," replied Pelz. "Something important, though." He jerked his thumb towards the adjacent office. "Keller's in there with some big shot. And they cleaned all of Willi's things out of his locker in the bunk."

"That so?" Frisch enquired lightly. "But where is Willi? If this is a bunk matter, how does he get off? Rating special favours, eh?"

"Special favours is good," observed Hoiseler. "Where do *you* think he is?" He smacked his lips in crude imitation of a kiss. "With that woman of his – where else? He didn't sleep in tonight – special reward for his War Service Cross." Hoiseler sighed a little. "She's the real goods, that baggage. Imagine being able to tickle her every night."

"And twice on Sunday," interrupted old Rufke joyously.

"Damn, but I envy Willi," Hoiseler sighed. "I'm going loony before this war's over. My old woman's safe in Sudetenland, and I'm safe here – but I'd a hell of a lot rather be back in Stettin,* going to sleep in a cellar. You could do things in our cellar. How the devil has Wegler been able to get himself a woman around here and I can't?"

Old Rufke, the barber, commenced to giggle. Frisch knew instantly the type of comment to expect from him. Rufke was a particular pal of Bednarick, the foreman in his shop. They had nothing in common except the peculiar bawdiness which possesses some old men. They talked sex like fevered adolescents, both of them pretending that they were still lions in the bedroom. Rufke, like Hoiseler, was a man whom Frisch utterly despised. He was a model of stiff-necked patriotism and national pride, who talked of German superiority over all other races as though it were one of the original Ten Commandments. As a man who had fought in the first World War and had an aviator son in this one, he had already divided up the world to his own satisfaction. He was the strategist of their bunk, too, complete with coloured maps and the latest radio bulletins, crowing over victories and excusing defeats. Giggling now, Rufke said, "Hoiseler, the difference between Wegler and you is to be seen at a quick glance when you're both stripped. Willi, now, he has parts like any normal man. But you – I don't know – sometimes I think there's a couple of peppermints there – other times I don't even see anything." Rufke rocked with laughter, his false teeth clicking in his mouth. Then he snapped out a comb in a flamboyant gesture and began combing his fine white head of hair.

Hoiseler, as usual, paid no attention to Rufke, although his dark face grew surly. He never liked to have fun poked at himself. Only Frisch, with his special brand of gentle satire, was able to make him accept a jest in good humour.

Frisch, eager to steer the conversation back into a fruitful channel, asked, "Do you suppose anything's happened to Wegler?" He was enormously agitated by the bit of news they had dropped – that the SS men had removed Wegler's things from his bunk. That fact, coupled with Wegler's continued absence, introduced a question he did not have the courage to face: if Wegler's approach to him that afternoon had been honest... If he, Frisch, had thrust off a good man, letting him go his own way alone...

Eggert, sucking a cold pipe, looked over at Frisch and asked indifferently, "Something happened to Wegler? What do you mean?"

Frisch paused for a moment before replying. His eyes searched the other man's face. Blandly, Eggert stared back at him. He was a thick-lipped, snub-nosed man with flinty blue eyes.

"I mean, perhaps Willi is sick... or had an accident."

Eggert grunted and looked away.

"He grunts," Frisch thought to himself with bitter weariness, "he grunts and he grunts as though he were a swine rolling in mud. Only, he is not a swine! There is a brain in that head, and there are thoughts behind that wooden face. And you, too, Weiner, you're another fine grunter, you are. Eggert sucks his pipe as though he's a baby with a nipple, and you fuss at those big ears of yours like you're the village idiot. Only, Eggert's not a baby, and no idiot could handle the work you do. How many Sunday nights I've tried to get you both to open up! You get drunk sometimes, but you never drop a word about rationing or casualties or anything like that, do you? The war's going fine, the world's lovely, everything pleases you! Only, I don't believe you, my friends. Your world isn't lovely, and you know it. I'm tired of your grunts. It's time for the pigs to come out of their wallow!"

"Say, Jakob," said Hoiseler, a flicker of interest coming into his tired eyes, "you haven't heard: I got another letter from my brother tonight. The kid's really in clover now. You want to hear?"

Frisch nodded, although he had no interest whatsoever in what he knew was coming.

A grin came to Hoiseler's loose mouth. "He's been promoted – a lance corporal. They moved him to Piraeus. Now just listen to this. The first night there he gets billeted in a private home – swell, too: the house of a lawyer. Educated people, he says, who even speak German. What do you think? There's a young girl in the house, fifteen years old, not a day older, and ripe as a plum, my brother says. He swears she has breasts like young pumpkins, like she was twenty-five and had two kids. Anyway, he gets one look at her and he thinks 'Tomorrow I start a private little blitz. There's a sweet piece I want under the sheets.'"

"Under him," old Rufke interrupted joyously. "What good is a wench under a sheet?"

"So he gets into bed," Hoiseler continued with a frown, ignoring Rufke, "and what do you think? Two minutes later there's a knock on his door. 'Who is it?' he calls. The door opens, and there the girl is. And who do you suppose has her by the hand? Her mother!

"'What do you want?' asks my brother.

"'A loaf of bread,' the mother says. 'If you'll give me a loaf of bread, my daughter will stay here to thank you...' Just like that, mind you, no beating around the bush. So my brother hops out of bed, naturally, and goes to his knapsack. 'I don't have any more bread, but here's two cans.'

"'What's in them?' the mother asks, like she was buying something in a department store.

"'Both fish,' says my brother.

"'Very good. But can you get bread tomorrow?'

"'Depending,' says my brother, who's no fool.

"'Naturally,' says the mother. 'My daughter will thank you each time. If she has no reason to thank, she won't.'

"'She'll have reason,' says my brother.

"'Goodnight,' says the mother. 'Christiana' – that's the filly's name – 'thank the German soldier properly. If you do, we'll get food every day. You hear, Christiana?'

"'Yes,' the girl says.

"So there you are. The mother goes out, and my brother, who must've been born under six lucky stars, throws the girl on the bed without any more talk. He's been riding her every night since, and he swears she was a virgin... Well, is that a way to enjoy foreign travel or isn't it, Jakob?"

"Yes," replied Frisch softly, "yes, indeed. Germans will be remembered in those countries, eh?"

"Ha! Ha!" Hoiseler exclaimed, with a burst of laughter. "You hit it right that time, pastor. The Greeks will have blond kids from now on. Racial improvement in the old-fashioned way."

Miserably, Frisch thought: "Fifteen years old... a girl born to be a mother. Poor Christiana. Poor, hungry Greek girl. Now you know what it is when Supermen make war."

"There's only one thing wrong with the story," said old Rufke. "It's a lie."

Hoiseler's thin, long face turned black with choler. "A lie, is it? You stinkpot! You old idiot! My brother's a fine man. He was a bank clerk. He's educated. He never lied to anyone in his life! What do you think he is, a greasy barber? You watch what you say, or I'll take your pants down and give your bony ass a hiding."

"It's begun," Frisch thought wearily. He was sick to death of this too. Men talked about women, then they grew angry over some triviality, and then they fought, sometimes coming to blows, like beasts. If they had Sunday night liquor in them, it only accelerated the process, but, drunk or sober, anger seemed to be seething within almost all of them – anger at nothing, just anger seeking an outlet. And after they had fought, they talked about women again… So it had become in their land, until now brutishness was the only pollen in the spring air.

"I can *prove* it's a lie!" old Rufke said seriously, with calm malignity of tone. "He said she was a virgin, didn't he?"

"He said so, and so she was!"

"I give you a commonly known medical fact," the old man retorted. "There isn't a girl of twelve in any of the Latin countries who's a virgin any more. I read it in a health bulletin just a few months ago. That includes even our ally, Italy. And the Greeks – why, the women are whores from the moment they're born. Everyone knows that. Rich or poor – if you pay them, they'll roll right over. So your brother lied about the girl. So the whole story is a lie!"

Excepting for Hoiseler, who took everything seriously, all the others knew that Rufke had invented this testimony on the moment. He was not to be trusted in anything he said, and he had a child's gift for believing his own imagination. It was therefore something to prick Frisch's attention that Weiner suddenly got up from his seat and walked across to the old man. Thick-necked and barrel-bodied, Weiner planted himself before Rufke as though he meant ugly business. His large ears, which stood out unbeautifully from his head, were flushed with blood, making him look somewhat comic.

"Listen," he said quietly and very unpleasantly, "you talk too much, you old windbag. I'm a Catholic, see? And you're talking about Catholic countries when you talk about Italy. From now on you shut up with those lies about Catholic women."

"I read it in a book," old Rufke retorted belligerently. "I can show it to you."

"Show it to the Devil!" said Weiner. "If I hear you again, there'll be trouble." Suddenly, as though a volcano had erupted somewhere deep inside him, he thrust out one hard hand and caught Rufke by the front of his skinny neck. "I'll twist this right off!!" he shouted. He subsided just as suddenly, and walked back to his seat. He pulled angrily at one ear lobe and then the other.

"Did you see that?" cried Rufke, choking with rage. "He tried to do me in. He threatened me. I'll report it, sure as my name is Rufke."

"Oh, shut up," Pelz told him. "We were all here. He didn't say a thing. Report him and see who gets in trouble."

The room fell silent then. Frisch stared covertly at Weiner, astonished and excited. In all the months they had been together, Weiner had never uttered that many words consecutively. But if there was this much locked in his soul, if he was not just a clod but a man with a capacity for anger... why then, he had possibilities too.

"I'll tell you a funny story," young Pelz said suddenly. He was a sensitive youth and alone amongst the others he seemed to have a hatred of quarrelling. Obviously he was trying to change the atmosphere in the room. "Speaking about someone who's lucky, I remember someone who was so unlucky it was funny as the Devil. This time two years ago I was in France. Our tank platoon was moving up to the front, through a village. We had a crazy loon as our platoon leader – Schmitke, his name was. All of a sudden Schmitke yelled to us over the radio, 'Short cut, lads! We'll join the other road there – right through that barn on the left.' We started to laugh. We knew Schmitke. Whenever he saw a barn, he just had to go through it. So he started, and we followed. Well, Schmitke's tank cut a hole through the barn, squashed a couple chickens, scared the water right out of two horses and went right through the other wall. Only... on the other side there wasn't a road like we thought. Instead there was a river. We hadn't seen it, see, on account of a hedge along there. So Schmitke's tank goes through the wall and through the hedge and then it drops into the river, where it turns turtle. Damned if the whole crew wasn't drowned, Schmitke included. I tell you we laughed for two days after."

"Pelz," said Frisch softly, "I want to ask you something about that. I'm curious."

"Yes?"

"You were telling me the other day you didn't like factory work. You wished you could go home to the farm, you said."

Pelz's sensitive face warmed at the sheer thought. "I should say. If I only had my two arms again, damn it. You can feed a machine with one hand, but a one-armed man on a farm is a stick of wood. Would I like to go back, though! You city men don't know what a good life is!"

Frisch took off his eyeglasses, wiping them slowly. He peered over at Pelz with his large, soft, near-sighted eyes. "Didn't it... Well, didn't it upset you a little to go through a barn – to kill chickens and suchlike – hey?"

Pelz shrugged as though he had never thought of it before. Then he said, "At first, maybe I didn't like it so much, now I recall. But in a war you don't care. You don't give a damn for anything, y'see, Jakob? What the others do, you do. You think, 'What the hell – maybe I'll catch one tomorrow.' You're out for some fun while you can still have it. Anyway… it's not as though it's your own barn. It's a Frenchman's barn. 'Why care about him?' you think. 'Life's too short.'"

"I see," said Frisch. He put his glasses back on again. "Yes, I understand. I sometimes wonder, though… If the French, say, or the Russians, should ever get a chance at us" – he was choosing his words carefully – "it would be just too bad, wouldn't it? They'd remember things like that."

Pelz looked a bit uncomfortable. "I suppose so. We damn better win, I suppose."

"What nonsense," interjected Rufke. "Better win? I like that. Have we won already, or haven't we? Why, we're sitting on Europe like a mother chicken on its private little egg."

"That's so, that's so," said Frisch. "I was only wondering."

"Don't you men ever look at a map?" Rufke continued in an amazed tone. "Why don't you look where we are in Russia now? In another week we'll have Stalingrad and the oil fields. Why, damn it, their industry's smashed, they have twelve million dead already and it'll be all over by—"

"All right, all right," Hoiseler interrupted. "Don't get wound up now, Field Marshal Rufke."

"I'm only—"

"Oh, shut up," Hoiseler told him. "Nobody wants to hear you. We can read the newspapers, too, you know."

"Damn it all!" Pelz exclaimed irrelevantly. "I'm tired of waiting around here. What's this all for, anyway? Maybe they've forgotten about us. Maybe we should go in there and tell them to speed things up a bit, whatever it is. I'm an ex-soldier. I don't see why I should be treated this way. I need my sleep."

"No," said Frisch.

"Why not?" The youth stood up. "I'm going in there. Why not?"

"You were told to wait, I gather," Frisch replied softly. "You better. You know who I think must be in there with Keller?" He lowered his voice. "Gestapo is my guess."

"You mean it?" said Pelz. He sat down. "*Hm!*" he exclaimed with a nervous little laugh. "*Hm!* Maybe we better wait."

2

In the adjacent office Fritz Keller and Gestapo Commissar Kehr were arriving at an unpleasant conclusion. After half an hour of searching question and answer, it was clear that Keller couldn't offer insight into the problem of Wegler's sabotage. This was a particular disappointment to Kehr, because Keller had been living with Wegler, and observing him, for over six months. The Gestapo commissar had looked to Berthe Lingg for direct information and had been baffled there. Now, in search of a character clue, as he called it, he found himself equally defeated. Kehr felt weary, sleepy, and – a bad sign for a detective – he was becoming tense. The time problem was his chief antagonist. He had no doubt that given a fair chance he would pick up a thread somewhere. But he was faced by the possibility that on the next evening the British bombers might return – and he would have accomplished nothing. He even might not be able to prevent a follow-up signal by some confederate of Wegler's.

Summing up his feelings, Kehr said humorously, "My friend, I'm getting to the point where I wish I were a woman, not a detective. You're acquainted with the ways of women? As a female I could now develop one of those unmentionable illnesses peculiar to the sex, and retire from this case with a good excuse. As a man all I can do is suffer from biliousness – and keep going. I tell you frankly, you're not helping me."

Keller, a rather stout, jolly man of fifty, screwed up his plump features in what he hoped was a proper expression of sympathy and said nothing. Secretly his only basic wish was to be clear of Kehr and safely out of the room. Although he honestly wanted to help the commissar and had racked his brains in an attempt to recall anything that might be useful, he was also gravely uneasy. Inevitably the whole situation was a reflection on him. He could hear already the muttered remarks of his Party comrades: "There must have been something to be noticed about Wegler" – or "Keller's all right, I suppose, but he must be blind", and so on... And although he might always retort "It wasn't me who gave Wegler a War Service Cross", he knew it wouldn't do much good. In a situation like this, someone became the goat. He was already resigned to the likelihood of being demoted from Cell Leader.

As a matter of fact, however, the possibility of a demotion didn't worry him. He had not sought the functionary's post – it had been bestowed upon him as senior Party member. All his life Keller had avoided responsibility, and one of the things that secretly bothered him about the National

Socialists was that they never left one free of duties. In the old Germany he had been a skilled machinist (as he was still), a man earning comparatively good wages. He was a member of a trade union and of the Social Democratic Party – but only as a matter of course. It was equally a matter of course that when the Nazis grew powerful, he smelt the way the wind was blowing and joined up with them. He would have done the same with the Communists or any other party. What he cared about in life was getting along and having a bit of fun. Right now, after six months of being Cell Leader, he was so sick of the word "duty" that even the necessity of preparing a weekly report irked him beyond the effort involved. To be relieved of the responsibility would only delight him.

On the other hand, he was desperately afraid of any unpleasantness. Demotion in the Party would make life difficult, and he certainly didn't want that. As a result, his testimony in respect to Wegler necessarily had been favourable. Since he couldn't present Wegler as a man who had given grounds for suspicion, his only self-defence was to build up the reputation of a saboteur. Yet, since that too had its dangers, Keller's uneasiness was doubly compounded. Right now, exhausted, anxious and driven, the one thing he no longer cared about was whether the Wegler "plot" was unravelled. He wished only that Kehr would have done with him and let him crawl back into the security and oblivion of his bed.

"Keller – look here," the commissar said to him suddenly, "there must be something you're overlooking. After all, there are only several possibilities here. Wegler must fit into one of them. Now look" – he stood up, stroking his chin, his handsome brown eyes fixed on Keller – "I give you the first possibility. Wegler is a biological destroyer. By a 'biological destroyer' I mean this: a man who's an anarchist or a Communist, or suchlike. People of that sort, I've become convinced, are born that way. They actually can't help themselves. We find them in all periods of history, in all races. For instance, Karl Marx was a German, Lenin a Russian, Robespierre a Frenchman. Like a cat born without a tail, these vermin are born without moral sense. You follow me, Keller? I'm talking science and philosophy now. A biological destroyer has no capacity for respecting law and order. On the contrary, something always makes him want to rebel. One can't do anything about them either – just root them out… Now, then, I know this is putting the matter philosophically, but the older I become, the more I find that the very key to man is to be found in philosophy. You understand, Keller, I wouldn't say this to everyone. But you're an intelligent man… I think you understand me."

"I do understand, sir, I do," said Keller. "And believe me, it's very well put. But I swear Wegler is not of that kind. I know these 'biological destroyers', as you put it so cleverly. In the old days, you see, there were always some Communists in the factory. I could smell their kind of thinking a mile away, and I tell you there just isn't any of it in Wegler. I'll even say this: of all the men in the bunk, Wegler is the most respectful of law and order. I watch that kind of thing, you see. You can tell it when they get drunk. Others around here, they get tipsy and they start to fight. Not Wegler. He'll just sit quiet. And you can be sure it isn't because he's a coward. He's a big enough man to smash anyone's head around here. Once I even saw him separate two men by just holding them with his hands. 'Germans shouldn't fight like beasts,' he said to me afterwards. 'They're not beasts, are they?...' I tell you such a man is not of that 'destroyer' kind. I feel sure of it."

"Very good," said Kehr. "We rule out the first category, then. Possibility number two: Wegler has a personal grudge against someone here – a leader like Baumer, let's say, or a foreman. I understand Baumer refused him permission to work on his woman's farm. Maybe that?"

Keller shook his head. "I don't think so, sir. Wegler told me about that. It was just yesterday, the last time I saw him, in fact. Just for a moment, in the bunk."

"Wasn't he angry?"

"If he was, he didn't show it, sir. The fact is, Willi was friends with everyone. The men around here all liked him. He was always quiet, not talking much, but you could feel he was decent. Everybody had respect for him, too, because he worked at the steam hammer. Man, that's a job for a lad of twenty who has guts like iron, not for one past forty. But Wegler handled it, and never complained, either. In fact, if you ask me what sort Wegler was, I'd say this: a typical German worker."

"Typical German workers don't commit sabotage," Kehr interrupted. "Damn it, Keller, there's a rottenness here, and we've got to root it out. The one thing you can't call Wegler is a typical German."

"I'm sorry, sir," Keller replied boldly, "but if you ask the others, I think you'll get the same answer. After all, why was Wegler given a War Service Cross? Because—"

"I know, I know! I know all about that damned Cross," Kehr interrupted again. "Wegler was an exemplary German worker, I know all that. Only, he committed sabotage – so he was not what he seemed, was he?"

Keller shrugged helplessly. "It's a riddle, sir. I'm the most surprised man alive."

"All right – we'll proceed scientifically then, and not give up so easily. Possibility number three: Wegler was a British agent... That I can answer for myself. No evidence. We've already looked at it backwards and forwards. No evidence at all. Correct?"

"I'm afraid so, Herr Commissar."

"Number four – listen carefully... If I say the word 'guilty', does it mean anything to you? Could Wegler have felt guilty over anything?"

"It doesn't mean anything to me, sir."

"Yes – it's really meaningless," Kehr muttered. "Now, let's see. We've ruled out biology. We've ruled out money, because that's the only way he would become a British agent. We've ruled out a personal grudge. And there's no evidence he had any underground contacts... Wait a minute... This man Frisch, in the bunk, the ex-pastor. What about him?"

"I've watched him like a hawk, sir. I've never heard a wrong word, a wrong idea."

"Proves nothing. He would be careful with you, naturally."

"But I've kept track of what he's said to others too. So far as I can tell, the Gestapo note on his dossier – that he's to be considered reformed – is correct." Keller was not calling on the reputation of the Gestapo without purpose. Like the War Service Cross in Wegler's case, it was his rod to lean upon.

"But what contact has Wegler had with Frisch? Were they often together? Buddies?"

"Definitely not, sir."

"Sure?"

"Sure – because they worked different shifts, sir. When Wegler came off, Frisch went on. Their only possible time together was Sunday – and all these last months Wegler's been at his woman's farm when he's had time off."

Kehr sighed. "Nothing there, then." He looked up at Keller with a frown. "Think back over the seven months now – isn't there even one thing you can pick out about Wegler that seems suspicious?"

Keller studied the question with furrowed brows. "I'm afraid I can't, sir."

"He never made a criticism about a Party Leader?"

"I would have reported it at once."

"Or told one of those jokes that circulate?"

"No, sir. Believe me, I watch those jokes too!"

"Can you recall – did he ever say anything about that woman of his that would cast any suspicion on her?"

"No, sir. The fact is, he never talked about her much."

Kehr paused. "You mentioned before that he didn't talk much. Would you say he was a secretive personality?"

"No, sir, not that. Just quiet. The truth is," he added quickly, "I watch that too. I mean – I would report a man if he said the wrong thing, but I'd also report a man who didn't say the right thing at the right time – like 'Sieg Heil'* at the end of a meeting, or expressing approval when the news of a victory comes over the radio. You know, sir?"

Kehr nodded. "Then there's nothing there?"

"No, sir. His behaviour was always patriotic."

"I see... You said you saw him yesterday?"

"Just for a minute. I had to go to my bunk for something at lunchtime. Wegler was lying down. Said he wasn't feeling well."

"Did he say anything else?"

"No, sir. I congratulated him on the Cross, and then I had to leave. I did ask him why he wasn't working, of course. He said that Baumer – I mean, excuse me, Labour Front Leader Baumer – had given him permission."

"Then you don't know what he did with his time the rest of the day?"

"No, sir."

Kehr paused to scratch his moustache. "Well then, here's my very last possibility. Think it over carefully now... What basis is there for believing that Wegler suddenly went insane?" He stared at Keller with an intent frown.

Keller considered the matter in silence. The instant Kehr had uttered the word "insane" his heart had begun to pound with relief. If it could be accepted that Wegler acted out of insanity, there would be no possibility of impeaching Wegler's Cell Leader.

"I don't know, sir," he answered cautiously. "If you ask me, 'Did Wegler ever show any signs of insanity?' I answer, 'No.' But if we consider that maybe he had a brain tumour or something like that – like a man I once knew who suddenly went loony in the shop one day and began to smash the machines with a hammer – why then, it becomes a possibility. I tell you this frankly, sir: it's more logical for Wegler to be a saboteur out of insanity than for any of the reasons we've taken up."

Kehr chewed his thick underlip. "Such a mess," he thought to himself wearily. "Our Führer has made us a Germany where a detective can no longer proceed by rules of logic..." "Well, Keller, thank you. I'll call you later if I want you again. Keep your mouth shut about this, of course."

"Yes, sir. Do you think I can go to bed now?"

Kehr nodded. "Send in Hoiseler, please."

"Yes, sir. *Heil Hitler!*" With a curious feeling that he was a sort of beetle who had just scurried out of the way of a steam roller, Keller walked quickly to the door.

3

All eyes turned to Keller as he came into the fetid waiting room. "At last," exclaimed Pelz. "So what's doing in there, Fritz?"

Without replying to Pelz, Keller said "He wants you!" to Hoiseler. Then he took out a dirty handkerchief and stood mopping his face and neck.

Pelz waited until the door had closed on Hoiseler. "What's doing, Fritz? Who's 'he'? What the devil's up?"

"I like that!" Keller replied with a burst of righteous anger. "You want me to betray Party information? What I know, I know! What you're supposed to know, you'll be told. Otherwise, keep your nose out."

Astonished at all this heat from a man who was usually so even-tempered, Pelz retorted, "What little louse bit you, Fritz? You're not supposed to tell – don't tell! But how should I know? Why jump down my throat over a simple question?"

"I'm sorry," Keller muttered instantly. His shoulders slumped. "I'm ready to drop," he exclaimed to no one in particular. Standing there, a round-shouldered, heavy-bellied man of fifty, he knew that he – who had always loved people – was now beginning to hate them. People were becoming a terror to him, because they were always demanding what he had no capacity to give. And as he turned slowly and walked from the office, his dismay with life was written in large script on his sweating face. Once, he knew, he had been a man with a capacity for simple joyous living. Where had it gone? What was there to existence now to cleave a man to life?

When the door closed, Pelz turned to Frisch with a wink and a grin. "Old boy's been through a session all right – like he's been in a sweatbox.* Ten to one it *is* the Gestapo."

Frisch nodded. The very necessity of waiting was making him anxious again. Primarily to occupy his own mind, he said to the others, "Did I ever give you my imitation of the old woman buying apples?" He got up, hunched his shoulders and shoved his glasses down to the tip of his nose. He was about to begin when the door opened. SS man Blumel came in, closing the door behind him. It was he who had driven Robert Latzelburger to his home a little while back. He was a youth in his early twenties, rather good-looking, with a swagger to him. "Is he busy?" he asked, jerking his thumb at the inner office.

"Who do you mean?" asked Frisch. "We don't know who's in there."

"The Gestapo commissar, of course," replied Blumel. "What do you think you're here for, coffee and cake?"

"Yes, busy," answered Pelz. With an almost imperceptible smile he congratulated Frisch for the manoeuvre. "Hoiseler's in with him."

Blumel hesitated. "Well..." Abruptly he opened the outer door again. "Come in," he ordered loudly, with a gesturing thumb.

The man who entered was the Pole who worked on Berthe Lingg's farm. That he was a Pole could be seen by the large yellow "P" sewn on his breast. But even without this, all of the Germans would have known it.

There is no creature on earth so bitter to look upon as a man who is utterly defeated. Stooped, as though he were expecting a blow, unclean, dull-eyed, the Pole stood in the doorway. He was tall and very gaunt; his head was shaven to the bone of his skull; his cheeks were hollow. He seemed to be fifty, and was actually thirty-three... He looked like a Polish slave in Germany, and these German workers knew him instantly, for they had seen others equally defeated.

Blumel motioned him in. The Pole obeyed in silence, and Blumel shut the door after him. In order to make room for him on their bench, Frisch, who was later to regard it as a grave error of conduct, pushed closer to Rufke.

"What are you pushing for?" asked old Rufke instantly, in a belligerent tone. "He" – jerking his thumb at Blumel – "can sit in Hoiseler's place."

"What about him?" Frisch enquired.

"What are you talking about?" Rufke demanded indignantly. "You want me to sit next to a Polack? Are you crazy?"

"A Pole?" said Frisch quickly. "I didn't realize. I can't see very well, you know. Excuse me."

"I like that!" muttered Rufke, still insulted.

SS man Blumel, sitting down on the bench opposite, stretched his legs out comfortably. "When I look at a specimen like that," he philosophized with a yawn, "I wonder why it took more than a single day to reach Warsaw. Transport difficulties, I suppose. Honestly, did you ever see such a race of people in all your life? Look at the way he stands."

"Maybe he has clap," old Rufke suggested with a joyous laugh.

Pelz, SS man Blumel and Rufke guffawed. Frisch smiled. Eggert and Weiner, who had closed their eyes again after the arrival of the Pole, continued their quiet nap.

With a breaking heart Frisch thought silently, "I pray God, you Pole, that you don't understand German. I pray God that it will not be Poles like you alone who sit in final judgement on us Germans. I pray God there will be judges who will at least call me in testimony, as well as you. For on my back, too, there are the marks of the German lash..."

The Pole stood against the wall, his shoulders bowed, his eyes cast down to the floor. If previously Blumel had bothered to enquire, he could have told them that the prisoner understood German very well. He was a pharmacist, and he had studied German in school. He even came from a border district, where German was spoken by the peasants. It so happened, however, that he hadn't been listening to Rufke's joke. After a year in Germany, he no longer listened to anything Germans said... unless it was an order.

Looking at the prisoner, wishing there were some way, some wordless language, some magic of music or heart, by which he could reach into the soul of this man and speak to him, Frisch thought fiercely to himself, "This, too, you have to know, you Pole: this is not a simple matter. Before Germans came to make you grovel, they murdered other Germans and made still others grovel. Do you hear me? I tell you this: he who judges out of suffering alone will judge wrongly. I warn you, Pole! You will judge wrongly. You will cast down new seeds for future suffering. And even in your blind pain, you will be guilty, too. Do you hear me, Pole?"

In silence they waited their turn with the Gestapo commissar.

4

3:55 a.m.

"Has Doctor Zoder called?" asked Baumer as he came into the Party office.

Frieda, the phone girl, was flaxen-haired, pretty and very serious about her work. "No, sir," she replied. He could see that it required effort for her to keep her heavy eyes open.

"Get him. He's at the hospital." Baumer sat down wearily, opening the collar of his shirt. As the girl plugged a wire into the board, she said, "Major Deterle called."

Sharply: "Why didn't you let me know?"

"He said not to, sir. He only wanted to leave a message."

"Oh... What?"

"Three anti-aircraft batteries will arrive by noon. Four more by six in the evening."

"He said 'batteries', not guns?"

"Yes, sir – batteries."

Baumer nodded. He thought with relief that it was something, at least. Not what they needed – a hundred guns would be more like it – but if the British did come, they could keep them high. For the past several hours his mind had been plagued by an ugly fantasy: of Wellingtons* coming down to five hundred feet to drop their eggs. They damn well wouldn't do that now – not with thirty-two guns to throw lead at their bellies.

"Can't you get Zoder?"

"No answer, sir."

"Keep ringing." Irritatedly he thought that probably he would be obliged to walk to the hospital. Feeling as he did, the three hundred yards there and the three hundred yards back would be as burdensome as a ten-mile hike. What was wrong with him, anyway? For several hours he had managed nicely. He had rushed from building to building, speaking to the key Party men, asking for an immediate report on any out-of-the-way behaviour, explaining the situation, warning that all rumours must be scotched. For a while the feeling of exhaustion had left him... but now it was in his bones again, settling like a cold damp.

"Still no answer, sir."

Perhaps, he thought, it was Kehr who had unsettled him again. He had just come from seeing Kehr. Not only was the commissar without a grain of useful information, but his only theory so far was that Wegler might have been insane. Here they faced a cold political act, well conceived, well executed... and a so-called Gestapo commissar was willing to explain it by brain fever. Multiply that brain fever and you had a Communist upheaval, nothing less. What stupidity! His first impression of Kehr had been right – an old-line hack! Surely the Gestapo knew that wars could not be won by hacks...

"Hello," said the girl into the mouthpiece, "Labour Front Leader Baumer is calling Doctor Zoder. Put him on, please." There was a moment of silence. "You don't understand," said the girl. "This is the Labour Front Leader calling. Please get Doctor Zoder instantly." She waited another moment. "This is ridiculous! Who is this? What's the matter with you?"

Baumer got up, tapped the girl on the shoulder and gestured for her to give him the earphone. He leant over to the mouthpiece as he heard a stubborn female voice insist, "Wollweber, and I'm trying to make you understand that the doctor has had a hard day. It's absolutely essential for him to get a few hours' sleep."

"Sister Wollweber," said Baumer hoarsely, "if Doctor Zoder isn't on the telephone in sixty seconds, I'll have you sent to a concentration camp!"

He heard a gasp at the other end and an almost imperceptible, "Yes, sir!" Grinning, he shook his head at Frieda. She smiled back.

Frieda was an earnest Party member whose manner was always serious during working hours. But her sudden smile, which was wholehearted and charming, transformed her for an instant into pure female, soft and marvellously pretty. It made Baumer wince to see it. Behind that handsome face, as he well knew, there was a mind that appalled him. The Friedas of the generation ten and fifteen years his junior were nicely tailored to the SS men of their own age, like Blumel – but not to him. These youngsters no longer thought about life as he had done at their age – they merely repeated what was being said on the radio. And of all that had transpired in Germany in the past ten years, it was this which distressed Baumer most. For when he dared examine the meaning of it, he was forced to conclude either that he was out of step with life, or that the new educational system, under the direct guidance of leaders he revered, was turning out a generation of handsome morons with whom, beyond a set of slogans, he had nothing in common. The comradely hopes, the idealism, the bitter passion of the bitter years, which had created the slogans they now uttered, were gone... In their mouths the words were empty and had assumed a different meaning. And he didn't know what to think about it or what to do about it – other than to say now, as he had said often before, "I have faith in the Führer. What he does cannot be wrong!"

He heard footsteps through the earphone. "Hello," said Doctor Zoder, "is that you, Baumer?"

"Yes. Is Wegler conscious yet?"

"No."

"I want you to wake him!"

"I'm sorry, but—"

"Damn it, Zoder, you're not cooperating. In an hour I face a meeting with Superintendent Kohlberg. I've got to see Wegler before that. Why can't you use smelling salts, or give him some drug? What sort of a doctor are you?"

Zoder gave his short, meaningless cackle. "It's this way, Baumer. I might give Wegler a strychnine injection—"

"Would it bring him to consciousness?"

"It might, but—"

"Give it to him!"

"Just listen a moment, please. I promise you I'll do anything you say – but listen to the facts first."

"I'm listening."

"The strychnine might bring him to consciousness, agreed. It might also kill him."

"I'll take the chance. He's no good to me this way."

"But wait a moment. He's still under the ether. Even if the strychnine did awaken him, his state of shock would remain. He won't know what he's talking about. You've got to understand, Baumer – a man in shock doesn't have a brain that functions normally. All you'll get from him is rubbish."

"When will he be out of shock, then?"

"I don't know that yet. I'm hoping that the treatment he's getting will show results by morning."

"Morning… What hour is morning?"

Zoder calculated rapidly. His medical chatter was pure deceit. Not only was strychnine one of the specifics for shock, but Wegler was no longer in a shocked state. Zoder was expecting him to come to consciousness momentarily. Inasmuch as Baumer was accepting his nonsense, however, he felt that he could choose a later hour than he had planned. He was more than ever determined to talk with Pastor Frisch before allowing Baumer to see his patient.

"Nine or ten o'clock, Baumer. If he's ever going to be conscious at all, ten o'clock surely."

Baumer cursed. "You're as much help as my foot, Zoder. I can't wait that late."

Zoder cackled with amusement. "In the future, my dear friend, have your sharpshooters consult me before introducing steel into a man's peritoneum. If every doctor in Germany were here, they'd still be helpless before that."

"We have an appointment for eight sharp," Baumer ordered. "I'll deal with Kohlberg some way or other. But at eleven o'clock the entire factory is to meet. By that time I want what's behind this business of Wegler's if I have to tear it out of his guts with pliers. You hear me?"

"Do my best," said Zoder with a laugh. Eight o'clock was a complete victory. "Let's merely hope septicaemia doesn't develop. In that case—"

"Damn septicaemia, and damn you too," said Baumer. "You'll try the strychnine at eight o'clock, no later."

He hung up. He looked at his wristwatch. It was 4:03 a.m. "Frieda... I'm going to lie down in my office. If I fall asleep, be sure to wake me by four fifty."

"Yes, sir."

"At four forty-five call Herr Kohlberg. Tell him I said he's to drink some black coffee and be ready for a meeting at 5 a.m. I'll come to his house."

"Yes, sir."

Baumer went into his office. He took off his jacket and his shoes, and brought out a folding canvas cot from behind a file. As he stretched out, there was a knock on the door. Frieda came in at his call. She was carrying a paper bag.

"Excuse me, sir. I wonder if you aren't hungry. I have a sandwich here." She smiled, her sudden, flashing smile.

"It's your lunch, isn't it?"

"Please take it. I'll be going home when Martha comes. But I know what *your* schedule is. If you don't take something now, you'll go all day without eating."

"Thank you. It's very thoughtful of you, Frieda." He took the proffered sandwich.

"Don't even mention it, sir." She hesitated. "Can I say something, sir?"

"Of course."

"I just want to say... Well, naturally, I've watched you, sir... and I just want to say that I always talk about you, and we're all really inspired, sir, by your example. We're proud to have you as our leader."

"Are you? That's good to hear," he replied wearily, but with gratitude. "Thank you for telling me."

"Yes, sir." She waited for a moment and then, as he remained silent, went out, closing the door softly.

"So," Baumer thought, "I'm an inspiration... except that I don't feel like one. I feel like a rag. The old Party fighter is developing aches and pains, it seems... the bright wine has lost a bit of its ferment..."

He lay quietly, chewing the tasteless sandwich. The bread was coarse and stale, the cut of pork like a thin sheet of rubber. His head was buzzing. He thought of his conversation with Kehr and became angry all over again. While he refused to accept Kehr's insanity theory, there was an aspect to it that worried him – the possibility that Wegler had acted alone. Sabotage was bad – but when it was committed by an organized group, it could be handled. One took for granted that some diehard elements still remained in the German community. But if Wegler was not of that stripe – if he actually was what his record showed him to be – a hitherto patriotic German – then the implications were vastly more serious. Once men of a reliable character began to turn against the National Socialists, then... then it would be 1918 all over again.

Baumer sighed and thrust the anxiety out of his mind. Kehr might come to absurd conclusions, but *he* damn well wouldn't. He had too many burdens to allow such theories to agitate him.

He turned over, pressing his cheek to the rough canvas of the cot. He thought of Frieda, of her sweet, youthful beauty... and then he thought of his wife. He had not heard from his wife in weeks. She was somewhere in Finland by now, nursing strange men. Did she miss him – as he missed her? he wondered.

The image of his wife's fine, intelligent face stirred his mind. She was almost as old as he was. Like him, she had come to the Party through idealism, not routine osmosis. She would understand that there were problems, that Germany might indeed lose. He could talk about such things with his wife... but he no longer trusted anyone else. Either his friends were so arrogantly confident of victory that they would report his doubts to the Gestapo... or else they would be sure he was unbalanced. Well... why did he have fears then where they didn't? Was it because he was a dual personality, still an architect inside, an idealist instead of a practical man? Did that make him different?

His thoughts drifted back to a summer night, almost a year before. It was the eve of his wife's departure for nurse's training. Things had been so different then. The bombings had not begun; the German armies were knifing into Russia without serious opposition; the factory was still in Düsseldorf, running smoothly. When he had held his wife in his arms, he had not felt himself a mere man enjoying the embrace of his beloved, but a god holding his goddess. They were *Germans* – and the whole universe seemed to be unfolding like a lush carpet under their feet. How intoxicating that moment had been! In the early days he had dreamt only a humble dream: of a Germany in which men like him could live in decency and quiet, in real brotherliness, without parasites or profiteers to choke them. But later, in the first period of the war, his fancy had become enkindled by the incredible success of German arms. Life became drunken, an orgy of unending victory, and the vision of a quiet existence faded before the impact of a Wotan fable come to reality.* He had begun to see Germany as the ruler of the world, to see men like himself as rulers of peoples and states…

Now the dream life was gone, and the quiet life too. What he had wanted first, he had not. What he had dreamt remained a fable. Once again, life had been temporarily… postponed.

In the morning of that last day, just as it was time for his wife to get dressed, Baumer had asked her to pause for an instant. He pulled the blankets back so that she lay before him in nakedness. He wanted desperately to fix the image of her body in his mind… That image, too, was blurred and cold now.

"I'll tear Wegler to pieces!" he thought suddenly. Fury swept through him. "He'll never even get near the axe. So help me, I'll take a knife and I'll strip his skin off inch by inch. I'll let him know what it means for a German to try sabotage!"

He lay back, staring at the ceiling. The cold exhaustion was in his bones…

In 1929 Baumer had been twenty-five, a university graduate with a degree in architecture. When he added up his assets, he could list his skill, his decent middle-class breeding, his youth. His debit column was heavier: no job, no money, no prospects and no hope. It is a hard world that produces a defeated man at twenty-five – but there were many men like him in Germany in 1929, too many to blame each individual. To say that Baumer was a revolutionary is to be mild: he was bitterly prepared for anything. He tramped the streets of Leipzig, of Bremen, of Hamburg, willing to clean lavatories for a salary, finding that even such jobs were at a premium. Twice, when he was sleeping in parks, he walked to a river edge to drown himself, and never knew why he didn't go through with it.

Then, one day, he came upon his future – a soup kitchen established by the National Socialist Party. There he found, in addition to a daily bowl of stew, the opportunity to earn a few pennies by handing out leaflets. And shortly he learnt that there were rooming houses where young Nazis, if they were fighters, could secure floor space without cost. A month later he joined the Party.

It was quite natural that Baumer should have become a National Socialist, and his decision had nothing to do with any interest in politics. The world needed patching, and many men were joining one party or another. Baumer had surveyed the Communists, and even though he had walked in a number of their unemployed demonstrations, he had found them distasteful. It was not to his pleasure to sing in the company of shabby men about a new world to be made by workers. He was an architect, not a worker, and he had no intention of becoming a worker. The Brown Shirts no less than the Reds, he found, promised a bright new world – but it was to be a *German* world, and it was this he cared about. He cared nothing for the working class of the world, about which the Marxists were so concerned. So far as he knew, it was the French workers who had robbed him of his father, and the English workers who were enjoying the Versailles plunder.* When the Nazis spoke of making *Germany* strong, of providing a good life for all of *German blood...* that meant something real.

With the Nazis, Baumer's self-respect returned, and with that... hope. The Party discovered in him a talent for speaking and organizing. Within three months he was a full-time functionary at a small salary. When the local group wanted someone to rouse the dispossessed or the frustrate, they called on Baumer. And Baumer could recruit them by droves, because he communicated to others the new hope given to him by the Party.

The years from '29 to '33 were hard... and they made Baumer hard. In the first two months after he joined the Party, he was in six street fights, all of them the result of raids on Marxist meetings. In that bloody period it was live or die, and he followed an inevitable path in what he did... and in what he became. The architect learnt the ways of the thug, learnt to use a knife when it was necessary, or a gun.

But finally, when State power fell to the Nazis, Baumer had considered that his political days were over. He had never stopped thinking of himself as an architect, or his political work as a stopgap. To his dismay, the Party refused him permission to abandon full-time work. The consolidation of power was just at its beginning. "Later," they told him. "Wait a bit until we have things in hand." So, for another three years he had remained a functionary, assigned to Labour Front work. But then, at last, he did achieve his personal goal. He was given a release, and a six-month stipend to carry him through a refresher course at a university. After that, for services rendered, a job was made for him in a firm that handled State business.

It was the deepest irony of Baumer's life that the years that followed had been bitterly disappointing to him. It was not his personal career that troubled him, but Germany. Month after month he had waited for the full Party programme to materialize... And as it did not, he had become more and more uneasy. He would lie awake at night and argue with himself: on the one hand Germany was rearming and becoming strong. He wanted that! The pledge to liquidate unemployment had been kept; the unity of the nation, the foreign policies, were being brilliantly achieved. But on the other hand... where was the Party promise to limit all salaries to one thousand marks a month? What about the liquidation of profiteering – or the protection of small business? For years he had given his heart's blood to a programme that would be both National and Socialist. Why was it, he asked himself, that only one half of that programme was being carried out now? He found no answer, and each month brought a new question, a new bitterness. By the time the war came, he was an unhappy and disillusioned man.

The war caught him up sharply. His patriotism and his years of effort flamed together at the danger to his fatherland. He realized now that "guns before butter" had been a necessary policy, and he put himself down for a carping fool.

In a blaze of enthusiasm he went to the Party. He asked for active military service. His Party superior smiled, patted his shoulder and told him that victory would be won by youngsters of twenty-two, not men of thirty-five. Meanwhile, there was other work. In this war the morale of the working class would be a decisive matter. It was up to men like Baumer to see that the home front did not repeat the stab in the back of 1918.

Within a week Baumer was once again a functionary. Just before the fall of France* he was promoted to be Labour Front Leader of a tank factory in Düsseldorf, a job of considerable responsibility. When he looked back now at the first two years of the war, the period seemed to have passed for him in a kind of impassioned ecstasy. There had been problems, but they had been as nothing before the triumphs of the new, revitalized Germany.

Now the ecstasy was gone, and the problems loomed up like an endless chain of mountains. One climbed, grew weary, and never saw the end. One paused at a moment of crisis to stare things in the face – only to discover that the face was ugly, that the goal was lost in a gloomy, inscrutable haze. The dream was still unfulfilled... The promise had been temporarily... postponed...

Baumer sighed. He passed his hand over his face and shivered a little in spite of the soft night air. He fell asleep.

5

Wegler climbed to consciousness slowly, like a diver who ascends only gradually from the deep sea floor to the surface. And precisely like a diver – who must grope upward from entombed darkness through layer upon layer of murk, who suffers varied pressures and dimly perceives changing forms of life about him – so Wegler only gradually swam upward to the light and air and familiarity of the surface world. Somewhere in his blind ascent there came a point at which his mind commenced to function again… but wearily, with the dull torpor of a thing hard risen from the grave. He was not aware of it, of course – there is no magic so great as this of the body's chemistry, or the thin, taut strand we call a human thought. But to his mind's eye the world of blackness was no longer wholly black. It turned red, and very dimly, as if through ultra-dark, red glasses he saw running figures and tongues of distant flame. Then thought began.

"What will happen?" It was this that troubled his brain first. It held no meaning for him, but his mind repeated it monotonously: "What will happen?" And then, "I'm waking up. I've been asleep… No, I've been sick. I must be sick because in sleep… What's happened to me? My God, what's happened?"

Just before he opened his eyes for the first time, he had a sensation that Doctor Zoder could have predicted, since it was typical of his wound. In his abdomen, at the point where a rubber drain had been inserted, he became aware of a painful throbbing. Zoder could not have known, however, that for quite a long moment the pain gave Wegler the illusion that he was in the factory, and that the throbbing in his belly came from the beat of the giant steam hammer at which he worked. It had been like that for twelve hours each day in the factory: when the six thousand pounds of fury descended upon the casting he held, the floor itself would seem to lift with a groan, and there would be an answering throb deep in the core of his gut.

He opened his glazed eyes. In blurred focus he saw unpainted walls of pine, the far end of his cot. There was no one in the room – and the room itself had no meaning for him…

He licked his lips. They were dry and felt cracked. He smelt the sweet, sick heaviness of ether about his person. His mind registered the information incorrectly. Hazily it said, "Gas." Instantly his sense memory cast up an unpleasant vision. Many years before he had done something of which he was deeply and irretrievably ashamed. He was about thirty, then, living in Cologne.

An unusual errand had brought him to a wealthy suburb. Resting for a moment in a park, he overheard two nursemaids in animated conversation. One of them, by her accent, was English. Since they were separated from him only by a thick hedge, he listened to their chatter without being observed. Both, he gathered, disliked their work and abominated their charges, who were infants. He listened idly, with amusement, until suddenly he heard the English girl, called Emily, offering her friend a bit of advice. "When mine yells," she said, "there's one thing I do that always shuts him up. I can't manage it when the madam's around, of course, but she's out most afternoons, thank God. And even though the cook knows, she doesn't care. I turn the gas on in the oven, see Marlene? Then I just shove the little brat inside for a minute. Believe me, there are no more howls out of him for the rest of the afternoon. The gas makes him sleep like a kitten."

"But isn't it dangerous?" the other asked in an uneasy, excited tone.

"Not a bit. It doesn't hurt them, y'see. Of course, when they get about a year old, it won't work any more. They kick too much. But I never hire out to older kids anyway... Too much nuisance, I say."

"My goodness... if I thought... But what if one died?"

"Don't be stupid, Marlene. What a thought! Naturally you don't hold them in long. But it's better for them to sleep than to howl all afternoon, isn't it?"

"I don't know. It scares me."

"Oh, you're stupid! If there's one thing I can't stand, it's a baby howling. But you do as you like."

"Well... I'll see. It's an idea, though."

The two girls moved on, leaving Wegler stunned. Loving children as he did, idolizing his own young son, the conversation seemed to him too monstrous to be real. He wanted to believe that it was only a jest – but his uneasy heart told him it was not. The girl had been too pleased with herself, her tone had been too coarsely gay.

As he sat, the two maids, pushing their carriages, moved around a bend in the path and passed before him. He knew instantly which of the two was Emily. She was the larger one on the outside, prattling now about a pair of shoes – a tall, full-fleshed girl of twenty with a moon face. To follow her and locate the house in which she worked would be simple. It was late in the afternoon – likely the child's mother would be home, or someone else in the family. He would ring the bell and say, "Excuse me, I don't want to bother you, but there's something you ought to know... I have a child myself..." But the instant his imagination carried him this far, a host of anxieties rose up to confuse him. In later years, recalling every detail and every thought, he was astonished at his timidity. The duty he owed this unknown family was so clear – an unqualified human obligation. For if a man did not even have this basic consideration for others, if a man and his brothers were so separate that one had no thought for the welfare of another, then what meaning was there to life – and into what degradation had the human spirit fallen?

These reflections came to him only later, however. At the time, he remained sitting on the bench, paralysed with indecision. His confused thoughts ran this way. What if the mother didn't believe him? He was only a working man – she obviously, with a nursemaid, cook and all, was a wealthy aristocrat... What if the girl denied it and had him arrested for slander? Could he prove the charge? No. There was even the other one as a witness against him – she would naturally stick by her friend. My goodness – he might be fined, he might even be sent to jail. Or – even if the mother did believe him and was grateful – it was likely *she* would have the girl arrested, and then, too, he would have to appear in court. At a time when so many men were out of work, he would certainly lose his job. A man had his own family to consider, had he not?

He sat on the bench, torn, sweating as though in a fever... and did nothing. Presently the two maids disappeared around a bend in the path. He knew that before it was too late he ought to leap to his feet and race after them. But he continued to sit there, like a dunce or an unfeeling brute – neither of which he was – and finally when he did jump up, they were not to be seen.

Wegler did not know then, nor did he comprehend later, that he was a victim of a fundamental law of our time: the unwritten code that in our society a man must weigh decency with care and cunning lest he be betrayed – the hard fact that this best possible of all worlds is constructed so as to mould men otherwise than they might like to be, to make them at once more fearful and more selfish than a man need be. He knew only that his failure to follow his heart, no matter what the consequences, had left him deeply shamed. In the still of the night, or as he gazed with pleasure at his own son, he would remember the bench, the coarse, pleased voice, the moon face. With the passing of time the memory plagued him less often, but it never quite faded away. And now it returned again in a hazy, uncomfortable vision, as though the ether he smelt were the gas in a cooking oven, as though the full-fleshed arms, the moon face, were hovering over his bed in unforgiving commemoration of his sin…

Gradually his brain cleared. The throbbing in his belly became more acutely painful. Presently he realized that he was not at work, and that it was not the steam hammer he felt, but something else. And abruptly full memory returned… even of the last moment when he had been shot down. In that moment he had seen a kneeling Elite Guard and the flash of moonlight on a rifle barrel. And although his body had stiffened in awful fear, he had remained where he was in order to strike one more match and drop it upon the arrow of hay. He realized that he must be in the factory hospital, and that the SS man had shot him.

Calmly he set about discovering his condition. There was the pain in his belly: likely he had been wounded there. As he tried to reach down in order to feel for a bandage, he found that he could not move his left arm. He turned his head, raising up a bit. He saw the rubber tube leading down to the needle; he observed that his arm was strapped to the bed. Weakly, feeling the cords of his neck tremble, he sank back on the hot pillow. The apparatus confused him. Had he been shot in the arm too? He moved his right hand down under the covers. He found that he was naked below the waist, whereas his trunk was covered with a coarse nightshirt. Commencing at his lower ribs and extending all the way to his groin, there was a heavy bandage of adhesive.

So then… a belly wound it was! He had served for two years in the World War – he knew what it meant when a steel-jacketed bullet tore into a man's gut. On the battlefield such men were usually finished. Perhaps now, however, there were new methods for saving them – or maybe he had been lucky.

This passing thought – that he had been lucky – exploded in his brain. For the first time since coming to consciousness, the full meaning of his situation became clear. Dead, he would have been safe. Wounded, he was trapped as not even a rat ought to be trapped if there were mercy in the world. After what he had done (his heart felt suddenly numb), there was no horror that they would not visit upon him. Now, at this moment, he, Willi Wegler, was in *their* hands, and the only road that lay before him ended in a lime-strewn grave.

Sick with fear, Wegler sought to steel himself. What could he do? He knew what this wound meant – he was aware already of the flabby weakness of his body. He could only lie there, preparing himself to suffer unspeakable anguish. The next hours were clear: so soon as they knew he was conscious, they would be after him. Baumer would come. He would demand to know who his accomplices were. What could he answer? And Baumer would want to know why he had signalled to the British. He had not been able to tell even Berthe, so how could he explain to Baumer? How could he speak of what he didn't fully understand himself?... Yet it was in order to force him to speak that they had brought him back to life and thrust him into this hospital bed. He knew the consequences if he dared remain silent.

The obvious solution occurred to him, and he grasped it with bitter eagerness. Obviously, he must kill himself – and quickly too! He knew enough about this wound to be certain that he need only rip the bandage from his belly. Death would be swift then, and as sure as their damned axe.

Had he come to it, then? It seemed he had. For him there could not be the sick man's faith in recovery, or the old man's ignorance of the moment, or even the condemned man's hope for reprieve. He was utterly and irrevocably doomed – and now, *this* moment, was the moment to save himself.

He lay very still, licking his lips. In truth he was too recently rescued from death to be biologically frightened of it. It is the unconscious life force in the healthy that fears oblivion. The deeply sick, the very old, the mortally wounded, these find death as natural as a tired man finds sleep. And he was all of these things and more – sick, wounded, and a century old.

Yet still he postponed what he knew he must do. The force which had brought him back to consciousness remained to quicken him. He was... curious. He had set fire to an arrow of hay in a frenzy, in an emotional explosion that had commanded him irresistibly. Yet beneath his frenzy there had been conscious purpose. Now every fibre of his being wanted an answer. Had the British pilots seen the arrow? And would they return?

Soberly he tried to examine the question. Provided his signal *had* been observed – what then? The possibility existed that even so there was no telling when they might return. Air warfare was complicated, as he knew from the newspapers. It might be necessary for them to take photographs or reconnoitre. In that case, it would be days or weeks before they returned to bomb. But Baumer and his headsman would not wait weeks, or even days.

Was it hopeless to believe that they might return the very next night? They were not stupid, these British. They might conclude that a camouflaged factory was inadequately protected – and so risk a hurried raid in the hope of a prize. As to the problem of photographs... since the target was obviously hidden in a wood, the wood itself defined the target. Incendiary bombs could take the place of photographs. And if all this occurred to him, why wouldn't the British think of it? It was not too unreasonable, was it?

Trembling suddenly, Wegler wondered if he dared make this decision for which his heart hungered. He *wanted to know*! He wanted to remain alive until the following night. If then the planes didn't come, all would be over for him – and he would die as stupidly as he now felt he had lived. But if they did come...

He licked his lips. His mouth, his throat, felt hot. Tomorrow night! Was it absurd for him to hope? How did he know, for instance, that weeks – or at least several nights – had not already passed? Biting his tongue over this new anxiety, he thought for a moment, and then slipped his hand beneath his gown. At work, two days before, he had been burnt by a spatter of hot oil. His fingers felt along the rib case on his left side. He found the spot. It was still tender.

If it had been this night, then, what time was it – and was it now day or night? And how long exactly must he wait before the planes might come?

Eleven o'clock was the hour at which they usually passed overhead. In that case, he must have been wounded shortly after. With a bullet in his gut, they had undoubtedly operated. (Doctor Zoder, the one who had examined him yesterday in Baumer's office to see if he were fit for the army...) How long did such operations take? An hour – two? He could only guess. But he must have been unconscious for several hours at least.

The answer came abruptly. He saw the obvious – that the blackout curtains were drawn over the window, and that a small night lamp burned on a table near his cot. By six thirty in the morning, when he always had breakfast, it was already light. Therefore it was now between midnight and six. Allowing for his period of unconsciousness, 3 or 4 a.m. would be accurate enough. In that case, he had about twenty hours to wait for the planes to come... or not to come. And he had twenty hours of life before he ripped the bandage.

He groaned aloud as a pain stabbed low in his belly, with savage lack of warning. He licked his lips. How dry and parched his throat was!

Now, with sudden anguish, Wegler remembered his war days again and realized why he was so thirsty. In the trenches, when a man was hit in the belly, he always wanted water – but water was the one thing they were told never to give him. Heinz, for instance, the lad who had been mess sergeant in his company...

* * *

An image of Heinz, as he had seen him in the hospital, came back to Wegler vividly, carrying terror with it. Before he went into the ward, the sister had told him that Heinz was doing fine. But she added that the first two days were very hard. If Wegler wanted to sit with Heinz for a little while, she'd get him a saucer of water and a piece of gauze. It was all right to keep wetting the lad's lips, even to let him suck a damp piece of gauze, but it would be disastrous if he allowed Heinz to have even a small drink, no matter how much he begged for it.

When he went in, the youth who confronted him was not the stout mess sergeant he knew so well. This man had grey, sunken features and glassy eyes. But his cadaver's face lit up excitedly when he saw Wegler, and he beckoned instantly for him to come close.

"Water, Willi – get me some water!" he whispered.

It was frightening. The youth's eyes, always so warm and intelligent, blazed suddenly with a cunning one could only call animal.

"Water," he demanded, "Willi, I want you to get me some water."

"Heinz," Wegler began, "the nurse…"

There was no chance for him to finish. Once Heinz knew that Wegler had been spoken to by the nurse, he counted him also amongst his enemies. He sank back on the pillow with a groan of despair and hatred, and from that instant on he was no longer interested in his visitor. And as Wegler observed, it was not that Heinz was delirious – he was quite conscious and thoroughly alert. But this Heinz was beyond interest in a mate from his company, or even in hearing Wegler tell him how lucky he was to cop a furlough. Heinz was on fire – throat, belly, breast – and beyond water there was no meaning in life for him, and no desire.

The memory frightened Wegler. He had calculated on twenty hours. But would he be like Heinz a few hours from now – a creature begging for water, caring for nothing else? What if Baumer held a glass of water to his lips? Heinz, too, had been a man before he was wounded. There was a point, surely, at which the will and pride of any man turned to jelly. And the more he denied Baumer information, the more violent Baumer would become – that he knew.

There was one little thing he could tell, of course – what he knew about Pastor Frisch. But God's Grace upon Pastor Frisch, and damnation to anyone who would betray him!

What ought he to do? They would be coming soon!

Slowly Wegler's confusion eased. A smile came to his lips. And then, as the full meaning of his own power came to him, a cry of bitter triumph welled up in his heart. It was of no matter to him that Baumer would make demands, or that a doctor might come spying upon him. It was he, not they, who was the sole judge of how long he lived. There was no power on earth that could make him yield to them – provided he wanted it so. He had only one task: to make a pretence of unconsciousness until nightfall. So long as he appeared unconscious, they would leave him alone. He must not answer questions; he must lie still; he must fight his thirst as long as he could. But if at any time their demands or his own pain mounted beyond bearing, then surcease was always at his command. At that moment he need only reach down to the bandage.

He lay very still for a moment, weary in brain and body from so much intense thought. But he felt deeply, quietly exalted. This was a plan indeed! To play a swindle for twenty hours. And then, God willing, to hear bombs dropping upon the factory. It would be worth a few hours of pain and thirst – for he would be dead a long, long time.

He licked his lips again. He lay still, his eyes closed. His square, large-featured face was flushed, but his forehead was free of perspiration now. The low pound of a heavy machine came to him through the night muted and distant, as though from another world. It gave him no pleasure to reflect that it might be his own steam hammer.

A groan burst from his lips again. This was the second time he had felt a sharp, cutting pain in his abdomen, quite different from the steady throbbing there. A bit wryly he told himself that it would never do. Pain or no pain, it was essential to keep his teeth locked together. For the next twenty hours he had a race to run: there was he himself on one team (Willi Wegler, the fool), and on the other team was Baumer... with a headsman at the finish line. He would somehow have to sit on his pain... and ignore his thirst... and pass the time.

This, too, was a new thought. How did a stupid wretch with a hole in his belly pass the time? He might think of the good things in his life, perhaps – of Käthe, his dead wife, and of sweet days... And perhaps, if he dared, he might even ponder over his muddled years and try to make some sense out of them. He was forty-two years old, and he was about to die. He had never been a liar or a cheat or dishonest – he had obeyed the laws, accepted each government in its turn and worked like a dog. And yet it had all ended in a muddle, and he didn't know why. He only knew that somewhere, somehow, he must have been inadequate.

Wegler's body stiffened a little even before his tired brain warned him that the door was opening. His heart commenced to pound violently. It was only with difficulty that he mastered the impulse to open his eyes.

Laughing, Doctor Zoder entered with Sister Wollweber. "But I insist," she was saying. "How much sleep did you have? Five minutes only! You're like a dishrag, Doctor Zoder. You won't last until tomorrow night."

"In that case, you may have the privilege of putting two ersatz pennies on my eyes. Now leave off. My patriotic patient needs me."

"Nonsense he needs you, doctor. Look at him. He hasn't stirred since I was last in!"

"And he won't stir until eight o'clock tomorrow morning," Zoder replied. "If Baumer comes around a second earlier, he'll be wasting his time."

Sister Wollweber folded her plump arms and snorted loudly. "You're going to give him morphine, I suppose?" On general principles she was opposed to injections.

Zoder fingered the pulse in Wegler's wrist. "Clever lady... Now keep quiet."

Wegler held himself relaxed to the doctor's touch, but he was deeply agitated. A narcotic would be his enemy now. He needed to be awake if anything happened, and he needed to hear what was said in his presence. He had only one weapon in his struggle – his own brain. If that were put out of action, he would surely lose.

"Pulse... 105."

Sister Wollweber marked the chart. "You see," she exclaimed in triumph, "no septicaemia."

Zoder grimaced as he whipped down a thermometer. "You'll guarantee it won't be a hundred and twenty in an hour?"

"I'll guarantee it! I have a feeling for these things."

"Oh yes, your Aryan intuition!" He placed the thermometer in Wegler's armpit and thought to himself, "Good God, how easy it is to be a fool. Why do I let her get me into these arguments? She pulls me down to her level, damn it – while I go along as though I were as stupid as she is."

"I'll make a bargain with you, doctor."

"What now?"

"About the injection—"

"That's none of your business!"

Placidly: "Of course, doctor... But after you inject, will you go to sleep until morning? I'll watch over him."

Zoder didn't reply. He bent down over Wegler, feeling his palm, examining his fingernails. The man had definitely passed out of shock – it was a little difficult to know why he was still unconscious. The effects of the ether would surely have worn off by now.

"Well, doctor?"

Still silent, Zoder felt over Wegler's skull with gentle, inquisitive fingers.

"A cranial injury?" asked the nurse.

Zoder shrugged. "I don't see any signs of it. But I don't quite understand this extended unconsciousness." He reached for the thermometer. "What was the temperature at post operation?"

"Ninety-nine and five tenths, doctor."

"It's a hundred now." He stared at Wegler reflectively. "Temperature, pulse, respiration are in good shape. I can't see why he isn't coming around. Look at him – he lies there like a log. Doesn't even stir."

"Will you go to sleep, doctor? You haven't answered me."

"I want you to look in on him every fifteen minutes, sister."

"I will. I promise."

"Will you call me the instant he comes to?"

"Absolutely, doctor. On my honour."

"In that case, I'll wait with the injection."

"You'll go to sleep though, doctor? Really asleep?"

"Oh, woman, woman!" he exclaimed harshly. "I'm fifty years old. Will you please let me decide my own conduct? I really can't stand any more of your jabber."

"I'm sorry," she whispered. Without warning she burst into sobs. "I try to do my best."

Her face turned very piteous with her weeping, but Zoder felt no sympathy for her. Instead his heart exploded with sudden venom. "Weep, you scum!" he thought. "There aren't enough tears in Germany to wash this poor, bleeding world clean again. Weep until you're blind – weep the blood from your damned bowels. Your kind has made the whole earth weep already!"

He turned away, staring at the man on the bed. "And you!" he thought. "I was managing fine until you came along. Now I'm as muddled as an infant. All I can think to do is wait until morning so I can run to a pastor. God damn you, too!"

"Oh, shut up!" he said aloud to Sister Wollweber. "Don't be such a stupid old goat." He strode angrily from the room.

Sniffling, the nurse dried her tears. It wounded her dreadfully when Zoder burst out at her like this, as he did every so often. At her age there was no obligation upon her to be slaving in a hospital. Zoder's scorn was shameful reward for her patriotism – yes, and for her steady sacrifice, her devotion.

The more Sister Wollweber felt sorry for herself, the more she became enraged... at Wegler. It was Wegler who had kept them both up all night, Wegler who was really the cause of their quarrel. And yet they hovered over him as though he were a decent human being and not an evil scoundrel who had tried to murder them all.

With growing rage she glared at the man on the cot. Her plump, earnest face became crimson with indignation. Execution was too good for a reptile like that, she told herself. He should be torn to pieces, made to suffer, the monster! "Oh, you!" she exclaimed aloud, with a moral indignation she could not contain. "Oh, you beast! How could you do a thing like that?" She moved closer to the cot and stared down at him, muttering to herself. Wegler's face stared back impassively. It troubled her extremely that he should have the cast of feature he did. If he were not there before her eyes, if someone had merely informed her of his treachery, she would have imagined an evil, wart-faced creature, a bloodthirsty Bolshevik – or a slimy, hook-nosed Hebrew, or a wild-faced madman. For who else would betray his own fatherland – a crime that, as every German learnt from infancy, was lower even than betrayal of parents or lover or family? Yet this blond, Teuton-faced, almost handsome man – yes, really handsome – had committed that crime. It was beyond words, the shame of it. Either he was truly mad (and not even that would excuse him), or else somewhere in his blood there was a hidden taint. "Oh, you vermin!" she exclaimed aloud again, to relieve her feelings. "What kind of a devil are you? You just wait... what you'll get!" And before she could quite realize what she was doing, she spat in his face.

She remained quiet for a moment, panting, muttering to herself. Suddenly a dreadful yearning welled up in her heart – an aching hunger for the war to be over, for her sons to be home, safe and whole, for life to be joyous and peaceful again.

She left the room, sighing audibly, thinking to herself that, with poor Sister Scheithauer still incapacitated, tomorrow would be another long day for her.

* * *

Even though he knew they had both gone, Wegler peered around the room through half-open lids before he wiped his face. He was too detached emotionally to feel anger towards the nurse. As a matter of fact, what she had done provided a useful caution. Now, no matter what happened, he would scarcely expect a woman's compassion from her, or anything except betrayal from the doctor.

He realized also that the visit had provided a gigantic piece of information. In cases like his own, evidently, there was the possibility of skull injury. He need only "lie like a log", as Zoder had expressed it, and see to it that no murmur of pain passed his lips. And in that case, the eight o'clock appointment which Zoder had arranged for him with Baumer might be permanently postponed. All in all, he had gained a lap in the race, thanks to the doctor, for now he was to be free from molestation until morning. After that, with any luck at all, he would have a chance of fending them off until night.

He lay quiet. During the ten minutes past, when Zoder and the nurse had been in the room, he had not felt the throbbing in his belly. Now it returned again with redoubled vigour. He locked his teeth together and swallowed painfully. It would be hard, this day of trial – there must be no mistake about that...

Well, then, he thought, he would begin now to occupy his mind. There was much to dwell upon. Yes – certainly. He could also hum songs in his head – the selections he had played on his accordion. Yes, the prospect was not at all bad. He would surely find it easy to occupy himself for a mere twenty hours.

All at once, Wegler's cheery mood departed. "I'm going to die tonight," he thought, and was seized by melancholy, by a sense of the galling futility and waste of his life. He thought of Berthe Lingg, who had been his betrothed. It was sad – sad and very bitter that she had betrayed him. If not for her, the arrow of burning hay would have blazed up unhampered.

And yet, even now, Wegler could not wholeheartedly hate Berthe for what she had done. Even in his own transport of passion he had observed that she was hysterical with fright. Perhaps, if he had trusted her more, or tried to explain more fully what was in his heart, she would have helped him instead of betraying him. He had been too confused himself, too tortured in mind and soul to be cautious or thoughtful about her. In that sense it was he who was the more to blame. Berthe was a good woman, and she loved him. He had bungled it for both of them.

Berthe's future, too, was dreadful to contemplate. She was thirty-six years old, unmarried, with his child growing in her womb – a child that would be branded the seed of a traitor. What would happen to her now – to warm-hearted, frightened Berthe, who wanted only to be happy?

Wegler sighed. He was sorry for Berthe from the bottom of his heart. Now their dream was gone. For a little while it had been sweet to contemplate – the farm; a decent, warm-fleshed woman as his companion; a growing child as evidence that they had indeed found a second life together. He had been drunk with that dream – as though it were not Nazi Land in which they were living.

Ah, God – what sort of man was he? Why had he lived as he had – why had he now done this?

What made an idea suddenly come to a man – grip him, hold him fast, force him to do what he had done? He was forty-two years old, but he really knew nothing about himself. And he had only twenty hours in which to learn why he had chosen to die in this way: a traitor, an outcast, a man to be spat upon by his society.

The cutting pain stabbed in his loins again. He ground his teeth together and prayed for the first time in years.

"Dear God," he whispered, "make the British planes come. Please! And help me think of something. I must not give in to this pain."

Out of the twisted web of his years, Wegler's searching, unhappy mind drew a thread, and then another. A phrase came to him: "Willi the Whistler". His friend Karl had always called him that, saying it with affectionate disdain. And now for the first time in his life Willi asked himself bluntly, "Was Karl right about me? He used to call me a big dumb ox. How is a man to know whether he did right or wrong with his life?"

It was in the trenches, in 1918, that Karl had first bestowed the nickname on Willi. "Whistling, always whistling," he exclaimed exasperatedly one day. "By God, when are you going to get serious about life?"

"Serious?" Willi had replied grinning. "Man, I'm serious as hell. Otherwise I wouldn't whistle. You and me are serious about different things, that's all."

While it was true that just then Willi was whistling out of nervous bravado, since they were preparing for an attack, it was also true that Willi had already learnt how to whistle at life. Karl, who was more sombre, had one slogan: "This war stinks – it's for the profit of the munitions makers and nothing else."

To this Willi would invariably reply:

"Sure it stinks, but like my father used to say, 'A wise man makes the best of things.' Here, you grouser, take a drink of schnapps and shut your trap. We're still alive, aren't we? All I know is I've got my blue-eyed Käthe at home, and a little one on the way. Man, I'm going home to *that*, if I can. I want some fun."

"A wise man makes the best of things," Willi would say, and whistle a few bars as he kicked the mud from his boots. "You know what my father always said?" he asked Karl once. "'Life is like a honeycomb,' my father always said. 'You've got to learn where to put your mouth and where to suck, what to swallow and what to spit out.' Now, that's straight thinking, Karl. It comes from a man who knew. What the hell, if you look at the dark side of life, it's all lousy. Do you think my old man had a good life? The hell he did. He worked like a dog, and he had painter's colic for ten years before he kicked off from it. But he made the best of things, see, and he always had a grin on his face. Now, you take me – I've been working and supporting my mother since I was fifteen. One week after I got called up she died from pneumonia. So what the hell! The way I see it, you can't figure life out one way or another – you can't even plan. Make the best of things, that's my philosophy. Have some fun, don't get too worried, take life like it comes."

"You and your philosophy..." replied Karl good-naturedly. "What to swallow and what to spit out! I suppose if a bullet smacks you in your ugly mug you'll decide to spit it out?"

"That's different."

"The hell it's different. Peace or war, if you're a worker – you get bullets."

Invariably Willi would answer such arguments with affectionate derision. "Hooray for Karl Marx," he would say, because his friend was the son of an ardent socialist, and had been named after Marx. "You go back and make revolutions, Karl. That's all right with me."

"And where will you be when I'm making a revolution?"

"Who knows?" Willi would reply, and start whistling. And he would whistle as he wrote his daily letter home. His wife, only just turned seventeen, was the daughter of a neighbour. For as long as Willi could remember, they had been indifferent to each other's existence. Then, during the ten-day furlough he received after his training period, they found a sudden, passionate attachment. In complete disregard for the wishes of her parents, who were convinced that their daughter would be left on their hands as a war widow, they married before his leave was over. Käthe had even abandoned her home rather than hear Willi criticized by her unrelenting, bitter mother. She was living alone now, rather miserable, on the meagre government stipend allotted to army wives. Willi knew that she was alone, but of her dreadful loneliness he never heard a word. As they were to confess to each other later, their letters had been mutually a confection of love and deceit.

"Darling Käthe," Willi would write. "I'm fine and more in love with you than ever. Where I am now all is quiet, no sound but the birds. You wouldn't think there was a war going on." (This was one of his persistent lies.) "The General Staff has decided that at all costs Willi Wegler must be returned to his wife safe and sound. The picture you sent was worth ten thousand marks to me. Imagine a husband without his wife's picture! You're looking a little thin, Käthe dear, but never mind. After the war I'll fatten you up. Did I tell you I learnt to play the accordion? I was in the hospital with the flu." (A second lie – it was a shell fragment in his head.) "I learnt there. Some fun. When I get home, I'll play for you every night – between kisses…"

Willi the Whistler… He whistled, and he laughed, but when Karl was wounded in the last retreat, Willi carried him four miles on his back. "Don't think I did it because I like you," he told Karl when they were safe. "I did it only because my father was a member of the building union, whatever the name of the damn thing is, and because your father is a member of the bakers' union – and the sons of union men ought to stick together. That's what's called class solidarity, isn't it?" And Karl, in spite of the pain from a punctured foot, burst out laughing. Willi whistled, but when the soldiers mutinied in his company and refused to move up to the front, he stuck with them, even though he didn't see the sense of it. He was war-weary too, but Karl couldn't convince him that mutiny was the way out – or that there wasn't something reprehensible in shooting your captain. And when they were surrounded by a loyal division and disarmed – when every tenth man was ordered shot – he stood up with the rest who were being counted off not welching, but saying to himself, "What am I doing here? I didn't want to mutiny. I only want to get back safe to Käthe, if I can."

The war nightmare ended, finally. The Armistice came, and he did go home. He walked up the four flights to the cold, bare room where his Käthe sat, bulging in pregnancy, hollow-cheeked and tired-eyed, and folded her in his arms. A huge, blond, square-jawed giant of nineteen, with the odour of death still evil in his nostrils, he said softly, "Ah, darling" – and he either had to cry or do something else… so, quite absurdly, he whistled as loud as he could.

But now his Käthe was dead, and Karl was dead too, and he, Willi, was lying on a hospital cot, worse off than both. It was not the dying he minded, but the muddle. Somewhere his whistling had led him astray. He sensed that now. But where, and in what manner?

His thoughts turned back to Karl again – to the chunky, tough-bodied youth he had loved so dearly in the frightened comradeship of the trenches – and then to the man that Karl had become…

Living in different cities, Willi and Karl did not see each other for some years after the war. Although they tried to maintain a correspondence, Willi found letter-writing an uneasy matter, and their exchange lagged. But in 1928 Karl and his wife turned up in Cologne. Willi was wholly delighted to see him and indifferent to the news that Karl was now a minor Communist functionary, devoting his energies wholly to his Party. So far as Willi expected, he and Karl would continue their fine friendship where they had left off.

The first part of their reunion was more than amicable. Karl and his wife were childless – quite obviously they enjoyed this contact with settled family life. In contrast to their single, furnished room, with its brown wallpaper, roaches and stale smells, here was a bright two-room flat with gay curtains sewn by Käthe, with solid articles of furniture handsomely stained by Willi – and with a ten-year-old who sweetened the dinner table with his bubbling conversation. Karl and his wife had never played "I spy with my eye something in the room that's blue – what is it?" or "I'm thinking of an animal in the zoo that's big, has a striped skin but no fur, and isn't fierce – what is it?" – or any of the other games by which adults carry on a relationship with a child. Willi could see by Karl's face that his friend was wistful over a treasure like this, which other men had but he did not. Secretly he decided that when he was working steadily, he would have Karl and his wife over for supper every week or so.

But later, when Richard was put to bed (he slept in the kitchen), and when the adults had moved into the bedroom to continue their talk, Karl steered the conversation to politics. Thereafter the congenial atmosphere began to sour.

"Willi," Karl asked, "what do you do with yourself these days?"

"Do with myself? What do you mean? I work. I have my family. That's a full-time job for a weakling like me."

"No trade-union activities?"

"In a way. I belong to our Union Sport Club. Sunday evenings we practise gymnastics." Willi laughed. "You know me: I'm bottom man for a team of four – the dumb piece of concrete. We're not so bad, though. Last year we won the inter-union contest."

"Fine," Karl answered with a slight frown. "But gymnastics... After all, gymnastics won't beat the Nationalists at the next election... or make jobs for the unemployed."

"I tell you, Karl," said Willi, "that's true enough, I suppose. But with me it's like this: I like to live quiet. There are men I know who play cards all day Sunday in a beer garden – you know? And there are others who are so hot for politics you can never find them home on an evening. They're off to their Party meetings, or things like that. But I guess my nature is this: I'm a man who likes family life. Sunday comes, Käthe and the boy and me take the trolley across the bridge. We get out into the country – the kid and I fly a kite maybe – then we have a picnic lunch. That's the way I like to live, see Karl? That's my beer and politics."

Karl grinned. "Same old Willi, eh? Still whistling."

Willi guffawed and whistled a bar from a song. "Same Karl too, eh? Always wanting to change things." To Irma, Karl's wife, he added, "Does he argue with you too all the time? In the trenches I could hardly hear the bullets for all his hot air."

"What a liar!" said Karl affectionately. Irma, Karl's diminutive wife, smiled at both of them and then turned to Käthe. "And do *you* have any political activities?" she enquired.

The question quite startled Käthe. She glanced up from her darning in surprise and shook her head. "Why, no," she replied wonderingly, "how is a woman like me to be mixed up in politics?"

"Käthe votes, though," said Willi. "Election time comes, she votes."

"And how do you vote?" Irma persisted.

"Oh... the way Willi votes," Käthe replied comfortably.

Even Willi grinned over her tone.

"Do you know who Lenin was?" Irma asked.

Käthe nodded a bit dubiously.

"Lenin had a saying: 'Every cook should learn all about politics.' How does that strike you, Käthe?"

Käthe shrugged, then giggled a little. "Maybe Lenin didn't know how to cook."

Karl burst out into an absolute roar of laughter. "Go on, answer that," he said to his wife.

"Certainly I will," Irma replied seriously. "But what are you laughing so hard about?"

"It was a funny answer, that's why."

"You see," Irma persisted, turning to Käthe, "what Lenin meant was that no society is well organized until everyone has a part in deciding its politics. It's as important to you what sort of government and laws we have as it is to a banker."

Käthe nodded and continued to darn Willi's socks.

"The next time we see you, I'll give you a pamphlet that Lenin wrote on the woman question. That is, if you'd like to see it."

Käthe nodded politely. "That will be fine, Irma."

Willi grinned and tiptoed into the kitchen for his accordion. He found Karl's wife fascinating to listen to – not particularly for what she said. Irma was a tiny woman, delicately boned in face and figure, with large, intense black eyes. She looked no more than sixteen, for all her thirty years, and Willi was enchanted whenever this seeming adolescent spoke in a mature woman's voice, and with an adult's poise.

He returned to the bedroom and sat down with the accordion on his knees. "How about an old soldier's song?" he asked Karl.

"Fine. But I'd like to ask you something serious first, Willi."

Willi grunted, his eyes smiling in anticipation.

"Your politics is confined to voting, apparently... But how do you vote? What party?"

"What party? Oh... I'm not particular. Now one way, now another. Usually the Social Democrats, though."

For the first time that evening Karl lost his usual good humour. "Oh, for Christ's sake, Willi," he exclaimed, "you ought to know better than that."

Willi, like any German worker, even the unpolitical ones, knew of the deep fissure between the Social Democrats and the Communists. He replied with a grin, "Why? Last time I saw you what were you? How's a simple-minded man like me to keep up with your somersaults?"

"Now listen," said Karl, who knew his friend well enough to be aware that Willi was ragging him, "don't give me any of that. I was an SD up until the time Noske linked up with the damn Junkers. Don't play naive with me, you old fox. You know the role of the Social Democrats as well as I do – or you ought to."

"Well," Willi replied, "maybe I know, maybe I don't. The fact is, Karl, I hear the SDP lads denounce you Communists, and so far as I can tell, they have a case, too. Anyway, how about a song now?"

"Scratch a Social Democrat and uncover a Social Fascist," interjected Irma bitterly. "You'll live to see it, Willi. They sold out the German worker in 1918 – they'll do it again. They're just as chauvinist as any old-line Prussian general like Hindenburg."*

Willi shrugged, indicating his amiable confusion with these arguments and counter-arguments.

"Damn it, Willi," Karl said, "it's your duty to decide who's right and who's wrong. Truth is truth, Willi. Facts are facts. As a worker, you should find out."

"I'll tell you, Karl," Willi replied affectionately. "If I had two lives, I would find out about politics in the second one. But I have only one life. Now look: I work. Or if the job shuts down, I look for work. That keeps my days busy. In the night-time, or weekends, I'm also busy. A family takes time, you know? I make things, for instance. That bureau over there... I designed it and built it and painted it. Saves a bit of money, y'know? Also, I like it. Now, meetings and politics – they take time, and they cost money. If I can save any money, I'd rather buy myself a farm some day instead of paying Party dues. I've always had a taste to live in the country."

"Yes," said Karl, "I remember you did. But look, man, all over Germany peasants are being forced *off* their farms. Don't you know that?"

"Maybe we won't have a farm, then," Willi replied a bit uncomfortably, for he had given up hope of actually acquiring one. "But a man has to live like he wants."

"You know, Willi," Irma said quietly, "I always wonder about a man like you. You know why?"

"Why?"

"You love your family – yet you have no interest in protecting your family's future."

Willi grinned. "I know. Next you're going to say why don't I work to make a better Germany by joining your Party, eh?"

"But isn't it true?" Irma asked with passionate seriousness. "The bankers don't care a penny what happens to people like the Weglers. You've seen the unemployed living in shacks on the edge of town. More are moving there every day, living like animals almost. What'll happen to you if you lose your job? The same thing, won't it?"

Willi grinned. "So far, when I lose one job, I pick up another. We've gotten along."

With mingled irritation and wonder, despite her desire not to be unpleasant, Irma exclaimed brashly, "But, my goodness… so long as you're getting along, don't you care what happens to anyone else? I don't understand such a selfish attitude."

Whereas Willi would have shrugged at the remark and let it pass, Käthe rushed to his defence. Bristling over this criticism of her beloved Willi, she exclaimed hotly, "Why, how dare you? What do you know about Willi? Why, only last month they dispossessed Frau Baumeister downstairs. She's a war widow with a sick child. Do you know what Willi did? He carried their furniture right back up the minute he came home from work. And when the police came, he barred the door. 'The child in here is sick,' he told them. 'I'll smash the face in of the first one who tries to move her.' Why, I was so afraid he'd be arrested I almost died. And when the union declares a strike, do you think Willi scabs? Two months he was on strike last year, sitting around the house. But that isn't enough for you, I suppose? Well, we're quiet, respectable people. We don't believe in stirring up trouble. Maybe you feel the only decent people are revolutionists – but we don't think so."

"Now, now – let's not get upset," Karl said, keenly upset himself at this outburst of temper. "You were wrong to say what you did, Irma. I know Willi – the best sort in the world. But y'see, Willi, that's just the reason—"

Willi interrupted, with a burst of discordant sound from his accordion. "Music hour, Karl. It's ten o'clock soon, and bedtime."

"Right," said Karl, yielding graciously. "You play and I'll whistle. How's that?"

"Just one thing first," Willi said lightly. "Just for the future… You two are the kind who want to make the world a better place to live in. Fine! And maybe all your hard work will accomplish things. Believe me, if you make your revolution, I won't stand in your way. But we're a different kind. I can't eat my heart out working for a world I'll never see. We used to have the Kaiser – now it's a Republic. I can't see it's any better. No, Karl, I'm just a little bug, and I want to live in my own little nest in my own little way. So from now on, old boy, you come around and let's talk over old times and sing a song or two – but don't waste your breath on us. We leave politics to the politicians."

It ended there, and in the years to come Karl's visits dwindled to one every six months. But that night, as they were going to bed, Willi told Käthe something that he had been quietly laughing about during their argument. "I'll tell you, Käthe," he said, "there's something else to all of this, I bet." He was sitting on the edge of their bed, and he caught her arms, pulling her over in front of him. "You had a look at Irma. I'm sure she's smart as a whip. But you know" – he began to rumble with laughter – "Irma hasn't got hair like yours." He ran his hand lovingly over Käthe's soft, corn-coloured hair. "And Irma's face is kind of thinnish. She hasn't got the prettiest little mouth in the world like yours. Do you know how pretty your mouth is, Käthe? It's really the prettiest thing about you."

"Is it?" Käthe asked, flushing with pleasure.

"Didn't I ever tell you? What sort of a husband am I?"

"You've told me. But I never believed it. I'm only glad you think I'm pretty. No one else thinks so, I'm sure. Look how fat I'm getting."

Laughing, Willi drew her face down to his and kissed her hard and long. "Is that so? Nobody else thinks you're pretty. Well, well... Maybe that's good." He slapped her plump bottom. "And do you know," he continued, "Irma looked kind of like a Grade A cedar board to me – smooth and flat. She doesn't have anything like these to interfere with her beauty." He cupped Käthe's pert breasts between his big hands, stooping to kiss them through her nightgown. "And Irma looked in the behind like if I took a feel I'd touch sandpaper." His hands thrust under his wife's gown, squeezing her soft flesh as he burst out into loud laughter. "So all in all I think my poor friend Karl spends so much time on politics because he hasn't got anything nicer to do." Lifting Käthe up, he lay back on the bed, swinging her down upon him. "What do you think?" he asked, as his arms folded her close.

"I think you're blind," Käthe replied. "I'll say this for Irma: she's pretty as a picture. I wish I had a waist like that. And such eyes."

"Pretty? I'd feel like I was breaking the law. She's got the figure of a twelve-year-old."

"So all men don't like fat women the way you do!"

"Fat... you're not fat. Thank God there's something a man can put his hands on."

"Anyway, Karl must love her, or he wouldn't have married her. He doesn't look like a cold-blood to me."

"You're crazy. Karl married her because he's so mixed up in politics he doesn't have time for a woman. You think if he was going to bed tonight with you, he'd think of politics?"

"Why not?"

"*Do* you?"

"Why not?"

"*Do* you... Hey?"

"Willi, don't squeeze so hard," she giggled. "No, I don't think so either..."

The sharp pain stabbed in Willi's belly. He bit his lip. "Willi the Whistler," he thought... "Yes, it's easy for me to look back now and say, 'Maybe Karl was right... maybe I was too easy about things.' But the truth is I still don't know if Karl was right. Jesus Christ, I've got no reason to lie to myself now. A man is what he is. How can a man help his nature? I never had a head that was interested in politics. I've got no reason to think now that if I could live my life over I would live it differently. Only... only, perhaps, I wouldn't whistle quite so much. The whistling seems sour now. It's ended... flat."

He licked his lips and then he began to laugh, silently, with pain. "Oh God!" he thought. "What a damn muddle it is! Who ever knows what's wrong and what's right? You walk on a dark road, you lose the way, but you don't find out until the end – when you fall into a ditch like a drunken fool. But when that happens, how can you look back and say, 'I should have gone this way or the other?' All you know is that you came out to a bad end... But Jesus Christ, I never wanted it this way. I didn't! I didn't!"

Quietly, with his lips clamped tight together, Willi began to cry. He thought of Käthe, of their simple, sweet life, of their boy, and the salt tears stung his eyes. For the second time he whispered, "Dear God, make the British planes come. Please..."

Chapter 6

The oral report delivered by Elite Guard Blumel to Gestapo Commissar Kehr contained the following data. Concerning the prisoner of war recently purchased by Berthe Lingg in the town marketplace for seventeen Reichsmarks, Blumel established that before and after Wegler's sabotage, the Pole absolutely had been locked in the barn. The only key to the padlock was in the possession of Berthe Lingg, who swore that she kept it on or near her person at all times. Furthermore, as Blumel advised Commissar Kehr with unmistakable pride, he had carefully examined the walls of the barn, the surrounding grounds and the windows, in order to be positive that the Pole did not have any means of secret egress. This being the case, Kehr concluded that the man was to be considered free from suspicion. Nevertheless, in order to establish his own thoroughness before the officials who would presently study the record, he had the Pole brought before him.

It was at this point that Kehr made the only error of his entire investigation. The mistake was inevitable. Like most Germans, the commissar had learnt in childhood that Poles – more or less through a decree of God Himself – were his inferiors. Later in his life this decree on the part of the Lord had been buttressed, enriched and developed into a system of statehood by one Adolf Hitler. Now, as an adult, Kehr not only continued to believe these early teachings in the careless manner in which most peoples of the earth regard at least one other race as being inferior to themselves, but he honestly assumed them to be scientific fact. Thus he had accepted at ten, and professed with utter sincerity at fifty, that a Pole was dirtier than a German by reason of a racial sloth, and a greater tendency towards greasiness in the sweat glands; that a Pole loved money with a sordid, grasping love; and that a Pole could always get the better of a German in a bargain because he was unscrupulous, whereas the German was not. It made no difference to Kehr, since he never reflected upon it, that he also felt the same about Jews – or that the Turks, by odd coincidence, spoke in the same way of the Armenians, the English of the Irish, the Americans of the Negroes. Kehr, like others the world over, was merely in the grip of a long inheritance of cultivated legend that had been passed down by generation after generation of his fathers, and was no less credible to him because it was unscientific, no less firmly rooted in his shrewd mind because it was stupid, and no less embedded in the genuinely charitable corners of his heart because it was wolfish. And because of this, he made an error with the one witness who could have given him a piece of real evidence in regard to Wegler's sabotage.

One of the facts which Kehr took for granted about all Poles was that they were by racial nature invariable liars. Therefore, when it came time to investigate the war prisoner, he assumed as a matter of course that the Pole would answer every question that might accrue to Kehr's benefit with an evasion or a deceit.

He began as usual: "Your name is Bironski?" He addressed the man in German, since Berthe Lingg had told him that the prisoner spoke their language.

"Yes, sir. Stephen Bironski."

At this point Elite Guard Blumel reddened with anger and pressed his lips together venomously. It made no difference to Blumel that the prisoner had understood every contemptuous word spoken about him in the waiting room – but it was a deliberate insult for the Pole to have listened to their conversation without advising them he spoke German.

"Pharmacist, eh?" asked Kehr, looking up from the man's record.

"Yes, sir."

"You don't look like a pharmacist," the commissar observed. His tone expressed the genial contempt he felt for the man's appearance. "It's no mistake?"

"No, sir."

"You actually have a university degree in pharmacy?"

"Yes, sir."

"What university?"

"Cra-Cracow, sir," the prisoner answered with a slight stammer.

"Well, then, Pan* Bironski, my educated Pole, how would you like to go home – to Poland, I mean... to your very own home in Poland?"

The prisoner raised his head at this, but the excitement that Kehr expected to see in his face was not there. His gaunt, unclean features remained dully immobile; his black eyes were toneless.

"You *would* like to go home, wouldn't you? You have a family there, I suppose?"

"Yes, sir." (His wife and two children had been dismembered by the same stray mortar shell on the second day of war.)

"And if I tell you there is a way in which it can positively be arranged for you to go home, do you believe me?"

"Yes... yes, sir."

"We'll see then." Kehr paused for a moment to belch. "Now, then, Pan Bironski, did anything happen last night outside the barn where you sleep?"

Ever since Blumel had come to fetch him, Bironski had been prepared for this question. And if ever a man had reason to lie, it was he at this moment – for he knew that Wegler had been his friend. He did not lie, because to speak an untruth to a Gestapo commissar requires character and courage. Bironski had neither. There had been a time, of course, when he had been what is called a "human being". He had lived quietly with his wife and two small girls, and had laboured earnestly in his pharmacy. But the man who stood before Commissar Kehr had been six months in a concentration camp, and then, for more than two years, a member of a forced-labour gang engaged in road building. A medical examination would have established that he was suffering from a kidney ailment and from anaemia, and that another four months of such living would see him drop dead in the field as surely as an autumn leaf drops from a tree. Even more revealing, however, would have been an enquiry on the part of his priest, or a skilled psychologist, into the state of his soul. It may be taken for granted that other Poles – and Russians and Frenchmen – who were suffering a similar captivity, were at this moment as hard in their hearts as an iron bar is hard – in their veins there was a distilled hatred and a thirst for vengeance that their captors knew and feared. But not all slaves become strong in their slavery: some are turned into a wretched and hopeless putty – and Bironski was of their number. With him the Masters of Europe had been entirely successful. He was now their creature – limp body and sick soul – until that day when he dropped dead in the field. And so at this moment he had no capacity or purpose, no desire or strength, with which to lie about Wegler. He told the commissar exactly what he had seen.

The air-raid alarm had interrupted his sleep the night before. He awakened in a sweat, as he did every time it sounded. Despite his physical exhaustion, it invariably took him the better part of an hour to fall asleep again – as a result, he was awake when a sudden commotion began in the field outside the barn. In the wall, above the straw pallet on which he slept, there was a small air vent. By climbing upon a box he was able to watch most of what transpired from the time Berthe Lingg came out into the field until the moment when there was a shot and Wegler fell to the ground. His description of the affair agreed precisely with the account given earlier by Frau Lingg.

"Now, then, Pan Bironski," Kehr asked, "do you have any knowledge of Wegler's motivation? Did he have any confederates that you know about? Did you see anyone else with him?... If you can throw some light on this, my dear Pan Bironski, I will absolutely guarantee that you'll be returned to your family." He paused for a moment and then added with paternal sternness: "But remember, it will go hard with you if you lie."

"Yes, sir," the prisoner muttered. "It is forbidden to lie. I know, sir."

"Well... anything to say?"

"Yes... yes, sir."

The prisoner's forehead knotted in concentration. What he had to tell had happened only two nights before, but he, who had once learnt the Latin names for an infinity of drugs, now found it very difficult to remember anything beyond a few hours' span. This particular event had been so astonishing, however, that he had not wholly forgotten it.

"The German, sir... I forget his name..."

"Wegler?"

"Yes, sir. He came to the barn and talked to me."

Kehr snapped up, his eyes opening wide. "He spoke to you? When? Was it before he lit the fire – last night?"

"No, sir... before that."

"Exactly when?"

"It was... at night, sir... before, sir."

"You've only been on the farm two nights – which night was it?"

"Only two nights, sir? Then it was the first night."

"Are you sure?"

"I... think so, sir. I'm sorry... it's... it's hard for me to remember things." He began to weep suddenly. "I'm sick, sir... sick... I need a doctor."

"Stop that!" Kehr ordered sharply. "Stand up straight!"

"Yes, sir."

"Let's say it was the first night... What about it?"

"He wanted me to escape, sir, but I wouldn't."

"You're lying!!"

"No, sir – I swear, sir."

"Don't try inventing something because you think I'll send you home. I'm not so stupid."

"No, sir. It's forbidden to lie. I know, sir."

"You still say he wanted you to escape?"

"God's truth, sir." Bironski crossed himself twice. "God's truth. He came to me in the barn."

"Go on!"

"I... ah..." He stopped, his forehead knitting painfully as he tried to recall. Suddenly the frown vanished and he smiled in triumph. The smile was ghastly on his unshaven, dirt-coloured face, as though it were a corpse smiling. "I remember, sir. All of it. He spoke to me, sir, through the little window. First he gave me a cigarette. But I... I told him it was forbidden for me to smoke in a barn." He said it eagerly, in triumph. "I wouldn't smoke the cigarette, sir – I obey all orders."

"Go on," Kehr told him. His eyes narrowed. He was commencing to feel sceptical already.

"Then he... he said he would write a letter for me to my home... But I said it was forbidden, sir."

"Come to the escape!"

"Yes, sir. Then he... he said he would break open the barn door for me any night. He said he would bring me clothes and... and some money... and some food... and... and *his own police papers, sir.*"

Blumel looked at Kehr and Kehr looked at Blumel. They said nothing.

"And... and that's all, sir."

"So why didn't you escape – money, clothes, police card... And you speak German – why didn't you?"

"It's forbidden to escape, sir."

"I see," said Kehr sarcastically. "And did he tell you why he wanted to do all of this for you?"

"No, sir. Just that he wanted to help me, sir."

"Did you know him some place before?"

"No, sir."

"Did he ever speak to you before two nights ago?"

"No, sir."

"Why should he want to help you, then – for your good looks?"

"I don't know, sir. I thought..."

"What?"

"I thought he... was only trying to test me – or to get me into trouble. But I knew running away was forbidden, sir."

To Kehr, whose appetite had been whetted for a moment, the story was a patent fraud. Obviously the one thing Wegler would not have done was to offer Bironski his police card. Even if the Pole had paid him a fortune, he would have offered him all assistance barring that – because where could any Pole go that he would not be captured sooner or later, and then what would happen to Wegler if his papers were found on an escaped prisoner? No – the whole story was absurd. Obviously the Pole had invented it on the spot.

"Sir," said Blumel, bending over Kehr and whispering, "if there's any truth in this tripe, I can find out in two minutes. If you let me have him—"

"I know, I know," Kehr interrupted impatiently, "so you'll beat him. So a wretch like this will say anything you want him to say. Please – I've been a detective too many years to need such methods."

With a flushed face young Blumel retired from the desk. He looked hotly at the Pole, who was the cause of the rebuke, and kept silent.

Only one thought made Kehr hesitate. The situation made it inevitable that the Pole, like any of his kind, would lie, yet this ridiculous story might make sense *if* Wegler was insane. Any German who would make such an offer to a strange Pole could only be insane – there was no other reasonable explanation. Yet he would become the laughing stock of headquarters if he offered the evidence of a Polish prisoner to support an insanity thesis. Tactically speaking, it would prove wiser to offer the analysis on general grounds, and to omit the Pole's testimony altogether. After all – *he* didn't believe the Pole. Why should anyone else?

"Take him back to the farm," he said abruptly to Blumel. "We've wasted enough time."

"Sir... I... Sir, you promised..." the Pole pleaded weakly.

Kehr jerked his head impatiently. As Blumel gave the Pole a shove towards the door, he began to cry again. They went out.

Kehr picked up his pen. He commenced scribbling his notes on the unproductive interview with Stephen Bironski, ex-pharmacist.

2

While all this was going on, Jakob Frisch and young Pelz were still awaiting interviews in the room outside. Their bunkmates, after only short sessions behind the closed door, had been allowed to depart. No one of them had opened his mouth on the way out, or had dropped any hint as to the nature of the investigation. Finally, when Blumel and the Pole were summoned, Frisch turned his attention to Pelz. ("My name is Frisch, and I am a ferret by profession; this youth is of interest to me.") Even though

Pelz had been in his bunk for over seven months, they worked different shifts and were not well acquainted.

As usual in making an approach, Frisch commenced by asking Pelz about his home. It was a rare worker, however tongue-tied about other matters, who would not pour his heart out to a sympathetic listener about his lost life in Essen, Cologne or Düsseldorf ("Is the house still standing, I wonder?...") Pelz, whose longing for farm life was acute, warmed up instantly and began to chatter like a canary. Frisch listened, asked an occasional question, smiled, and wherever possible probed for political reflections. Suddenly the youth startled him by breaking off in the middle of a sentence to stare closely into his eyes. He said nothing, but his thin, blond face turned pink. He gazed at Frisch intently, turned away, then looked back again. Finally he muttered, in an awkward stammer, "I... You know, Jakob... I've wanted to ask you something for several weeks."

"What is it, Ernst?"

"Everyone calls you 'Pastor'! You *were* a pastor once, weren't you? It's not just a nickname?"

"I was a pastor, yes – ordained and with a pulpit."

"I see."

"Is that what you wanted to ask me?"

"No, I'm coming to that. You see, I had a feeling you *were* a real pastor."

"Did you? Why?"

"Well... You... Because you don't hurt people, I've noticed," Pelz explained simply. His mouth twisted a little. "You're not one to call a man, 'Hey, One-Arm!' Oh, they don't mean anything by it. They understand I got it in the war. It's just a way that people talk. I expect I was the same before it happened to me. Only you don't, Jakob. I've seen that."

Frisch nodded a little. Behind his thick glasses his large eyes were limpid and warm, and Pelz, who had always liked this colourless, vague-featured little man with his earnest manner, felt comforted. He knew Frisch wouldn't betray his confidence. "I felt you were the one I could come to for some advice, pastor."

"I'll tell you the best I know, Ernst."

"Can I ask you something else first?"

Frisch nodded. He wondered mildly where all this was leading.

"Why haven't you got a pulpit now?"

"I don't quite know how to tell you, Ernst. Perhaps because I found it necessary to examine my heart again, quietly, before preaching to others. After the war I hope to have a pulpit again." This was the formula he had used since coming to the factory. It was not the whole truth, but so far as it went, it was not a lie.

"I see," said Pelz. He seemed satisfied, even though the answer was this general. "Pastor… it's this way… I'm only twenty-one, going to be twenty-two next month. I suppose I'll work in a factory for the rest of my life… about the only job for a cripple like me – some simple machine to feed, or stock work like I do now. Anyway, something to give me wages of a sort. But…" The hurt was naked in his eyes now. "There's more to life than just a job."

Frisch nodded.

"I always thought to get married and work a farm. I have to forget that now. A well-to-do farmer with only one arm can hire help. A man like me, unless he and his woman work their ten acres themselves, it's no go. You see, pastor? If I'd been lucky and had a part of my arm left, they could have given me an artificial hand. But off at the shoulder the way it is, I can't even have that."

"Yes, Ernst."

"Well… I'm resigned to it. I'll get along. At least I wasn't killed. I have that to be thankful for."

"And you can always feel proud of having done your duty," Frisch added deliberately. "You gave your arm for Germany, for the Führer." He wanted to see whether the lad would echo the sentiment – or, more significantly, let it pass as bombast.

"Yes, of course," Pelz replied seriously. "You mustn't think I ever forget *that*, pastor. There are men who lose an arm or a leg in a motor accident. It seems to me chaps like that would go out of their head over their bad luck. They have nothing to take comfort in, have they? But I don't forget I helped save Germany… and when I'm feeling at my very worst over my arm… in the middle of the night sometimes… I think of *that* – it means more to me than you can realize."

"Of course," nodded Frisch, with an inward sigh. He thought to himself sadly: "Anoint man with a honeyed creed, and what corruption will he not accept? The spider, the crayfish, the wolf, cannot be led astray as can man. They have no souls – they cannot aspire, or be gulled."

"Still, Ernst," he said aloud, "a man can't build his life on the basis of a duty once performed, can he?"

"No, Jakob – and that's what I've been leading up to." Pelz reddened a bit. "A man – a man needs to have a woman. You know how I mean it, pastor?"

"Of course."

"Girls used to like me." It was said flatly, without boastfulness.

"Don't they still, Ernst? You're young and handsome. The war hasn't changed that."

"It's changed more than you think," said Pelz gloomily. "Look, Jakob, I met a girl soon after we came here. She's from a farm the other side of the village. We... well, she liked me, and she let me be free with her. I really liked her, too. So I thought 'Why wait? I probably won't find anyone I like better' – so I asked her to become engaged."

"Well?"

"She told me right out, pastor... 'No!' She liked me too, she said – but not for marrying." The youth paused for a moment to take a noisy breath. "'Making love in a clover meadow is one thing,' she said, 'but marriage means kids, it means having more than a hole in the wall to live in...' And she told me right out, honest: a one-armed man would always be at the bottom of the ladder, taking the lousy jobs no one else wanted." Pelz swallowed. Then he continued stubbornly, in spite of his inward pain, "She was right, you see – even I admit it."

"I'm not so sure she was. Who is to tell what a man can achieve with a woman to help him in life – to encourage him?"

Pelz was silent for a moment. Then he said, a little irritably, "Pastor... I don't want hot air from you. I know what I know – let's be frank. Damn it – what's the average man's life, after all? He has to work like a dog to get along. It's not like I was so special. I'm just average, too. Now with one piece of me gone, I'm less than average. I want to ask your advice, but I don't want just a pat on the back. This is one time when I have to think clear."

"Go on," said Frisch. Before this honesty he felt rebuked, and more than a little ashamed of his careless generality.

"Three months ago, I read in the paper that a matrimonial bureau was being set up by the Führer himself – to arrange marriages for crippled ex-servicemen, see? So I..." He reddened again. "I wrote to the bureau – just out of curiosity." He stopped talking for a moment, then corrected himself fiercely. "No, damn it, not out of curiosity at all: out of hope, damn it. I felt most girls would be like the one who refused me – but that a girl who was willing to arrange marriage through this bureau, why, she'd have a different attitude, see?"

"And?"

"So... Well, there were letters, and papers to fill out, and pictures back and forth, and so on... but the short of it is that I'm supposed to be married next week. All done by telephone – you see, pastor?"

"Who is the girl?"

"Her name is Elsa Seiffert. She's a nature teacher in a camp for children in East Prussia."

"You don't know her, I gather?"

"Just by letters and her picture." With embarrassment he drew an envelope from his pocket. He plucked out a snapshot. It was of a young girl surrounded by half a dozen children of nursery-school age. The children were naked, and the girl wore an abbreviated sun suit.

"She's very pretty, Ernst." She was... extremely pretty, a girl of no more than eighteen, with an eager, handsome face and an athletic figure. "It seems to me you're in luck, lad."

"I don't know," replied Pelz gloomily. "Look here, pastor, in her very first letter she said she had fallen in love with me straight off – that I was her ideal and all that."

"Well – what's wrong?"

"It's rubbish, that's what's wrong. I can look at her picture and say to myself, 'There's someone I'd like to sleep with.' Maybe she's thinking the same of my picture, if girls think things like that – I don't know. But to swear she's in love with me and all that... it's rubbish. She's in love with the idea of making a war hero happy – she wants to do her duty by the Führer, that's all."

Frisch was silent.

"And now that the time has come to either go through with it or not... I'm getting cold feet. One part of me wants to marry her, sure – to try and make a go of it. When I think of being lonely for the rest of my life, of living alone and going like a dog once a week to a different whore, I can put a bullet through my head. 'When will I get a better chance than this?' I ask myself. Sure, I want to marry her." He swallowed painfully. "But the other side of me looks at it with common sense. How is she any different from the girl who refused me? That one already knew me, and had been free with me, and even wanted to continue, she said, because I... Well... She liked me that way a lot, she said. It's clear how Elsa's different, pastor – she's eighteen, while the other girl was twenty-three. It's the difference between having dreams in your head and being practical. Right now Elsa feels she's being patriotic. But when the war ends... when she's forgotten that once she got her picture in the paper for marrying a one-armed veteran... when she's twenty-five, thirty... What will happen then? Listen..." His blue eyes became clouded. "I'd rather live alone than have it thrown up to me ten years from now that my wife wasted her life by marrying a cripple. And I know in my head that the day will come when she won't be able to stand it any more. She'll see other men getting on and her husband not – or she'll have to keep working herself because I can't support her properly... But damn it – the day she tells me she's sorry she married me, I'm going to kill her!" The venom died out of his eyes, and his face became miserable. "Only, after I've killed her, she'll still be right. It would be a mistake for any girl to marry me." He smiled wryly. "Except, maybe, one of those spinsters of thirty-five who can't get anyone else. You ought to see some of the pictures I've gotten." He gestured aimlessly. "So that's it, pastor. I don't know how I expect you to give me advice. I suppose I just had to tell someone about it." Pelz bent forward, his head in his hand, hiding his face from Frisch's gaze. "But I'm in a damn muddle over it, I tell you that."

"Marry her," said Frisch quietly.

The youth looked up. "You mean it?"

"Yes."

"How about..."

"You don't give the girl enough credit, that's what I think. How do you know *she* hasn't thought this over too? The farm girl here – she didn't want you. The other girl is willing. That's the difference between them – not that one is practical and the other isn't."

"I wish I could be sure," Pelz muttered gloomily.

"You know, lad, nobody can be sure of any marriage. You're so sensitive over being one-armed, you don't give yourself a fair chance. You want guarantees in advance that nobody can have. And sometimes, you know, when a man starts off with a handicap in life... there's Goebbels, for instance... he gets very far *because* of it, you might say.* A marriage can be the same."

"Yes, I can see that," Pelz admitted. "Ah, damn it," he exclaimed harshly, "why did this have to happen to me? Why, pastor?"

Frisch was silent.

"Pastor... you've been educated. What are we here for?"

"I don't understand, lad."

"Men, I mean. Why are men born? Why do they live? Why does someone like me, with only one life, only *one*, have to be crippled?"

"You had to defend your country," Frisch replied softly.

"But why?"

"Because Germany was attacked." Only by an effort could he keep the bitter sarcasm out of his voice.

"I don't mean that, pastor." Pelz struggled for the right words. "I mean… Why was Germany attacked at all?… I mean, why is there war at all? Why do there have to be Jews in the world to start wars? I mean… A man wasn't born to be crippled, was he? If not for the Jews there wouldn't be war, would there? So why did God make the damn Jews at all?"

"Dear God!" Frisch thought. "Where does one begin – and how? An hour ago I told myself this lad had possibilities. His one sweet life has been blighted… But in what way can I reach into his hurt? What formula can make the multitude of his kind vomit this brew they have drunk?" Frisch stared at the floor, defeated, sick with a rotten despair. No, he could summon no words that would take the ass's head off this youth… And yet… there was hope of a sort, perhaps. Words might be useless with this lad and his kind – but as a drunken man must first fall into the gutter to know he is drunk, or a blind man topple over the cliff to know he is blind, so maybe this youth, this German multitude, would finally and painfully learn through catastrophe… "I don't know," he said softly, "I can't answer your questions, Ernst. Perhaps the future will."

"Maybe the war will answer them," Pelz muttered. "Once we bring German culture to the world, maybe there can be peace for all time afterwards."

"Tell me," said Frisch slowly, "do you feel sure we'll win the war?"

"Don't you?" asked Pelz with astonishment.

"Yes… But I was asking you because you've been a soldier, you know military matters."

"What can stop our army? Nothing. We're invincible."

"Of course. It's good to hear you say it."

"Anyway, you think I should marry her, pastor?"

"Yes. Marry her and have many sons, lad. Your Germany will need them."

They both looked up as the door to the inner office opened. The Pole came out, followed by Blumel. The Pole was crying, blubbering weakly and noisily. As they crossed to the outer door, Blumel winked, jerked his thumb towards the prisoner and burst out laughing. After they had gone, Pelz said softly, "Look at that poor wretch, pastor. I feel sorry for him."

"Do you?"

"Why did God make Poles, I mean? Why didn't he make the whole world Germans? What's a Pole got to live for that he should even be born?"

"I don't know, lad."

"I never used to ask so many questions, pastor. I never thought about any of these things."

"Is that so?"

"My head is full of questions nowadays. I wonder why?"

"I don't know, lad."

"Anyway, thanks for the advice, pastor. I think... maybe I'll take the chance... get married, I mean."

The door opened. "Ernst Pelz!" Kehr said sharply, peering out at them. Pelz jumped to his feet, snapping up his arm in salute. "*Heil Hitler!*"

He walked inside smartly, his empty sleeve swinging with each stride.

Frisch leant his head back against the wall and closed his eyes.

3

4:15 a.m.

After the interviews with Commissar Kehr, Berthe Lingg had been brought back to her farmhouse by Elite Guards Blumel and Latzelburger. There, for the first time since she had seen Wegler shot down, she found herself alone. With no need any longer to maintain a façade of behaviour, she had walked into her bedroom and abruptly collapsed.

Now, still fully clothed, but helpless to move under the exhaustion that gripped her, she lay upon her bed and wept bitter tears for the man she loved.

Berthe had not betrayed Wegler to the factory guards through calculation, but hysterically, and in a state of terror – terror of what might happen because of his sabotage, fear of the British bombers overhead, dread of the unusual. Now that she was alone, now that there could be no screen of patriotic sentiment between her shocked soul and the implacable face of her conscience (the guards had congratulated her enthusiastically: she was a noble and courageous woman, a pure German), now her mind echoed these patriotic fineries to no avail. No logic could quiet her aching heart, no celebration of patriotism ease her guilt. In her mind's eye a horror dwelt: of a man's living head lying upon a block, and of a gleaming axe blade that rose and fell in an endless, measured beat, lopping the skull from the trunk, sending a great jet of bright blood into the air... the head of her lover... the head of particular shape – of blue eyes, of the wide mouth she had kissed with hot pleasure... the head that had dwelt upon her pillow.

Yet still her mind fought for peace and justification, turning over arguments already cold, seeking new ones – the brain asking of the heart: "What else could I have done?" And even her heart was confused, for a corner of it hated Wegler bitterly. It was *she* who had really been betrayed. Wegler had violated the sworn promise of their future – taken their fused lives into his hands and ripped them apart. To her his act of sabotage had no sense or meaning. "Why – why did he do it?" her mind kept asking. And there was no answer she could find – it was a stroke of vandalism that she would never forgive.

She told herself this incessantly. But beneath all her thoughts, one truth lay quiet and sharp, a knife edge pricking at her brain. Beyond all else she had come to feel a single thing about Wegler: that he was a good man! A man is the sum of many things, and Berthe, no longer an adolescent girl, had measured Wegler in a practical way. She knew he could be the working partner she needed on the farm, she found him a quiet, easy companion, and she was grateful for his virile manhood – that in their physical love she cleaved to his great body with exaltation and delight. And all of this made a second husband who would be a miracle of good fortune to a farm woman of thirty-six. But beyond this she had known from the first that, as men go, Wegler was singularly upright: honest, a human being of rectitude and simple dignity – a good man. But why then had a good man done what he had – committed the awful sin of sabotage? And if a good man had acted so, what was she, who had betrayed him?

This she could not answer. Other arguments turned flabby when her heart faced this. And at such times her hatred of him, her anxiety over her own position, yielded to the single hysterical desire to crawl abjectly to the side of his hospital bed, to kiss his hand and beg forgiveness.

And so she wept, and neither heart nor mind could find ease in this muddle of pain and confusion.

It was shortly after four thirty in the morning that Anna Mahnke arrived at her farmhouse on Latzelburger's bicycle. Berthe did not hear the creak of the gate, or Anna's vigorous knocking on the door, and it was only when she entered the kitchen and called loudly that Berthe started up in fright. Her heart contracted with dread at the notion that she was being summoned again before the Gestapo commissar. In self-protection she had not told Kehr all that had occurred that evening, or revealed even a part of what Wegler had actually said to her. If it came to a second interview, she had no confidence in her ability to defend herself.

Then, as Anna continued to call her name, she recognized the voice of the Community Welfare Leader. She responded with instant cunning. Pretending sleep, she muttered, "Who is it?" – and at the same time did quite an extraordinary thing: she quickly pulled off the handsome sweater she was wearing and stuffed it under her pillow.

This sweater, which was a gift from her son, was infinitely precious to Berthe. The previous December, when there had been a drive to collect warm clothing for the soldier lads in Russia, Anna Mahnke had come around with so many arguments that she had been forced to contribute the only sweater she possessed. Now there was another "warm-clothing campaign" in the offing. Once Anna saw this new sweater of hers, it would be whisked into the grab bag before she could even bid it goodbye. She was determined to avoid that, if possible. The poor lads who had to endure the awful Russian winter needed warm things, it was true (thank God her own son had escaped that agony so for) – but after all, the winters in Germany were cold too. What was a farm woman to do when she had to work out of doors half the time? And who looked out for a body in this world unless they looked out for themselves?

"I have to see you, Berthe," called Anna loudly. "Get up, please."

"Coming, coming," Berthe replied sleepily. She stepped out of her skirt, pulled down the covers of her bed and tousled her hair. Then she slipped into her patched bathrobe and opened the door. Anna was playing her pencil flashlight around the room. She had already closed the blackout curtains.

"I must say," she exclaimed, "for a woman who's been through what you have tonight, you're a calm one to sleep so soundly. You poor girl, what a tragedy to befall you."

Berthe shrugged.

Anna switched off her flashlight. "Put on a lamp, my dear. You and I need a serious talk."

Berthe hesitated. She knew her face must be puffed and blotchy from her weeping, and she didn't care to have Anna observing signs of remorse. "My lamp is broken... I have no candles, either. If we open the curtains, there'll be enough light."

Anna shrugged and played her light on the floor, while Berthe drew back the curtains. A pale light, half of the night and half of the imminent dawn, illumined the room. "Some business, eh, Berthe?" Anna exclaimed animatedly. "Imagine... your betrothed a saboteur! It doesn't seem possible you didn't notice anything in advance."

"The idea!" Berthe exploded. "What are you trying to suggest? I—"

"Now, now – my goodness," the other interrupted hastily. "Don't get angry. It was just a manner of talking. I don't mean it the way you think."

"A nasty manner of talking," Berthe insisted furiously. "I've been through enough. I don't want insinuations from anybody. The smart alecs at the factory didn't notice anything, you might remember. They gave him a War Service Cross."

"Of course, of course," Anna replied soothingly. "Let's just forget what I said. I apologize. After all, you saved the factory. I know that. In fact, you have my heartfelt congratulations."

Berthe sat down. "So… why have you come? It's in the middle of the night. If you're only here because you heard the news and want to gossip about it…"

Anna felt rising irritation with this unaccountable belligerency. "Now, Berthe, that's silly. You know I wouldn't come out here at four in the morning for a reason like that."

"What then? If you please, tell me quickly, and then let me get a bit of sleep. It will be light in a few minutes, and I'll have to tend the cows."

"So, what do you think I've come about?" the other exclaimed coldly. "To exchange recipes? Or have you forgotten that you're carrying Wegler's child?"

"Oh!"

"Oh!" Anna repeated, a little mockingly. "Now you don't have so much to say? Anna Mahnke's not a fool any longer. She hasn't come just to gossip. We might even say she's come three miles by bicycle, at four in the morning, because she has Frau Lingg's welfare in mind." She sat down and laughed suddenly. "Anyway… let's stop being silly. We two have an important decision to make. We can't decide correctly if we're angry."

"What is there to decide?"

Even in that pale light Berthe could see the look of astonishment that played over Anna's face. She winced inwardly, realizing she had said the wrong thing.

"You think there's nothing to decide?" asked Anna softly. "You're – how does one put it? – you're content to bear a tainted child? To have the whole community know your shame?" She gazed at Berthe with wonder.

Berthe was silent. Then, even though she recognized that it would involve her deeper, she said, "The child will be Aryan, won't it? What's wrong with that?"

"Oh, nothing, nothing," retorted Anna harshly. "But also the spawn of a traitor – not so?"

Berthe said nothing.

"Berthe," Anna continued in a more conciliatory tone, "I know you don't like me. Why, I can't say. But it doesn't matter. I'm here in the interests of your welfare. Frankly, I'm sorry for you, Berthe. Wegler's brought enough heartache to you already. Why should we expose before the entire community that you're bearing a traitor's child?"

Berthe maintained her silence.

"So, then… Do you want my cooperation in keeping this a secret? It's up to you."

Berthe still said nothing.

"Well… are you dumb?"

"What do you want me to do?" asked Berthe softly.

"First of all – how many people know you're pregnant?"

"Only you… and Wegler, of course."

"What? You haven't told anyone else?"

"No one."

"My goodness, what luck!" Anna exclaimed jubilantly. "It makes everything so much easier."

Berthe nodded stiffly.

"Now the main question: exactly how many weeks gone are you? But exactly, Berthe."

"What difference does it make?"

"Can't you see for yourself? I'm thinking about arrangements for a rest home, naturally. I've got to write… a reply takes time – such things can't be handled in a day. Remember: you'll want to leave before your pregnancy can be noticed. Also, arrangements must be made for the care of your farm while you're away. Therefore we both have to speak to Peasant Leader Rosenhart. But I'll see that Rosenhart cooperates, don't worry."

Berthe said nothing.

"Naturally," continued Anna, "once the child is born, you have a real decision to make – provided the child is healthy, of course. If *I* was in your place, I'd leave it with the authorities to bring up, especially if it's a boy. But that's up to you… Meanwhile, I have to get busy. So… what's the answer?"

Berthe remained silent.

"Don't tell me you haven't counted the weeks?"

"I'm not going to have a child at all," Berthe interrupted, in a rather loud, harsh tone. "No arrangements will be necessary."

"What?" Anna was flabbergasted.

"It's just as I say. I... lost it."

"You lost it?" Anna gazed at Berthe with hostile eyes. "When did you lose it?"

Berthe hesitated. "Right after I told you I was pregnant."

'You're lying," Anna said immediately. "My goodness, Berthe, don't you realize I'm here to help you?"

"I'm not lying."

Calmly Anna said, "You must think I'm a fool. I saw you in town only two days ago – the afternoon the Poles were sold. Didn't I ask you how things were going with you inside? And what did you answer – hey? I'll tell you if you've forgotten."

Berthe bit her lip. She had entirely forgotten that chance meeting. "Fine," she had told Anna, "not even an hour of sickness, thank God." Her brain raced furiously, but she could think of no way to squirm out of the lie.

"So let's settle it this way, then," Anna exclaimed angrily. She jumped up from her chair. "I apologize for worrying about you – I apologize for riding three miles at night just to help you. Tomorrow morning I'll go straight to the Party. 'Berthe Lingg's pregnant by the traitor Wegler,' I'll tell them. 'You decide if anything is to be done.'"

"So then – I'll tell you the real truth," Berthe replied softly, giving up the fight. "I never was pregnant in the first place."

A look of such pure bewilderment crossed Anna's ugly face that Berthe would have burst out laughing if there had been an ounce of strength left in her.

"You lied about your pregnancy?"

"Yes."

"There was not even a miscarriage?"

"No."

"Why did you lie? What reason?"

"I lied to Willi because I wanted to make him marry me," Berthe explained sadly. "We had a quarrel. I felt he was an honourable man. If he thought I was pregnant by him, he'd offer to marry me. And he did." She took a deep breath and then added sullenly, "And I lied to you to stop your nagging at me. 'Have a child by him – have a child.' Twice a week you were after me from the time we first started to go together. So I lied to you too. I was sick and tired of your nagging."

"My goodness," Anna muttered in bewilderment. "I never heard such a crazy business in all my life." She stared at Berthe across the dimly illuminated kitchen. "Now I don't know what to believe."

"You can have a doctor examine me, if you like," replied Berthe, with the same sullenness in her tone. "I'm not pregnant – I never was. So you don't have to go to the Party, and there's no need for any arrangements – and you came out here at four in the morning for nothing. Now, if you please, I'll go back to bed."

"A fine thing," Anna muttered, "a fine thing!"

"What?" Berthe asked sarcastically. "Aren't you glad? I should think you'd be pleased to know I'm not pregnant by a traitor. Or are you more disappointed because it'll be one less baby to your credit?"

"Mind how you talk to me!"

Berthe laughed out loud.

"At least one thing is clear from all of this," Anna observed coldly, interrupting her laughter. "You're scarcely a German to be trusted. You, a hereditary peasant!"

Berthe shrugged and looked away impatiently.

"And if you think I'll tear up my case record, you're mistaken. *You* can tell lies all you want to – but not Anna Mahnke. Into your record it goes: 'Case closed because Frau Lingg lied to the Party Welfare Leader about her pregnancy.'"

"Good!" said Berthe with rage in her voice. "I always knew you were a troublemaker. Now you'll try and have my farm—"

"I... a troublemaker? Because I—"

"You – yes, you! Always butting in where you don't belong!"

"You shut up – or I'll report you! It's my responsibility to encourage births in this district. If you attack my work, you're attacking the Führer."

"Oh, get out of here!" Berthe shouted. Her face turned beet-red from choler, and the words tumbled out of her mouth in a flood of stammering, incoherent passion. "Just look at you: you used to be a good woman when you were only a schoolteacher. I respected you! Ha! Ha! Do you know what you are now? A swine! So I didn't want a child until I was married. I'm old-fashioned, I admit it. The word 'bastard' I still don't like. Go and have your own bastards, you patriot, you hypocrite. If you didn't keep nagging people, they wouldn't lie to you. So now report me... go ahead... get me in trouble... have my farm taken away from me, you swine!"

Anna burst into tears. She sobbed bitterly, her hand pressed over her mouth as though in shame. Exhausted by her tirade, Berthe stared at the Community Welfare Leader in growing wonder. She had never seen Anna – the disciplined Party comrade Anna – break down like this.

"How dreadful… how ugly it is," Anna muttered between her gulping sobs. "Everything turns ugly. Such sacrifices I make – the energy I give. And then it's thrown back in my face: I'm a swine for doing my duty."

"Oh, well," said Berthe. She jumped to her feet, disconcerted by Anna's tears. She didn't want to feel pity for Anna – or for anyone other than herself. A quarrel would have suited her inner needs much more. "I didn't mean… I'm upset too."

Suddenly Anna stopped weeping. "What a fool I am! To let a word from such as you turn me into a child." Abruptly she rose to her feet, standing very straight in all her thin height, looking down at Berthe scornfully. "Very well, you snot-nose, I'm a swine. But to real Germans I'm a patriot. And if this traitor of yours… if he gave you a disease, then don't come running to me. There'll be no decent doctor to care for scum of your kind. Not while I'm the Welfare Leader."

"Ha! Ha! You…" said Berthe to Anna's departing back. "What man would be interested in giving you anything? As well get satisfaction from a board."

Anna swung around, her face going bloodless with rage. "Very well!" she replied in a choked whisper. "You think I won't report you? Very well. I'll make it hot for you, don't worry." She ran out.

Berthe remained where she was. She was frightened now. Anna had Party connections. There was no telling what trouble she could make. It had been stupid of her not to watch what she said.

Presently she began to whimper. "Oh, Willi, Willi," she said aloud, in a forlorn tone. She sank weakly into a chair. Her mind's eye saw the big head on the block, and then the sheen of a swiftly falling blade… and she began to scream softly and piteously as the bright blood spurted before her face, blotting out the world with its irretrievable stain.

4

4:30 a.m.

"Well – so you're the pastor?" exclaimed Commissar Kehr with interest, as Jakob Frisch came into his office. "Sit down, pastor."

"*Heil Hitler!* Thank you, sir." Feeling exactly as though he were settling down in a trap that would presently snap shut, Frisch lowered himself stiffly onto the seat of the straight-backed chair before the desk. He began at once to clean his eyeglasses.

Whenever Frisch became nervous, he manoeuvred for time by diligently cleaning his glasses. People usually waited for him to finish before continuing conversation, since with his glasses removed, his blinking, stupid manner conveyed the sense that he was deaf as well as blind.

Commissar Kehr did not wait. On the contrary, he instantly asked, with a friendly smile, "Why are you nervous, pastor? Is there something on your mind?"

"Sir," replied Frisch after a moment, "I'd tell you, sir, but I don't know who you are. There *is* something worrying me, yes, sir, but I've been forbidden to talk about it freely."

"Adolf Kehr, Gestapo commissar."

"Yes, sir. I see." He settled his glasses on the bridge of his short, fleshy nose and looked timidly at the bulky man across the desk. "May I ask if you have my record, sir?"

Kehr nodded.

"In that case… Frankly, sir, any investigation frightens me. As you know, I've been in a corrective camp. That's why I'm nervous, sir. That's all."

Kehr nodded. He fixed his shrewd, handsome eyes on Frisch in an unblinking stare and awaited developments. This business of quietly staring at a man was one of his familiar techniques – sometimes it brought results, sometimes not. Since he had no particular suspicions of Frisch, and no hope of extracting pertinent information from him, the stare was almost as routine as the interrogation. Not quite, however. Frisch was a bit of a character. At four thirty in the morning, when Kehr was tired, sleepy and thoroughly frustrated, he was ready to seek diversion in any quarter. In this case, he was curious about the psychological workings of a pastor who had been in a concentration camp.

Under his pitiless stare, Frisch wriggled like a bug on a pin. He had been quite calm during the long wait in the outer office, but the instant his turn came, he was once again beset by the fear that Wegler had betrayed him. Panic fluttered up in his breast like a field bird taking wing from its hiding place. Wegler had seen him in the woods two nights previous, and had guessed that it was he who had painted the anti-fascist slogans – as he had. And even though the logic of the investigation pointed more at Wegler than at him (since it was Wegler's effects which had been cleared out of the bunkhouse), panic and logic have never been more than first cousins in any human being. Under Kehr's cruel, prolonged stare, Frisch paled, dropped his eyes against his will and cursed himself silently for a coward.

In the back of Frisch's mind there was a thought which nourished his self-abasement. At various times in the past six months, minor acts of sabotage had occurred in the factory. Once a power cable had been severed in his own shop; he had heard of similar events through the gossip of the workers. In each case, however, the sabotage had been so cleverly executed that it indicated the coordinated activity of more than one individual. Frisch could be certain of this: he had given countless hours of thought to the problem, but had always found it impossible to carry out any of the plans he invented. As a result, he had yearned desperately for contact with the underground cell or cells which he knew must exist among the workers, and his heart had bled with anguish over the knowledge that other anti-fascists *were* there. Now, however, he told himself that his isolation was a blessing. Where a man had so little courage as he, how could the security of others be entrusted to him? He answered his question savagely, saying that it could not. He was a coward… a frightened lump of flesh who forgot principle when he merely recalled the concentration camp… Yet now, even in his panic, his heart wept with shame.

Presently the commissar tired of his play. The fact that Frisch was displaying nervousness did not weigh with him. He was too experienced not to know that an honest citizen was often more uneasy in the presence of a policeman than a criminal. He picked up the papers that constituted the dossier of JAKOB FRISCH, PASTOR, and said quietly, "You're not under suspicion of seditious activity, pastor, so calm yourself." Glancing through the dossier, he began politely:

"Some questions about your background, first of all. Born in Stettin, I see?"

"Yes, sir."

"Father an electrical worker… died in 1917… Did he die at the front?"

"No, sir. A factory accident. He was electrocuted."

"Well, well… rather hard on a boy of eight, hey?"

"Yes, sir."

"It doesn't say here how your mother got along financially."

"Well, sir… there was some compensation… and for a few years some assistance from the trade union…" Kehr's eyebrows lifted a bit. "A bit of insurance, too. Also… my mother did flower work at home – artificial flowers, that is…"

Kehr nodded. "Did fairly well, eh?"

"Not exactly, sir. The sums were small. In fact, money ran out by the time I was sixteen, except for the artificial flowers, which didn't pay much."

"Yes," Kehr nodded, "it does say you started working at sixteen."

"My father's factory – electrical apprentice, sir."

"You were in the trade union, of course?"

"Yes, sir."

"And naturally, since the trade union had helped you with money, you felt quite friendly towards the idea of unions – hey?"

"I really didn't think of it, sir."

"Come, come," said Kehr, "don't start *that* way with me. I'm not trying to convict you of anything. We both know the function that the trade unions performed under the Republic. Now, of course" – his voice turned formal – "the German worker is protected against exploitation by better means. But if you begin by denying the obvious, my dear pastor, we'll get nowhere. I have to believe you'll stick to the truth."

"Believe me, sir, it's the absolute truth," said Frisch earnestly. "I can explain it this way: my mother was very religious, you see, and… Well, sir, I grew up the same way. She always wanted me to be a pastor, so when I went to work I kept on with my schooling. At night, sir."

Kehr nodded. He paused to rub his small moustache, which for no good reason had begun to itch violently, and asked, "What's that got to do with your attitude towards trade unions, however?"

"Just that I never thought about them at all, sir. My head was full of other things – of my studies, and my hopes of some day leaving factory work."

"Nevertheless," observed Kehr quietly, referring to a paper in his hand, "I see that you became a member of the Socialist Party in 1926."

"Why, no, sir," replied Frisch timidly. "That's an error."

"It says so in your record." It did not: Kehr was fishing.

"But sir, I was brought up to be hostile to the ideas of the Marxist parties… on religious grounds. My father was a Social Democrat, but I never even attended a Socialist meeting. I wasn't interested."

"I see," said Kehr. He pulled the thick lobe of his ear and surveyed Frisch for a moment. He had wanted to uncover the extent to which the pastor's opposition to the State had possessed a Marxist coloration. But the tone and appearance of this scared little man, with his feminine eyes and his vague, undistinguished features, made his protests convincing. He *looked* to Kehr like a man who would turn to religion rather than politics if life became hard for him.

"Anyway, in 1935, you managed to get into a seminary, I see. You were then how old?"

"Twenty-six, sir. My mother died that year. Since I didn't have to support her, I was able to matriculate for full-time study."

"And what was your attitude towards the National Socialist Party and the government at that time?"

"I gave them full support, sir," Frisch replied truthfully.

"With your record? I don't believe you, pastor."

"If you give me permission to explain, sir... My creed was this: I believed that a minister of the Gospel must only concern himself with spiritual matters. 'Render unto Caesar the things that are Caesar's.'* I believed that, sir. I still do." It was true that he had once believed it – it was a lie that he believed it now.

"If that was really your creed, why did you end up in a concentration camp?"

Since Frisch had formulated an answer to this delicate question long ago, he had no need even to choose his words. "Well, sir," he replied with a contrite, yet seemingly straightforward air, "I was a Confessionalist. I made the mistake of being influenced by Pastor Niemöller. At the time it seemed to me that the National Socialists were interfering in the organization of the Church, as Pastor Niemöller said – in the 'things that were God's', that is. Now I know he was wrong."

"Why?" asked Kehr with curiosity.

"For this reason," said Frisch. "Any organization, even an inter-Church council, has its secular aspects. I can see now that it was inevitable and correct for the Party to concern itself with Church organization." He didn't believe a word of this.

"*Hm...* I see," said Kehr. He thought this over for a moment, and then decided that the discussion was becoming too technical for him to pursue it any further at four thirty in the morning.

"At any rate, I'm to take it that at this moment you are fully in accord with the policies of the Party and of the government?"

"Yes, sir. 'The ruler of the people is ordained by God', sir! I believe that." (Another lie.) "I don't know if it says so on my record, but as soon as war broke out, I volunteered for the army."

"Yes, it does say so. Rather interesting in view of the fact that you were still in a concentration camp. Why *did* you volunteer, pastor?"

"My fatherland is as dear to me as to any other German, sir... And I believe with Pastor Niemöller that a German owes his government absolute obedience."

"I see, I see," said Kehr. He scratched his moustache. These ecclesiastical hair-splittings were beginning to confuse him, and anything which confused him he considered boring. "In that case, pastor, you would have no use for a man who committed sabotage on the home front, would you?"

"None, sir. A traitor! I'd shoot him myself."

Kehr nodded. Then, watching Frisch carefully, he told him about Wegler's attempted sabotage.

The incredulous astonishment which played over Frisch's face was not manufactured. At the same time, coupled with his astonishment, he felt a wild elation – triumph flooded through his veins like a hot liquor.

"Imagine!" he exclaimed with soft hypocrisy and a shaking of his head. "It's unbelievable – unbelievable. To think Wegler would do a criminal thing like that!"

"Can you throw any light on it?"

Frisch's eyelids blinked rapidly. He took off his glasses to clean them again. "No, sir – you see, I really had very little to do with Wegler. We worked different shifts." His eyes blinked stupidly at the commissar.

"I know," said Kehr. "Tell me – what does the word 'guilt' mean to a pastor?"

"Guilt, sir? A man feels guilty when he has sinned in some way – against God or against his fellow man."

"Do you have any notion why Wegler might have felt that he had sinned?"

Frisch put his glasses on again. Diffidently he enquired, "May I ask if he indicated anything like that, sir?"

"To his woman, Berthe Lingg. He felt guilty 'because of the Pole', he told her. Yet the woman swears that he didn't even know the Pole who's working for her. Our investigation bears her out."

With a heart so swollen with excitement that he feared his exaltation must surely burst out of him, Frisch replied softly, "I don't know, sir."

He did know. Then and there he would have wagered his life that he was right. But he had no intention of communicating his guess to Kehr.

"I just don't know, sir," he repeated. "It seems a bit wild to me – crazy. Either there's more to it than that, or else the man was out of his head. No reasonable man feels guilty towards someone he doesn't know, does he?"

"Exactly!" exclaimed Kehr. He made a mental note to use that phrase in his report. It was an excellent way of putting the core of the entire case. "Look here, pastor, you're obviously an intelligent man. Now, do you agree with me that men act for definite reasons, and out of definite passions?"

"Yes, sir, I do."

"I grant that they are sometimes complicated motivations and complicated passions," Kehr continued. His voice waxed a trifle oratorical, as it always did when he stepped into realms of thought that he considered philosophic. "But underneath all of the psychologizing, my dear pastor, I've always found a hard nut of self-interest or cupidity or jealousy at work in all human beings. Something selfish, at any rate. Do you agree with me?"

"I do, sir"

"'Find the woman in the case!'* we detectives say. Or… 'Is there a money motivation?' And if there isn't anything tangible like that to explain a crime, why then, we absolutely know we're dealing with an erratic* of some sort."

Frisch nodded with an expression of humble admiration on his face.

"Now, of course," Kehr continued, "I don't discount the class of erratics either. There are the biological destroyers, for instance, which is my term for Communists, anarchists and that sort, and there are other categories. But Wegler fits into no one of them. Ergo, I have begun to conclude that he must be insane."

"Very reasonable, sir," murmured Frisch, with soft humility. "I think your logic is air-tight."

"Yes," said Kehr. He sighed. "The trouble is that one doesn't only have to deal with intelligent men. Others may not see it so clearly."

Frisch nodded sympathetically.

"Well," Kehr sighed, "I expect that's all, pastor." He stood up and came around the desk as Frisch, too, rose to his feet. "You know, pastor," he whispered, "I must tell you that I'm sorry you had those two years in a camp. I know they were hard." He gazed down at Frisch with the appropriate degree of sympathy.

"Perhaps, sir," Frisch replied, also in a whisper, "perhaps I have a truer knowledge of God and mankind than I had before. But they *were* hard. And I'm very grateful for your sympathy."

Kehr nodded. He squeezed Frisch's arm. "I'm not one of those who've turned their backs on God," he whispered. "I want you to know that." Then he cleared his throat and returned to normal voice. "By the way, if you hear anything that'll be of help to me, I'll do my best to wipe out this black mark on your record. You can count on that. I play square."

"Thank you, thank you," replied Frisch humbly. "I'll keep my ears open. I'll come to you if I hear anything at all, sir." He added to himself: "The hypocrite. He hasn't thought of God for thirty years."

Kehr squeezed his arm again, nodding and smiling, pleased with his little stratagem, and Frisch left the office. And while the backbone of the State, as Kehr earnestly regarded himself, returned to his desk to begin the laborious work of examining the dossier of everyone in the factory who had ever been in a concentration camp – since every last one of them would have to be interviewed – the erstwhile pastor walked slowly back to his machine shop. Kehr would never know it, of course, but he had bestowed upon Pastor Frisch the only moment of complete exaltation that he was to experience in his life. Years before, in the pulpit of a little church, Frisch had felt a soaring joyousness, but commingled with fear. And on the day he left the concentration camp, there had been a moment, too, when his heart had been proud with victory. But now he was not exulting over his own courage or his own victory, but over something much more profound: the soul of Man. And after long years of quest and bitterness, of frustration and suffering, he felt that at last – in the deed of a worker named Willi Wegler – he had found the meaning of man's existence on this earth. And presently, presently, he knew he would find again the God he had also lost. For when he had lost his understanding of Man, he had lost the face of God. And this had happened to him on a bleak night in the cold of the year, when he had walked on his hands and feet beneath the bright light of a railroad platform – and at the command of a number of God's creatures had howled like a dog.

Chapter 7

As the SS squad car drew up noisily before the little cottage in which Edmund Kohlberg, superintendent of the factory, lived, the door opened and Kohlberg himself appeared. He was wearing a bathrobe over his rumpled pyjamas, and his hairy face was unshaven. He nodded a frankly irritated good morning to Baumer as the latter stepped down from the car and abruptly walked back into his house, leaving the door ajar by way of cold invitation. Baumer burst out laughing. He swung around to Commissar Kehr, jabbed his arm and whispered, "There you are, Kehr! That's what the Party has to contend with. The whole line-up of production bastards, stock-exchange bastards, financial bastards! This is one of the production bastards. Oh, I'll give him his due: a first-rate man at his own problems. But where would any of them be without the Party – hey? Knifing each other for crumbs in a second-rate Germany! Here we present them all of Europe so that they can suck honey out of it like it was their personal, gilt-edge tit – and what happens? They think they managed it. Look at him – angry because I've gotten him up two hours early. He knows I've come on some Party matter. Politics don't interest him, the bastard. Or else he thinks he can handle politics better than the Party!" Baumer spat and shook his head with bitter amusement. "Well, let's go in," he said. He strode towards the open door, and Kehr, smiling quietly, followed at his heels. Kohlberg's cottage was a small affair of only four rooms that had been erected on the same hasty basis as all of the buildings auxiliary to the factory. But in compensation for these rigors of war, since a man in his position was accustomed to live much more comfortably, the cottage had been built at the very edge of the factory acreage. It nested sweetly in a grove of elm trees, removed from the clamour which accompanies the manufacture of tanks, and was protected from drunken trespassers by a twenty-four-hour guard of SS men.

"Herr Kohlberg, may I present Gestapo Commissar Kehr?" said Baumer as they entered the living room.

Kohlberg nodded and muttered grumpily, "*Heil Hitler*... Sit down, gentlemen. Excuse me if I continue with my coffee."

Whatever the house appeared to be outside, it was elegantly furnished within. Kehr guessed accurately that Frau Kohlberg had commandeered more than one factory truck in order to transport her things from Düsseldorf. He reflected without bitterness, but with a modicum of envy, that the wealthy somehow kept going in spite of war and taxes. By the fragrance of Kohlberg's coffee, it was real coffee; by the look of the cream he was pouring into his cup, it was real cream; and by the sweet smell of his cigarette, it was real tobacco. And who couldn't enjoy a war on that basis?

"Well," said Kohlberg without preliminaries to Baumer, "what is it?" He looked up from his coffee cup with a level stare that compounded irritation and curiosity. He was in his late forties – a short, stocky man, whom the workers called "Old Hairy". The source of the nickname was obvious: the superintendent was obliged to start shaving at his cheekbones and to continue down until he reached the neckband of his shirt. A more bristly-faced male Kehr had never seen – but a rather handsome one, nevertheless, with a face and muscular body that exuded power, and eyes that were like two black marbles, bright and impenetrable at the same time.

"The business is this," said Baumer. Calmly, although he didn't feel calm about it, and smiling, although nothing about it amused him, he told Kohlberg the story of Wegler's sabotage. His calm was deliberate, and it was designed to irritate Kohlberg. He assumed it as part of their long-standing feud, in which each tried to trap the other into a trifling error, a foolish statement, a loss of temper. The feud existed because the two men approached their factory problems from varying points of view. Kohlberg, a businessman, judged all problems by the slide rule of profit, loss and the plant's yearly financial statement. He was a patriotic German, but he kept in mind that his factory was owned by the Reich's Steel Trust, not the State, and it was solely as a representative of private industry that he received a handsome salary and (if all went well) a yearly bonus. Baumer, on the other hand, as the political representative of both the government and the Party, was determined that the plant at all times must serve the best interest of the nation. These varying attitudes caused no conflict when it came to major policies like winning the war – or like substituting four thousand Polish prisoners for four thousand Germans. But in small, rather petty matters – such as whether or not production might be interrupted for fifteen minutes while Baumer made a speech (Kohlberg regarding it as fifteen minutes wasted, Baumer as part of a necessary campaign to sustain morale) – in matters like this, they often found themselves in sharp disagreement. Hence it now suited Baumer's book to inform Kohlberg about the sabotage as though he were a housewife relating a shopping venture.

When he was finished, Baumer sat back with a quietly irritating smile to watch Kohlberg first grow pale, then leap to his feet and storm up and down the room like a drunken sailor. The factory was not only Kohlberg's responsibility: it was his pride, his beloved, his past and his future. But finally he quieted down, and then, after they had discussed the results of Kehr's investigation – which were exactly nil – Baumer said, "Well, do you have anything to propose?"

"Propose?" Kohlberg exclaimed in a fury. "Certainly! I propose to remind you that you have an army of SS men around here who are being given free bed and board solely to prevent sabotage. I also propose to put on the record that it was *I* who wanted the Service Cross given to a Party member, and *you* who insisted that it go to someone like Wegler. So all right! You were full of bright theories about how giving it to Wegler would cement unity between Party and non-Party workers – so now propose! Propose yourself out of this pickle! Propose what you'll say to the High Command if the British bomb this factory to hell... Well? Do I hear anything? Or are you suddenly dumb, you bright young man?"

Knowing Kohlberg, Baumer had been prepared for an explosion. He found it hard to keep his own temper, however, in the face of an attack so unprincipled. There had been no need for him to consult Kohlberg about the Service Cross. It was purely a Labour Front matter, delegated to him by the Munitions Ministry – he had discussed it with Kohlberg solely as a gesture of courtesy. Now, to find the superintendent repaying him by a stab in the back was almost too much to bear. Nevertheless, he satisfied himself now by a mental note not to forget it. In the emergency of the moment he had a duty that came before everything else: that of making plans for the protection of the factory. This he would fulfil despite Kohlberg, Kehr or any other obstacle.

"Well, Edmund," he replied acidly, "have you let off enough steam, or do you need more time before we can get down to business? Personally I have a lot to do this morning."

"Go ahead, go ahead," Kohlberg grumbled. He sat down heavily, drank off his cup of coffee in one absent-minded gulp and poured a second from the large silver pot. "My job is to keep the production belt going. I'll do that until the British planes, by arrangement with your friend, Wegler, turn this place into a junkyard. But that's all I'll do! The rest of it's your responsibility."

"Of course," said Baumer, "my responsibility it is! Only, I'll need your cooperation."

Kohlberg drank down his second cup of coffee noisily and said nothing. Inwardly he was not only seething over the news, he was badly frightened. The memory of the awful Düsseldorf bombings turned his flesh to water. There, at least, he had been able to run down to the cellar of his house, which had been purposely constructed as an air-raid shelter. But here one had nothing. He thought of his wife, who was asleep in the next room. He decided that she must leave immediately for some village out of range of the factory. Yet no sooner had he told himself this than he groaned with self-pity. As he knew from experience, he was always forlorn without his beloved Maria at his side. Until they were reunited, he would suffer unremittingly from tempers and constipation. But when he faced the thought of asking her to stay, he knew he couldn't. Any malaise he suffered was as nothing to permitting her to remain in this danger spot. Unless... unless, of course, he could arrange to go with her. His heart leapt at the idea. Why not? he wondered. Why couldn't he spend his nights twenty miles away, and yet manage the factory in the daytime?... The hope died. Baumer, he knew, would be sure to report it. It was all Baumer needed – a little item for the Party such as that Herr Superintendent was not on twenty-four-hour call.

With his bull neck swollen and his hairy face a pained, ugly red, Kohlberg listened in silence to Baumer's proposals.

"The first matter to dispose of," said Baumer, "is the meeting we scheduled for eleven this morning."

"That *you* scheduled, not me," interrupted Kohlberg.

"*I* scheduled," Baumer agreed calmly. He turned to Kehr. "The idea of the meeting was to turn the conscription call into a demonstration of patriotism. Get it? I intended to have Wegler volunteer for the army. Others would follow. It would be written up for the papers, and we'd have photographs taken."

Kohlberg laughed out loud. For an instant a flush spread over Baumer's handsome face, then it receded, leaving him a bit white about the lips. He continued quietly:

"Since the conscription call stands, I see no reason to alter plans for the meeting. As a matter of fact, the only change is this: in place of Wegler, I'll ask one or two of the Party men amongst the workers to speak. They've been primed to volunteer anyway. So that's settled. Correct?"

"Except if none of your unprimed workers volunteer," observed Kohlberg. "Dammit, Baumer, I'm a Party man too – and a good one. But to me a conscription call is a call – why do you have to surround it with a vaudeville act? We'll lose an hour of working time."

"I thought we had this out last week," replied Baumer wearily. "Do you think these men are hot-headed Hitler youth? The devil they are. They're middle-aged and tired. They've been bombed out of their cities, their families are somewhere in Sudetenland – they don't even know if they'll have homes to return to. If you can't appreciate why patriotic inspiration is necessary to such men, when they're being sent off as soldiers, you're less intelligent than I think you are, Edmund... Besides, there's also the effect it'll have on the home front, isn't there?"

"All right, all right," muttered Kohlberg. "It's settled."

"As a matter of fact," Baumer added, "I don't see how any work'll get done today anyway. We'll have to shut down the factory."

Kohlberg looked up with his sharp stare. "What are you talking about?"

"We have to dig trenches, Edmund. And damn quickly! Up until now we've relied on camouflage. If the British saw Wegler's sign, what good is our camouflage any longer? We've got to make some provision for the workers."

"Yes," Kohlberg groaned. "Oh, damn it! You know who's due this afternoon? Herr von Bildering! He's on a tour of all our plants in Europe. I wanted to show him that this one was running smooth as silk. Oh, damn it!"

"Maybe you can put him off?"

"No – he's on the way, already. He's motoring – called me last night."

"Can't be helped," said Baumer. "I'm sorry, too... Anyway, my idea is this: let the night-shift men sleep – except the Poles, I mean. All day-shift men and all Poles are to start digging trenches the instant the meeting's over. We'll have to scrounge out every possible digging tool, from shovels to spoons. I have Captain Schnitter, of the Anti-aircraft Defence, already drawing up plans for where and how deep, and so on."

"My God!" Kohlberg interrupted with sudden excitement (forgetting that it was against Party etiquette to call upon God). "What about *that*? We need some anti-aircraft here – we need plane protection!" His ruddy face had suddenly become drained of its colour.

"Attended to already," Baumer told him. "The planes, naturally, will operate in whatever manner the Air Force Command decides. As to guns:

we'll have sixteen emplaced by noon – thirty-two in all by evening. At least double that by the end of the week – I hope."

Kohlberg nodded nervously.

"Mind you," said Baumer, "I don't expect a bombing. I feel sure we put the fire out too quickly for the British to see it. This is merely in the nature of precaution."

Kohlberg shrugged gloomily. "Düsseldorf had an armoury of guns. Little good it did us there. Little good it'll do if they come here."

Kehr cleared his throat. "Excuse me, gentlemen," he said deferentially, "I don't want to meddle, but what explanation will be given to the workers for this hasty trench-digging?"

"The truth!" replied Baumer easily. "What else? I'll tell them about the sabotage. I expect the results will be not at all bad. Since the sabotage endangers them, they'll be indignant. Production will go up – you'll see."

"*Maybe* it will – maybe," Kohlberg muttered. "Maybe they'll be indignant, and maybe not. You're telling them that a German worker who just received the War Service Cross for his devotion to the fatherland… why, man, it's more likely to give some of 'em ideas. If you trust the loyalty of our workers, I don't. As traitorous as Wegler, nine tenths of them. Every one of them hostile to us in his heart."

Both Kohlberg and Kehr stared questioningly at Baumer. He, in turn, merely grinned. "Maybe so, maybe not so," he replied. "In any instance, we run no risk of giving them any ideas, as you put it."

"How don't we?"

"The sabotage was not committed by Wegler," Baumer explained softly. "Wegler is sick with pneumonia. A sudden illness. Tomorrow or the next day he'll be moved to some city hospital so he can get the treatment due a man of his patriotism. And presently the news will leak back that Wegler has died, poor fellow. We may even stage a commemorative ceremony for the bastard, who knows?"

"Then who committed the sabotage?"

"Why, a Pole, of course. A specific Pole, in fact. The Pole who works on the very farm where the sabotage was committed. It's simple, it's logical, it's believable. In addition, it'll prevent any friendliness from arising in the hearts of our German workers towards the Poles here."

The two others pondered this in silence for a moment. Then Kohlberg said shortly, "That's clever, Baumer." He poured himself a third cup of coffee. Kehr remained silent.

"However," Baumer continued, "in the event that Kehr here succeeds in getting some information we can use to better advantage – or if I can get something out of Wegler this morning – we'll possibly revise the plan."

"Whatever you say," agreed Kohlberg, "but I think the Pole is an ideal solution. If it was my affair to decide, I'd hang him in the village square and herd every Pole there to watch it. I'm afraid of them. You're going to have to keep those swine in line, Baumer. Every one of them with a heart black with treachery. You'll see! At the first opportunity there'll be an army of guerrillas within our own borders."

"You know," Kehr observed uneasily, "there's a problem attached to the Pole. I—"

Baumer interrupted. "You mean that a number of people already know it was Wegler?"

Kehr nodded.

"Half a dozen or more of my SS men know. They can be silenced. Doctor Zoder and the woman, Berthe Lingg, know."

"I can talk to *her*," said Kehr. "I have to see her again anyway. But there are the other men in Wegler's bunk. Even though I warned them not to speak of it, they ought to be seen again."

"So all right! You'll assemble them the minute we return," said Baumer. "And I'll attend to the others. What's there to be uneasy about?"

"Nothing, I guess," Kehr admitted. "Agreed. It's a very good plan. I congratulate you."

Kehr was lying. He didn't like the plan. Not on grounds of its effectiveness. On that score it seemed very clever to him also. The truth was that he had a moral objection to it. In a lifetime of police work he had witnessed, and occasionally been a party to, a good many unsavoury dealings. But to take a bribe, to hand a criminal a more severe sentence than he deserved, or to use one's police powers to climb in bed with a woman – those were innocent types of transgression. Hanging a guiltless man, even a Pole, was somehow flying in the face of that basic middle-class morality which seemed to him the foundation of a State. It was typical of the ruthless brigandage of the National Socialists, which always left him secretly uneasy. "Whatever is necessary is right," the Baumers said fervently, and this they considered idealism. Perhaps it was... Only, in a den of wolves, how could one tell who would be devoured next?

"There's only one more matter, then," said Baumer. "An air-raid rehearsal. We've become rusty. I suggest having it at five in the afternoon, so that the night-shift men can participate before they go to work."

Kohlberg nodded. He was wondering again if he could manoeuvre a way of being absent from the premises at night.

Baumer stood up. "Well, Edmund," he observed with a small, twisted smile, "when we've won this war, we'll really have earned our peace, hey? The early days of picking off a country in a few weeks, with lovely new plants for your Steel Trust to incorporate, seem to have gone."

"Yes," Kohlberg muttered, "yes." He didn't dare add his real opinion – that the Führer had made his colossal mistake in attacking Russia. After Dunkirk, England had been a rotten apple. They could have consolidated the Continent without any of these bombings, and left Russia for later. Now they were bleeding at every pore.

Baumer smiled. He knew Kohlberg was frightened of the possibility of a bombing, and it pleased him. Not that he would enjoy it himself, but he would be a man about it. "Well, cheer up, Edmund." He laughed coldly. "We'll pull through. By fall everything will be different. We'll smash the Reds this summer, and then we'll turn the whole Luftwaffe on England. They'll learn what it means to bomb women and children."

"Yes, yes," said Kohlberg. "I look forward to it."

He accompanied them to the door and nodded an absent-minded good-bye to Kehr. Then he shut the door. He stood for a moment, rubbing his hand over his hairy face. Quietly he padded across the room to another door. He went inside.

His wife was still asleep. He lay down beside her on the warm bed, turning so that he could gaze at her face. She was a plump, blond woman, ten years his junior, who had found her life's satisfaction in adoring this able, successful man of hers, in petting him, flattering him, offering herself to him as mother, social hostess or abandoned woman, whatever his extravagant moods demanded. The creaking of the bed awakened her. She opened her eyes with a sleepy smile. "What is it?" she asked quickly, sensing his unhappiness.

"My darling," Kohlberg muttered. He fumbled at the buttons of her nightgown, pulling back the silk until he exposed her heavy breasts. He bent down, his hands moulding the warm flesh to his closed eyes. Her arms went about him comfortingly. "Ah, darling," he murmured again, "when will this war end?"

2

There was the time when Richard had recited:

> Chug, chug,
> I'm a little tug,
> I pull the big boats,
> Chug, chug, chug.

That was when he was five and a half, as Wegler recalled. And at about the same age, with hot excitement: "Daddy, listen to what *we* saw: Mommy an' I saw a rainbow today, an' it was all *coloury*." Or the time that he was learning to brush his own hair – and very serious about it, too. Wegler was shaving one morning when the lad climbed up on a stool in order to peer into the mirror. He brushed furiously at an unruly sprig at the top of his head, exclaiming aloud the while "Now I'll get that big feller" in an enraptured chant, "now I'll get 'im. An' those big fellers in back – I'll get *them* now, too."

A little boy! A little boy learning to do what the grown-ups did – brushing furiously, brushing clumsily, brushing with delight the very own hair of himself...

They were born naked and they were born innocent, and it was more than the heart of a parent could enfold to watch the tiny lump of flesh grow so sweetly. Only a few days ago he had thought to have another with Berthe. It had welded him to her, this news that his seed had leapt into life in her belly. As nothing else it had given him hope of making a new life for himself again. Now, God help her, she would have to bear a bastard – or else cruelly rob it of life. And he wished he could beg her forgiveness for that...

Wegler stirred on his cot. He sighed, licked his lips, swallowed painfully...

He remembered something that went back to the first week of Richard's life. He was standing over the crib when Richard suddenly sneezed. Without thinking, and with delight, he exclaimed excitedly to Käthe, "Did you see that? He's almost human" – and then stammered before her gale of laughter, trying to explain what he really meant... Yet perhaps he had really meant *that* – the becoming familiar, the taking on of shape and abilities, the helpless mewing flesh that commenced to see, that learnt to smell the nipple in its approach... at six months striking the bottle with lusty joy as he sucked, at a year learning to grasp it in proud possession between two tiny hands whose strength was incredible... to proclaim by loud babbling: "This is mine. I own it. I expect it as my due. I understand this first rule of property..."

But then the child became strong-limbed and a man – and the man, one found, was carved to a special destiny. For he died conquering the land of another people – a people who fled before him on snowy roads in the bitterness of winter, carrying mournfully their innocent, naked children... And when he died, you, Willi Wegler, his father, asked softly, "What was it for? Why? The passion and the birth, the nourishment and the bringing up... for what... to what purpose... why?" And found no answer...

Wegler swallowed – licked his lips. He thought fretfully: "My pillow is hot. Why is it so hot? Why doesn't Käthe come and change it?" He groaned as the moment of somnolence passed, and he heard the distant beat of the factory. His Käthe was no longer real, his Richard, brushing silken hair, was no longer alive – there was only the throbbing in his belly, the punctual stab in his groin, the parched, aching throat.

He thought: "Where did it all start? Yes, I hate the Nazis now. But why didn't I know about them earlier – a year, five years earlier? How is it possible for a grown man to live like a sleepwalker?"

But then, even more sadly, he thought: "Hah! Suppose I had known earlier – what would I have done? Christ, how stupid it is to look back and say 'If...' It's not so long ago. Why lie? I remember how I felt about things. I went along, whistling like a dummy until... until they took my Richard away from me, I suppose. But then it was too late. By then I was... I was in a muddle, I suppose. In a muddle... and scared. Yes, Jesus Christ, why lie? There was nothing to do, I said. What could one man do?"

When 1933 came, and Hitler was made chancellor of Germany, Willi didn't believe that things would become different. There were some, like his friend Karl, who argued vehemently that the National Socialists were the enemies of workers like him. "That may be," Willi replied, "and don't think I voted for them. But now that Hitler's chancellor, he'll have to respect the laws, won't he?"

No matter what Karl or others said in the first weeks of the new regime, it seemed incontrovertible to Willi that law was law. Besides, a government had to be respected. The wise men had been echoing this creed for as far back as Willi could remember – his teachers, drill sergeants, the newspaper writers. Many things were going badly in Germany – men like Willi could see that, even if politics didn't interest them. And Hitler claimed he had a solution for them. "Well," said Willi, "it's not likely, but time will tell." A man like Willi wanted his work, his family, his cold-water flat – only a little world. When the Republic gave it to him, he was tolerably satisfied, and if the National Socialists would give it to him, he would be satisfied with them too. "Wait and see," said the Willis. "We can always vote him out."

So Willi waited. But then things began to change. The newspapers began to use a new language – words like "Folk" and "Aryan" and "Racial Purity" that no one had ever bothered about before. Soon more and more people began to use that newspaper language, not only the Nazi Party members. But still, they were only words, and words were not as important as the contents of a lunch basket.

There were emergency decrees, too, particularly after the Reichstag fire. Germany was declared to be in a state of alarm, and rules were issued about Jews and Communists, who were conspiring against the State – or so the papers said. Willi might hear that the owner of a store where he once bought a suit had been arrested because he was a Jewish profiteer. Or a Communist worker, Ernst, might not turn up on the job one day, and the whisper would go around that Ernst had been arrested for illegal activities. These things were unusual and disturbing, especially since Willi knew that Ernst was a war veteran like himself, a good lad whatever his ideas – or that the Jewish shop owner made so little money out of his shabby store that he never could afford any help – but still these things had not happened to Willi or to his family. And even though it was whispered that a great many people had been arrested, still the streets were as crowded as usual, and Willi had not actually seen anyone arrested. Once, in the early days, he tried to look up Karl. He wanted to know what his old friend would have to say about these developments. But Karl had moved from his lodging house, and the landlady shut the door in Willi's face when she heard the name.

Of course Willi didn't like it when the trade unions were abolished. Unions helped a man with his wages, every German worker knew that. But at the same time it was officially announced that the National Socialists were setting up other unions. Maybe those would work out well, too, Willi thought. He was sceptical, but... Well, he'd wait and see. Who wanted to stick his neck out or get into trouble? And what could one do about it anyway?

And presently, even before Willi knew quite why or how, he developed the habit of breaking off a conversation when he heard other people complaining. And he developed the habit of not speaking his own thoughts aloud if they were at all critical of the new regime. "You'll get into trouble," the whisper ran. It seemed wise to pay attention. Formerly one knew what the word "trouble" meant. Trouble came when you violated a clear rule on a clear statute book. But now trouble came from all corners, like fog stealing in upon a sleeping city. And so if Willi heard that a former leader of his union had been arrested, he didn't like it at all, but he tried to forget it. Frankly, yes, he didn't want to get into trouble. And frankly, yes, he was confused. For over the radio and in the press, from the endless marching columns and daily on the job, he heard that things which seemed wrong were right, and that things which needed doing would be done, and that this Germany he lived in was being reborn – and he didn't know: he was confused, terribly confused.

After a while, without his quite realizing it, even Willi's ideas changed a bit, too. The Versailles Treaty was a millstone around Germany's neck – was it not? Even the Social Democrats had said that. And Germans in neighbouring lands were being cruelly oppressed. Willi hadn't known this before, he wondered about it – but everyone said so: there were even atrocity pictures in the newspapers – and it didn't seem just. If Hitler wanted to correct these evils, one couldn't oppose him on that. Besides, as the years wore on, the other nations like England and France didn't oppose Germany over her demands. It seemed as though there would have been *some* opposition from the other nations if Germany's cause had not been just. Or so everyone said.

And after a bit Willi heard so much talk about the Jews, and how they had poisoned the life of Germany, that he didn't know what to believe. He didn't know many Jews, so how could he judge for himself? "Where there's smoke, there's fire," he heard people say. Anyway – he was not a Jew. The government claimed things would get better when the country was purged of the Jews. Who could tell whether it would happen that way or it wouldn't? Willi didn't know.

All this, however, was before a remarkable change of lands took place in Germany. Willi didn't realize at first about the change of lands. He learnt it only when his son moved out of the ancient land, Germany, and into the new land, which was Hitler Land.

Richard was close to fifteen when Hitler became chancellor. At sixteen he was wearing the uniform of the Nazi Youth movement. And suddenly Willi realized that the world had spun one day when he was busy dreaming, and that it had whirled quite out of his reach.

* * *

"Father," Richard said one day, "I want to have a heart-to-heart talk with you." He was just home from his year of Labour Service, and he said it very quietly, with the over-serious mien of a youth of eighteen who is feeling commendably earnest about life.

"Talk," replied Willi, with an affectionate smile. They were walking in the meadow land on the outskirts of town. They had walked there many times before, with Richard bouncing piggyback on his father's shoulder. But now he was as tall as his father, and almost as broad, and he had the same big-jawed, blond face, and Willi was very proud of him indeed.

"You know that I respect you very much, Father," the youth began.

"I'm glad."

"But there's something now... Well, it disturbs me," said Richard, flushing a little. He wished he might have found a more felicitous word. It was not the phrasing suggested to him the day before by the Party Block Committee.

"Father – now that I'm older and can see things with more mature eyes, I can't quite... feel about you the way I used to."

"No? And why not?"

"Because I've come to the conclusion that you're... well, you're selfish, Father." ("Put it to him ethically," they had said.)

"Selfish?"

"You only live for yourself."

"I? For myself?" Gently: "And not for you – for your mother?"

"That's the same thing, don't you see?" Richard explained in triumph. "My generation is learning to live for *everyone* – for the People, the State." His voice waxed lyrical. "To live any other way is to be selfish, Father."

Willi felt relieved. "I was afraid I'd done something terrible – like robbing a bank."

"Don't laugh it off, *please*. I want to be proud of you, but how can I be when you don't take an active place in the common effort? You should be a Party candidate."

"Well, lad, it's this way: meetings, politics – they've always been a little out of my style..."

"That's no reason you shouldn't change."

"No, but think of it in this manner: I like to play the accordion. I tried to teach you, but you never took to it. Now tell me – did I ever say you *had* to play it?"

Grudgingly: "No."

"Well, why? Because I know that different people have different ideas. They think differently, they like to do different things."

"But we're not talking about accordion playing," the youth argued. "I'm talking about more serious things, about duty – idealism. All the easygoing democratic nonsense about some people having duties and others not, that's been done away with now, don't you understand? Every German from now on must have one duty, one idea, one will!"

Willi was silent. The word "nonsense" hurt.

"Father… you wouldn't be a good German if you let me have ideas contrary to the health of the State, would you? And I wouldn't be a good son if—"

"Different people have different ideas," Willi interrupted stubbornly. "That's only natural."

"No, it isn't!" his son cried with indignation. "Not natural at all! You'll have to excuse me, Father, but this is one principle I know better than you. We had a dozen lectures at the camp on it. What you're saying is the heart of Jewish-democratic thinking. Just look how it's poisoned your mind. No, Father… you've simply got to realize that from now on every German must have only one idea – our Führer's!"

Willi turned to stare at his son, at his angry, impassioned eyes, his fervent expression. And for the first time in their life together he knew a father's deepest agony: that Richard, while kin to him in flesh, had become violently alien in spirit. It left him trembling.

"Lad," he said despairingly, taking the boy's arm, "I'm willing to try these new ways, to keep up with your generation. You know that I'm not against the National Socialists."

"That's all I ask," the youth interrupted with enthusiasm. "Just try."

"But there's something I want to ask of you."

"Ask anything. I'll bring you the proper books to read, I'll take you to our meetings—"

"Something else." Willi's tone became husky, beseeching. "Right here where we're walking, lad, I remember another day. It was when you were only a shaver of three or so, just learning to talk so a body could understand you. You and your mother and I were having a picnic on a Sunday. We were napping on the grass – right over there by that tree, I think. And you woke up suddenly. A butterfly had brushed over your face, y'see. You jumped to your feet and you ran after it, like a kid will. And you called out, 'Look… the flybutter is flyning… see how it's flyning.'"

Richard laughed. "Did I say that?"

Willi didn't laugh with him. Instead, with eyes that were humble in their pleading, he went on hastily, stammering a little. "Listen, lad – you'll never know until you have a boy of your own how much a thing like that becomes… well, becomes part of the heart of a father. When I look at you now, I don't only see a fine, handsome man – I see you like you were on that day. And I – I see you when you were only four, Richard, trying to learn how to fly a kite. You were a little too small to do it proper, yet somehow you had the idea that all it took was to run with it and it would go up. You would run like crazy, your little face growing redder and redder until you dropped down in a sweat. Then you'd rest for a minute and jump up to try all over again. And I see you the first day you went to school, boy, when you were frightened and cried. And so many, many things I see! And lad, all of it and more is what it means to be your father – this… this storage trunk full of things, so to speak. And if now I can't look at politics just the way you do – don't you turn away from me on that account. There's so much to this world outside of politics. I love you, lad, and I'll always love you, no matter what your politics are!"

"Of course, Father," said Richard with genuine feeling. "And of course I'll love you too."

They left it at that. But they both knew that Willi had begged the issue between them, that he had fogged it over with sentiment. Between them, for now and for ever, there was an abyss. Their formal love never bridged it.

In the years that followed, Willi often pondered over that conversation with his son. One phrase in particular remained to prick him: "You'll have to excuse me, Father, but this is one principle I know better than you."

It was true. His son had principles. His son lived, acted and judged all events according to certain principles. And when his son married Marianne – a dove-eyed beauty whom he had met while on his Labour Service – why, it turned out that she likewise was running over with principles. She was not particularly bright, this dark-haired daughter of a postal clerk, but her head was stuffed with principles – certain and exact, immutable and all-knowing principles. And Willi, who was twenty years her senior, asked himself suddenly one day, "What principles have I to equal theirs? By what principle has my life been guided?" He found no answer. He searched his heart and became only more and more confused.

"My goodness, Käthe," he exclaimed one night in a sudden explosion of bewilderment, "what's happening to Germany? Do you know who I met today? Arthur Schauer – do you remember him? He came to see us in Cologne once with Karl. We were in the same company together in the war."

"Schauer?" Käthe replied in a whisper, even though they were in their own kitchen. "He was a Communist, too, wasn't he?"

"Yes. I guess so. Anyway, he came and stood by me while I was waiting for a trolley car. 'Aren't you Willi Wegler?' he asked me. I didn't know him. He looked like an old man of sixty, I tell you – all bent over like he was humpback, with his hair almost white…

"'I'm Arthur Schauer,' he told me. I couldn't help myself, Käthe. I just said it right out – 'Have you been sick or something? You don't look good.'

"You know what he told me? He looked around to see if anybody was walking nearby. Then he whispered to me. 'I had pneumonia,' he told me. 'I was in a concentration camp for politicals until a few months ago. I haven't recovered.'

"'Pneumonia,' I said like a dummy. 'But—'

"'The camp is fine, you understand,' he said to me. 'It's just that the climate is so unhealthy. Nearly everybody gets pneumonia. You remember Karl?'

"'What about Karl?' I asked him. 'I haven't seen Karl in—'

"'Karl's dead,' he told me.

"'Dead?'

"'He was in there with me. He got pneumonia the first week.'"

Willi stared at his wife, his big face twisting with anger. "Don't you understand?" he asked. "They killed Karl – that's what they did! I don't care what Karl's politics were. He was a decent man, a war veteran. To do things like that… It's… it's criminal. No good can come of it."

"Willi, Willi, keep your voice down," Käthe implored anxiously.

"And that's another thing," he whispered in anger. "Here we are in our own home, but we have to whisper. It isn't right, Käthe. You know what I'm beginning to think? I tell you, it seems to me that the National Socialists… why, they say one thing but do another, it seems to me."

"But look," said Käthe, "there are no more unemployed now. They kept their promise over that. If you forget that you were unemployed all through '32, I don't. And they stopped all that dreadful street rioting. They brought peace and order, didn't they?"

"I know… but to kill a man like Karl… what sort of order is that?"

"Of course that's what Schauer said. You don't know. He might be lying."

"But I've heard things from others about those camps. You have too, Käthe."

"Yes – but what can we do? Is there anything to do, Willi?"

Her question left him silent, as it always did, even when he asked it of himself.

"And look how Chamberlain* and all the others had to come here to make a treaty,"* Käthe continued. "If the Führer isn't doing right, would they come?"

"I suppose not," Willi muttered, "I suppose not. It's hard to know what's happening any more."

"We're getting along – aren't we, Willi? Things are harder with all the deductions – but you've kept working."

"Yes."

"We'll just have to wait and see. What else is there to do?"

"I suppose so."

...And in this manner, in the years that led up to the outbreak of the war, Willi Wegler remained a solid citizen of the country in which he lived. When there were irritating regulations on the job or special taxes... deductions for a promised motor car which he didn't want, or an increase in his working hours – he didn't like any of them. But life was still not intolerable. And Willi continued to say to himself, "Maybe things will get better. Maybe everything is going the right way, like they say." Meanwhile, he had his work and his Käthe. Meanwhile, there were visits from his son, who was in the army. Meanwhile, there was the reasonable succession of day to night, and night to day, as it had always been. All about Willi there were others, into whose hearts he could not see, who appeared solid, quiet and satisfied. Perhaps they were not, but he dared not ask. And so Willi remained quiet and meek and confused – a solid citizen.

And this, although Willi did not know it, composed his principle of living. To accept his fate, as most men since the beginning of time have largely accepted theirs, moving only slowly to alter it; to accept the lot bestowed upon one by birth; to accept the rule of the great, vague beings of the universe; to remain meek and quiet unless one's daily life became utterly and abominably intolerable – this was Willi's principle, as it is the principle by which most of humankind has always lived. And upon none of this did Willi ever reflect. He merely lived it – as did so many of his fellows, for it was the iron code taught to the innocent and the naked by the grim totality of their lives.

When war came, Willi accepted it as he would a sickness. He didn't like it – but there was nothing he could do to change it. The war of 1914 had left a horror in him that no propaganda could alter. When the German armies quickly overran Poland,* he was glad – not because it meant victory, but because he hoped that then there would be peace. And when peace didn't come, his spirits sank, and for a time he blamed the English and the French for not ending the war. The Führer was willing to make peace, the papers said, but Germany's enemies refused.

After Poland came Norway,* and with Norway the war reached home. Richard was a parachutist, and he was killed in the first days of the action. When the news finally came to the Weglers, it was not merely as a death notice. Richard, it seemed, had died quite heroically. A posthumous award was to be presented to his widow.

Käthe was prostrated by her son's death. Willi went alone to the little village near Düsseldorf where Marianne lived with her parents. She had taken her child there for the war's duration.

There was a public ceremony on the steps of the town hall. A colonel of the paratroopers bestowed the Iron Cross on Frau Marianne Wegler. There were speeches, and there was appropriate music, and it was all very inspiring, people said. During the ceremony Willi stood stiffly – a big blond man with his face painfully empty, his heavy shoulders sagging. Occasionally he rubbed one hand over the other, slowly and awkwardly, as though they were cold. His brain said "Richard is dead", but his heart couldn't comprehend. In his heart Richard was running down the street with his yellow hair tangled into curls… in his heart Richard was reciting "Chug, chug, I'm a little tug…" and bursting out mischievously at the dinner table, when they had guests:

Red, red
Wet your bed
Wipe it up
With gingerbread.

In his heart Richard was so fiercely alive that it couldn't be the colonel was right – it couldn't be! But it was, and he knew it.

That night Willi watched Marianne put his grandson to bed. Not for one instant in that long day had she displayed any grief – not even when the Cross was thrust into her hand. She had worn her head high and proud, and Willi had overheard more than one comment applauding her patriotism. But now, as she buttoned her lad's pyjamas and asked him if he would like to hear a story, Willi could see that she would burst into tears the instant she was alone in her room. It was then that he learnt the meaning of the word "principle" as he had never understood it before.

"Tell me the story of the sparrow," the child said.

Marianne smiled mechanically at Willi. "It's the one he wants to hear every night," she explained. She leant close to the boy so that his cheek was pressed to hers. Her lovely face was a mask, her fine eyes were hot with pain.

"The spider kills the fly," she began. "Then the sparrow kills the spider... and the hawk kills the sparrow... then the fox kills the hawk... and the dog kills the fox... then the wolf kills the dog... and then what?" she asked her son.

"Then what?" he echoed.

"Why, you know... Who kills the wolf?"

"You tell me," the lad said in his slurred baby talk.

"Why, a man!" his mother replied. "And that's the way the world is, Dickie boy. The strong always win, and they kill their enemies. Will you be strong when you grow up?"

"Hm-hm..."

"Will you be the strongest man there is and kill all your country's enemies?"

"Hm... hmmm..."

"And what will you be when you grow up?" she asked, as she turned half towards Wegler with a proud smile.

"A solya," the child answered.

"That's it: a soldier," Marianne repeated.

"A heeo," the child continued.

"Yes, a hero like your daddy," Marianne said.

"An' fight for my Führer," said the child, thrusting his hand out in salute.

"Yes," said Marianne, and even though her mouth suddenly trembled and her face went white – not even then did her eye become clouded by a tear.

And Willi? He merely stared at Marianne and could not speak. Later he realized that his face must have expressed the full horror in his heart. For under his pained gaze Marianne flushed.

"Well, what?" she exclaimed angrily. "You don't like it?"

Willi said nothing – but no, he didn't like it. If wars came, they came – but what was the world coming to when mothers prepared their children for death?

"Then don't like it!" said Marianne furiously. "But my child will be brought up properly – he'll learn the principles of German manhood as his father would have taught him!"

And perhaps not until then had Willi fully realized the extent to which Germany had been transformed into National Socialist Land. For in his

Germany adults always gave certainty to growing youth. But now it was an adult like him who was uncertain, who felt himself to be no more than a dumb log rolled over and over by a tossing sea, whereas the youths, the tiniest children, strode the world with absolute assurance. They had a response to all questions, they had a clear roll-call of good and evil, and they knew at five that they would kill at eighteen.

And this was principle. And what principle had he to oppose theirs?

Willi opened his bloodshot eyes. He stared unseeingly at the walls of his hospital room. His tired mind thought: "*No, you never had a principle, Willi. And you have none now. You never understood about the Nazis… what they were… you still don't understand. All you know is that a rottenness has come from them.*"

He lay quiet, licking his dry lips. Once again, as though brain and heart were impaled on the knife point of this new concept, he thought: "*No, Willi, you had no principle before, you have none now. But why does a man without principle throw away his life? Answer that, Willi. Can't you answer even that?*"

Upon the bare pine boards of the ceiling in his hospital room Willi saw a leaping flame. Heartsick, he closed his eyes. But now a fiery sky was painted upon the hot parchment of his lids.

"*It began there,*" his heart whispered. "*In the fire that burned Düsseldorf. An anger came, and after that a shame. So now you know, Willi. Even you have a principle now, a small one of your own – one of anger and of shame…*"

His eyes remained closed. His heart was pounding.

BOOK TWO

THE WRATH OF JEHOVAH

December 1941–August 1942

Chapter 8

Willi was at work when the British bombers came to Düsseldorf. He emerged from his factory shelter in a fiery dawn to find the five-storey tenement in which he lived sheared in half. Käthe had been in the cellar with numberless others. He helped dig their bodies out. As an old soldier, he knew enough about death to be aware that Käthe had not suffered. Still, even for an old soldier, it was not good to look upon the body of his wife and see it without arms, its viscera exposed.

He cursed the British that day. He stood upon a carpet of rubble and broken glass and raised his fists to the heavens. And when he had ceased cursing these foreign marauders, he fell silent, remaining as tearless and graven as a lump of statuary. To any bystander, his mien must have seemed the very incarnation of grief. It was not. It was quite beyond grief. It was numbness, it was a new state of being, it was the state of a man whose soul has gone to sleep.

Only a few weeks later he stood silent, in a silent row of men, upon the bleak platform of a country railroad station. It was a Sunday, seven in the morning, wartime.

On the horizon, at the hazy rim of an expanse of brown farmland, a cold-faced sun was rising cheerlessly to greet them to their new home. Miserable, exhausted, the men gripped their pieces of baggage – a suitcase or a duffel bag or a cardboard box. For many of them, like Willi, the lone box contained the sum total of their household property after forty years of life and toil. For the remainder, even though they had been more fortunate in the recent bombings, it would amount to little more in the end. Their wives and children were being shipped to unknown destinations in the East; their apartments had been padlocked. They nourished small hope of finding their possessions intact when the war was over. One way or another, it was sure to turn out badly – of this they were morosely confident.

They stood silent, although here and there someone broke out into a muffled, hacking cough; they shivered, they waited in orderly lines, because that was how they had been told to wait. There were many from Düsseldorf, some from Cologne, a few from Duisburg and Essen. They had been twenty-eight hours en route, too crowded together for sleep. And as they stood on the platform, the same ugly thought possessed all minds in common: that the war was no longer a picnic! No longer now could they expect a pound of yellow butter weekly from their Gerhardt in Denmark, their Otto in Norway. No longer were there parcels of bacon from Holland, of silk stockings and needles from France, of sweaters and shoes from Belgium. The loot had given out, the gravy had been sopped up, the lands of milk and honey had been sucked dry. Now there were only the bitter pieces of paper from the War Department: *We regret to inform you that your son, Paul... your brother, Heinz... your father, Thomas... on the Eastern Front... It will be a violation of patriotic duty to wear mourning.* Now the war had come home!

They waited, shivering in the cheerless dawn. Presently, as some trucks arrived, they were marshalled into columns of three. Under the supervision of a swarm of SS men – healthy, well-fed young athletes who had slept well the night before and were warmly dressed – they deposited their belongings in the trucks. "Remember your truck number," the SS men bawled. The motors roared, the wheels spun on the frosted earth and the trucks shot off down the road that led through the village. In columns of three, shuffling in their weariness, they marched at a command to the other side of the railroad platform. Presently more trucks began to arrive. They piled in, standing up, the wind biting at their faces.

In this manner, a thousand strong, the first contingent of workers to arrive at the village of X entered upon their new life.

2

Willi was assigned to the forge room as a labourer. When peace came, his lifetime skill as a plumber might be once again considered useful. But there were no water closets or sinks to be installed in medium tanks. In Düsseldorf, a few months before war came, he had been ordered into an arms plant. They had used his girth and strength at heavy labourer's work. He was assigned similarly here.

The very first afternoon Willi did something which surprised the other workers more than it did him, but which he understood no more than they. He volunteered to work at the "Giant-killer".

The "Giant-killer" was a drop forge, a great mechanical steam hammer that pounded home twice a minute and shaped cold metal to its die like

clay under a man's fist. As the workers said: there were two industrial diseases a man could get from wrestling the "Giant-killer". One was hernia,
provided his nerves held out; the other was a nervous breakdown, provided
his intestines held out. Either way it was the machine that sooner or later
conquered the man. When the hammer came down with its six thousand
pounds' pressure, every foot of the concrete floor rumbled and every worker
in the building thought to himself, "I'm glad it's not me." Usually the lad
who took it on was in his twenties and had the strength of a bull. Even so,
in six months or a year, he either quit or gave out. And never had it been
known that a man of forty-two would volunteer for the job.

It came to pass in the following manner: the drop-forge man was
Schenk – a squat, enormously broad-shouldered youth of twenty-four
who had been deferred from the army because of his bad hearing. He
had worked at the hammer for some months in Düsseldorf and had been
reassigned here. The second afternoon, without previously having uttered
a word of complaint, he came over to Hartwig, the foreman, and said
with a bewildered groan, "Sir, I'm passing blood." Hartwig had been
thirty years in the forge room at one job or another. He didn't need to
ask questions. He merely sighed, shut off the power that operated this
beast of a machine and said, "Go to the hospital." Then, with a downcast
face, he climbed the ladder to the catwalk and went into the office of the
shop superintendent.

Fifteen minutes later work in the forge room was interrupted for a meeting. Those workers who were relatively new, like Willi Wegler, waited to
hear what was up. The older hands merely grimaced cynically. They knew
exactly what to expect: there would be an appeal for a volunteer – and
the sentiment of the appeal would be equally divided between patriotic
exhortation and emphasis on the high rate of pay that came with the job.
So it proved to be, but no one volunteered. Patriotism was fine except
where a man had to pass blood for it. Even the Party members thought
stubbornly to themselves: "Let 'em bring a young parachutist back, or a
tankist who can stand a pounding. It's crazy for any one of us older men
to volunteer. We'll only bust our insides for nothing."

Willi raised his hand. Why he did, he never really came to understand,
although subsequently he pondered the matter. He only knew that he felt
a need to pit his strength against the cold fury of that pounding tower
of metal.

The superintendent, Herr Kuper, asked his age.

"Forty-two, sir."

Herr Kuper looked at Hartwig, Hartwig looked back at Herr Kuper, and both looked dubious. Wegler was a big man, obviously stronger than average. But at forty-two!... Finally Herr Kuper nodded. This was one job where the worker had to be willing. They had no choice but to let Willi try.

The job itself was simple. Hartwig explained all Willi needed to know in a half hour. It was a matter of rhythm and of stamina, and that was all. By six thirty that night, when the shift ended, Willi was half dead, but he was the new drop-forge man.

3

The hours of each workday succeeded one another imperceptibly: they became a morning, then an afternoon, then another day slipping into vague memory. For Willi the weeks passed in a fantastic, dreamlike manner. But his nights were dreamless. He ate supper, washed and then rolled into his bunk to sleep like a corpse until the morning whistle. It was the hammer that turned his days into a drugged phantasm and his nights into oblivion. But it was precisely this he had wanted of the hammer without knowing why or how. His soul had sought the hammer, knowing instinctively that in their combat he would find the surcease he needed from thought and memory. In those first months after Käthe's death, the "Giant-killer" was his means of survival.

He was too old for the hammer, but he would not yield to it. He had never been a fleshy man, yet the hammer stripped his frame in the way that water, as it runs down a rocky hillside, strips away every last particle of earth to leave only inflexible stone. There was no meat on him after two weeks at the job. There was only taut skin over iron muscle, a face that was sunken-eyed and sunken-cheeked, a body that seemed itself to be cast out of some blond metal. The hammer was terrible, but the man became terrible too. Like giants of equal strength, they fought in silence, day after day. And their struggle never varied: Willi stood before the hammer, his legs spread powerfully as he gripped the floor. After the first half hour, his face was marked with dirty runnels of sweat, his thin, blond hair was tousled. The hammer, as at all times, lay waiting for him. It slid up and down at the top of its oiled shaft, back and forth, noiselessly, down two feet, up two feet, always ready, always waiting. Willi swung to the left. This was the first movement, invariable, a pivoting at the hips. With his long steel tongs he gripped a heavy casting from the pile on the cement floor. (A labourer with a wheelbarrow kept it eternally replenished.) Again he pivoted, this time back to centre, the muscles of his arms and back and thighs cording and swelling with the effort. He dropped the casting onto the base of the hammer, holding it in place, just so, by the iron grip of his tongs. That was the moment of contact. In one instant, in the imperceptible flicker of an eyelash, the hammer came down. It came down with a smashing thud, six thousand pounds of fury. It hit the casting, and the steel lump was instantly shaped to the mould of its die. And when it hit, there was a low, ugly man's grunt, "Uhhh!" Willi would hear it as he swung his tongs to the right to drop the casting on the moving belt there, and each time, with curious, never-ending surprise, he realized that it was he himself who had uttered that cry, uttered it involuntarily, a protest torn by the sheer force of the hammer from the core of his gut. He heard it, and then he pivoted again, tongs swinging. The pile of castings was ready, the hammer was waiting... And this was the magic of it: that no matter what painful notion came into his mind, it was always gone the instant the hammer came down. Willi asked no more. And if he had thought about it, facing it honestly perhaps, he would have realized how curious it all was. Not quite three years before, when he first stepped into the forge room in Düsseldorf, he had turned pale at the sheer head-splitting noise of the machines. It didn't seem possible that a man who had been accustomed to comparatively quiet work on construction jobs could even live in a din like that. Every moment he expected that the ear-shattering noise must surely stop. When it didn't stop, when he realized that according to the new war rules he was to work there seventy-two hours a week, he began to tremble in every nerve of his body. But now it was altogether different. Now the factory was his source of life, noise, hammer and all. Now the roar of the forge room had become a pleasant thing to him, like the beat of a surf when a man is lying out on a beach at night. Yet perhaps it was not quite like a surf, but more like the good pounding in a man's head when he is drunk and has a terrible need to be drunk, when there is a great roaring in his body and he lies on a bed knowing oblivion will come, he lies suspended and feels no pain, no deep anxiety – he experiences no worry or shame... he is... sweetly anaesthetized, so to speak.

It was a good job for Willi – a job for a man who was benumbed... and who wanted to remain that way.

4

This was the routine of Willi's existence six days of each week. But Sunday had its own routine as well. Since there was no morning whistle, the men slept late. It made no difference as to food: there were only two meals on the Lord's day anyway, at noon and at five. Willi would stay in bed until the noon meal. Afterwards, for an hour, he would do his washing – the overalls he had worn all week, the three pairs of socks he owned, the patched suit of heavy underwear he used as a sleeping garment. It wouldn't have taken Käthe all of an hour to scrub out a few trifles like that, but Willi dawdled over it, keeping busy. Afterwards he returned to his bunk to lie there smoking one flat-tasting cigarette after another until his week's ration of tobacco ran out, as it did every Sunday afternoon. He spoke little, and then only when one of the others addressed some question to him. Yet those like Hoiseler or Keller or Rufke, who chattered incessantly about one thing or another, did not regard him as a morose man, but merely as a taciturn one. When they asked him a question, he replied amiably enough; when Frisch did one of his comical imitations – the palsied old woman milking a cow, or the near-sighted train conductor, or their particular favourite: Emil Jannings playing Oom Paul Kruger, the Boer leader* – Willi smiled or laughed along with the rest. They liked Willi, they admired him for being able to handle the steam hammer, and they knew as little of his heart as he knew of theirs.

The witching hour of the Sunday routine was five o'clock. A few minutes before the hour they would get dressed in their holiday finery, which was shabby at best. In Willi's case it consisted of a blue serge suit which he had bought some nine years before. It was shiny, but not otherwise in bad condition, except for a spreading seam down the centre of the back. His work at the hammer had swelled his shoulder and back muscles until now the suit was too tight for him. Actually Willi would have been happier if the British bombers had left him some of his other possessions instead – a pair of genuine leather shoes he had owned, or his accordion, or the photograph album he had compiled with Käthe over twenty years. But since the King of England had decided that Willi Wegler was to be granted his blue serge suit and nothing beyond, he wore the suit on Sunday, as he had done every Lord's day for nine years – and that was all there was to it.

They dressed, and then they walked to the commissary. "No rutabagas today, boys," they would say to each other, "today's Sunday." This five o'clock Sunday meal was always the tastiest of the week. It was not to be compared with Sunday dinner as they had known it in the old days, in their own kitchens... but it was a bright spot in the week's monotony, nevertheless. Bread, soup, potatoes, a lump of salt pork, an apple apiece. Or sausage and fried potatoes, or a vegetable and meat stew, and so on. Of course, once they would have spat at the meagre portions they now received. But in the years of preparing for the war, the years of sacrificing butter for guns, they had learnt that their bodies could do a day's work on a quantity of food that wouldn't have made a single meal before. They never took much relish in their meals – and they always felt a bit dissatisfied afterwards, a bit hungry. But they got along... and they worked.

That was the five o'clock meal, and then, following it, came the high moment of the week: the excursion into the village. The very best part of this excursion was the beginning of it, when they walked through the woods to the road. At this time, whether or not they admitted it, most of the men held one lush fantasy in common: that of meeting some lonely housewife whose husband was off in the army and getting her into bed. Since they had been all week building this fantasy for themselves, their minds were hotly inflamed by the time their walk began. The woman no longer mattered, really. At first they had looked for a pretty face or a figure that pleased them. But after a few weeks, however much their secret imagery might still evoke a woman who was moulded to their special tastes, their eyes were won by almost anything in skirts. They were desperately hungry, and that was all there was to it.

And yet, actually, their hunger was not primarily physical. Even though a man like Hoiseler talked endlessly of his past conquests, even though Keller snipped dozens of photographs from the pornographic magazines which flooded the factory compound, what the men really wanted was a decent life again, their own homes, their children, and an end to the war... and when they spoke bawdily of women, it was this for which they were yearning. They were tired men, overworked and underfed. If they had been at home, they would have dropped off into exhausted sleep on most nights without even touching their wives. But in this sort of nightmare existence they acted like fevered adolescents.

The walk through the woods was the high moment, but it was soon over. Once they reached the road, they set foot upon the real world. The road led to the village, three miles from their bunkhouse, only an hour's stroll. And no sooner was the village in sight than they knew in their hearts that all of their fine-spun inventions were nonsense. A good-looking youth like Pelz, in spite of his dangling sleeve, could meet up with a farm wench and presently wave them a gay goodbye on Sunday nights. But the factory was swarming with men, and the village was small. In the race for the outnumbered women, only a portion of whom were willing to be faithless to their husbands, what chance had a fat-paunched man of fifty like Keller or the sour-visaged Hoiseler? They had none, and they knew it after the first two Sunday nights spent in quest. Nevertheless, they set out each week as usual, and so long as they were advancing upon the village, they remained gay with anticipation. Their spirits began to drop after they had passed the first house. Their sweetly imagined Anna was not on the sidewalk to greet them; their plump Maria was not changing her bodice behind an unshaded window, as she had been doing all afternoon in their fantasies. And so, by the time they reached Poppel's beerhouse, they were back to reality again. And then Hoiseler would turn to Keller and say, "What about a little drink?" And Keller would thrust his hand into his pocket, feeling for his few coins, and answer with a shrug, "Why not? What else is there to do?" And that was Sunday. They went into Poppel's, where the air was sour with beer smells and tobacco smells and the smells of tired men, and they got as swinishly drunk as their funds would permit. They talked loudly, they sang, and sooner or later some of them came to blows. And when the vocal ones like Rufke had settled what was to be done to England and what parts of Russia would be left to the Russians... and when the silent ones like Weiner had sat frozen over their glasses until their money ran out... then they all staggered home in the darkness with swimming heads and sour stomachs, and fell into bed to snore until the morning whistle.

That was Sunday, and so the week was rounded out. And so Willi Wegler lived too. Willi had never been much of a drinking man, but he became one now. In the first few weeks he had learnt that a Sunday spent alone in his bunkhouse, or even walking through the woods, was a Sunday of anguish. For six days of the week he was too exhausted to think. But when he was by himself on Sunday, his mind's eye recalled Käthe – never as he had known her in the good years of their life together, but always as she had been in that last moment: an armless corpse, the body mutilated and ripped open. And when he tried to think of Richard, even trying to recite to himself

Chug, chug,
I'm a little tug...

– even that was impossible, for his mind refused to dwell upon that Richard at all. Instead it was the Richard who had come back from the labour camp that he recalled, and the son of that Richard, who had held out his hand in proud salute and said, "A solya… A heeo… An' fight for my Führer." And he couldn't bear to live with these things – he felt strangled by them. And so, like the others, he made his way to Poppel's beerhouse on Sunday night, to sit in silence over the cheap beer and the raw schnapps, to benumb his numbness, to still his mind by becoming swinishly drunk.

He lived like this for the first four months at the factory. It was then that he met Berthe Lingg. After that his life changed.

5

April 30, 1942

There is no telling beforehand by what device of fate a man and woman will become lovers. In the history of Willi Wegler and Berthe Lingg it can be ironically recorded that they were brought together by an act of sabotage – a deed of no great moment, conceived and perpetrated by a number of men whose names they were never to know.

It came about in the following manner: at exactly ten minutes past 9 a.m. of an average workday the power in the forge room suddenly went dead. The cavernous structure, always so ferociously alive, turned deathly quiet in the next instant. Willi, like the other workers, stood helpless before his machine and blinked in stupefaction. His flesh, whipped by routine into intimate knowledge of a working day, could not comprehend this interruption; his ears ached under the weight of the unexpected silence. "How? What? Why?" his face said idiotically. "Something is wrong?"

He glanced up at the conveyor belt. Its little wheels, which grated noisily on the overhead track twenty-four hours a day, had suddenly come to rest. The varied metal shapes it carried hung suspended, dead, like prisoners that had suffered execution. He looked around. Even the clattering spot welders were silent: they uttered no more sound now than a dead fly. The whole cavernous forge room had become a catacomb.

Finally Willi, like most of the others, said to himself suddenly, "A meeting!" And abruptly he relaxed, at ease at last, because he had found an explanation for this disorderly interruption of his day.

But there was not to be a meeting. After a little while Foreman Hartwig was summoned up the catwalk for a word with Herr Kuper. When he returned, it was to announce quietly that a generator in the powerhouse had broken down. The entire plant would have to be idle for the next twenty-four hours.

There was no official pronouncement concerning sabotage, of course. There was even disagreement amongst the plant executives as to the cause of the breakdown. The superintendent, Herr Kohlberg, consulted with his engineers, but could reach no satisfactory conclusion. He pointed out to Baumer that in most German factories machines were beginning to wear out at a rapid rate. It would be foolish, he maintained, to become excited over a disagreeable – but inevitable – mechanical failure. In fact, they would have to expect more of them.

To all of this Baumer replied with one word: "Rubbish!" "Mechanical failure, eh?" he said sarcastically. "But why a mechanical failure on the day before May First?"*

Kohlberg shrugged. "It's a coincidence."

"It could be – but it isn't!"

"Your proof?"

"My nose is my proof! I can smell sabotage here! Dammit, Kohlberg – look at the facts: May First is the Marxist holiday. We ourselves have declared it a free day. Why? Because it was the only way we could be sure half the working class wouldn't get sick on 1st May. So what happens? This year we issue an order: 'Due to the National Emergency, work will continue on Friday, 1st May.' Fine – only a generator cracks up on 30th April! Mechanical failure? Not in a million years!"

"All very reasonable," replied Kohlberg, "only, it's not what I would call 'evidence'… At any rate, no work until the night shift tomorrow."

"I'll call a meeting of all leaders," said Baumer morosely. "The official explanation will be a mechanical failure. Rumours to the contrary are to be reported to me. Meanwhile, I'll try to turn it into a morale factor: twenty-four hours off for all workers… no one required to report in until tomorrow night. The best thing we can do is accept it with a pleasant face."

Naturally, none of this behind-the-scene activity came to the knowledge of Willi Wegler. He knew only that for twenty-four hours he was to be deprived of the ferocious and deadening routine which kept him at ease with himself. It was not a matter of conscious reflection on his part. He merely experienced a grave uneasiness of soul, as might a prisoner suddenly removed from the security of his bars. He had been given a day off – and he didn't know what to do with it.

For an hour or so he tried to pretend it was Sunday. But it was not Sunday, and he found it useless to pretend. He watched his mates at a game of cards, and tried to whip up interest in guessing who would win the bar of soap that they had put up as grand prize, but he felt restless and agitated. Finally, when their midday meal was over, he made a sudden decision: he would go off to Poppel's beerhouse, and he would go alone.

The decision to go alone was evolved out of necessary cunning. Willi would have preferred company – when others were around, he could always fill his head with their jabber. But he knew that it was too early in the week for his bunkmates to have any money. What with iron savings and the multiple other deductions from their wages, most men went around with empty pockets from Sunday night until the following Saturday. There were only a handful of highly skilled workers who could afford to get drunk twice in one week. Because of the "Giant-killer", Willi was of their select number. And since he had only enough money in his overalls to finance his own stupefaction, he asked the Labour Front Office for a pass and wandered off quietly after lunch, telling no one where he was bound.

It was a raw, misty day, this last day of April, and Willi was thoroughly chilled by the time he reached the village. Since it was still early afternoon, Poppel's was empty. Willi sat down by the stove with the aged and garrulous proprietor for company. Poppel jabbered and filled Willi's glass; Willi nodded and drank Poppel's spirits. It was schnapps he was pouring down his gullet, or at least it passed by that name. "Raw varnish," Willi would say each time.

"Ha ha!" the proprietor would reply.

"Raw varnish!"

"Ha ha. Be glad for what you get, sonny. I won't have anything soon but that stinking beer they're sending me. I make no claims these days. Ha ha. I get what I can – I sell what I get."

"Another, if you please," Willi would say politely. "And this time I'll follow with a glass of that fine beer."

By dusk, when habit reminded Willi that it was time to return to the factory for his evening meal, he was utterly befuddled. Politely he wished Poppel a good night. He knitted his brows in desperate concentration and heaved his big frame up out of the chair. Employing that slow, automaton's gait peculiar to intoxicated men when they are ashamed of being drunk, Willi manoeuvred himself to the door. He wished Poppel a polite goodnight for the second time and then staggered outside.

The cold night air almost felled him. He leant his head against the brick wall and smiled foolishly. As though suddenly possessed by a clever notion, he bumped his head against the rough stone. It was quite a blow, and it hurt him. He put his hand to his forehead, groaned with pain, and then, abruptly, staggered off down the road in the general direction of the factory.

The mist, which had blanketed the countryside all day, was now heavy with raindrops. Willi wore only a thin sweater and overalls, and both garments were soon clammy. He didn't mind. The liquor in his body kept him warm, and he liked the rain on his face. He began to sing, reaching back into his dead life for the folk melodies he had once played on his accordion.

Once or twice he tripped over rough spots on the dark road and fell heavily, but it bothered him not at all. And once he wandered off the road into a potato field, and then circled back in a great arc to the road again – all as if it had been purposeful and he were a farmer inspecting his field.

So, in that superb state of contentment which liquor can momentarily impart to an unhappy man, he made his way towards the factory.

The barbed-wire fence which kept trespassers off factory property also marked the end of the twelve acres of land belonging to the widow Berthe Lingg. Willi had passed her farmhouse countless times on his journeys to and from the village and had scarcely glanced at it. There is no telling why he chose to stop by her gate on this night. He had no intention of going inside the yard or of knocking at her door. He was merely captivated by a drunken, idiotic desire: to swing her wooden yard gate back and forth, and to discover if it creaked.

The gate did creak, and quite loudly. Willi stood in the rain, his hair plastered down wetly over his big skull, a broad and foolish grin on his face, and swung the gate back and forth with intense joy. His simple pleasure was short-lived. Out of the darkness, with the almost inaudible snarl of the truly vicious watchdog, came Frau Lingg's dog. She was a mongrel bitch, two thirds black water spaniel, the rest brown shepherd, as ugly to the eye as she was ill-born. She came with a rush, and the snarl ripened at the last moment into a blood-curdling growl.

Had the dog not been in such earnest, it would have been comedy. The fence was high and the bitch was both squat and thick-bodied. Willi might merely have kept the gate closed and remained secure. Instead, as he heard the growl, he swung the gate open to the distinct advantage of the dog. Short-legged as the animal was, she nevertheless was dominated in spirit by her shepherd parent. As the gate opened, she leapt with a killer's snarl straight for Willi's throat.

The comedy deepened. The dog's capacity for jumping was not equal to so tall an objective. Although her jaws snapped shut, they came away with the middle button of Willi's sweater and no more. Instantly she leapt again, but this time with less momentum to aid her. Willi kicked out. The kick was not born of fear, for he was too drunk to appreciate either the savagery of the dog's attack or his own peril. Actually he was laughing. He was in that fine stage of intoxication where a man will carelessly walk in front of a motor car or lie down in a pool of water for a night's rest. The kick was merely instinctive reaction to this dog object, and it was as blundering and amiably befuddled as anything else he had done that evening.

The comedy ended abruptly. His foot struck the dog a glancing blow on her flank, knocking her ten feet away, but not hurting her. At the same moment he stumbled and fell heavily to his knees.

The fall shook him up, and an awareness of his situation suddenly came to him through his drunken fog. Yet because he was so drunk, his peril seemed enormously magnified. He was gripped by an irrational, paralysing terror, and he remained where he was, on his hands and knees, as the dog charged towards him again. Only at the last instant did his senses respond sufficiently for him to raise one arm before his face.

It was the arm that saved him. Another dog would have chewed his flesh at random, but this snarling mongrel was determined to find his throat. And as she leapt again and again, only to be thwarted by the barrier of his arm, he recovered his ability to act. He swung his fist blindly, like a mallet. It struck the bitch squarely on her snout, knocking her backwards into a screaming heap. She rolled over, howling. Again she attacked. And again Willi struck down with his huge fist, this time hitting her skull a terrible blow. The dog fell and never moved. Her legs twitched a little, and that was all.

Probably the animal was stunned rather than dead, but that could never be ascertained. Berthe, who had heard the howling which followed Willi's first blow, ran out of her house in time to observe the result of the second. She shouted at Willi and ran over to the fence. But by that time it was too late to save her dog. With a curious, unthinking reversion to a technique of killing that he had been taught as an army recruit, Willi staggered to his feet. He leapt high over the dog with his knees bent – and straightened his legs just as he came down. Even from the other side of the fence Berthe could hear the snapping of the dog's rib case. She cried out with horror. And Willi, quite amazed by her sudden appearance and frightened by her scream, stood stupidly, looking from the dead dog to this strange woman, and back again to the dog. His head was swimming from all this violent physical activity, and he was suddenly sick to his stomach. He felt horribly guilty over what he had done.

Berthe ran to the motionless animal and got down on her knees by her side. She called to her loudly. There was not a quiver of response. She lifted the limp head, she prodded the thick body with her hand. Finally, with revulsion and dismay, she realized that the bitch was thoroughly dead. Jumping to her feet, she let her rage burst forth in a series of the coarsest peasant curses she knew. Just as abruptly, she fell silent. To her astonishment the murderer had vanished. She looked down the road, but he was not to be seen. She ran a few yards towards the factory, since it had been immediately apparent to her that he was one of the workers there, but she found only darkness and mist. Raging, she returned to the dog.

It was not out of affection for the dead animal that Berthe felt so badly. The bitch had been her husband's, and she had never liked the evil-tempered thing. Nevertheless, there was a place on the farm for a dog, especially when she fed herself by dining on the rodents that infested the barn and fields. Only the week before Berthe had received a proposition from Friml, the village butcher: she was to have four marks, provided she kept her mouth shut, and Friml would have the dog for his own purposes. Although she had refused the offer, it was with a promise to think it over. On the one hand there were the rats; on the other hand, times were hard, and four marks weighed in the hand. Now, of course, the rats would breed in joy and security – and there was little likelihood that Friml would accept the animal in this condition. Or if he did, she reflected, he was Jew enough to cut the price. Since it was a Black Market deal, she would be at his mercy.

Bitterly upset, Berthe decided to carry the dog down into her cellar for the night. In the morning she would hurry into town with the corpse, and do what she could with Friml.

Dragging the heavy, resistant body, she reached the doorway of her house, which she had left open as she ran out. She lifted the dog by the scruff and pulled it over the threshold. Then she stopped, almost frightened out of her wits. There, with his back towards her, calmly drinking a glass of water at her sink, was the murdering drunkard.

If Berthe had been carrying a stick when they were both out of doors, she would have cracked Willi's head open in complete disregard for consequences or of danger to herself. But now, finding him in the close confines of her kitchen, she became frightened. She could not know that Willi had wandered into her house with as much purpose as earlier he had marched into a potato field. Or that, upon seeing her water tap, he had become conscious of a gigantic thirst, and so had remained to drink one glass of water after another, of which this was the fourth. She saw him only as an intoxicated and violent male who had invaded the security of her home and who was, perhaps, as willing to murder her as her dog.

She watched him in trembling silence for a moment as he finished one glass of water and filled another. Then she shivered and got control of herself. Quickly she opened the front door again. She wanted a means of exit in the event he tried to attack her.

"Now then," she cried harshly, "what the devil are you doing in here? Get out, quick!"

Will turned around slowly, his mouth gasping open as though he were an idiot, the half-filled glass in his hand. He was not a prepossessing object. His bloodshot eyes, his wet, tousled hair, his soggy work clothes which the dog's teeth had ripped at arm and chest, made him appear more a wandering tramp than a worker. Above all, he frightened Berthe because he was so big. She was accustomed to brawny men, but this one, even in the sag of drunkenness, had a terrifying body. Nevertheless, she felt more indignation than fear. "Don't you understand me?" she shouted. "Get out of my house!"

Willi only stared at her. He was not quite sure who she was. But then, seeing the dog, he made the connection. He grunted with embarrassment. "Your dog," he muttered thickly. "I didn't mean—"

"Will you get out?" she cried threateningly. Her voice rose. "I have a telephone here." (A lie.) "I'll call the police!"

Willi started for the door immediately, in fright.

"Put my glass down! Are you trying to steal my glass too?"

He stopped dead, staring at the glass. Then he set it down hastily on the edge of the table. The glass toppled off and crashed on the floor.

"Oh God in heaven!" Berthe cried. "Now my glass!"

"Excuse me, excuse me," Willi muttered thickly, in embarrassment. He dropped down on his hands and knees to gather up the shattered pieces of glass. Then, before she could even shout at him to let them be and get out, he pitched forward on the floor in an awkward, humped-over position, closed his eyes and went instantly to sleep.

"Get up!" she yelled. "Get up now – this instant!"

From Willi there came an audible full-toned snore.

"Oh!" she cried. She ran over to the prostrate man and kicked him on his backside with her wooden-soled shoe. Her reward was a second snore, as dulcet and contented as the first. With indignation she ran to the sink. She filled a pail with water, returned with it and rolled Willi over on his back. She flung the water onto his upturned face. Willi responded with as much life as would his steam hammer in similar circumstances. Finally Berthe took to belabouring him on the ribs with the heavy wooden pail – keeping it up until she burst out into dismayed laughter. At that point she gave it up as futile.

After a bit she sat down to finish her cold supper. And then she went to bed. She moved a heavy chest before her door and placed the largest kitchen knife she had on a chair by her pillow. She started to laugh again at the idiocy of the whole business, and ended up by becoming angry once more. Finally she fell asleep.

6

The sun had not yet risen when Berthe awakened. She dressed quietly, opened her bedroom door a crack in order to peer out cautiously and then tiptoed into the kitchen. Willi was still where she had left him, sleeping blissfully on the remnants of her shattered glass. She hesitated, not knowing what to do first. She had chores which demanded attention – the cows and chickens. She wanted to bicycle to town with the body of her dog, and to arrive there early enough so that no kind friends might be about to enquire into the contents of her basket; and yet she dared not set about her duties with this man still in her house. Who knew what he might do? Burn the house down or steal something, surely...

Hoping that this time she would be more successful, she filled the wooden bucket with water. Willi stirred as the contents poured down on him. She repeated the process. After the third bucket Willi's eyes opened. He sat up with a groan.

"Well," said Berthe, retreating instantly to the table where the knife was, "so you're awake at last? Now get out of my house. And quick, or I'll call the police!"

Not knowing at all how he came to be in a house with a strange woman, Willi stared at her dumbly. His sleep had almost wholly wiped out memory of the night before. The last thing he could recall clearly was sitting in Poppel's, drinking schnapps.

"Well?" she demanded. "Are you going?"

The obvious explanation presented itself to Willi. He had somehow made the acquaintance of this female and she had taken him to her home. One of the village women, obviously. But still… when a man went home with a woman, he didn't wake up on the floor. Nor did the baggage* shout at him the next morning in this vixenish manner. What had occurred? Had they ended up by fighting? What about? He was a peaceable man… he never fought with anyone.

Groaning under the weight of his head and feeling an aching stiffness in the ribs, Willi rose laboriously.

Berthe retreated a little, clutching the knife firmly in her hand.

"If you please," said Willi with embarrassment, "how did I get here?"

"You broke in. Like a robber! That's how!"

"Broke in?" He was sure she was lying.

"I suppose you don't remember?" Her voice turned high-pitched and whining as she mocked him coarsely. "'I didn't mean it… I was drunk… My mind's a blank!' Oh yes… I know you men. Pigs, every one of you!"

"Please," said Willi wretchedly, "I'm so sorry. I'll leave right away. Only tell me where I am."

"In *my* farmhouse – that's where! You're from the factory, I suppose?"

He nodded with embarrassment.

"The factory's down the road. And a pity you couldn't land there, where you belong, instead of coming in here and breaking things up like a madman!"

"Breaking things up?" he asked in weak consternation. "What did I break?"

"There. That glass."

"Oh… Don't worry. I'll pay you for it."

"And the dog? Will you pay for her, too?"

Willi stared. "What do you mean?"

She pointed. "My dog – that you killed last night."

Willi gazed dumbly at the dead animal, which lay stiff and unhandsome on the threshold, and wondered if the woman were making this all up out of her head. How on earth could he have killed a dog? Why? But then… how had he landed here in the first place?

"I killed her? Truly?" he asked.

"Does she look alive to you? You hear her barking, you brute?"

"How did I kill her?"

"You jumped on her. First you knocked her down, then you jumped on her. Crushed her to pieces, and such a dog! A dog I loved. Well… will you pay for her too, or do I have to go to the police?"

"I'll pay, of course I'll pay," Willi assured her hastily. "I'm an honest man. If you say I killed your dog, I'll make good. But how is it possible? Why should I want to kill a dog?"

Berthe, of course, knew perfectly well that her evil-tempered mongrel must have brought about her own fate by attacking this man, as she had others in the past. And since the dog's character was known in the neighbourhood, Berthe's threat of going to the police was as empty as air. But Willi's hasty agreement to make restitution made her catch her breath at the opportunity.

"Look here," she said, "what's done is done. Don't ask *me* why you killed her. All I know is she never harmed anyone in her life. Gentle as a lamb, she was. Probably she ran up to you to be petted, and you, brute that you are, killed her in cold blood."

"This is terrible," Willi muttered. "Poor little dog."

"Never mind the false sympathy. If you want to be honourable about your crime, pay up."

"I'll pay. I told you I'll pay!"

"She was a trained dog, I'll have you know. Not just an ordinary one."

"I'll pay. Just tell me how much."

"When it came time to bring in the cows, did *I* ever have to go? Not once. I'd just say to my dog, 'Get the cows' – and off she'd go."

"I'm sorry, I'm so sorry," Willi muttered wretchedly. "Believe me, I'll pay."

"And such a pet she was. A protection to a widow living alone. Where will I get another dog like her?"

"I'm sorry, I'm sorry," Willi said desperately. "If I could bring her back to life, I would. But I'm an honourable man, I'll—"

"All right, if you're honourable like you say… eighteen marks, and that'll take care of the glass too."

Willi faltered. "Eighteen marks?"

"Hah! Honourable in words only, I see."

"But… eighteen… for a dog? Why a fancy dog only costs—"

"Don't talk to me about fancy dogs!" Berthe interrupted acidly. "What does a farmer like me want with a fancy dog? I need a work animal that's sharp – not some pedigree with a curly tail. And besides, who said I was asking for what the dog cost four years ago? No! There's the years of training, that's what counts. I'm asking for damages, for what the dog was *worth* to me. So now – pay up or I'll go to the police! The police'll make it higher, don't worry. They won't be as soft-hearted as me. With the police there'll be a fine to pay too!"

"All right, all right!" said Willi hastily. "Eighteen marks! I'll pay it!" He put his hand into his pocket and came up with two pfennigs. "Oh," he muttered.

"Oh!" she mimicked.

"I promise you I'll get it. I'll bring it to you tonight."

Berthe's heart sank with disappointment. Now her bird was flying the coop. She'd be too afraid to make it a police matter.

"Look," said Willi, misreading her expression, "here's my identification card. You can notify the factory if I don't come back with the money."

Berthe studied the card. "When will you come? Can you come tonight?"

"Yes."

"All right, tonight then – or I go direct to the police tomorrow morning."

Willi nodded. He hesitated awkwardly for a moment, muttered an embarrassed goodbye and then left.

Berthe tiptoed to the doorway. She stood gazing after him as he crossed to her front gate. With a peal of inward laughter she said to herself, "A lummox if I ever saw one." She glanced down at the stiffened body of the dog, then prodded it with the toe of her shoe. "Good riddance to you," she exclaimed aloud, with muffled laughter. "At eighteen marks a very good riddance."

In this rather disagreeable manner a man and a woman who were destined to be lovers were brought together.

Chapter 9

It was not until late in the evening, when Berthe was already preparing for bed, that Willi returned. He had slept most of the day, and then it had taken him several hours to borrow the five marks that he now had in his pocket. He had gone patiently from one acquaintance to another, receiving a coin here, another there. And all evening he had been berating himself for spending his last penny at Poppel's. It was not a practical regret, but a moral one: that he had made a swine of himself. For even though his pride was weaker than the dark need which drove him to schnapps, he could not free his soul of an attendant shame.

He arrived at the farmhouse about nine in the evening. When he saw that all the windows were dark, even though the blackout curtains were not drawn, he didn't know quite how to proceed. Was the woman away, and ought he to wait? Or asleep, and dare he awaken her? As a factory worker whose bunk was illumined by electric light, Willi was not aware of the meagreness of the kerosene ration. But to a lone farm woman like Berthe, who had to sit in darkness for most of each evening, the kerosene ration was one of the bitter pills of the war. At the moment she was sitting in the kitchen soaking her feet. Her new "Victory" shoes, with their wooden soles, were giving her corns.

Willi compromised with his uncertainty by knocking very gently. The sudden loud reply from the dark kitchen – "Yes, who's there?" – made him jump.

"It's me... Wegler... from the factory."

"In a minute," Berthe called, leaping up with excitement. She ran barefooted to close the curtains and light her lamp. She opened the door hastily. "Come in, come in," she said warmly, with a simple greed she could not conceal. "I..." Her mouth dropped open and she became dumb. It didn't seem to her that this possibly could be the same man. As people do, she had dwelt all day on the only image she had of Wegler – a huge, tattered marauder with an idiot's look on his face. Between that man and the one who now stood in her doorway there was only a physical bulk in common. Willi had dressed up – blue serge suit, clean white shirt, tie, shoes scrubbed free of mud. Quite consciously he was attempting to correct the impression that he knew the woman must have received of him. It was not out of interest in Berthe that he did so. Actually, all he remembered of her was that she had a loud voice and a shrew's tongue. But it was one of the deep springs in his character that he couldn't bear to have people think ill of him. And so tonight he had spent half an hour in preparing for this journey of atonement, slicking up as though it were a celebration.

Willi was more successful than Berthe ever let him know. Instead of a brigand she found herself confronted by a neatly clothed, respectable – yes, even handsome – man. She felt like blushing over her own appearance, for she had run to the door in her bare feet; her dress was shabby and soiled, and her hair... before she knew what she was doing she put her hand up to see if her braids were in place. Finally, recovering her voice, she said, "Well... aren't you coming in?" She added a little haughtily, "You're very late. I was going to bed."

"I'm sorry," Willi apologized. He stepped into the kitchen diffidently. "The fact is..." He stammered. "I had to borrow, you see. It took time."

"Oh... you had to borrow," Berthe echoed with some embarrassment herself. Friml had paid her two marks for the dog already. Twenty marks in all was almost a sin. To hide her embarrassment she exclaimed loudly, "Well, then... in the future maybe you won't go around killing dogs."

"No, no... you mustn't think... I'm not that sort of a man."

"Well, then?..."

"Well then... The fact is that I have only a part of it tonight. I couldn't borrow it all."

"Oh!"

"But by tomorrow night I'll have the rest."

Berthe frowned. "You said tonight."

"I tried my best. Believe me. Here... I have five marks now. On Sunday I'll surely have the rest." He held out the coins.

"You said tomorrow. Tomorrow's Saturday, not Sunday."

"Yes... Saturday," he corrected with a stammer. "Tomorrow night positive. We get paid."

"Well then, tomorrow." She held out her palm, and he tipped the coins from his hand into hers.

"Yes, tomorrow," he repeated like a dunce. "Well then..." He shifted from one foot to another. Now that he was sober, he could observe that this woman was not wholly unpleasant. He felt that he owed her a more elaborate apology.

"Well then?" Berthe asked with a slight mocking smile. This extreme diffidence on the part of her brigand was commencing to amuse her.

"Well then, tomorrow. Goodnight."

"Goodnight."

Willi turned to go, but stopped so abruptly that Berthe began to wonder if he were slightly touched in the head. What sort of man was this big lump anyway? He killed dogs with his fist, yet he paid eighteen marks in return. He was drunk as a pig one night, and like a choirboy the next. He stopped and he started, he said goodnight four times like an idiot, and now what?

Willi was staring at a corner of her kitchen. As Berthe's eyes followed his gaze, she saw that it must be the accordion that so attracted him. "Well?" she exclaimed.

Willi started. "You have an accordion?"

"Not a piano."

"An accordion," he said softly, as though it were a honeyed word he liked to hear.

"So?"

Willi turned to her, and his blue eyes were suddenly so bright that it made Berthe wonder about him.

"I always played the accordion," he said softly. He felt choked by a bittersweet nostalgia. "I... liked it. But mine was smashed in a bombing."

Berthe said nothing.

"Do you play it?"

"My husband did."

"He's in the war?"

"I'm a widow."

Willi nodded. "Well... goodnight, then." He had not taken a step before he hesitated again. "Frau?..."

"Lingg."

"Frau Lingg... it... would it be asking too much to let me play it for a minute? The accordion?"

"Now?"

"Well... I meant now. But if..."

Berthe shrugged. "For a few minutes, perhaps."

"Thank you." He crossed with haste to the makeshift box in which she had set the instrument. He picked it up fondly, looking it over with eyes that sparkled. Berthe watched him closely, struck again by the sudden warmth in his eyes, and wondering about him. Now that he had come through on their money agreement, turning up as he said he would, she no longer felt hostile towards him. Whatever he might be drunk, obviously he was not a man of rough behaviour when sober. In fact... her murdering tramp was quite attractive. His physical bulk had frightened her the night before when she didn't know what to expect next, but now she regarded his big shoulders and powerful body with a different eye. There was one thing about Willi that confused her, however: the impassive quality of his face. It seemed to her that she had never seen a man with so stony a face – not cruel or selfish, as some men's faces were, but utterly without expression.

She watched him closely. Willi sat down with the accordion on his knees. He ran his fingers lightly over the keys, then dusted them off with the sleeve of his jacket. He sat for a moment, staring abstractedly at the instrument. He had apparently forgotten her presence. She could not know that the years were rolling back for him, or that the accordion was the one object of his past that remained sunlit.

"Well?" she asked.

He looked up with a slight start.

"I thought you wanted to play?"

"Yes," he said hastily. He lifted his fingers to the keys, spread his legs and began to play. It was a soft, sad melody, one Berthe had never heard. Almost at once she said to herself, "He plays better than Johann did." She sat down with a quiet sigh, gazing at him. After a bit she looked away and closed her eyes. The music was beautiful to her – but it also made her grieve. A man playing an accordion at night – it was the touchstone of all she had lost when her husband died. She always reflected bitterly that a town woman could get along when she lived singly. She worked in a factory, perhaps, where there were people to talk to, and at night there were crowded streets, friends to see, or a neighbour across the hall if she wished to chat. But on a farm it was... dreadful. Things had not been so difficult for her until her son was taken by the army, or even while she still had the hired man, surly as he had been. So long as there was *someone* nearby through the long days! Someone at breakfast and at supper, someone for the evening so that one needn't sit alone in darkness. How dreadful that was, to sit alone at night after a day of loneliness – to go to bed alone, and to know that you would rise alone! Now her son had been away almost a year, and the hired man for two months; and the presence of this man in her kitchen playing the accordion was cruel... it was too much to bear because it made all of the nights to come even more lonely than they need be.

"That's enough," she exclaimed suddenly, in a rough tone. "I want to go to bed."

Willi stopped in the middle of a chord. He got up hastily, flustered. He didn't understand this sudden change of mood on the woman's part, and he resented it. But without argument he set the accordion back in its box. "Thank you, Frau Lingg. A fine instrument. It was a pleasure to—"

"I'm sorry I let you play it," Berthe interrupted harshly. "Go away now. I'm tired."

"Yes," he stammered. "Excuse me." He left hastily, thoroughly bewildered.

"Now, mind you," Berthe called, running to the door after him, "the rest of the money on Saturday or I go to the police." She shut the door angrily. She was in tears before she reached her bedroom. She undressed, sobbing quietly, so filled with an inexplicable hatred for Willi that she could have killed him. She lay sleepless for over an hour. The last thing she remembered was the factory siren screaming "Blackout", announcing that British planes were on their way. She said to herself bitterly, "It's men who make wars, not us. It's men who like politics and killing each other. How easy it is for them to die and leave us alone, the swine!"

Then she fell asleep.

2

As Willi walked along the road the next evening, he concocted a plan. It was this: to make a friend out of Frau Lingg so that after this night, even though his debt was paid, he might still visit her. The goal was simple, but Willi's motivations were complex, and he was only superficially aware of them. All that he felt clearly was a yearning to repeat again the ten minutes in her kitchen. Music had always delighted his senses, and he had left the farmhouse with soft memories crowding into his mind. For a few hours at least his heart had felt eased. To possess again this freedom from utter bleakness, to cling to the miracle of a clean, quiet kitchen with a woman in it – even an unpredictable, somewhat sharp-tongued woman – it was this that constituted his simple, conscious longing.

Behind it was something else: Willi's spirit had been whipped into stupefaction by a decade of events beyond his understanding. He had sought surcease in the primitive manner of an animal that crawls deep within a cave to endure its wounds in silence. But even as an animal must finally emerge to light and air and food again if it is not to die, so Willi's soul needed to emerge from its comatose state. And all of this, the music, the kitchen, the woman – the sheen of a frying pan, the creaking of a gate, the odours of a house – represented a life that was *alive*, and that beckoned to the buried hungers in his soul. He was not yet ready for death, and this taste of a decent existence had stirred him profoundly.

On this night, as he went through the creaking gate, he saw a sliver of light under the door. And this time it was he who was astonished at the person who confronted him. Berthe was no longer the ogress she had seemed on the night of his drunkenness or the suspicious, unkempt peasant of his second visit. She was smiling, her face was more than agreeable, and she looked... pretty.

Berthe had prepared for Willi with care, hope and deliberation. Her coarse dark hair was neatly braided; she had bathed; she was wearing the most pretentious dress of her meagre wardrobe: a tight-fitting garment of cheap black satin. In that instant she became a woman to Willi, a sexual object – and she could see it in his eyes. She saw it, weighed it, and was pleased – for she had planned it that way.

"Good evening," she said quietly. "Come in, Herr Wegler."

"Good evening," he replied slowly, still gazing at her. And then awkwardly, "It's not raining tonight."

Her smile broadened a little. "No. A fine night. You'll sit down for a bit?" She indicated a chair.

"Thank you." He sat down, stiff and bulky on the edge of the chair. She chose a rocker nearby. A tiny, secretive smile clung to her full lips.

"I have the rest of the money..." Willi began, with some embarrassment. "But what a fine-looking woman," he was thinking. "How is it I didn't notice last time?" He fumbled in his pocket and put the money on the table. "You want to count it?"

Berthe shrugged. She replied slowly, smiling. "I expect it's correct. I expect, Herr Wegler, that when you're sober, you count correctly."

Willi flushed in contrition. "I know money doesn't make up for the dog. I'm so sorry I killed her, Frau Lingg. Believe me."

"So now let's forget it," she exclaimed hastily. His honest humility was disconcerting. She had cheated him brazenly over the dog, and to have him offer further apologies aggravated her acute sense of guilt. She jumped up, swept the money off the table and crossed with it to a crock in the cupboard. "Now it's over, Herr Wegler. You've done right. We'll forget it."

"Just one thing," he added eagerly. "I'm not... I don't want you to think I'm the sort of a man who does things like that. Often, I mean."

Berthe shrugged. She said nothing. Her attitude, and the ensuing silence, made Willi feel that he was a fool. He had paid the woman – clearly that was all she wanted. He got to his feet, wretched with disappointment.

"Wouldn't you like to play the accordion again?" she asked quietly.

"Yes... surely," he exclaimed, absolutely delighted. "I hoped... But last time it upset you."

"It won't upset me," she smiled. "I like it."

"Thank you. I was hoping..." He went at once to the box in the corner of the kitchen. Berthe watched him. As his hands touched the instrument, she saw again, as she had the first time, the quick softening in his eyes. She wondered at it, and liked it – but she said to herself sadly, "Why does his face have to be so hard? What makes a man like him get drunk and become a beast? Women have their troubles too, but they don't become beasts."

Above all else in life, Berthe hated the violence in men, and, like most women – although she was not usually aware of it – she resented the male rules that governed her life. From childhood on it had been necessary for her to struggle against the contempt of women that she found in her world – against man-made codes a thousand years old, which were now ascribed to God or to Nature or to the State. And it was this that made her respond to Willi's diffidence. She had only to look at him to know that he was no weakling, and indeed it was not a weakling she wanted in a man. But just as she had been revolted by his drunken violence at their first encounter, so now she quickened to the sense that he was a man who would not carry contempt for a woman. He had apologized to her with guilt, not condescension, and out of thirty-six years of manoeuvring in a man's universe she instantly felt the difference.

It was in this moment, as Willi sat down with the accordion on his knees, that their wooing began. He looked up at her with a shy, grateful smile as he began to play, and although neither of them knew it, they were already falling in love.

Berthe listened and watched him with a veiled glance. Willi's body had relaxed with the music, and an abstracted smile softened the firm line of his mouth. She could see a gentleness in his face now – a tempering of the hard set of his features. And after a bit, because she already needed to know his answer, she asked: "Where are you from, Herr Wegler?"

He looked up. "Düsseldorf. But for many years I lived in Cologne."

"Ah... Düsseldorf." And then, with only the faintest embarrassment, "You have a family, I suppose?"

"No," he said. He stopped playing, and a sense of aching dejection filled his heart. His blue eyes went blank; his face took on the dead look she had already marked. In a flat, unemotional tone, as though he were reciting something he had repeated many times before – or as though it were an old tale that no longer interested him – he said: "I had a boy and a wife, Frau Lingg. My boy died in the attack on Narvik. My wife was killed in a bombing. Now I'm alone." He sat silent, stony, resenting her for the inevitable question, as he had resented all of the other inquisitive ones before her.

Berthe felt dreadful. She wanted to say something in sympathy, but his blank eyes, as he continued to stare at her, seemed to forbid platitudes. Finally, out of her own private sorrow, she said simply, "I hate the war too. The war killed my husband. In such a silly way – just as stupid and as… cruel as war is. He went to the city on business. There was a practice blackout, and he was run over. By an ambulance, imagine! How stupid!"

They were silent for a moment. "It's two years now," she added quietly. "And it's almost a year that they took my son. When the Russian war started. He was only seventeen, imagine!"

"Yes?" said Willi. "When I was seventeen I was in the last war."

"My boy's in France, thank God. There's no fighting there. I pray to God he won't be sent to the Russian front. He's such a fine lad," she added with open pride. "Straight as a birch tree, and so good-hearted. I'll die if anything happens to him."

She saw Willi's fingers tapping the keys softly, nervously. "Play," she said softly, "play again."

So now she knew – he was not married. She had felt it must be so. On the night that he came so humbly to meet his pledge and sat in her kitchen with the accordion on his knees, her heart had whispered: "This is how it should be… this one you will want." She had been afraid to admit it before this moment, too suspicious of herself. She knew that she had been hungering for a man at her side, that for the past year she had been seeking a new husband. The farm was going to ruin without a man, and she herself was bereft. She needed the benison of a man's love, she wanted to wash a man's sweaty clothes, to seed the fields beneath a hot sun at the side of her husband. She was nothing, dead flesh, without a man, and she knew it. It had always been so.

But she had not wanted Rosenhart, the local Peasant Leader, even though he had been in earnest. He was… not the man she wanted. And she had not wanted the SS men or the others who had come only on female hunting

– who wanted to use her as a whore, without paying her, as she had told one of them in rage. And she had begun to feel that it was hopeless, that in this world of men at war she was destined to dry up like a plant robbed of nourishment, that soon she would be too old for any attractive man to want her. And then, stealing in upon her despair, Willi had come to play the accordion in her kitchen. He was not elderly like Rosenhart, he was more than strong enough to be a good farmer; he was free; he was attractive. And he had come out of the night, a man belonging to no one and to no place, as though something had directed his drunken footsteps to her farmhouse – as though he, too, were seeking a companion and a home.

Suddenly, out of an old terror of what men could hide about themselves, she said aloud, harshly, "But why do you have to drink like a pig? Why do you turn yourself into such a beast?"

Willi stopped playing. Slowly he took his fingers off the keys. A flush of shame spread over his big, hollow-cheeked face. He answered without thought, the first words that occurred to him, but they were more revealing to her than he knew. "I never drank before," he said awkwardly. "I don't like to get drunk, even now. It's just that... well..." He stopped, biting his lip.

Berthe felt ashamed. Men did drink, and this one, who had lost his family, drank for obvious reasons. Yet he had not been drunk when he came to visit her. Why couldn't she have been satisfied with that?

"Excuse me," she said uneasily. "It's only that men... I don't like men who drink. My husband... Well, he was a good man, truly. But sometimes, when he went with others, he would take too much. And he became... not like himself then... he was cruel to the animals, and to me."

Willi said nothing. She jumped up suddenly. "Would you like a cup of coffee, Herr Wegler?"

He nodded politely. "You have enough?"

"Yes."

She smiled happily at him and ran to the stove. A cup of coffee for him would mean a morning that week without coffee for her. But she didn't care. "Play, please," she urged, turning around. "I like it so much. You play so fine."

Willi played, and as he played he watched Berthe and thought about her. Earlier that evening he had listened with disinterest to the bawdy chatter of his bunkmates, who had observed him with affectionate envy as he dressed for a special night out. Now he remembered their suggestions. He was not blind. Frau Lingg had dressed up for him. She had not sent him away once he handed over the money: she offered him coffee – she was a widow.

Why not, then, if she was willing? He would ask to call again, and they would see. Perhaps the future would offer more than the accordion alone.

Willi was not thinking of marriage. To think of a woman in terms of marriage is to think of life in terms of a future. But Willi had no more thought of his future than a stone. He was living from day to day with only one conscious object: to be free as much as possible from pain, from deep thought and from memory. And he was turning now towards this woman as he had to his steam hammer, seeking only an anodyne for his senses. As any woman, in any kitchen, could have met his soul's need for a taste of life again, so any woman who was not too ugly could satisfy his sexual need. He was thinking of Berthe exactly as she didn't want him to think of her – and what he wanted of her was the very opposite of what she already wanted of him.

He watched her, and he mused, and he estimated her body. He found her very attractive – a pleasing face and a strong, full figure. He wondered if she were the sort who would go to bed with a man.

"I like that song," Berthe said, turning around at the stove. "My husband used to play that, but not so well. He always made mistakes and had to start over." She smiled happily, turning back to the stove. Willi nodded and continued to play. He stared at her thick legs, her flanks, the white, warm nape of her neck above the collar of her dress. He slipped into sexual fantasy, thinking how pleasant it would be if she would give herself to him without fuss. "Such a business people have to go through," he thought. "You shake hands for a longer while than necessary, and that's the first step; then a goodnight kiss; the next time a longer kiss; God knows how much rigamarole* it takes till you land in bed. Or has it changed nowadays? It's a long time since I was up against this sort of thing. If she'd just hold out her arms to me now and say, 'I know... It's the same for me too...'"

His musings ceased. Into his mind had come a terrible image: of Käthe, his wife – of her naked body ripped open from breast to loin, the viscera protruding.

The image oppressed him for only a moment. He had learnt in these past months that there were artificial techniques for forgetting. He ground his teeth together and bit his lips. He bent over the accordion, with his big face hidden from Berthe, and forced his fingers to travel over the keys. And presently his mind, his face, his eyes, became blank – for this was the technique which pain had taught him. Nowadays it was all he knew. "But how well you play..." repeated Berthe, as she brought the coffee to the table. "My husband could never play so well."

"I had lessons when I was a youngster," Willi explained slowly. "I was in a hospital for a little while in 1918. A buddy taught me. Then, afterwards, I kept it up."

"Put it down now and drink your coffee while it's hot. Imagine, I have nothing to offer you with it." She sighed, but her sigh ended in a laugh. "Barley coffee and not a bit of cake. What a way to live!"

"This is fine, Frau Lingg." He was more grateful for the gesture of hospitality than she knew.

"I haven't been able to bake a coffee cake in God knows how long. It seems to me we eat like convicts nowadays. Imagine, even us farmers too! But everything is registered – I swear they know every last drop of milk my cows give, every egg that's expected, every potato. And they want it all. I should try to hold out a cup more milk than they allow me... Hah! I'd land in jail." She laughed softly, shaking her head. "One thing I'll never understand is this: I send my milk away looking like milk – but when people buy milk in town it looks like blue water. What do they do with it, I wonder?" She laughed again, her body quivering softly under the contempt of a peasant for townfolk. "They think they're feeding pigs, perhaps? 'Skimmed milk is for pigs and Poles.' That's what farmers always say."

Willi smiled absently. His eyes were on her round, gay face. He liked her face. The skin was coarse-grained, with some tiny pockmarks on her forehead and at one side of her stubby nose. But it was a warm, alive face, very womanly; her wide, full-lipped mouth, her gleaming black eyes, excited his senses. He would have liked to lean across the table suddenly and kiss that laughing mouth. He wanted to stroke her dark braids and pull her close to him so that her quivering breasts were tight and warm against his chest. Hotly he thought, "Why not? Why shouldn't I do it? I can't lose anything. Maybe that's what she wants too. And if it turns out otherwise, so to hell with her." But then he told himself, "Don't be a fool. Women don't like to be considered easy. She'll get angry. Why should you lose out on a chance like this for being so much in a hurry?"

Berthe was not at all unknowing of Willi's glances, or of their meaning. Even his hard face seemed to be coming alive as he stared at her. It made her heart swell with hope and happiness to see it. She chattered on gaily, making conversation, and all the while her eyes grew brighter under his molten glance. She too was ardently hungry for a lover's embrace, and if there had been only that on her mind, she would have been bold enough to suit him. She was no longer a child, and she was not plagued by guilt or virginal fears. But she already hoped for this man on a permanent basis, and if he didn't know it yet, he would soon find out. "Meanwhile," she thought to herself with inward laughter, "if he burns a little, that's fine. It's the same for me too, so let him treat me serious."

They drank their coffee, and Berthe continued her animated chatter. She talked about the farm – of how hard it was for her to manage it alone. They had mobilized her hired man and her horse. The fields had been badly ploughed by a battalion of city schoolboys who knew nothing about farming. The seed had come late this year, there was a lack of fertilizer – and yet all one heard was that the country needed more food, and that it was the duty of farmers to increase the yield. "How?" she asked with a forlorn laugh. "I work from sunrise to dark as it is. I'm a lone woman. If some of those wiseacres would only tell me how! And is it my fault that there was no snow this January, so that the frost spoiled my rye?"

"Yes, you need help – you need a man on the farm," Willi said. Berthe's heart thumped sweetly. She looked over at him with a timid smile. But he didn't go on as she hoped. He was thinking back twenty years, to his own dream of a farm.

"And imagine," she continued after a moment's silence, "we're coming into summer now. Everything will depend on what's done in the fields in the next few months. The young potato plants will have to be weeded, the hay should get two cuttings – nothing takes care of itself on a farm. If only there were a strong man about, I'd have no more worries."

"Yes," said Willi. He had finished his coffee, and he felt that social decorum declared it to be time for him to go. But he didn't want to go. He kept wishing she would do something that would give him an excuse to be bold with her – although he didn't quite know what he expected her to do. After all these years of marriage he needed to go off and ponder the question of how one approached a woman!...

"So that's it, you see," said Berthe. "It's no picnic for a lone woman on a farm."

"No." He smiled at her. "I'll tell you," he said suddenly, "I've lived all my life in the city, but years ago I had a plan – I wanted to save money to buy a farm."

"Truly? You know something about farming?"

He shook his head. "But I always thought I'd like it. I got the idea when I was in France, in the last war."

"To be a farmer you've got to know how. It's not just pushing a button in a factory."

"I know. But I figured I could learn. I'm good with my hands."

"So why didn't you do it – buy a farm?"

"I never could save enough," he replied with regret. "I'd get a little ahead, and then work would shut down. I used to raise onions in a window box – that's the closest I ever came."

"Some farmer," Berthe laughed.

He smiled back at her. "They were good onions." Reluctantly he stood up. "Well, Frau Lingg, so now it's time to go. I've overstayed, surely."

"I should say not. Don't think it. It's been a pleasure."

"I thank you for the coffee and the…" He gestured towards the accordion. "You know, if I thought you'd sell it to me, Frau Lingg…"

"A keepsake," she replied. "I couldn't. But then…" (as though it had just occurred to her) "why shouldn't you come back and play it sometime?"

"You wouldn't mind?"

"It'd be a pleasure."

"Fine… Thank you."

The farce between them ended as Willi laughed with a quiet gaiety she didn't know he possessed. "I'm a liar, Frau Lingg. I didn't want to buy it. I wanted you to invite me back, like you did."

Berthe laughed with him. Yet in the next moment, as she saw what was in his eyes, her face turned compassionate.

"You see, it's… lonely at the factory," he told her simply. "I… to be in a room like this with you… it's… I can't tell you how good it is to me."

"Is it?" she asked. And then, as the truth in her own heart refused to be bottled up any longer, her face became suddenly forlorn, and as nakedly revealing as a child's. "But not so lonely at the factory, Herr Wegler, as it is for me here. That's why I invited you."

They gazed at each other in silence. "Frau Lingg," he said softly – tenderly, it seemed to her, "Frau Lingg." Her mouth began to tremble, and an expression came over her face of such deep and utter submission that he became filled with wild desire. "Frau Lingg," he murmured again. His eyes were becoming hot and hard. She stood still, her head bent, her eyes averted from his. He put out his hand and touched her hair. "Frau Lingg," he whispered.

She sobbed deep in her throat and once again looked up at him with that involuntary, submissive expression on her face. She had not intended this – she did not want it as yet. But as though her words had been brewed out of some sickly magic, her simple admission of loneliness had loosed the longing in her heart. Her mind was warning her, saying, "Not yet. He'll think badly of you. You mustn't." But she felt drugged, with a hot languor in limb and breast that it was beyond her will to overcome.

Her knees unglued as he kissed her. She would have fallen if not for his embrace. He held her body tight against his, and his mouth was fierce upon hers, his hand bold and greedy at her breast. They stood locked, in a torment of desire that was different for each of them. His mouth would not relinquish hers, nor would the arms loosen that held her full and open against his body. She remained unresisting as he half led, half carried her to the bedroom. She was drugged with a desire far older than anything he, or any man, could evoke – and it was more urgent than all her plans, her pride, her code of behaviour.

The spell broke as quickly as it had captured her. As Willi pressed her back upon the bed, she opened her eyes. She saw his face, half in shadow, half illumined by the kitchen lamp. It had become savage; his eyes were brutal. With anguish she realized that it was a false tenderness she had felt in him, and that she had projected a false sympathy into his heart. And she cried out incoherently against what was happening, begging him, "No. Don't. Let me go."

Willi let her go – and never knew why. It was not out of sympathy. His own soul-sickness was too profound for him to be considerate of another. And it was not out of pity, for the cruelty she had seen in his face had really been there. There was no way for Willi to have known it, but upon his face at that moment there had been something quite horrible: the expression that had gripped his features when he killed her dog. As he had changed so suddenly from a befuddled, good-natured drunkard into a man who leapt upon a dog and crushed it to death, so, along with this sudden eruption of sexuality, there had come not tenderness – which even a libidinous man can feel for his love of a moment – but a hot cruelty. Over a span of ten years Willi had been immeasurably hurt: now, festering in the dark recesses of his heart, there was a confused and inexpressible hatred. And what he hated or whom, he did not know. But in wanting Berthe, he had desired even more to hurt her.

It is hard to know what made him remove his hands from her body, and then slowly stand up... to turn his eyes away from her and gaze dully out of the window. He never knew himself. But perhaps it was only this: that the brutish giant who became sodden with schnapps and stamped a dog to death was still the man who once carried a child piggyback down by a river. The soul of that man heard Berthe's cry – and felt shame. And so he let her be.

For a long while there was silence between them. Berthe sat up. Her body and limbs were shaking, but her eyes were dry. Slowly she arranged her clothes. She watched Willi as he stood, stony-faced and empty-eyed, staring at the shadowed moonlight on her fields.

"Oh, you!" she muttered, low-voiced, hoarse with emotion. "What sort of man are you? I saw in your face… You looked at me like I was the worst thing in the world to you… you didn't want me at all. I don't know what you wanted. Oh, you're just a pig! There's never a man who isn't a pig at bottom."

"No," he stammered, turning towards her. "I don't… I'm not…" He fell silent, bewildered by the aching furies in his heart.

"Oh, I'm a fool," she cried hotly. "I knew you'd hold me cheap. Get out of here. Get out quick. Don't come back again." She burst into tears, covering her face with her hands, sobbing in humiliation and defeat.

"Don't cry," he said. "Only don't cry. You're a good woman, truly. Only…" He stopped, and then burst out in a rage: "Damn it, stop your crying! Don't make like I've done something to you. I've done nothing. I paid for your dog, didn't I? And who asked me to stay tonight? If anything happened, it was your fault! I didn't want it. I only want to be let alone."

"My fault?" She jumped to her feet with a cry of anger. "Oh, get out of here, you pig! Get out, or I'll do something to you!"

Willi turned. He hesitated a moment and then left the room. She stood still, trembling, and listened to the scrape of his shoes across the kitchen floor. The salt tears began rolling down her face. Then she caught her breath as she heard him stop at the door.

"Frau Lingg," he said from the next room, "I'm sorry. Nothing was your fault, nothing. I…" She couldn't see that his body had begun to shake, but she heard the abject stammer in his voice. "I'm sick," he said with a groan. "I don't know why I do anything."

She crossed swiftly to the door of the bedroom. She had never hated any man more than she had hated Willi when she saw the evil disregard with which he was possessing her… And yet, a moment later, he had released her. Between those two moments lay the contradiction of this man… and the torment she had to resolve.

She began to speak to him. She spoke not out of conscious deliberation, but artlessly, from the deepest truth in her heart. The tumult of emotion she felt forbade pride or shame, manoeuvre or cheap reproach.

"I thought you liked me," she said. "I asked you to stay tonight because I liked you. You know what I had in my mind? I'm not ashamed. I'm lonely. I know you're lonely too. I hoped that after a bit, if everything went right between us, you'd ask me to marry you. You think I let any man kiss me

– any stranger? I don't. But I liked you so much I couldn't help myself...
and now you've spoilt everything."

She stood still, bleeding at every pore, hoping without hope that he
would somehow heal the wounds he had inflicted upon both of them.

Willi turned around, his face twisted.

"I know," he muttered. "I could see."

"Then why were you... why did you have to..." She searched in vain
for words.

"I'm sick," he said again with a groan. He suddenly hid his face
with his big hands, as though the confession of weakness were intolerable to him. "There's nothing left in me. I'm nothing... I'm nothing
any more."

"Why?" she asked, going closer to him. "What is it with you? What
makes you this way?"

He didn't answer her question. Instead he said, looking at her now:
"Yes, I'm lonely too. I'm so lonely and sick inside, I want to kill myself."

"Is it that you don't like me, then?" she asked. "Is that the reason?"

"No, I..." He began to stammer. "I like you. But in the bedroom I...
I don't know what happened with me. You made me... I began to think of
my wife." A groan burst from his lips. "I can't stand to think of my wife.
I see her lying on the ground with her face all cut up, and her arms cut
off, and her body looking like some butcher had dug his knives into her.
It makes me want to kill somebody. If only she had died from a sickness...
If there was a funeral, maybe, if I cried like a man should cry... But ten
times a day I bury her – and she's still there, all cut up on the ground."

She went to him then, too full of sudden understanding to hate him any
longer. And when she spoke to him, there was such sorrowful compassion
in her tone that Willi felt he would be torn to pieces by the stabbing ache
in his breast. "But we're both so lonely..." she said. "For people like us
it's needed to cry together."

"Oh don't," he said brokenly, "don't. I've told you now. Now I'll go
away. I'm sorry I came."

Perhaps once in the life of a woman like Berthe there comes a moment
of such profound sympathy for another human being that it is impossible for her to hesitate over what must be done, or to be wrong in the
doing. She took his hand and pressed it to her breast. "Stay with me," she
murmured lovingly. She raised up on tiptoe and flung her arm around his
neck. She kissed his face with a wordless compassion – small, soft kisses
on cheek and mouth and forehead. "Be with me, Willi," she whispered.

"We're strangers, but we need to love each other. I love you already. Willi, I'm without shame. If you leave me, I don't know what I'll do."

He said nothing, standing in her embrace with a shaking body.

"But why should it be so hard for you to cry with me?" she asked. "I can cry over your wife too. Look at me, I can't help crying over her."

And then she held him close as his years of confusion and pain burst out into raging grief – held him and stroked his head as he wept and wept, and his tears wet her face, and his huge, iron body shook with anguish. And in that moment she knew a depth of pity and love she had never known before, or would again.

Willi lay in her arms all night. He talked fitfully and chaotically about his life, yielded to uncontrolled bursts of weeping, then talked again. At daybreak, exhausted, they fell asleep.

Chapter 10

After that stormy night, Willi looked upon Berthe with eyes that were blinded by an inexpressible gratitude. Between them there was the ripening love of a man and woman who were lonely and well met, but beneath that adult love Willi was welded to this woman as child to mother, seeing her in a radiance of adoration. She had unlocked the festering grief in his heart, and hers was the reward of having healed him back to life. Sometimes Willi fumbled to express what he felt, but his speech always ended in a helpless stammer. And at such times he would merely embrace Berthe with fierce passion, trying to tell her by his flesh what he could not speak in words.

To Berthe it was all the same. As the weeks passed, she watched with a swelling heart as the strange, hard Willi she had come to love became less hard, less strange – a Willi who could laugh, who took to whistling as he strode through her gate in the evening, a quiet companion to be taken sweetly and quietly for granted. And as the heart of the man unfolded to her, all that was without guile in her own character quickened to the gentle decency she found in him. And sometimes, as she worked in the fields, she would stop to sigh in happiness and say to herself, "How does it happen that a woman of thirty-six, with a grown son, finds a new love and a new life like this?"

Of all the days in the week, Sunday had once been the bleakest for both of them – but now it became a day of sheer joy. Weekday evenings Willi was obliged to report back to his bunkhouse by eleven at night. He would walk to the farmhouse after his supper at the factory commissary. Usually Berthe would be just coming in from the fields. He would stay until nine – rarely later, because Berthe had to rise even earlier than he – and then he would go home. But Saturday night and Sunday they spent together. And each longed for the golden weekend like a prisoner awaiting parole.

With an intensity that amused Berthe anew each Sunday, Willi set about becoming a farmer. There was no chore he did not try to take off her hands, and if he so much as carried slops to the pig pen, he would boast loudly that he was already a farmer. In the morning, while Berthe scrubbed clothes for both of them and chattered at him through an open window, Willi, stripped to the waist in the warm sun, would saw up a week's firewood. He would put down the saw when his task was finished and go over to the window to whistle at her. "Any work for your hired man?" he would ask. Then he would reach in and pull her to the window, rubbing his sweaty face against her warm throat, kissing her again and again. "Ah, you," he would exclaim, "you're a witch – you don't let a hired man do any work for you. No wonder your Spindler went off to the army."

"So?" she would reply, slapping his hard chest. "So?" And he would grin at her as she hit him, proud of his strength. "Come on out, woman," he would say. "I'll show you some gymnastics."

"Ha! Ha! Gymnastics! Do gymnastics grow potatoes, I'd like to know?"

"You need exercise. You're getting fat."

"Exercise? When did a farmer ever need exercise? You think I push buttons all week, like you?"

"Push buttons!" he would say. "Hah – push buttons!"

When it was time for the milking, they would go down to the barn together, with Willi imitating the trill of every field bird that piped on the way. Each Sunday Berthe would shake with laughter to see him pull mightily and in vain at the teats of a protesting cow. "Oh, you dunderhead!" she would shout at him lovingly. "How will you ever be a farmer? You have to *squeeze* out the milk, not tear the bag to pieces. It's not a machine, you brute." And each Sunday Willi would be the one to crawl into the chicken house. He would emerge with the warm eggs in his big hands and an unvarying expression of astonishment on his face as he reflected on the ways of Nature. And he would stand by the pig pen, dumb with a city dweller's wonder as he contemplated the spectacle of six little grunters nuzzling the belly of a sow... until Berthe would exclaim with mockery, "So... so... are you coming or aren't you? Or do you want to get down there and suck yourself?"

In their free hours there was always the accordion to play, or a stroll through the sweet-smelling fields, or occasionally a walk to the village. And there Berthe would hold Willi's arm with naked pride and promenade down the street like a queen.

At night for the few hours before Willi returned to the factory, there was... themselves. They would lie with the moonlight like a cool blue shawl over their rapt bodies. Their hunger for each other was frenetic and insatiable, startling even to themselves. Once, bursting with a sense of happiness that he could scarcely contain within his grateful heart, Willi exclaimed, "What sort of a woman are you anyway? You make me feel like I was... I don't know... nineteen again... like my life was just beginning."

He was surprised by Berthe's reaction. In sudden, loving sorrow she replied, "You're too good a man for me, Willi."

"What?" he demanded. "Such talk…"

"Truly you are. I can tell. Oh, Willi, if I do things you don't like, try not to mind. Just remember that I love you."

"What are you talking about? And what sort of a man do you think I am?"

"You? You're perfect."

He guffawed. "Sure."

"Well… you tell me, then, what sort of a man you are."

"Me? Oh, I…" He fell silent.

"You're asleep?" She jiggled him in the ribs.

"Who knows what sort I am?" he answered moodily.

She raised up on her elbow to look at him. "What are you thinking?" she asked seriously.

"Nothing. What should I be thinking?"

"That's what *I'm* asking." She laughed. "Oh, you men!"

"Oh, you women," he replied with mockery. "I'll tell you: I like to play the accordion, I like to whistle, I like to work and…" – catching her suddenly to him in a wrestler's grip – "I like gymnastics."

"That I know," she laughed. "And what else?"

"Nothing."

"You like to go to church? After we're married I'd like to go some Sundays. Will you go with me? It's the way we farm people get together."

"Sure."

"You like to see friends?"

"Sure."

"I want you to meet the Guttmanns – and there's Irma Winz, my next neighbour. She's one of my oldest friends."

"Irma!" Willi exclaimed.

"You know her?"

"No. There was another Irma I knew once."

"I'm jealous. Was she your girl?"

"No. The wife of a friend."

"Who was he?"

Willi didn't answer for a moment. He had never spoken to Berthe about Karl, and he found now that it was very difficult for him. But finally he told her.

"Oh," she said. "But of course… if he was a Communist… good riddance to him, I say."

For the first time since they had become lovers Willi raised his voice in anger. (The next night he apologized abjectly.) "He was a good man," he replied harshly. "Why do you talk about what you don't know? He was a decent man, and it was not decent to kill him."

Frightened, Berthe stammered, "But... I'm sorry... excuse me. You're right. I didn't know him. I shouldn't have spoken." Then, as he remained silent, "Are you... You never talk about the... the Party or the government, Willi? Are you one of those who..."

"I never talk about them because I don't think about them," he answered harshly. "All I want is to live quiet."

Willi was evading. Nowadays, in his secret thoughts, he had begun to think about politics incessantly – even though he didn't want to, and even though he would turn his mind to other matters when he became aware of his thoughts.

"All I want is to live quiet," he repeated now in the same harsh tone. "I want to work... to be here on the farm, if I can... and to have you." He embraced her passionately. "I don't care about anything else, or what's happening next door even. If only we can live quiet and decent here."

"Of course we will – of course," Berthe told him fervently. "You'll see what a good wife I'll make you, Willi. And if there are things I do that you don't like, will you tell me, darling, so I can change?"

In reply Willi laughed long and loud. He stroked her face, gazing at her tenderly. "You don't know how I love you, Berthe," he whispered. "With you I forget everything from the past that I don't like to remember. You're like... I don't know what. But without you I'd be nothing."

In warm embrace they clung to each other. "Darling," she whispered, "sometimes... when we're like this... do you still think of... well, of your first wife?"

"No," he said softly, "no!"

"I never think of Johann either. Never, Willi."

They were both telling only a half-truth, but it was good that they were, for it was the way of a man and a woman who need to love each other.

2

Life had become good for Berthe and Willi – but it was also not wholly good. There were several reasons for this, and the first was Anna Mahnke. A few weeks after Willi became a steady visitor at the farm, Berthe received a formal call from the Community Welfare Leader. And after Anna had enquired briskly about Berthe's health and Berthe, thank you, about Anna's well-known gall-bladder condition, Anna got down to business.

"So," she commenced with a warm smile, "the first thing is to offer congratulations, eh?"

"About what?"

Anna's smile broadened. "Herr Wegler, naturally."

Berthe was flabbergasted. "How do you know about him?"

"What's the difference? I have my ways." She laughed with not a little pride.

"But I want to know," Berthe insisted. It was not out of curiosity, but out of dismay that she asked. Deeply as she already loved Willi, it couldn't be said that she knew everything about him. Some men boasted of their women. Had Willi been making a parade of her at the factory? "Please tell me," she insisted. "I have my reasons."

"Well, it's no magic. When one of the factory workers takes to staying away from his bunkhouse regularly every Saturday night, the authorities want to know where he goes. That's all."

"Someone followed Willi, you mean?"

"So what's the matter with that? It's time of war. There has to be a check-up. Anyway, everything's fine. Herr Wegler is spending his Saturday nights with Frau Lingg. Splendid! Everybody is happy. Naturally the information is sent to my office. First chance I get, I come out here. So... here we are! And now tell me: how are things getting along?"

"All right."

"It's settled between you? You're to be married?"

"It's settled."

"Splendid. You're pregnant already, I hope?"

"No."

"What's the matter?"

Silence...

"Monday morning Doctor Zoder, from the factory, holds a clinic in town. You'll come in and he'll examine you."

Berthe scratched the tiny pockmarks at the side of her nose. "Why should he examine me? I'm *healthy*."

"Why? To see why you're not pregnant."

"I know why I'm not pregnant. Because I don't want to be. When I'm married, I'll have a child. Not before."

"So that's it!" Anna's voice turned cold. "In the year 1942 a German woman to speak like her grandmother!"

"In the year 1942 a bastard is still a bastard."

The remark made Anna absolutely furious. "Don't use that word! There's no such word any more. A child is a child. You think you can dirty an innocent German child by using a dirty word? Only your own mind is dirty. You should be ashamed."

A shrug from Berthe... She stood gripping the earth stubbornly, her strong, thick legs set wide, her hands on her hips. There was an extended silence.

Anna, deciding to be conciliatory, adopted a new approach.

"By the way – I've been meaning to ask you... Your record card says you gave birth to three children, but only one is living."

"Rudi. He's in the army."

"Rudi, I know. A splendid boy. But the other two must have died before I moved here?"

"Yes."

"Ill health, was it? It should state on your card. The way they kept records in the old days is a scandal."

"They were both small when they died," Berthe told her quietly. "Girls... The little one fell in the well when they were playing – at least, that's what we figured – and the other tried to help her."

"What a tragedy – dreadful. But at least it wasn't ill health."

Silence.

"When do you intend to get married, then?"

"Rudi wants to meet Herr Wegler. After that! Rudi's coming home on furlough soon."

"So it'll be soon?"

"A few weeks, I expect."

"A few weeks only? Then why shouldn't you start the child now?"

Berthe grinned slyly. "If it's only a few weeks, why can't I start the child then?"

"Who knows what can come up to interfere later?"

"Hah – who knows indeed? That's why I'm waiting."

"But how can you think only of yourself, Berthe? You're not the selfish kind, surely. Hitler expects every fertile woman to do her part in this war. That means bearing children."

Silence...

"Well?"

Silence...

"Berthe – you must understand that these matters are no longer private. I don't come here as a busybody. This is the business of the Folk."

Silence…

"*Ach*…" Anna laughed. "You peasants! When you want to be stubborn, it's like pushing against a stone wall. Very well – I'll be in to see you again. Goodbye, Berthe."

"Goodbye."

This was the beginning of their struggle. A week later Anna returned. Had Berthe heard from Rudi? Oh! The furlough was postponed, was it? There – what a waste of time! Months might be lost this way. What was the sense of it? And how unpatriotic!

Anna was tireless in her arguments. But since persuasion alone couldn't make Berthe pregnant, the situation between them became slightly comic. Indeed the whole affair would only have amused Berthe if it had not been for Willi himself. In a way that Berthe could not define, she gradually began to sense things about Willi that troubled her. It was as though a thread of shoddy had intruded into the fine fabric of their relationship, and, try as she might, she could not pull it loose.

The trouble commenced when they came to discuss their marriage in practical terms. Eager as Berthe herself was for the consummation of their relationship, she was forced to raise the question of her son. Legally, on the basis of the new decrees concerning ownership of the soil, the land belonged to Rudi. If Willi and Berthe were to look forward to a stable future on the farm, Rudi's approval of their union was essential. And although Berthe now wanted Willi above all else in the world, she also wanted her son's love, and the right to live on the farm.

"But what if he says no?" Willi asked when she first informed him of all this. "Anyway, it's crazy for two grown people to ask a boy of eighteen for permission to marry."

"He won't say no. It isn't really his permission we're asking."

"If that's so, then why don't we get married now?"

"That I *can't* do, Willi. After all, my own son… In decency I have to let him know beforehand. I've explained the law to you. We're hereditary peasants now, and—"

"I understand the law. But what if your boy does say no? What if he feels one man on the farm is enough?"

"He won't. I promise. Two men are needed here."

"You don't answer me, Berthe. I say: let's get married. If your son doesn't like it, too bad. You think I need this farm to support you? I don't!"

"But why can't you wait, Willi? How long will it take for him to answer a letter?"

"I say: let's get married."

And in the weeks that followed, as they waited for Rudi's answer, Willi kept up the single refrain: "Berthe... why don't we get married? Let's get married, Berthe." He didn't shout it, and he didn't beg. And yet after a bit Berthe began to notice that whenever he said "Let's get married" it was always in the same tone of voice. The tone puzzled her, and she tried in vain to understand it. There was something wistful about it, and something lost, and something hungry. And it was all so mixed-up she couldn't grasp what lay behind it.

Nor did Willi understand it. He only knew that he had an acute hunger to begin upon his new life. The factory had begun to oppress him now, for it carried memories of Düsseldorf. He needed to be able to say: "*This* is my life – *this*; there has never been any other."

It was not long before a similar conflict arose between them over the question of a child. One night, as Berthe was telling him about the farm and her troubles with it, Willi suddenly interrupted her:

"Berthe, there's something I've been wanting to ask you."

"Yes?" ("You haven't been paying any attention to me, have you, darling?")

"You said... Once you said that you could still have children. That's so, Berthe?"

"I think it is. One can't be sure, but my mother had children until she was forty-three."

"Well, so... you think maybe you're pregnant already?" he asked eagerly.

"No."

"How do you know?"

"I know."

"You've had a period?"

She laughed. "There are other ways of knowing."

"How, Berthe?"

"You booby... I use something... I don't want to become pregnant yet."

Willi fell silent. He was hurt by her answer.

"You don't want to, Berthe?"

"Not until after we're married. What do you think?"

"Of course, but then... why don't we get married, Berthe?"

"Willi, Willi... we've talked about it a dozen times already. You know why."

"I know. Darling, I know – it would be better to wait until we were married, but…"

"But what, Willi?"

"But I… want a child, Berthe. Not if it would be dangerous for you, but—"

"Hah! I can still have a whole litter, I'm positive," she interrupted proudly. "I'm healthy as a sow. And you" – leaning over the table to kiss him avidly – "I think you could make me pregnant if I was sixty. The way you go at a girl."

"Then… since we're going to be married anyway—"

"No!" she interrupted. "Not until we're married."

"Yes… I suppose so. It's better to wait." His tone was troubled, and he was frowning.

"My goodness, Willi – let me ask you something. Why are you in such a hurry to get married and have a child? Why can't you wait for a month or two?"

"I… don't know, Berthe." He began to laugh a little. "It's silly, isn't it?"

"You know what I've been thinking?" she observed shrewdly. "There's something behind all this hurry."

"What?"

"Hah – if I knew, do you think I wouldn't tell you long ago? Maybe you don't like factory work any more – you're in a hurry to be a farmer. You think farm work's easy. Is that it?"

"Hm!"

"Hm!" she mocked. "What?"

"I don't know. I'm thinking."

"All right, my sweetheart, you think. But I'm a farmer and I'm going to sleep now. I don't have any machines to work for me. There's no little steam hammer to pull my weeds for me. So off with you – back to your bunkhouse."

"'Little steam hammer…' Someday you'll see it," he told her jestingly. "You'll see what sort of a man I am."

"Ah, I know, I know." She flung her arms around him. "I know." She bent over him, kissing his face softly. "My darling, don't be worried about anything. We'll be married. And we'll have a child, more than one."

Willi pressed his face to her breast. "Ah yes," he said. "Yes, I want it."

"Oh, Willi – maybe I… Maybe a woman should hide her feelings more – but I can't. You don't know how much I love you, darling." She began to laugh softly. "If you told me to steal, I'd steal. If you told me to…

anything – I can't hide it, Willi. I'd crawl down the street for you, if you told me, like a dog..."

"Just let's get married, Berthe."

She burst out laughing. "Oh, you!... Like a phonograph record. Goodnight, my phonograph record, I'm going to sleep now. And listen – you fall right asleep too. Don't start worrying over your stupid worries, whatever they are."

"Worry? Who worries? I never worry."

"You do. It's no use lying to me. I wish you could get another job. It's that terrible hammer, I bet."

"You know, Berthe, I'll tell you: I've started thinking the same thing myself. I don't like the hammer so much any more. It seems harder now. But I spoke to the foreman yesterday, just hinting like, and he doesn't want to let me off."

"Well, never mind, Willi. Soon we'll get married, won't we? And then you'll come to live on the farm."

"That's what I've thought. For another little while I can stick it out."

"Goodnight, darling. Sleep well."

"Goodnight."

But sleep no longer came easily to Willi. Berthe had eased his heart so that it was no longer necessary for him to deny life to himself. He could accept the events of his past now – not without bitterness, but as an old sadness that could be borne. And yet it was not at all the same Willi who stepped out of the grave as had numbly entered it. For this Willi felt an angry uneasiness towards life that he had never known before – a vague, powerful discomfort that he could not understand or control. He would lie awake sometimes, his body exhausted but his mind in a ferment, and he would ask himself, "What's the matter with me? What am I so upset about? It can't be Berthe, surely. I love Berthe. Is it the damn hammer? What sort of a fool am I anyway? Why don't I go to sleep?" But he would continue to lie awake, feeling so hot all over that he would suddenly throw back the blanket and groan in physical distress.

And this new Willi was plagued by a burning need to *think* – to examine his life and the life of other men, to understand his past, his son, his friend Karl... to try and abstract some meaning from the careless years that had ended so badly.

And out of this confusion and uneasiness would come his repeated wistful plea: "Let's get married, darling. Let's have a child." For it seemed to him that all would be well if only his new life came to flower.

It was this that tainted Berthe's happiness. Sometimes she would talk to Willi about matters of the utmost importance – only to discover that he had not even been listening. "Oh what a day today!" she told him once. "Listen to me, Willi, tell me what to do. I went to see Rosenhart today. He's the Peasant Leader in our district. Did I ever tell you he was after me to marry him?"

"No," Willi replied. It was a warm June evening, and they were sitting out of doors. "What a night! Smell the air, Berthe."

"Listen to me. I want to tell you about Rosenhart."

"I'm listening."

"Erich's an important man around here. A nice man too, and an old friend. He wants to meet you. Anyway, I went to see him. 'Erich,' I said, 'for God's sake – I need some help on my farm. A woman can't tend twelve acres alone.'

"'Help is coming, Berthe,' he answers me. 'They've promised us labour gangs.'

"'You told me that weeks ago,' I said.

"'I can't help it,' he yells at me. 'I'm not keeping them in my kitchen.'

"'But look, Erich,' I said, 'be reasonable. The Farm Bureau gave me cattle from Denmark, correct? Fine animals. But even Danish cattle have to eat, don't they? So all right – I have three acres in hay for winter feeding. Two cuttings those acres will need this summer. Who's to do it? I have three acres in sugar beets by your orders. But will you order the hogs to harvest them when the time comes? And my potatoes, my soy beans... How can a woman alone care for all of this? Even when my hired man was here – but now he's gone...' You see how I told him, Willi? I told him straight all right. So then Erich gets mad. He's a nice man, but he always gets into a temper...

"'Go home,' he said. 'You're not the only farmer around here in a fix. Maybe you don't know we're at war.'

"You think I went home, Willi? Ha ha – not me. I know better. If I make a fuss now, I'll get help when help comes. That's the only way. So just like I was deaf I said to him, 'All I want to know, Peasant Leader Rosenhart, is what my swine will eat in January if no one is brought in to harvest my sugar beets. You think I'll let you take my farm away when I have to slaughter my hogs?'

"'You slaughter your hogs without permission, and you'll be in a concentration camp before you can wink your eye.' That's what he told me. Can you imagine?

"'So send me help,' I said.

"'Dammit! Dammit! Go home now. You could be weeding a whole acre of potatoes instead of gabbing. When help comes, you'll get it.'

"So I went home, Willi. When Erich says 'Dammit! Dammit!' I always know it's time to go home. But I'll be back to see him next week, don't worry. I know what I'm doing... But you see how it is. I have problems enough to drive me crazy."

And after all of this, when the least Berthe expected was a word of comfort, Willi suddenly said, "Think of it – ten thousand dead today. That's what the war means."

She was astonished. "What?"

"Just think of it, Berthe. That's what this war means. Today ten thousand men died in this world. Twice as many, perhaps."

"You mean to say you weren't listening to me at all, Willi?"

"I was listening. Of course." He cracked his big knuckles in embarrassment.

"So tell me something I said. And don't do that, Willi. I can't stand it when you crack your knuckles. It sends shivers through me."

"I'm sorry... About Rosenhart it was."

"And what did I say?"

"I heard you, Berthe. Only I began to think: 'Today, in one day, how many men died? Women, too, probably, and children.' I remember how it was in the trenches in 1918. I'd look at the moon and I'd think, 'The same moon is shining over peaceful, sleeping towns. How is it possible?' That's what I started to think now."

"Yes, it's horrible," Berthe agreed, shrugging. "But what good does it do to think of it?"

"Why should it happen? That's what I keep thinking."

"What do you mean? We're at war. Now, why aren't you like me, Willi? I try not to think of the war. Whenever the notion comes into my head that my Rudi might be sent to the Russian front, I forget it right away. What's the use of such thoughts? There's always trouble in the world – war or no war. There's always people dying for nothing, I suppose, and some going hungry. But what's to do? You have to think of yourself, that's all. You can't think of the whole world..."

Why was there war at all? Willi would ask. Who was responsible? Was it the same gang in this war as in the last – the munitions makers, as Karl had always said? And when would peace come? And what would life be like afterwards? Would the old days ever return – the old Germany? Or were the National Socialists in for good?

His questions, more especially his sudden, brooding silence, frightened Berthe. He was thinking too much, she told him. If others heard such questions, he might get into trouble.

And Willi, gazing at her with his blue, abstracted eyes, would muse softly, "Yes, trouble. There's a word to think about, too. Trouble. I never wanted to get into trouble, did I? No, that's right."

"So who ever wants to get into trouble, Willi? What are you talking about? What are you trying to say?"

"Nothing, Berthe, nothing," he would reply softly. "I'm just thinking. I'm trying to find out."

"What are you trying to find out – what?"

"I don't know. There's something."

"You're talking like a loony. Stop thinking now. Play the accordion."

"Yes. Yes, I'm a duncehead," he would agree suddenly. "What am I worrying about?" Then, whistling, he would go into the house for the accordion. He would come back to lean over the instrument, hump over it in apparent concentration, but Berthe could see that he was still thinking, still wondering. And invariably at these times he would play one song over and over again. It was an aria from Handel's *Messiah** that he had learnt by rote. He didn't know the composer's name, or the words: "*He was despised and rejected of men, a man of sorrows and acquainted with grief.*" But he played it endlessly, as though this music and no other could satisfy what was in his heart...

And all of this grieved Berthe, became the ugly taint in their happiness. But at such moments she too told herself that once they were married, once Willi had come to live on the farm with her, all would be well. So the weeks passed, of spring and of early summer.

They heard from Rudi, finally. While his letter settled nothing absolutely, it gave real promise. Even Willi admitted that the lad was being fair. Rudi replied that a second marriage was solely up to his mother. She was still young, and he could understand her desire for another husband. On the other hand, since they would all have to live together on one farm, he asked her to delay the marriage until he met Willi. That, he said, would be very soon. He was expecting a furlough at the end of July.

That evening was the happiest Willi and Berthe were ever to spend together. It was a Saturday night, and they lay in each other's arms talking joyously of their years to come, of the farm, of how blessed it was to have each other. And for the first time since Willi had emerged from the bomb shelter in Düsseldorf, he felt absolutely confident that the future held a secure place for him.

At eleven that night, when the factory siren warned them that British planes would soon be passing overhead, they lay in warm embrace, listening and laughing quietly. The war and the world were just outside – but they were free of both. On this bit of earth they had marked an island. On this they would remain.

Chapter 11

It was late afternoon. A warm sun poured through the curtained windows of Berthe's kitchen, tinting the floor with a filigree of gold, making her feel as though God Himself were blessing her home. Not since the first day of war had the household worn so festive an air. Wild flowers graced the room in a dozen places – in vases, in a garland over the mirror, on the table. The worn floor gleamed in its cleanliness, the brass kettles shone, the kitchen was savoury with the rich, sweet odours of roasting pork and new potatoes.

Quietly Berthe tiptoed around the room. She set the table with the lace cloth she had received at her marriage; it had been used only a dozen times in twenty years. She peered into the oven, sniffing, now and again basting the fat meat that was slowly turning to the softness of butter.

The table was set for three. Again and again with hot pride Berthe whispered to herself, "My two men at the same table." And every so often she stopped to glance into the mirror. Each time she viewed herself she would see a radiantly smiling face, a face unable to repress the rapture in her soul. And constantly she watched the old clock, waiting for the hand to mark five.

Her son was home. He had walked into the yard before noon, his bulging knapsack slung over one shoulder, a heavy package tied over the other, his cap at a rakish angle. He had looked so handsome in his uniform that Berthe almost died with pride as she rushed out to meet him. Rudi had gone to war an apple-cheeked lad, an unmistakable farm boy whose round, good-natured face seemed young for his hulking body. He was more than a year older now. She saw that at her first glance. His face was thinner, and there was a thrust to his heavy jaw. And his body was both bigger and leaner. Maturity had come in this year, and it was with a sweet bitterness that she recognized it.

"Well, Mamma," he said as they hugged each other, "how do you like your farmer now?"

"Rudi, you're so handsome! You're taller, your shoulders are bigger… Hah!… What Hedda Guttmann will say when she sees you!" She kissed him feverishly, seeking words for her love, angry that she had nothing to say except silly things, such as her reference to Hedda Guttmann. "Oh darling, a whole year it's been… such a long, hard year."

"Now, Mamma, what do women always have to cry for?" he asked pettishly.

"Never mind. If I want to cry a little, I'll cry. You're well? You've been all right?"

"Strong as a bull." He couldn't repress a boastful grin. "God knows farm work takes muscle. But the army makes a man of you, I can tell you that! You ought to see my chest now, my legs."

"You, a man! Not yet nineteen. A baby."

Grinning, Rudi swung her up in his arms. "Into the pigpen with you! From now on it's Herr Lingg, master of the house… Well?"

Berthe hugged him in overflowing pride. "Correct. From now on it's Herr Lingg. I won't even dare call you Rudi." His manliness thrilled her. Her mind's eye could remember him so clearly as a young toddler – the black, bushy hair, the pudgy cheeks, the two crooked front teeth. The man still had those angular front teeth – but now Rudi was lean and tanned and husky, and his bushy hair was a close-shaven bristle, and his thick neck looked almost swollen against the tight military collar. "Well, Herr Lingg," she asked laughing, "and does it feel good to be back home?"

"Home!" Rudi said. "You don't know. I won't say I haven't liked the army. So far it's been a picnic, in fact. But home!" He began to laugh, his hearty, good-natured laugh of old. "When the war's over and I come back, I won't even budge over to Poppel's beerhouse. Come along now, Mamma…" He seized her arm. "Show me the farm – I want to see everything."

They had spent the first hour examining the stock and the growing crops. Rudi had shaken his head over the hay – it was getting dry and long past cutting. "You wait much longer and it will flower, Mamma, it'll be no good." He had listened, for the moment all farmer, to Berthe's tale of her difficulties, of the impossibility of running the farm by herself. And then, inevitably, they had come to the one matter they had not hitherto mentioned.

"So," he said jovially, "now I see why you want to get married. You need hired help, eh?"

"Not only that." She flushed a little. "A woman as young as I am – she still wants a companion."

"Sure," said her son genially. He stood off and gazed at her. "You know – you're not such a bad-looking woman."

"*Ach* – stop it."

"I mean it. Before this you were only... my Mamma. Now I've been away, I can see you differently. Well... so what sort of a man is this one, eh?"

In glowing terms Berthe described Willi: he was respectable, capable, strong enough to do anything, still young.

"Is he a Party man?"

Berthe hesitated. "I don't think so."

"Too bad."

"His son was awarded an Iron Cross," Berthe told him anxiously.

"So?"

"He was killed in Norway."

"Very good – but I'm sorry Willi isn't an old Party man."

"How is it you're so strong for politics now, Rudi? You never cared much."

Rudi shrugged. "You learn things in the army. Lectures all the time. I'm educated now. I'm no dumb farmer any more."

"So what about Willi?"

"Well... I have no real objection... provided it's understood that the farm is mine."

"Of course it's yours. By law. Willi understands that."

"I'm not talking about that. I know the law too – the farm is for me and my eldest son. I don't like arguments is what I mean. When I come back, I want to run the farm without anybody trying to tell me how."

"Why should he try to tell you? You're the farmer. Not him."

"Who knows? That's why I wanted to see him first – to size him up."

"A quiet, good man, Rudi. You'll see. He's coming tonight."

"All right. If we get along, fine. You can get married tomorrow. If not..." He shrugged. "I'm no baby any more, Mamma. I've thought this all over. You can get married if you want to, of course, but I don't want anybody on my farm who'll be a nuisance."

"You'll like him – you surely will, Rudi."

"All right, we'll see tonight. Right now let's leave it. I'm sleepy. I haven't slept for two days."

"My poor baby. You mean it?"

"Had to stand half of last night too. The trains are... you just can't imagine."

"But what about tonight? In the letter you sent from the railroad station you wanted me to ask people for tonight. Your very first night home – I didn't understand why."

"Did you ask them?"

"Yes, but now you're tired."

"An afternoon's sleep and I'll be fine. You ought to see us on manoeuvres sometimes – march all day, sleep four hours, march again. I'm used to it… So, who's coming tonight?"

"Well… you asked only the Guttmanns. That's all I invited. Willi too, of course."

"How's Hedda?"

"Hedda I haven't seen since you left. She's been working in the factory. And not even her mother. Since they took the horses away, right after ploughing, nobody can visit at all. You've been writing to Hedda?"

"No."

"Why all this interest in her?"

"Well…" Rudi grinned. "I always liked her. When I started to think of a furlough, I started to think of Hedda. Who knows… I may want to get married after the war."

"Off to sleep with you, then. Hedda mustn't see you looking dead. Your room's all ready."

"Got anything to drink for the party tonight?" he asked as they went into the kitchen.

"No… a half-bottle of some blackberry wine."

"You mean the same stuff we had when I went away?"

"Yes."

Rudi guffawed. "A baby couldn't celebrate decently on that. No… I think maybe we better have champagne tonight."

"Champagne? Surely! Of course! And what else, Herr Lingg?"

"You think I'm joking?" He tore open one side of the bulky package he had brought home and began to pull out straw-covered bottles. Grinning, he set them on the table in a spectacular row. There were seven in all. "*Voilà* – as the Frenchies say. Tonight we'll have champagne."

"Rudi… it must have cost you I don't know how much! Such a waste of money."

He grinned. "In France a German soldier can buy things for nothing. Now, Mamma, another thing. Let me smell you." He pulled her close and sniffed her neck ostentatiously. "*Pfui* – you smell like a farmer." He opened his knapsack. He fished around and brought out a small coloured box. "You know what perfume is? Or are you such an ignorant peasant woman you never heard the name?"

"Of course I know," Berthe replied excitedly. "You bought it for me?"

"Not for the cows. Ever have any?"

"Once. Your father brought some from the city once. But not like this. I can tell how expensive this is," she said excitedly as she opened the box. "I've seen in the advertisements. Real French perfume, imagine! I'll smell like fairies." She sniffed. "It's like flowers, Rudi, like heaven."

"And now, Mamma," he said, standing off to look at her, "it seems to me you wrote in a letter last winter that you had to give up your sweater in the collection."

"You didn't get me a sweater too? You didn't, Rudi!"

Rudi fished in the bag. "I'll tell you the truth: it's not exactly new – a sample in a store. But just as good as new." Triumphantly he brought out the garment. "Do you know how much a sweater like this would cost in Germany?"

Berthe's eyes glowed. It was pure wool, wine-coloured and soft. "Oh, Rudi darling, I can't believe it. You couldn't even buy a thing like this in Germany. If you were a millionaire, maybe…"

"You like it?"

"Do I like it? Ha… Anna Mahnke should try and get this one from me. I'll murder her first."

"And how about this?" He pulled out two pink nightgowns. They were of fine silk, trimmed with lace at the bodice.

Berthe was left speechless. The tears came into her eyes, and she caught Rudi to her, kissing him. "Ah, God, what it is to have a son who loves you!"

"Now, Mamma, crying again!"

"How can I help it?" She laughed. "I won't even dare wear such things. I'll look like a cinema actress."

"You mean you won't wear them?"

"Of course, of course I'll wear them. I'll feel like a queen. But who ever thought? My God, how rich those Frenchies must be!"

Rudi burst out laughing. "Not so rich any more. The stores are cleaned out by now, I can tell you. The soldiers didn't leave a thing."

"But how much all this cost, Rudi!"

"It's like I told you, Mamma. The rate of exchange makes everything dirt cheap – twenty French francs for one mark. We go into a restaurant… order a meal… we have wine, beer, meat, pastry… and the whole thing costs one mark. So now… I'm off to sleep. Strict orders: wake me up by five o'clock. I want to shave, take a bath…"

"I'll start hot water on the stove. But six o'clock will be time enough. Willi doesn't get here from the factory till seven."

"Five o'clock. Those are orders! I want to look over the farm again."

"Yes, my soldier," she said laughing. "Five o'clock!"

Rudi went off to sleep. And Berthe, in a glow of happiness, set about preparing for the evening's party.

Now, peering at the clock again, she saw that at last the hands had moved to five. She stopped before the mirror for a last glance at her handsome sweater. Then she walked quietly into Rudi's room.

Asleep, his face relaxed, Rudi looked so young that she winced at the thought of one like him facing the agonies of war. Other women's sons might be killed, but it couldn't happen to her. God would surely spare him. She bent over, kissing his forehead softly. How much he was like his father! she thought. He had her own dark eyes and hair, but the rest of him was wholly like his father – the thick nose, the heavy brows, the square, heavy chin. He was no movie actor in looks, but like his father he had the look of a man – of a German farmer with sound stock behind him. It was character and blood that counted, after all, not cute noses. Not every woman had a son who would think of his mother as Rudi had thought of her – writing letters so faithfully, bringing back presents when he came on furlough. The father had been a good man and a good farmer, and his son would be too.

"So, Rudi," she said, shaking him gently, "it's five o'clock."

Rudi's face took on a strained, anxious look, then his eyes flicked open.

"My goodness – what's the matter?" Berthe asked.

He relaxed with a slight laugh. "Would you believe it – I was dreaming about the damn French." He shook his head and began to guffaw, but with half-hearted amusement only. "I remember now. A Frenchy came into my barracks with a knife in his hand. Dammit, it was as long as a bayonet. He was just bending over me when I woke up. Those pigs! They've got everybody nervous these days. You don't know what kind of people they are, Mamma. No culture. And ugly-tempered. Real swine, I tell you!"

She stroked his forehead. "Poor Rudi. How awful the war is."

He yawned, showing his strong, crooked teeth that were discoloured by tobacco stains. "I'm still sleepy."

"Well, Herr General, you told your lieutenant to wake you up at five o'clock. It's to the minute. I obey orders, Herr General. I'm disciplined."

"Mamma, how nice you look in the sweater. Hm! Like the wife of a banker, I swear, of a Reichstag deputy."

"It's not too tight?" she asked anxiously. "I was afraid it fitted a little too tight."

He eyed the prominent mould of her breasts. The sweater was a size too small. "No," he lied. "It's just perfect. Wear it in good health." With amusement he thought to himself, "You have too much in front, Mamma. The Frenchy didn't have so much. Regular pumpkins, you're carrying." Instantly he felt a surge of guilt. It was dirty to think of his own mother in that manner. But then he began to laugh to himself. "What the hell," he thought. "I didn't come from a tree, now, did I? Papa lay on top of Mamma and they did what all people do. I suppose when this Willi sees Mamma in that sweater, he'll want to have her right off. It's funny. Seems like my own mamma wouldn't want anything like that. But that's only a kid's notion. That's what you think when you're twelve, when you first hear about it. Hell... that Frenchy was no younger than Mamma."

"Well, lazy," said Berthe, "your hot water's ready. Should I pour it in the tub?"

"Fine. What do I smell cooking?"

"Nothing. Supper tonight won't be much."

"Mamma! It's roast pork!"

Berthe's face glowed. "And new potatoes. The Farm Bureau will have a few less potatoes this fall, and one less little pig, but my Rudi will eat some good meals while he's here. You know what I did this spring? I held out one little pig when Erich Rosenhart came counting."

"You didn't. If you'd been caught—"

"Don't worry. Erich likes me. I wasn't afraid. If it'd been anyone else... Anyway, do you know what we'll have tomorrow?" She saw the change of expression that came over his face, and her burst of happy chatter ceased.

"Tomorrow, tomorrow," said Rudi quietly. He grimaced. "I'm afraid we won't eat together tomorrow, Mamma. I was going to wait until later tonight to tell you, but I suppose it makes no real difference."

"You're not staying the ten days?" She asked it although she already knew the answer.

He shook his head.

In sheer desperation: "A week only?"

"Now don't cry, Mamma. I'm leaving tonight."

Berthe's face went white. Her mouth began to tremble.

"Not tonight. Surely not *tonight*?"

"There's a train coming through at one thirty in the morning. I have to take it."

"But it's so unfair. A whole year you've been away without a furlough."

"War, Mamma."

"If you were an officer, you'd get furloughs," she observed bitterly.

"Now, Mamma – don't talk like that! It's not respectful. Officers are officers."

"In your last letter – the one before the train – you said you'd have ten days positive."

"Yes, but listen – you know where I'd be now if I wasn't going to school? In Russia. My division went on one train, I and a few other lucky ones came home. Be glad, Mamma." He patted her hand. For a moment a sly, humorous look came over his face, making her wonder what he was up to. She knew that look well – the son had learnt it from the father.

"So?" she asked knowingly. "What are you hiding from me?"

Rudi began to chuckle. "I'll tell you, Mamma. I figured we'd be sent to Russia. So I applied for admission to the Elite Guard." He nudged her in the side with his thumb, the laughter rumbling just beneath his words. "I'm patriotic as the next man – but why should I go to Russia if I can help it? Most of the Waffen SS divisions stay... you know where?"

"Where?"

"Right here at home."

"Rudi!"

His laughter burst out. "So maybe I'll be guarding Russian prisoners for the rest of the war. Hell – you know what the lads call Russia among themselves, Mamma? 'The land of the meat-grinder.'"

Berthe too began to laugh. She squeezed his hand, and her black eyes glowed. "In the Lingg family we're smart, eh? Oh you... I knew you were up to something."

"You knew! How did you know?"

"I could tell. You and your father both. I remember..." She began to quiver with laughter. "Do you remember about the ducks, Rudi – the time your father sold the ducks?"

Rudi grinned.

"You were only a lad then, but—"

"Sold them by the pound, eh?" said Rudi, guffawing.

Berthe shook with laughter, remembering it. Almost fifteen years back, a party of city people had stopped off at their farm with cash in their pockets and a taste for duck in their mouths.

"You have ducks?" they enquired eagerly.

Rudi's father had nodded in silence, but Berthe had observed that sly, humorous look beginning to capture his face – the look that always meant he was up to something clever.

"Will you sell us four ducks? We're to have a picnic, you see. We're going to a camping ground."

Again he had nodded.

"At what price?"

"What price do you pay in the city? The same, naturally."

"In the city there are no feathers on a bird."

"I'll pull the feathers."

"Ah, but what we pay in the city is not what you sell for here," the leading vacationist had pointed out shrewdly. "There are middlemen. They make a profit from both of us."

"True."

"In that case, let's split the difference. We'll buy cheaper than usual, you'll sell higher. We'll pay by the pound." He mentioned a figure.

"Agreed. You want fat ducks or lean?"

"Fat! Fat! It makes better eating. But prepare them quickly, please, and for roasting. We have forty miles to go."

"Fat they will be," said Rudi's father. And on his face Berthe had seen the very expression that had crossed Rudi's features a moment before. Later she discovered the reason. Her Johann had put over an old farmer's trick, forbidden by law when selling to market. With a darning needle he had thrust a hole into the large vein in the breast of each of the ducks. Then, with a hose, he had filled their veins with water. It was a matter of only a minute to do the job, and never before or since had three-pound ducks left their farm weighing five pounds. They had laughed over that story off and on for twenty years. It was still a legend amongst the farmers of the community...

"Like father, like son," Berthe said with affectionate laughter. "In the Lingg family we're smart."

"The men are smart anyway," exclaimed Rudi, prodding her with his thumb again.

"Thank God. Some men have to die in a war, I know. But why should it be you? Every day you were gone, Rudi, that question came into my head: why should it be you? I'm patriotic too. But I'll let the other mothers say '*Heil Hitler*' and be happy if their boys are killed."

"You want to say '*Heil Hitler*' with your boy alive, eh?"

She hugged him, pressing her cheek close to his. "Thank God you're one to look out for yourself. In this world—"

"I know, I know," he interrupted jestingly, "in this world you have to look out for yourself. Now let me see: did I ever hear that before or didn't I?"

"Never mind. It bears repeating... You're really sure you won't have to go to the front?"

"One never can be sure. Some SS divisions have been used. But most are at home – or in occupied territories behind the lines. Maybe I'll be sent to Norway, for instance. Not bad, y'see. I hear the winters are cold, but the girls are hot."

"Rudi!"

He guffawed. "So what do you think – I'm still a baby?"

"Now then," she said, changing the subject. "The water's ready. Should I bring the tub in here?"

"In here will be fine." Rudi stretched luxuriously. "What a shame I can't stay a bit. This old home of ours is like heaven... Now, Mamma – no more tears."

"Who's crying?"

"You were going to. I could see it in your face. Be glad I'm here now, not in front of Stalingrad."

"I'm glad! I'm glad. What do you think?"

"We'll make a bargain, hey? We'll pretend tonight that I'm going to be here for weeks. We'll laugh, we'll get drunk, we'll have a good time – and if you see me pinch Hedda's behind once or twice when we're dancing, you won't say 'Rudi'. Is it a bargain?"

"It's a bargain," she replied, smiling.

"Now get the hot water, lieutenant. And see that it's hot."

2

Rudi wiped his mouth with the back of his hand and gazed over at his mother with an expression of ecstasy on his face. "What pork!" he exclaimed for the tenth time. "Like honey in the mouth. You don't even have to chew it, hey, Willi? It dissolves by itself. What a cook you are, Mamma! Willi... have another glass of champagne!"

Willi, who was commencing to feel the effects of four large glasses, glanced over at Berthe. He knew she wouldn't want him to get drunk. "Maybe not," he said apologetically. "Maybe you'd better save some for the guests."

"My God, be a man. There's five bottles yet," said Rudi. "Here, give me your glass."

"Go ahead, Willi," Berthe urged eagerly. "Why not? Tonight's a celebration." She smiled at her son, anxious to keep him in a good humour. "When did we ever drink champagne before, eh?" she added.

Rudi grinned and poured another round. "To everything there's two sides, even to war. *Heil Hitler.*"

Willi raised the bubbling wine to his lips with a contented smile. He found champagne delightful; he wished there might be a bottle of it at dinner every night. He glanced over at Berthe, nodded, winked, smiled.

Willi felt good. Despite the fact that nothing had been decided as yet about the marriage, he remained confident. Things were proceeding. He had arrived at the farmhouse an hour before to be greeted at the gate by a flustered Berthe. "He's here... Willi," she whispered. "Be sure you make him like you! If he likes you, we can get married right off, darling."

Very good. Merely to be pleasant was not difficult. Especially when the lad himself turned out to be a rather decent sort – high-spirited, friendly, affectionate towards his mother. The latter quality really warmed Willi. A lad who would come back from the army with an armful of gifts for his mother showed character and heart. Very good.

It was true that during the first half-hour at the dinner table Willi had been worried. They ate, they drank champagne and they talked of everything under the sun – except that which concerned them most. Whenever Willi made an approach, Rudi changed the subject. It disturbed Willi intensely – until he suddenly understood what was happening. The lad was making a game out of the situation. He would look over at Willi with a sly grin on his face and say "Well... so you're the Willi she's been writing about, eh?" – and then immediately talk of something else. Or he would exclaim, "Well... well... and from which end does a cow give milk, do you know, Willi?"

Very good, too. In Rudi's place Willi would have proceeded differently. He would have sat down with the prospective suitor, commenced a frank talk and then given a direct answer, yes or no. But if Rudi were choosing to conduct the matter otherwise, Willi understood. The lad was nineteen. He wanted to feel important. Very good. To have this woman he loved so dearly, to be established on the farm, was all Willi wanted. He was willing to flatter a young man to achieve that goal. Let the lad feel big. A few more drinks, a bit more laughter, and he would be ripe for a direct question.

"So... another!" Willi said, draining his glass. "When has a man ever tasted anything like it?"

"Ha ha!" Rudi replied. "Now there's a man."

"Another and another," Willi repeated, laughing heartily. "Why not, eh, Berthe? When your son comes home, it's a celebration. Another and another. Rudi – have you ever done gymnastics?"

"In training – on the parallel bars a little. That's all."

"I used to do pyramid building," Willi said. "I was bottom man for four."

"You don't say... Can you do a one-armed handstand?" Rudi asked with interest.

"Not now. That takes practice. But in a couple hours' practice I could." Willi felt slightly uncomfortable at this boasting, but it was deliberate. He didn't have much time in which to impress Rudi, and he knew that a youngster like him always regarded athletic accomplishment with respect.

"You ought to see Willi do his handkerchief trick," added Berthe proudly, taking up the cue.

"What's that?" asked her son. He picked at a string of gristle caught in his crooked front teeth and gazed at Willi with interest.

"Aaah – that one's easy," said Willi. "You put a handkerchief on the floor. Then from a knee bend you do a kind of hand balance; you pick up the handkerchief with your mouth, see? Anyone can do it."

"Show him, Willi," said Berthe eagerly. "He'll like to see it."

"Sure," said Rudi.

Willi laughed. "If I do it now, with three platefuls of pig inside of me, do you know what would happen? I should say not. Later, perhaps."

"Good," said Rudi. "You'll show me later. If it's easy, I'd like to learn it."

"A husky lad like you – you'll learn it in five minutes," Willi told him expansively.

"Fine," said Rudi. "Let's not forget... Now, Mamma – why are you so stingy with the potatoes? Look, my plate's empty. What a way to treat a fighter for the fatherland." He laughed joyously. He too felt good. The liquor was bubbling sweetly inside of him, and he felt like a king to be sitting at the head of the table, where his father had always sat. He had not thought to assume his place as owner of the farm so early in life. It was sad that one's father was dead – Rudi had been quite fond of his father, in fact. But to be a property owner at nineteen... that was magnificent. "So, Willi," he said with a grin, "we have to decide the first question first. The question is, 'Which comes first, the chicken or the egg?'" He guffawed loudly. "Do you think he knows, Mamma? Mamma, some more pork. Please, why so stingy?"

"And you, Willi," asked Berthe. "A bit more pork? And onions?"

He shook his head, sighing. "I'm splitting, Berthe. I won't be able to work for a week. I haven't had a meal like this for ten years."

"*Voilà!*" said Rudi, apropos of nothing. "*Voilà, voilà.* Mamma, start opening another bottle of champagne." He turned to Willi. "Your son was killed, eh?"

Willi nodded.

"Mamma says he won an Iron Cross."

"In Norway. He was a parachutist."

"Well!" exclaimed Rudi with respect.

Willi drained his glass of champagne. He wished Rudi had not brought up his son's decoration. It left him with a pain in his gut. It made him recall the morning he stood with his daughter-in-law before an oratorical colonel. He felt now as he had then – not proud, but miserable… miserable and angry.

"Say, Mamma…" Rudi looked around suddenly. "Where's our dog?"

Berthe blushed. Stammering a little she answered, "I had to sell her, Rudi."

"Why? Who bought her?"

"The butcher, Friml." She kept her eyes averted from both her men. Even though she had insisted upon returning the eighteen marks to Willi, the incident still shamed her.

"How come Friml?" asked Rudi in perplexity. "I know Friml from the time he kicked that Rolf I had when I was a kid. Friml hates dogs."

"It was not for a pet, Rudi."

"What then?"

"To… to eat," she stammered.

Rudi stared at her, dumbfounded.

"Sooner or later someone else would have done it," she explained anxiously. "Nobody can keep a dog around here any more. So I thought, 'Why should someone else get the benefit?' Friml was ready to pay me."

Rudi stopped chewing. He asked slowly, "Nobody can keep a dog any more?"

"You know what our meat ration is? Hm… You don't think we eat like this every night?"

"When I left it was…" – Rudi wrinkled his brows – "it was twenty ounces a week. Wasn't that it, Mamma? It's changed?"

"Now it's ten and a half. Since April."

"Ten and a half?" He stared at her, frowning. "There was no report of it in the army paper."

"That's why I sold the dog." She began to laugh. "'Roof rabbits' is what we call cats now. Go look in the butcher store."

Rudi put down his knife and fork. He said nothing, but he was obviously disturbed.

"And everything else the same," his mother continued. "Even potatoes are scarce. Since last winter."

"Why should potatoes be scarce?"

"Who knows? Ask Berlin," his mother replied sourly. "But if it was everywhere like here… Here we had a rainy summer such as I don't ever remember – and then an early frost. I lost almost half my potato crop. Not even good for the hogs."

Slowly Rudi poured himself a glass of champagne. He said wonderingly, "In the army newspaper it said things were fine at home."

"Hm!" Berthe snorted. "Try to wear my shoes for a day. Try to drink the tea we get."

"In the army paper it said things were good," Rudi insisted. "It said there were Dutch farmers in the Ukraine… that there was already a harvest this year."

"So where is it?"

"Maybe it'll be here soon."

"If it comes, that will be fine. But meanwhile your army paper is lying."

"The army paper doesn't lie!" Rudi told her sharply.

Berthe shrugged. They fell silent for a moment.

"Why didn't you write me about this?" he asked.

"It's forbidden. There's signs all over the post office: 'Civilians must keep up the morale of the soldiers. No complaining.'"

"I see," Rudi said. "Tobacco has been cut too?" he asked Willi.

Willi nodded. "Three cigarettes a day."

"Three? What can you do with three a day?"

"I save mine until Sunday. Then I smoke them all."

Rudi fished in his breast pocket. He tossed a package on the table. "Keep 'em. I have more. They're real Turkish."

Willi nodded in gratitude.

"So… things are tight here!" said Rudi. "Well, no matter. I'm sure what the army paper says is true. By Christmas you'll all be eating Russian bread. Things will get easier."

"Let's hope so."

"I guess I'm lucky to be in the army now. We get canned tomatoes, fresh bread, two pounds of meat a week – the best of everything."

"Ready for coffee now?" asked Berthe.

The men nodded. She began to clear the table.

"A wonderful meal, Mamma. Hey, Willi?"

Willi grinned.

"You know who had it lucky? The first soldiers who went into France. They used to spread butter on candy bars, they told me. The stores were half cleaned out by the time I came."

"How rich those Frenchies must've been!" Berthe said enviously.

"Rich, fat and stupid," Rudi added with contempt. "The French always used to boast of their culture. What culture?" He banged the flat of his muscular hand down on the table with sudden anger. "They're no more than barbarians. They have their minds on good living and money." He belched several times in rapid succession. Then he began to laugh. "But this champagne they make is some stuff, hey Willi?"

Willi nodded.

"Excuse me." Rudi got up abruptly, his face red from the food and the wine. He walked outside hastily.

In a quick whisper, Berthe said, "The Guttmanns will be coming soon. Any minute, Willi. You must talk to him."

"I will. Don't worry, I will."

"He feels good now. Keep after him. Don't let him put you off."

Willi squeezed her hand. "I've been waiting on purpose. I'll ask him right now."

He bent over, kissing her lovingly. Passionately she said, "I'll die if it doesn't turn out all right, Willi." She kissed his hand with eager, soft little kisses. Willi stroked her dark braids, his heart swelling with love and pride of possession. "Don't worry, my darling. We worried for three months, but now it's over. I could tell the minute I saw him. A fine lad, Berthe. He won't stand in the way. He's only trying to feel a little big by delaying things." He pressed his lips to her cheek. "No one can take you away from me now... No one, Berthe."

"Well, well," said Rudi from the doorway, "the love birds. Bless you, my children."

Willi cleared his throat. "Rudi, your mother has written to you." He stood up. "We want to get married. I assure you—"

"Man!" Rudi blinked at Willi as though seeing him for the first time. "You certainly are a big bastard, Willi. Excuse me, Mamma. I didn't mean to say that. I'm a bit tipsy to be honest. But where did you ever find such a bull?" He began to laugh. "Look at him, he's even coming out of his suit."

"Rudi," said Willi with a patient smile, "please say yes or no. You're leaving tonight. There will be others coming here soon. It's time you told us."

Rudi sat down heavily. "Yes, I'm leaving tonight," he repeated sullenly. "Leaving my farm." He looked up, his face sad. "Sure, why not? Get married. What do I care? They'll likely send me to the front. I'll get killed anyway. The young have no luck. Luck is for the old."

"Oh no," his mother cried. "What are you saying? You'll be stationed at home. You said so. Don't talk nonsense, Rudi."

"Who knows?" Rudi replied. He held his head in his hands. "I'm drunk. The cold air made it all go to my head." He looked up, his eyes bloodshot, a grin returning to his face. "So how about it, Willi? From which end does the milk come? You haven't told me yet."

"Which end, I know," Willi replied with patient good humour, "but the milk doesn't come for me."

Rudi roared. "A cow doesn't work by electricity, hey? You can't push a button."

"So?" Willi asked. "What about it, Rudi? All I ask is the right to work on the farm. I'm a good worker, you'll see. I'm handy. I can learn how to be a farmer, you'll see."

"Only I want one thing understood," Rudi said suddenly, almost with anger. "I run the farm. What I say goes."

"Absolutely." Willi crossed over to him eagerly. "I give you my hand on it. What you say goes. Say, listen… I've worked under a boss all my life. Why shouldn't I like it better to have you for my boss?"

Rudi belched and began to laugh. "But remember: from chickens only eggs come. Never try to milk chickens. They don't like it." He burst out laughing and slapped Willi on the back. "Go ahead. Kiss Mamma. I want to see you two kiss like a young couple should. My, what a pair of shoulders he has, Mamma. If there's no horse on the farm next spring, harness him up. He'll plough."

With a radiant face Berthe went over to her son. "You first," she said with her whole heart in her voice. She kissed him. "I ask God to bless you and bring you back to both of us, so that you can sit at the head of the table and be the head of our family." She kissed him again.

Rudi grinned. "You're a nice mamma. You're all right too, Willi. Go on, kiss her."

Willi put his arm around Berthe, stooped down and kissed her lips. "I love your mother," he said joyously. "I promise you I'll be good to her."

"Not too good," Rudi advised. "A woman has to be kept in her place. Hey, Mamma?… Well, now we're all happy. I hope to God you can get on the farm right away, Willi. Mamma needs help. The way this place looks, it breaks my heart."

"As soon as we're married, I'll go right to Rosenhart," said his mother. "He promised to help me."

"Good." Rudi rocked back on his heels, smiling. "A handsome bride, if I say so myself, eh, Willi?"

Willi grinned. There was a serenity in his heart that went beyond joy. "But this is really happiness," his mind was whispering. "Only after you've had pain do you know what happiness is."

"But that sweater now," said Rudi with amusement, "that sweater is a bit too tight – don't you think so, Willi?"

Willi grinned. He considered it a bit coarse of Rudi to mention it, but he didn't care. Let the lad talk. He was going away tonight.

"Ah, that sweater," said Rudi. He laughed with secret delight. "You can't appreciate it, you two. You don't know what I went through to get it for you, Mamma. Such an experience." He guffawed loudly. "Even if it is too tight."

Embarrassed, Berthe turned to the table. "We must have a toast, Rudi. How can we skip a toast?"

They stood with glasses uplifted. "I'll give a toast," said her son. His face turned serious for an instant, warm and affectionate. "To you, Mamma, and to you, Willi. I wish you a good life and much happiness."

They drank seriously, in silence. "*Ach*, I feel like crying," Berthe exclaimed. She turned to Willi, pressing her face to his shoulder. "Did you ever see a nicer son?"

"No," Willi replied, with a lump in his throat.

"Mamma, quiet," said Rudi. "I hear someone at the gate. Is it them?"

Berthe ran to the door. "Yes, they're here," she announced with excitement. She went out. Rudi rushed to the mirror. He buttoned his tunic hastily, rubbed a food stain from his mouth, lit a cigarette. Then he turned, standing very straight, a broad smile on his lips.

The first to step inside was Herr Guttmann. He was a bull-necked, bald-headed farmer of sixty, fleshy-faced, bulbous-nosed. He grinned when he saw Rudi and offered a meaty, calloused hand. "Well, lad, back safe and sound," he said hoarsely, with affection. "That's fine, fine."

Rudi grinned back at him, but kept his eyes on the doorway. Herr Guttmann nodded with polite curiosity at Willi, who nodded back, but Rudi was too absorbed to think of introducing them.

Berthe came next in the procession (to Rudi's annoyance), walking with her arm around Frau Guttmann's waist. The mother of the family was a thin, sour-visaged woman of fifty who looked as though she hated the world, as she more or less did. She had once been the beauty of their community, but five children and thirty years of toil had squeezed the sap from her. She greeted Rudi softly, kissed him, started to say something – but then ended up by being silent. It was obvious to Berthe that she was thinking of her own sons, who were in Russia.

When Rudi saw that the next to appear was Martha Guttmann, and that after she stepped into the room the doorway remained empty, he almost cried out with disappointment. He had expected Hedda to come running in first – a maiden eager to welcome the returning warrior. Mechanically he shook hands with Martha. Scarcely answering her greeting, he whispered, "Where's Hedda? Don't tell me she didn't come?"

"Of course she did," replied Martha. She turned around, calling, "Hedda – why don't you come in?"

After this stage play, Rudi expected Hedda to enter shyly, but he was mistaken. Hedda's smile, as she appeared in the doorway, was not at all bashful. It was positively saucy, and a bit unfriendly, as was her whole expression. She stood posed, tucking a wild flower into her auburn hair, surveying the room with the air of a haughty princess. In his stunned reaction to her beauty, Rudi didn't stop to analyse the meaning of that peculiar smile; later he was to remember it as having been bitterly significant. He had left a pert, winsome girl of sixteen – but this Hedda, only a year older, blazed with an almost imperious beauty.

Rudi was not the only one who was startled to see Hedda. Berthe, with a lump coming to her throat, cast a quick glance over at the girl's mother. It was Elsie Guttmann she was seeing all over again, the Elsie of a quarter-century before – a slim girl who had somehow escaped the broad-hipped mould of the peasant, a girl with a body straight as a birch, with a grace to her limbs and a sweet, soft curve to her breast, a girl whose face was not broad or thick-nosed or coarse-skinned, but lean and sculptured and classic in its loveliness.

Impetuously Rudi ran over to the doorway. It had not been his plan to betray interest like this. He had thought to stand slightly aloof, the stern soldier, and let the girl pay homage to him.

"Hedda," he cried rapturously, grasping both her hands, "but what's happened to you? You've become as pretty as an actress." He turned excitedly to Frau Guttmann. "Now I know why Mamma said you were the prettiest girl around here."

To his embarrassment Frau Guttmann said nothing, and her face expressed acid disapproval. He wondered with dismay if he had said the wrong thing. From now on he absolutely wanted to remain on the good side of the elder Guttmanns.

"Well, and are you glad to see me, Hedda?" he asked boldly.

"Yes, of course," she replied, and this time her smile was warm and genuinely friendly. "I'm very glad to see you. And you've changed too. You look... fine. A real soldier."

Rudi grinned, speechless with pleasure.

"My goodness," Berthe exclaimed, "what a dumbhead I am. I haven't introduced any of you to Willi." Grasping her lover's arm proudly, she commenced a formal introduction.

"Now, Mamma," Rudi interrupted with a grin, "why so bashful? Herr Wegler is from the factory – but nothing else?"

Blushing a hot red, Berthe said, "Yes, there is something else... Willi and I... we're to be married."

There was a moment of silent surprise on the part of their guests, and then Elsie Guttmann smiled for the first time. "My dear Berthe," she said, going over to her and kissing her, "that's splendid. I wish you all happiness. I do sincerely."

Grinning joyously and a little foolishly, Willi shook hands with each of the Guttmanns in turn. "I'm an old farmer, you should understand," he told them. "I know how to grow onions in window boxes."

Herr Guttmann guffawed, and even his wife smiled.

"Go on, Willi, tell them where milk comes from," said Rudi.

"Milk comes from a can," replied Willi happily. "Potatoes grow on trees and eggs are made in a factory. I'm an old farmer from Düsseldorf. I know."

The Guttmanns roared, liking him immediately for his humility about farm matters.

"Never mind," said Berthe, patting Willi's arm. She was delighted by the good impression he was making. "You'll see what a farmer he'll be a year from now."

"Well, and how about a toast with some real French champagne?" Rudi asked.

"French champagne? Really?" said Hedda eagerly. She shivered and laughed. "What's it like?"

"Like heaven," Rudi told her authoritatively, pulling a cork. "Hear that?" He began pouring the wine, his eyes on Hedda's face. She blushed suddenly and averted her gaze. Angrily she said, "Watch what you're doing. You'll spill it."

Frowning, Rudi poured the champagne. He wondered what on earth was wrong. He and Hedda had always been good friends. If now he was frank in his admiration, why did Hedda act so... he couldn't find the word... so upside-down? One moment she seemed pleased to see him, the next she was angry.

"A toast to the bride and groom," said Herr Guttmann in his hoarse voice. "Happiness and..." He stopped, having been about to say automatically "and many sons". Instead, he finished lamely: "And a long life to both of you." He drank off his glass with a perspiring face, but with an inward chuckle. It had been a narrow escape. They were not youngsters, after all. "God in heaven, what a drink," he exclaimed. "You mean to say the French have this all the time?"

"Not any more," Rudi replied. "Now we have it."

"It's like... I don't know what it's like," Hedda exclaimed rapturously. She belched prettily, laughed. "Can I have another, Rudi?"

He indicated the bottles. "Another and another. It's all yours."

"Hedda," her mother said sharply, "remember."

"Oh, it's all right," the girl replied in a pettish tone.

"Come, let's sit down and be comfortable," Berthe cried joyously. "Here's a chair for you, Elsie. And you, Hugo. Children, find chairs. Rudi, fill their glasses again. Tonight we have good reason to celebrate."

Elsie Guttmann sighed. "If only *our* sons were home!"

"Now, Mother!" said Martha sharply. She looked over at her severely. Martha was a girl of twenty-two, not nearly so lovely as her younger sister, but with a trim handsome figure. "So, how are things in France?" she asked Rudi quickly.

"In France it's a picnic," Rudi answered with an honest grin. "So far, a vacation. I can't claim any victories."

"No? But what about the French girls?" Hedda enquired with a saucy tilt of her head.

"The French girls are..." He stopped – he had been about to answer boastfully, but he changed his mind. "Are not so nice as the little finger on the hand of a German girl like you," he finished gallantly.

"You know? You're sure?" she asked with a provocative gleam in her bright eyes.

He couldn't resist that. "I know. I'm sure."

"Things are quiet then in France?" asked Herr Guttmann.

"We get bombed, of course... but nothing much where I was... near Orléans. No factories near my barracks. Of course, we have trouble with sabotage."

"Sabotage?" asked Willi slowly. He fixed his gaze on Rudi.

"In the newspapers they say all is quiet in France," Herr Guttmann exclaimed. "The French accept the New Order,* I read."

Rudi laughed, expressing his superior knowledge. "Sure they accept it, the swine. When we watch them, they accept it! When we stand over them, they accept it! And when we shoot them, they accept it! Otherwise not. Take it from me."

"So?" asked Willi. He frowned.

"But why do we talk of unpleasantness?" interrupted Berthe. "Elsie, how much did you put in vegetables this year?"

"What's the matter with the French, anyway?" Herr Guttmann enquired, ignoring Berthe. "Don't they know they're whipped?"

Rudi shrugged. "You'd think they would! Do you know what we soldiers were told when we first arrived in France? Strict military orders: 'Be nice to the French; be polite; make them see that Germans are their friends.' But what was the result? Sabotage. They wreck trains whenever they can; they burn grain; they stick a knife into any soldier they find alone at night – I tell you, that part of it's no fun."

"Hm! You said it was a vacation," Berthe commented, grieving instantly for what he had been through. "Some vacation!"

Rudi grinned, "Orléans is not Berlin," he replied with the foxy look coming into his face. "But neither is it Leningrad." He laughed.

"Imagine!" Martha exclaimed indignantly. "What a way to repay kindness!"

"Don't worry," said Rudi, nodding his head with the air of one who is giving a confidence, "they're not getting away with anything now. For every act of sabotage, they get ten times in return. We're teaching them who runs the show."

"Rudi," asked Hedda with her glowing eyes fixed on his face, "have *you* shot any Frenchmen?"

Rudi shrugged. "I've been on firing squads," he replied casually. "Everybody takes his turn."

"Have you been on *many*?"

"Three."

"How does it feel?"

"Oh… what is there to feel? You get used to it. The first one… well, the first one I felt a bit queer. But you get used to it."

"What do the condemned ones do?" Hedda persisted. "Do they cry, or do they—"

"Oh, enough of this sort of talk," Elsie Guttmann interrupted harshly. "Why do we have to talk of things like that? If some miserable people are shot, do you have to know all the details?"

"Miserable people?" Martha asked indignantly. "I like that. My goodness, saboteurs – people who stab our German boys in the back. Shooting is too good for them."

Slowly Willi said, "If it's so that the French people are sabotaging, Rudi, then… in case there is a Second Front, they'll be—"

"Don't worry," replied the youth, "our officers have explained everything. There are plans. In case of a Second Front we'll smash the English back into the Channel – one, two, three. They'll never get through our fortifications. And any of the French swine who try anything… well… they'll be sorry, that's all I can say."

"Hm!" Martha exclaimed bitterly. "It's enough to make you choke. We bring peace and order to France, we extend a helping hand to them – even though they brought war down upon us – and what's the result? They're ready to stab us in the back. There's a Frenchman for you."

There was a moment of silence.

"And what would we do if the French army was here?" asked Frau Guttmann suddenly. "You don't remember 1918!"

"But what sort of talk is this, Mother?" Martha asked in astonishment. "Are you comparing the occupation of the Rhineland by French nigger troops with today? I suppose we should move out of Poland and let them arm against us once more?"

"I want the war to end, that's all," her mother replied softly. "I want my sons home. Poland's nothing to me – or France, either."

"So do we all want the war to end," Martha replied tartly. "But before Germany can exist in peace, we have to smash our enemies."

"That's true, Elsie," her husband agreed. "What do you say, Herr Wegler?"

Willi remained silent. He sat stiffly in his chair holding an empty glass between his big hands, gazing at it abstractedly. And when he looked up finally to reply, Berthe's heart contracted to see the moody unhappiness in his eyes. "Whatever way there can be peace quickest is the best way," he answered – evading the question.

"Willi… how about playing the accordion for our guests?" Berthe asked. "You can't imagine what a good player Willi is," she boasted to the others.

"Fine, fine, let's hear," said Herr Guttmann.

"Rudi," asked Martha before Willi could make a move, "have you heard what the Americans have done?"

Rudi shook his head.

"It's unbelievable. They passed a law: every man of German blood has to wear a black swastika over his heart!"

"Gangsters!" Hedda cried indignantly.

Rudi nodded his head knowingly. "Like our major said," he added with a tipsy thickness to his tongue, "Germany can have no frontiers. It's either German culture or subhuman culture. There's no compromise!"

"So when will the war end?" asked Elsie Guttmann softly. "How can Germany conquer the whole world?"

"It will end when it will end," Martha snapped. "Don't you trust the Führer?"

Her mother tossed her head. "I want my sons back."

"Your sons, your sons," Martha said bitterly. "I'm ashamed of you, Mother. Before others, too. Don't you think I want my husband back?"

"Rudi, fill the glasses," said Berthe. "Tonight is a celebration night. Let's not be so serious."

"Correct," said Rudi. "Hugo – drink up. Willi, how about another?"

Silently Willi shook his head. He hated this sort of talk. He wished there were a way he might leave the room. Others could speak glibly of conquering the world – but he remembered 1918 in his marrow. Their talk meant only one thing to him: more months of war, more killings, more starvation – the whole bloody mess repeated. And for what? It was this he had begun to ask of himself. To what purpose? Where was Germany going? When the National Socialists had come to power, he had not welcomed it, but he had accepted it. When Richard had said "Father, I can't quite feel about you the way I used to", he had sorrowed and accepted it. When Käthe had died, he had raised his fists to the sky in impotent protest – and then, with bruised mind and battered heart, had dumbly accepted it. But nowadays, as he listened to these architects of the New Order – in the barracks, in the commissary, in Berthe's kitchen – his very flesh felt pained, and he found himself asking for the first time in his life, "Where is it all leading? To what end?"

"My goodness, Berthe, said Herr Guttmann, "I almost forgot. I have news for you from Rosenhart. Some little news first – a regulation. Farm animals are to have their tails shorn. You'll get a list. You'll leave only a little tuft at the end, so they can brush the flies away. Then you bring the hair in a bag to the Farm Bureau."

Berthe burst out laughing. "What next? Do you hear, Rudi? That's what it is to farm nowadays. What silliness."

"Now, Berthe, permit me," Martha said, flushing a little. "You ought to understand that no rule is passed foolishly. I happen to know all about this. The hair is needed for the textile factories – to make clothes. What's silly about that?"

"Of course, of course," said Berthe hastily, in an apologetic voice. "A rule is a rule. You mustn't think – but what's the other news, Hugo?"

Guttmann grinned. "How are you getting along on the farm all by yourself?"

"I'm going crazy. My hay will be all dry straw. My potato plants—"

"Starting next week you'll have help!"

"You mean it? How do you know?"

"I was in to see Rosenhart today. Labour gangs are coming."

"Oh, thank God!" she exclaimed fervently. "Rudi, Willi – you hear that?"

Rudi nodded, grunting. "About time. I want a *farm* to come back to, when the war's over – not twelve acres of weeds."

Berthe sighed ecstatically. "What news! What a day this is!"

Softly, Frau Guttmann said, "And Rosenhart's other news? Why don't you speak of that, Hugo?"

"Now, Elsie… we decided not to, didn't we?"

"What news?" asked Berthe.

Guttmann shrugged. "Nothing. I'll tell you another time. Rudi, how about another drop? Can you spare it?"

"I should say," he replied heartily.

"Rudi, do you know about my Ernst?" asked Martha, holding out her glass. "He's been decorated."

"Honestly? That's wonderful, Martha," he replied enviously. "Where is he now?"

"The same as when you left. In Africa…" She laughed. "Chasing the English. He writes me they'll be in Egypt in the next push."

"How the English can run!" Hedda exclaimed. "Rudi, if I get drunk on this delicious champagne it'll be your fault. The English know how to get other people to fight their wars – and to run. That's all."

"They have no morals, the English," added Martha. "No honour. Honestly, I wrote my Ernst that against the English he ought to get another decoration, or I wouldn't let him come home."

"Decorations!" her mother echoed softly. She turned her bitter, handsome eyes on her daughter. "You think war is made up of decorations, don't you? Our family has four men in this war. Do you think all they'll get is decorations?"

"Mother, that's open defeatist talk!" her daughter replied angrily. "Do you think I'm a child? No new world can ever be created without suffering."

"They had statistics in the paper, Elsie," interjected Herr Guttmann reassuringly. "Against all of our enemies we have so far suffered only three hundred and fifty thousand casualties, mostly wounded. Russia has already lost eight million dead."

"Statistics!" Frau Guttmann echoed with scorn. "Last week we heard from Gertrude, didn't we?" She turned to Berthe. "Her Lutz is dead."

"Gertrude Brandit's boy?"

Fury was seeping into Elsie Guttmann's face. "And Walter Baecker is coming home now – in time to dig potatoes in September for his father. Only, he has no legs any more, so it will be a little hard for him."

"Mother – will you stop it? This is just stupid," said Hedda. "It's defeatist."

"And Rosenhart's twins…" the mother continued implacably. "You remember them?"

"Elsie!" said her husband. "You promised!"

Berthe looked from one to the other. Her face became very pale. "They've been wounded?"

Elsie smiled bitterly. "Not wounded… not prisoners… not missing… two more statistics."

Berthe raised a nervous hand to her mouth. "Not… not dead, Elsie? Not those two fine, handsome boys?"

"Both dead. Both… both. Not twenty-two, and they're both dead."

"Oh, God in heaven!" Berthe whispered. She looked over at Rudi with anguish. "Oh, poor Erich!"

"Damn it, let's stop this talk," Rudi exploded angrily. "Let's have some fun."

"Herr Wegler," said Guttmann hoarsely, "Berthe says you play. Let's have a tune." He frowned severely at his wife.

Willi stood up. He stared at Elsie Guttmann with his eyes and face gone hard. Then, a bit unsteadily because he was drunk, he walked to the box where they kept the accordion.

"Something lively, hey, Willi?" Rudi cried. "Something with a snap to it." He glanced over at Hedda and wondered if he could move his chair closer to hers without being reproved by her vixen of a mother. "Here, let's turn around so we can all watch him," he suggested loudly, as Willi came back with the accordion. He hitched his chair close to Hedda's and began to applaud. "Curtain, curtain," he said. "Or, as the French say, '*Voilà!*'"

Willi sat down. He began to play.

"Hedda," Rudi whispered under cover of the music, "you've become the prettiest girl I've ever seen. Honest."

Hedda smiled and tossed her head a little.

"What I'd give if I didn't have to go away tonight! A year's pay. Honest."

"You're going away?" she whispered. "Your mother said—"

"Yes, tonight. Will you write to me, Hedda, if I write to you?"

She didn't reply. The smile departed from her face.

"What's the matter? You're so... upside-down tonight, Hedda. Don't you like me any more?"

"I like you," she replied softly. "I've always liked you. But you didn't write to me all last year. I waited."

"I'm... I don't know what to say," he stammered. "I wanted to write. I kept thinking of you. But I... Somehow—"

"Too many French girls, eh?" she asked saucily.

"No. Honest. I didn't even give them a thought."

"*Hm!*" she retorted. She applauded loudly as Willi finished his first tune. "How well you play!" she exclaimed loudly. She smiled tartly at her mother. Frau Guttmann had been frowning throughout her conversation with Rudi.

"Willi, give us a dance," said Rudi. "Can you play a dance?"

"I can play a waltz," Willi replied quietly.

"A waltz is fine." He jumped up. "Come on, Hedda."

"No," she answered stiffly.

"What? Not dance with me?"

"No," she said. Her face was definitely unfriendly. Martha jumped up, "*I* feel like dancing, Rudi. Dance with me."

"No," he insisted stubbornly. "I asked Hedda to dance with me, and I want her, not you, Martha. No offence meant," he added hastily, "but why shouldn't Hedda dance with me? Are we friends or aren't we?"

"Rudi," Elsie Guttmann said in a strained voice, "Hedda's not feeling well. Don't ask her to dance."

"Oh!" He was instantly contrite. "I'm sorry. Forgive me. Well then, Martha, if you—"

"Lies, lies, lies!" Hedda cried suddenly, jumping to her feet. "I'm sick of lies."

"Hold your tongue!" her mother shouted.

Hedda's fair skin flamed. "*You* can be ashamed, you old stick!" she screamed at her mother. "But *I'm* proud!" She wheeled around, facing Rudi. "Do you want to know why I can't dance? Because I'm pregnant. In seven months I'm going to be a German mother."

"Oh, you hussy!" her mother cried, bursting into tears. "Oh my God, what a life we live!"

"Well... aren't you going to congratulate me?" Hedda asked Rudi. On her face there was the same unfriendly smile he had seen when she first came into the room, cold and saucy and full of confident hauteur.

"You're... married?" he asked.

"No, I'm not married. Does a girl have to be married to do her duty by the Führer? I didn't want to be married."

"Ah, you," her mother burst out in a wail, "so why boast? Will you please tell me that one little thing – why do you boast in front of strangers?"

"Hush, Elsie," her husband said hoarsely. His fleshy face had turned grey. He sat biting his lips. "Times have changed."

"No, times have not changed," her mother shouted passionately. "A bastard is still a bastard."

"Mother! You stop that immoral talk," Martha cried indignantly, rushing to her sister's defence. "The baby will be adopted by the Führer, you know that."

Frau Guttmann commenced to laugh hysterically. She turned to Berthe, wringing her hands. "They've gone crazy, these young people. They all talk like the same phonograph record. Black is white – a bastard is a medal of honour. How do you like it?"

"Oh, you're such an old fool," Martha said with contempt. "Germany goes forward, but my mother stays where she is."

"She's not satisfied, my daughter. She wants her mother to be a whore too."

A scream of rage burst from Hedda's lips. "Don't you dare call me that. All decent Germans honour me."

"All decent Germans will look at your belly and laugh, you whore."

"I'll report you to the police," the girl cried. "I'll tell Anna Mahnke every word. You're an enemy of the State!"

"Report, report," her mother spit back.

"Please... keep quiet... I beg you," Herr Guttmann implored miserably. He turned to Berthe, his face agonized. "I apologize. The girl is young. She doesn't understand—"

"Oh, this is unbearable," Hedda cried, bursting into tears of rage. "I should be honoured by my parents. I'm giving a child to the State, perhaps even a future soldier. All my expenses paid to a home for Hitler maids. Everybody honours me except my parents."

"And the father," Frau Guttmann spat. "You forget him. He doesn't honour you enough to pay for a wedding licence."

"That's a lie!" the girl cried furiously. "We never intended to marry."

"Oh, goddamn it, *shut up*!" the father shouted. He stood with clenched fists, his face purple. "Not another word from anyone! No... You shut your mouth too, Elsie. I won't have this any more. I've got to have a little peace in my life. I'll kill myself!"

Silence descended upon the room. The mother wept brokenly. Berthe stared with a trembling mouth at Willi, and Willi – his face set in the hard, dead mould she knew and feared – gazed vacantly at the floor. Slowly Rudi poured himself a glass of champagne. He drank off the glass at one gulp, poured another.

"Are you toasting me, Rudi?" asked Hedda in an unfriendly voice.

He stared at her. Then he said dully, "Why not?" He drank the wine down quickly.

"Now we'll go home!" Herr Guttmann announced hoarsely. "Come, Elsie. Girls, come." He stood up.

"No," Berthe began, "please don't..." She stopped as Herr Guttmann turned his pasty face to her. "Anyway, thank you... for coming," she stammered.

Hedda stood, her eyes on Rudi. "Well," she asked coldly, "do you still want to write to me? I want to know."

Rudi flung the glass in his hand at the stove, shattering it into a thousand bits. "No, goddamn you, I don't. Get the hell out of here."

With a look of scorn and hatred Hedda said, "Pig!" She thrust out of the room. Quickly her sister followed. Herr Guttmann put his arm about his wife's waist. He led her to the door. There he paused for a moment, looked around at Berthe and gestured with his big, calloused hand. It was a gesture of confusion, of helplessness, of impotent rage.

The door shut after them.

Rudi sat down at the table, his face working. His eyes were sick with jealousy.

"Rudi," Berthe began. "After all, Hedda isn't the only—"

"I don't want to talk about it!" he interrupted harshly. He banged his hand on the table. "Do you hear me? I don't want to talk about it!"

"Of course, of course," his mother said hastily. She was close to tears in her sorrowful compassion for him. Feverishly Rudi began to open another bottle. It was the only one left of the seven he had brought home.

"Willi," Berthe whispered, "play a little."

Willi stared back at her stupidly. He said nothing.

"Willi?"

He got up slowly and went over to the table. He poured a glass of champagne for himself. He drank it down, poured a second – drank that one also.

"Oh, why did things have to be spoilt for us tonight?" Berthe cried in a forlorn, angry wail. "Damn the Guttmanns! Why did they have to bring their family quarrels to us? Rudi, I *will* say it: that Hedda may be pretty, but she isn't worth your fingernail. Do you think there won't be other girls for a handsome man like you?"

Rudi's lips twisted in angry pride. "And why not?" Thick-tongued, he added, "What's it to me? She's probably diseased too, the little tart."

"All right!" said Berthe. "Now we're finished with the Guttmanns. Let's be happy. We started out so happy tonight. Nothing's changed for *us*, has it? Rudi, you're going into the SS. You'll be stationed safe at home. And Willi – you and I can get married. You'll come to work on the farm. So now, I insist, we'll forget about the others and their troubles. There's always trouble in this world. You can't live if you think of other people's troubles."

"Of course," Willi said, "of course..." But his tone was not in harmony with his words. He was gazing fixedly at Berthe, yet his eyes were abstracted, turned inward. And on his lips there was a crooked, ironic smile. The smile angered Berthe. It made her want to yell out at him, "Oh, for God's sake, what's wrong with *you* now, Willi?" But instead she said feverishly, "Rudi, pour me a drink too. I want to celebrate. There's only a few hours left before you leave. Let's be happy." She glanced back at Willi again. The crooked, ironic smile was still on his lips. "Willi, play something for us!" she ordered loudly. "Something pleasant."

Willi nodded vaguely. He sat down, fitting his fingers to the keys.

"What champagne!" Berthe exclaimed. "Rudi, what a son you are to carry these bottles all the way from France! Play, Willi, play for us!"

Very softly Willi began to play: "*He was despised and rejected of men*," he played, "*a man of sorrows and acquainted with grief.*" The crooked smile clung to his lips.

3

Giving his knapsack a final pat, Rudi stood up. "Well, Mamma, now it's goodbye."

Berthe embraced him fiercely. "I've changed my mind. I'll walk to the station. It'll be an extra half-hour with you."

"No, that's foolish. You're dead tired. And with those shoes…" He laughed. "Willi would have to carry you back. No, you get to bed. The cows still have to be milked, don't they? The war hasn't changed that. Goodbye now, Mamma." He kissed her and patted her shoulder. "Take care of yourself."

"Write me your new address."

"As soon as I arrive."

"I'm so sorry tonight had to be spoilt."

"Who said it was spoilt?" Rudi tossed the evening off with an expansive drunken gesture. "You want the truth. I don't give that for Hedda. Plenty of girls in this world."

"Good. That's the way to talk."

Willi picked up the knapsack and slung it over his shoulder. "It's time, Rudi. You don't want to miss the train." He smiled at both of them – the same curious, crooked smile that Berthe had seen on his face while he was playing the accordion. It troubled her – it was not a good smile somehow. It was only a… pretence of a smile. It made her wish fiercely that Willi were a simpler man, without so much hidden from her in the private reaches of his heart.

"Say… you forgot to teach me that handkerchief trick," Rudi said. "Well… I'll learn it next time. I'm too drunk anyway." He turned to his mother. "Now mind you," he admonished gaily, "this sweater – be careful how you wash it. If it shrinks one inch more, all my trouble in getting it will be for nothing."

"Never you mind," she said, slapping his hand affectionately.

He put his arm around her, and they started outside. As they stepped into the yard, leaving Willi a few paces behind, Berthe whispered into his ear: "You like Willi?"

"Sure… He's all right. It's good you're getting married."

"I'm so glad, Rudi. Willi thinks you're a fine young man. He told me." They stopped at the gate. "Well, Mamma…"

"I'll walk down the road with you a bit."

"No. You stay here. The gate marks our farm. That's where you should be. Goodbye, now. And no crying."

They embraced closely.

"No crying now," he repeated. "Come on, Willi. If I miss my train…"

They stepped out on the road. "A beautiful night," Rudi said. "A moon and stars all in my honour. And no British planes. Where are those planes you told me about, Mamma?"

"I sent a telegram to the King of England. I said: no planes tonight." She gazed at him with a trembling mouth. "Now remember, Rudi, if there's any fighting, don't you try to be a hero. Just come back safe."

"Don't worry," he laughed. "Goodbye."

"Goodbye, goodbye, my darling. I'll pray for you every night."

She remained at the gate, fighting down her tears, until the figures of her two men became wavering shadows on the moonlit road. Then she began to cry softly. She watched until the shadows disappeared. "God in heaven," she thought to herself, "who wanted this war? Who needed it? Oh, damn the British! Such beasts they are!"

Weeping she walked back into the house. She sat down at the littered table and rested her head in her arms. "Dear God," she whispered, "protect Rudi. Don't let the Americans bring any of their soldiers over. Sink every one of their ships, dear God. Teach them to leave us in peace! Why can't poor, decent people like us live out one lifetime in peace?"

Presently she stopped crying. She sat up and dried her eyes. She surveyed the kitchen, trying to decide whether to go to bed or to clear things up first. She felt very tired, but not sleepy. Her brain was racing, turning over the events of the day. She decided to finish the dishes before getting into bed. It was Saturday night; Willi wouldn't have to return to the barracks. And tomorrow morning they could go back to bed after they had finished the chores. Besides, it would be pleasant to talk to Willi when he came home from the station. There was so much to talk about now – so much to plan. Perhaps they would walk into town to see Rosenhart tomorrow. She would find out definitely about the labour gangs Hugo had referred to. And she would start the wheels rolling to get Willi transferred to the farm.

"Oh those Guttmanns!" she thought with anger. "A family without any feeling. Hedda was the worst. A blind man could have seen that Rudi was smitten with her pretty face. Why couldn't she have kept quiet on his one night home, been sweet to him – given him a kiss, even? She had been free enough with her kisses elsewhere, the whore."

Berthe sighed. Nothing ever ran smoothly in life. Her Willi, now… what a worrier he was! The talk about the war had upset him – she could see that in his face. Why did men always have to worry about things that were none of their business? The trick in living was to keep your mind on the good things. "Oh, you," she thought suddenly, "I'll fix you. Don't think you'll come back and get me to talk about Rosenhart's boys being killed, or when is the war going to end. I'll fix you."

She began to laugh out loud. Willi would be home in an hour at most. She would make believe she was asleep. Let him view her for a moment in one of those new French nightgowns. He'd find out how much his deep thoughts mattered to him. She had tried the nightgowns on in the afternoon. Like the sweater, they were a bit too small for her, particularly at the bosom. When he saw her in the pink one, he would think some elegant French whore had gotten into his bed by mistake. Berthe's laughter rose softly in the quiet room as she thought of it. When she heard him at the gate, she would throw the sheet back and lie there wickedly in that nightgown. And by tomorrow morning he would have forgotten all his deep thoughts.

Softly, smiling, she began to hum as she washed the dishes.

4

Berthe awakened to the sound of the creaking front gate. Drowsily she told herself that it was Willi home from the train. She lay half asleep until she heard his heavy step in the kitchen. Then, recalling her plan, she hastily threw back the sheet. She smoothed down her nightgown where it had become ruffled. She lay back with a quiet smile, listening to the scrape of his shoes again, waiting for him to enter the bedroom.

He did not come in. Wondering at it, she twisted around in bed and peered out of the half-open door. She saw his shadowed bulk near the sink. He was standing, motionless, his back to the bedroom. As she watched, he moved slowly to the table. He sat down, half-illumined now by a silver play of moonlight from the window. She could not see his face, but she saw him put his hand down on the table with his big fist clenched. A wave of irritation swept through her. What now? she thought. How little it took to make a man unhappy! Had Rudi said something... or was Willi still thinking about the war?

She got out of bed. Barefooted, she padded into the other room. Willi didn't turn, but she knew from the slight stiffening in his figure that he had heard her. Silently she stood by his chair. She stooped down, pressing her lips to his forehead. Her fingers played in his hair. She was smiling, a smile at once loving and slightly disdainful. "Did Rudi get off all right?" she asked softly.

There was a moment of quiet before he answered, "Yes."

"Don't you want to come to bed now?"

He didn't reply. She moved a bit so that he could see her. "I wanted to surprise you with my new nightgown. I wanted you to come into the bedroom and see me lying in bed like a French aristocrat."

A shiver ran through Willi's big body. He stared at her, his eyes pained, saying nothing.

Crossly she exclaimed, "Now, what's the matter?" And then, as he was still silent, "Oh, you! What's the matter with you? Why do you have to be like this?"

"I have to talk to you, Berthe," he said in a low voice. "I have to talk."

Deliberately, although rancour ran hot inside her, she smiled. "Come to bed, then, Willi. We can talk there."

"Here," he said. "Now. Please."

"I'm cold." She approached him, bending over wantonly. "I'll sit on your lap, and you'll keep me warm."

"No," he replied. "I want to talk. Put on something if you're cold. Please."

She snapped erect. "No!" she answered hotly. "You say no to me, I'll say it to you. I'm tired. We can talk tomorrow. I'm going to bed." She stood still as he looked at her. There was a bright, feverish gleam in his eyes suddenly, the look of a man with a sickness in his vitals. "Willi," she asked in a changed tone, "what's the matter? If something is wrong, my darling, tell me what it is. I'll listen. Of course I'll listen. I was upset a minute ago. I expected you'd want to love me when you came home. I was disappointed…" She stopped talking.

"Please, Berthe," he said in a sick voice. "Oh, please, please – cover yourself up. This fine nightgown of yours – I don't want to see it."

Wholly astonished, she peered into his face, but he turned his eyes away from her glance. "All right, Willi," she murmured. She went into the bedroom and donned her worn nightrobe. She came back, silently. "Do you want me to put on a lamp?"

"No," he said hoarsely. "What I have to tell you should be said in the dark. You won't want to see me – and I don't want to see you."

She sat down at the table staring at him, her hands beginning to tremble a little from nervousness. "You had a quarrel with Rudi?" It was the only thing that occurred to her.

"No. No quarrel with Rudi…" he answered dully. "Berthe…" He drew a deep breath. "Berthe… I don't know how to tell you, my darling. Only listen to me."

"I'll listen, Willi." Was he very drunk? she wondered. He didn't seem so. "What's happened, Willi? Tell me."

"Everything's turned rotten, that's what," he replied miserably. "You and I… We want to make a good life together. I used to think we could live on this farm like… like it was an island, away from everybody. Now we can't."

"Why?" she asked softly. "Tell me what you're really thinking. Don't hide from me. I'm your wife, Willi."

He turned to look at her, his eyes softening with gratitude at her love. "Hold my hand, Berthe." He held it out to her across the table. "Let's try to keep our hands together now, dearest. Don't take your hand away from me. No matter what I say, darling."

She gripped his big hand in both of hers. "No, I won't," she whispered. "Nothing you can say will make me do that… so long as you love me, Willi."

"Yes, I love you. I don't know what I'd do if I didn't love you," he said passionately. Then he sighed. "Well, so listen…" He began in a dull voice: "Tonight we had a celebration. It's so nice to drink champagne, to smoke a decent cigarette. And Rudi brought you presents: perfume, some nightgowns. I'll tell you how Rudi got them, Berthe. Because Rudi told me. Rudi was drunk. He was boasting, the way one man does sometimes with another. I suppose he was angry, too, about Hedda. I'm a man. It's easy to know what he was thinking. He was jealous. If the girl would make love with some other man, why not with him? So in order to show me he wasn't jealous, he told me a story. He didn't need to go begging for a girl like Hedda, he said. He told me about his French girls."

Berthe's hands tightened on his. "I see!" she interrupted, bitterly. "Well… sons don't talk to their mothers about things like that… or husbands to their wives. But women aren't stupid. We know what men are like. Men are men. What can be done about it? I suppose you never went with a prostitute before you were married?"

"I went with prostitutes, yes."

"Well, then? Do you expect Rudi to be different? He's in the army. He's at war. A woman like me tries not to think of such things. What's the use?"

"A few days before Rudi came home, he was sent to arrest somebody, Berthe. A woman. There were others with Rudi, about a dozen. The woman lived with her boy of fourteen, Rudi said. They went early in the morning, when the woman and the boy were still asleep."

"Willi, why are you telling me this?" she asked bitterly.

"Berthe, if you leave go of my hand before I finish telling you, I… I don't know what I'll do…"

She sat silent for a moment, frightened. Then she said painfully, "Well?"

"The woman was a rich woman, Rudi said. She lived outside a small town. She had an estate, with a large farm and a large house. Her barn was filled with grain. The day before the trucks were to come to take away the grain – because she was not allowed to keep any of it – she burned the barn down. So Rudi was sent with the others to arrest her."

Willi leant his head against the palm of his free hand. His voice had become very tired.

"They didn't wait for anyone to open the door. They broke it open. The woman ran out of bed in her nightgown, a pink one, Rudi said" – Berthe gasped – "and she met them in the hallway upstairs. The boy was there too. Then Rudi's corporal, who was in charge, told the woman she was under arrest. She didn't say anything, Rudi told me. She looked like she was expecting it, he said. She asked the corporal if she could have a few minutes to get dressed. He told her yes. Then, when she went into her room, the corporal called the men together. 'Listen,' he said – this is how Rudi told me – 'that woman is going to be shot this morning. I know it. Why should we let her go to her death unhappy? You saw for yourselves… she's quite a piece. Will we have some fun with her or won't we?' That's what Rudi told me. So they went inside."

"Oh, stop it, stop it!" Berthe cried. Hot tears were dropping down on his hand. "What's the use?"

"The woman's lad tried to stop them, Rudi told me. So one of the soldiers dragged him over to the bed. The corporal kept telling the boy, 'Pay attention: this is how the stork brings babies!' Rudi thought it was so funny he couldn't help laughing again when he told it to me."

Berthe wept bitterly, in silence.

"Then, before they took her away, the soldiers went to her closet. The corporal told them, 'Help yourselves, boys – why should we leave these things for some Frenchmen to have?' So that's how a German mother got a fine sweater and two nightgowns, and a bottle of perfume."

Berthe's body shook. "I didn't take my hand away," she said brokenly. "Are you satisfied?"

For a long while they had nothing to say to each other. Berthe wept with sick anguish. Then she burst into a furious tirade. "What do you want me to say? It isn't women who make war: it's men. We women bear men, we try to make them grow up decent – and then what do they become? Men – that's what they become, men! And the older men teach the younger what a man should be like. What do you want from me?"

Painfully, fumbling for words, Willi said, "You don't understand, Berthe. It isn't Rudi. I was in the last war. I suppose when men go to war, some of them always act like that with foreign women. I saw it."

"Foreign women?" she interrupted savagely. "Take away your policemen and see what would happen here. You think German women haven't been dealt with like that by German men? Why, my neighbour, Irma Winz... It's you... you men... it's what you are in your hearts!"

"No," said Willi hoarsely, "you're wrong, Berthe, and you still don't understand."

"What don't I understand?" she asked with anger.

"It's that Rudi wasn't *ashamed*," he said slowly, painfully. "Men do terrible things, I know. When you've been in a war and seen men die all around you, you change, I know that. Once I killed a Frenchman with a knife – I stabbed him in the throat. When men do things like that and stay in trenches for months, it's not so hard for them to forget decency, to see a woman and to take her by force, perhaps. But after I killed that Frenchman, I wasn't happy. I killed him, or else he would have killed me – but I wasn't happy. I've seen soldiers after they handled a woman in the way Rudi and the others handled that Frenchwoman. There was always a... sickness in their faces. They wanted to forget what they did." His voice rose, riding on its pain. "They weren't proud of it, Berthe. Rudi was *proud*. And they didn't take the woman's nightgown, or her sweater, and bring them back as presents to their own mother."

Berthe remained silent, biting her lips. Willi stood up. He began to pace.

"Listen to me, Berthe," he said harshly. "There's a rottenness here – and I know where it is. When Rudi was telling me his story, laughing the way he did, boasting, I wanted to kill him. I picked up a stone from the road. I held it in my hand. I knew that with one blow I could take revenge for that woman."

Berthe started up out of her chair with a muffled scream. "You didn't hurt Rudi?"

Willi stared at her, and slowly she sat down. "No," he said. "But suppose I did?" He approached her, peering into her face. "Suppose I did kill him?"

"Oh my God, leave me alone," she cried, tearing her eyes away from his.

"Suppose I did, Berthe?"

"Then, so help me God, I'd see you hanged," she replied with a burst of hatred. "You'd be a murderer. The murderer of my own son."

"Yes," he said softly. He stared at her. The crooked, ironic smile twisted his lips. "You don't understand me. You don't understand what I'm saying. You're the only one in the world I love now, but you don't understand what I'm saying."

"I understand everything. But that Frenchwoman is dead. What happened to her is over. If you killed Rudi, you'd do worse than he did!"

"But the rottenness?" Willi asked with impassioned wonder and surprise. "Don't you understand where the rottenness lies? It's not in what Rudi *did*. Not that he is a bad boy. But that Rudi is a boy you and I call a 'good boy'; that Rudi loves his mother; that Rudi was kind to me; that Rudi is not an ape or a criminal – *and that he was not ashamed*, Berthe. That's where the rottenness is." Wrath came into his voice; his words beat at her. "You listen to me: I'm not a Dr Goebbels. I'm not a general or a university professor. I don't read books. I can't use big words. I'm not one who understands things in a minute. But what is decent, what is right, I know! What is wrong, what is shameful, what is sinful, I know! When a young man brings the clothes of a woman he has raped to his own mother, I understand that he is rotten. When a girl has a baby like it was a loaf of bread she was baking in an oven, then I understand!" He stopped, choked.

"Willi—"

"And one other thing I know," he interrupted harshly. "This rottenness I won't live with! *I won't live with it!* Not one minute. Me, it won't touch. Do you hear me, Berthe? *Me, it won't touch.* I can't live like that. I'm a decent man."

She stared at him, terribly frightened, misunderstanding. Her fears burst out in a single, agonized question: "What are you going to do?"

He didn't answer.

"You're going to leave me, aren't you?"

His astonished eyes sought hers. For the moment her question had shaken every other thought from his head. "Leave *you*? Don't talk crazy."

"You are," she cried frantically. "I can see it in your face. Your face is the way it was the night you first came to my house. I could see it beginning tonight."

"Berthe... darling," he answered passionately, "this is just crazy." He seized her hands, kissing them. "No! How could I leave you? I couldn't live, even, without you."

"But there's something," she replied in the same frightened tone. "I can see it. You're going to do something. I know it."

"Yes," he whispered. He kissed her hands again, and then pressed them to his face. "You've got to understand," he muttered, as though afraid to say it aloud. "My son... Richard... All the time I was telling you what Rudi did, I was thinking about Richard. It's like... I can't say it... it's like... what happened to me with Richard and with Käthe is all the same... like with Richard, it's now the same with Rudi... it's all one, somehow."

"But, Willi, what are you talking about?" Berthe asked in confusion. "Your wife was killed in a bombing, it's—"

"I know," he interrupted, "but it's the same. And I..." His voice burst out loudly: "I want to leave the farm!"

"Leave? Leave here? My farm?"

"With you, Berthe. You and me. We'll go some place."

"*Leave my farm?*"

"We can get another. This is *his* farm. I don't want to work his farm."

"Willi, my goodness," she cried. Her brain raced feverishly as she sought for arguments. "You don't want to live with Rudi, all right. But Rudi isn't here."

"It's his farm. I don't—"

"My God, let's be honest," she interrupted. "How do we know Rudi will ever come back? But meanwhile, why should we leave? You think farms are like stones... you go out on the road and just pick one up?"

"You don't understand," he muttered.

"I understand more than you think. This rottenness... you think I'm blind? But you're all mixed-up, Willi. If Rudi was here, it would be different. But to mix up your dead wife, your dead son..."

Willi covered his face with his hands. "Jesus Christ, I don't know what to think any more. I don't even know what I am."

"Oh, my darling," Berthe cried. "You're a good man, a decent man – that's what you are. I swear to you: you and I can be happy. We can tell other people to go to the devil. And we can..." She stopped, aghast at the lie that had leapt into her mind... Then, slowly, she said: "And we can be happy with our child."

It was her tone rather than her words that made him look at her.

"Yes," she said softly, "I'm carrying your child, Willi. I was going to tell you tonight. But you see – we can't leave the farm until the child is born, can we? Where would we go?"

"A child, Berthe? Our child?" he whispered.

"Yes, my darling," she lied.

"Oh!" he said. "Oh!"

In silence he gazed at her. Then, after a little while, she reached out her hand to him. "Now will you take *my* hand, Willi? I didn't take my hand away from you before, even though what you said was terrible for me to hear. Now take my hand, Willi, and say we'll stay here on the farm together."

Slowly he reached out. He pressed her hand and then he held out his arms. She moved to him. She kissed his face, his hot forehead, and she felt that her heart would burst with tenderness for this fine man, this decent, humane man, and his wounded heart. He held her close, in silence.

"Ah, Willi," she said, "my darling, my sweet love."

He said nothing, but he strained her body to his.

"Dearest," she said, "go outside for a few minutes. These things Rudi brought me... when you come back, they'll be gone. I'll burn them and they'll be forgotten. And when you come back, bring your whole heart to me, darling. Come into the bedroom, where I'll be. Lie down with me, and take me into your arms and call me wife. Go now, darling. Go outside until I call you."

He kissed her then, passionately, and his hand stroked her face. Then he went out.

Swiftly Berthe crossed to the bedroom. She removed her robe. Wincing under her private pain, she pulled the pink nightgown over her head. "My own son!" she thought, as she flung the gown to the floor. "What brutes men are!"

She donned her robe again. She rummaged in a bureau drawer for the second nightgown. Then she ran to the closet. She tore the soft wine-coloured sweater from its hook. Last of all, on her way back to the kitchen, she snatched up the bottle of perfume that had been so precious to her only an hour before.

She lifted the stove lid, stuffed a piece of newspaper into the black hole and lit it. With fury she watched the paper flare up. She thrust the pink nightgown into the flames. It was as though Rudi's face were burning there upon the silk. She covered his image with the second nightgown and sobbed in her throat as she watched the bright flame lick at the gleaming fabric. Then she stopped. With the sweater in her hand and her hand poised, she stopped. "But this is ridiculous!" her mind cried. "Clothes are only clothes. A sweater is only a sweater. There's no evil in a sweater. What am I doing? It's insane to burn good clothes like this."

For a moment she felt dizzy. What would Willi say?... Her mind answered quickly and easily: Willi need never know. She would put the sweater away. Later she would get her hands on some dye. Change the colour of the sweater and what was it? A different sweater. She could invent a story – a cousin had sent it to her. Six months from now, when it was bitter cold and she desperately needed a sweater, Willi would not remember. What Rudi had done... he had done. She hated him for it. But why should anyone get moral about a sweater? It was childish. The nightgowns were gone now, but that was little loss. They were only playthings that probably wouldn't have lasted two washings. But to destroy a fine sweater like this, or the perfume... that would be crazy.

She replaced the stove lid. She ran into the bedroom, folded the sweater neatly and hid it beneath a pile of her other things in a bureau drawer. She thrust the bottle of perfume into a second drawer. Quickly she returned to the kitchen. She observed with satisfaction that the room stank from the burning clothes. Willi would never know the difference. Softly she padded to the front door. She saw Willi standing at the gate, his broad back turned to her, his head bowed. "Darling," she called. He turned slowly.

"Come in, my darling." She ran back into the bedroom.

Willi entered the kitchen. His nostrils twitched at the pervading stink in the room. He could see the glow of embers through the portholes of the stove. He crossed to the bedroom, shutting the door. Berthe lay naked, a tremulous, loving smile on her lips. He sat down. His fingers plucked at the sheet.

"Berthe, sweetheart," he said softly, "thank you for... for burning the clothes."

"Hush," she said. "It's forgotten now. I didn't do it only for you, but for me too, Willi."

"Yes," he replied haltingly, "I know. That's why I... I love you, Berthe."

She pressed her lips to his hand. "You *weren't* thinking of leaving me, were you, Willi?"

"No. How can you ever believe it?"

"I was so afraid."

"But after the war—"

"Hush," she said. "Not now. Now lie down with me, Willi. Hold me."

"Please," he said, almost timidly. "After the war, when Rudi comes home, I'll want... We must leave the farm then, Berthe. I swear I'll get another farm for you, darling. Or perhaps, even... perhaps move to another country, maybe. Too much has happened to me here. I feel as though I can't breathe. I'm not so old. I can make a living anywhere, I'm sure."

"Hush," she said. "We have time to talk of that."

"But I want to know. Would you go with me, Berthe?"

"Yes," she replied softly. "So long as you call me wife, I'll stay with you."

"Thank you," he muttered, "thank you, Berthe. God bless you."

"Darling," she whispered, "now put those ideas out of your head. Put your face down on me... Here, where our baby is."

And slowly, with a glowing face, she drew his head down to her body.

"We'll make our baby like you," she said. "We'll make him fine and good – won't we, darling? Won't we, my sweet, fine Willi?"

She pressed his head deep into her soft, warm belly.

Chapter 12

Monday noon came as usual with the scream of the siren. The power shut down in the forge room. Willi stood for a moment, tired, blinking, feeling on his flesh the rhythmic beat of a hammer that had already ceased its pounding. He put down his tongs, wiped his face and chest as best he could with a pocket rag and went quickly to the locker for his jacket. The mess hall was a distance away, and they had to be back at their machines in thirty minutes.

All this was as usual. It had been this way every workday for seven months. And if Hartwig, the foreman, had been asked, or Hoiseler, who operated a stamping press near Willi, they would have answered, "Willi? Why, Willi's the same as usual. There's the hammer, and there's Willi. Willi will go on as long as the hammer does. He's some lad, that Willi – a lump of iron himself."

But nothing was as usual in Willi's heart. What Rudi had done plagued him as though he himself were tainted by the deed. No matter what Berthe had said, Rudi made him remember Richard and Richard's son, and Karl, and Arthur Schauer. Formerly these had been disconnected memories, however painful, but now they were linked by Rudi, and he kept feeling that they were like the scattered pieces of a puzzle that had to be put together.

It is not easy to begin to think. It is not simple to seek a pattern or a meaning in what has always been without pattern and without meaning. That there was now a rottenness, as he thought of it, in his land and in his people, Willi knew. But where it had started, by whose hand the well had been poisoned, he did not know. Ah yes, he could answer, "The National Socialist Party." But that was too simple, it seemed to him. He himself had lived under the Party all these years. It still didn't give him real understanding – or explain his own uneasiness. Now he wished he knew what had happened in the days of his careless sleepwalking, when he had lived from moment to moment, whistling. Now he wished he could remember what Karl had said to him in 1931, or recall the leaflet that had been pressed into his hand the day after the Reichstag fire... or add and subtract the numberless pinpoint events that must have built this rottenness. Above all, his mind returned to a single quest: what was the road for him now? Where was he going?

His brain had no answer. It offered him only a refuge – himself and his beloved Berthe, and the child of their flesh. At least *he* was without taint, he told himself, and Berthe was guiltless, and the child to be born – they would devote their lives to keeping the child's heart free of this rot.

But meanwhile, there was the outside world to reckon with, and other men and other women. All this morning he had been trying to examine the world and the men about them. Hoiseler, now... he kept wondering about Hoiseler. Until today the men in his bunkhouse had been merely voices and figures to him. But now he wanted to know about them – not complicated things, only a few simple matters. He wanted to know if there were some amongst them who would say, "Yes... a child is a child. A child is precious. It must not be dealt with like a loaf of bread." And were there some who would also say, "Sure... we've gone along with the Nazis this far, but when a man acts like a beast, he can't call on the glory of the next thousand years to excuse him. Crime is crime. Good is good. Evil is evil. Sin is sin. We know this." And were there some who would say "There's one thing we believe: there *is* such a thing as decency. Men must be decent. Men are not wolves"?

These things Willi wanted to know. With these simple, burning questions in his heart he gazed all morning at the workers about him, and stared at the men he passed on his way to the commissary, and whispered to himself, "There must be some. I'll speak to Pelz. And the pastor – I'll see him on Sunday. In the barracks these men never say a word against the National Socialists. But neither do I. Maybe they're keeping things to themselves too. Maybe, in their hearts, they're like me."

The morning had been as usual, but lunch was not. When Willi set his plate down on the table reserved by custom for the men in his bunk, he found an excited conversation going on. This was strange, and he marked it. Usually the men sat humped over their plates, wolfing their food in silence. It was only when they were outside in the hot sun, rolling a cigarette, that talk sprang up amongst them. But now there was a mounting buzz of voices from all over the huge room. "There you are, Willi," Keller, his Cell Leader, said animatedly. "We've been waiting for you. Sit down, lad, take the wax out of your ears."

"We're to have a political meeting with our lentils today," Pelz explained. "The—"

"All right now, no more chatter," interrupted Hoiseler. "You've been stringing us long enough, Fritz. Spill it." Hoiseler's long, dark face was as sullen as always, even though his eyes were curious.

"I know what's got Hoiseler excited," said Pelz with a grin to Keller. "He thinks you took up that petition, Fritz. They're going to send us some Greek girls, right?"

"Virgins," interjected old Rufke merrily. "Isn't that so, Fritz?" His false teeth clicked in his mouth.

"Gentlemen," said Keller, "we'd better get some new jokes. The one about Greek virgins is so stale it smells. Now listen: I've just come from a political meeting in the Labour Front Office. All the Cell Leaders were there."

"You told us that twice already," observed Hoiseler with irritation. "Come to the point."

"Willi didn't hear it, did he?"

"All right – now he's heard it."

"War's over," said old Rufke, "that's the news, eh, Fritz? The Reds have surrendered, England asks peace, there's a revolution against the Jews in America."

"Shut up, you!"

"The news is this," said Keller. "Our little community is larger by four thousand than it was last night."

"What?" Rufke asked. "A pair of thighs for every four men? What consideration! What an eye to our comfort!"

"Larger by four thousand Polish prisoners."

There was instant silence. The others looked at him with excitement. Willi stared at his muddy lentil soup.

"What for?" asked Pelz. "What do they want with Polacks?"

"Some are to be used on the farms. But most of them are to be trained for jobs in the factory."

Hoiseler clicked his tongue. "So it's one man to the army for every Polack, eh?"

Pelz grinned sourly and flipped his empty sleeve. "It's Russia for you, boys. Goodbye."

Keller shook his head. "Baumer said nothing about the army. Why can't it be that some of us will be transferred to another factory?"

Pelz laughed. "Take it from me – there'll be an army call in a week. This summer campaign has cost us casualties."

"Nonsense," exclaimed old Rufke, in a reproving tone. "We've had practically no casualties at all. I saw it just yesterday in the paper. We've been going through the Reds like a hot knife through butter."

Pelz shook his empty sleeve again. He laughed in derision. "Get ready for the army," he said to Willi, at his side. "I know."

Willi said nothing. He was staring at Keller, his brow furrowed. He recalled now what Herr Guttmann had said about labour gangs.

"Whatever it is, we'll hear when the time comes," said Keller. "Right now there are instructions. Pay attention." He pulled a slip of paper from his pocket. "First: there must be no friendliness between any German worker and any prisoner. Those of us who are called on to train individual Polacks must see to that especially. Understand?"

"Well, of course," snorted old Rufke. "What do you take us for?"

"How do you train a Polack when you can't speak his language?" asked Pelz.

"There'll be interpreters... Although I understand some of them are from a border district. That kind speak German." Keller cleared his throat. "Second, and very important: we're to keep the strictest watch for sabotage. From now on SS guards will be in every plant at all times. But there can't be a guard for every prisoner. Therefore we have our own duty in the matter too. These Polacks are our enemies. As Germans we must see to it that—"

"Listen," Hoiseler interrupted, "we're not kids. You think we're going to stand by and watch sabotage?"

"Don't jump down my throat, man. I'm only telling you what I'm supposed to tell you. Any suspicious action must be reported at once."

"Make an end to it," said Hoiseler, "I have to get to the latrine."

"Third: we must watch work pace, especially on jobs where there can't be a piece quota. The Polacks are liable to try slowing up. If they do, it's to be reported."

"If they do, how about a swift boot in the hind end?" asked Rufke merrily. "That talks in any language, eh lads?"

"Fourth and last," said Keller, "we must take it upon ourselves to see that, during the training period, production doesn't slow up too much. Therefore, while the prisoners are learning, keep a strict watch over every operation. We mustn't have a month in which the whole factory is turning out scrap."

"That depends," said Hoiseler. "Are they workers or farmers? Have they ever been in a factory before?"

"They didn't tell us. Probably all kinds."

"Well, dammit, I don't want a farmer to train in my work," Hoiseler said with disgust.

"Look who's talking anyway," Pelz observed. "Hoiseler, the hardware salesman. You've been boasting that you were never in a factory in your life before three years ago. I suppose you didn't have to be taught?"

"Sure – but I'm a German, not a Polack," replied Hoiseler with heat. "Don't you think there's a difference?"

Willi stared at Hoiseler. "A German, not a Polack." The words bit into his brain. Two nights before he had stopped Rudi on the road. In anguish he had cried out, "But how can you laugh about this, Rudi? Aren't you even ashamed? Will you do this to other women too? Wouldn't you care if others did this to your mother?"

And Rudi had become furious. He had replied, "Are you crazy? You son of a bitch, you're drunk. Is a German woman the same as a Frenchwoman? Do you want me to have the same respect for a French saboteur as for my own mother?"

Yes, Rudi had looked insulted – the way Hoiseler looked now. Willi stared in turn at Hoiseler, at Rufke, at the one-armed Pelz, at Keller. "Yes," he whispered to himself. "This is how it is. This rottenness is here too. A German, not a Polack. To a Polack or a Frenchwoman you can do what you want. There is no shame in what you do to them." And suddenly, as Willi gazed at his comrades, an odd and terrible notion gripped his mind: that behind their separate faces and separate voices there was a single face and a single voice that they possessed in common – a grinning face and a hard, clacking tongue... a tongue that said "A German, not a Polack" and a face that laughed as the tongue clacked. And as he stared at their faces and heard their metallic laughter, he began to hate them with a violent, consuming hatred that blazed in his gut like a flame. Yet at the same time the notion made him feel unbearably alone and lonely. He gazed around at the other tables, seeking a face that was not laughing, that would be sad, that would catch his eye and nod, saying, "Yes. This *is* rottenness. I agree with you." But there was no eye to meet his: there were only faces that told him nothing. And it left him feeling frightened and despairing and consumed with self-pity.

Then, from outside the commissary, there came a sudden shout: "Hey – the prisoners are coming." Instantly there was an uproar in the large room. The men leapt to their feet and began running for the door. "C'mon..." young Pelz said with excitement. "Let's take a look at what we'll have to work with!"

"It won't be much, I can tell you that," said Hoiseler, rising from his chair. "I was on the Eastern Front in the last war. Such stupid swine you never saw in your life."

"Well, Willi," Keller said, as they walked out, "how are you, Willi?"

Willi grunted. He ached to say: "I always liked you, Keller. Don't *you* see the rottenness here?" But he was afraid.

"You know – a couple of weeks ago we saw you in town with your woman. We were drunk, so I told the lads to leave you alone. Didn't want to embarrass you." He nudged Willi with his elbow. "But she's a handsome one. You're lucky."

"We're going to get married," Willi said suddenly. "I'm moving to her farm."

"Really?" Keller slapped his back. "I'm glad, Willi. I wish you all happiness. But listen... you sure Baumer will let you leave the hammer? You're a valuable man, you know."

"Yes," Willi muttered. "I'm sure of it. They need men on the farms. Once we're married..."

He didn't continue. From the mass of workers gathered in front of the commissary there came a deep-throated buzz – and then a sudden end to conversation. The first group of Poles had appeared.

There were about twenty of them, preceded and followed by an SS man carrying an automatic rifle. Flanking them there was one SS man on each side with a revolver at his hip and a heavy leather whip dangling from a loop around his wrist.

The Poles walked in silence, and the German workers stared at them in silence. The prisoners were big men for the most part, peasants with powerful frames. Their skulls were uniformly shaven, and the heads of many were scabrous, broken out with sores. They did not look ahead, or at the sky or at each other, but only at the ground. Their unwashed faces were hollow and gaunt, and the cords in their necks were visible, and they walked stiffly, as men walk who have been five days locked in cattle cars. Some were barefoot, some had torn shoes, and some had rag bindings on their feet. And they wore shirts and trousers, but that was all – except for the letter "P", the large yellow badge of their inferiority sewn on their breasts. And as they came up to the throng of watching men, they did not look up or turn their heads, or glance at each other, but kept their eyes upon the ground and walked silently on.

It took no special knowledge to know why these prisoners walked as they did. Willi understood. The truth screamed from their bowed, shuffling figures: that after three years of captivity some of them were now so beaten that their hearts were squeezed empty, and that these didn't know where they were and didn't care, and so they kept their eyes upon the ground as defeated men always do, but that there were others who had been strengthened by their servitude, who knew exactly where they were, and whose hearts throbbed with a hatred that no tongue could express – and so they too kept their eyes upon the ground, for they were afraid of what their eyes would show. But almost before the first of them had passed, it was no longer upon them but at his fellow Germans that Willi gazed. What were *they* thinking? In the disdainful faces he could see scorn and contempt plainly written. He knew those faces now. They said "A German is not a Pole" and laughed. But what about the others – the men with blank faces and expressionless eyes? Was it pity those men hid behind their eyes, or merely a heart that did not care? Were there some amongst them, perhaps, who clenched their teeth, who felt as he did that it was indecent to starve men as these Poles were starved, that it was evil to drive them to work at the point of a gun as though they were slaves? And as the whistle screamed from the powerhouse, calling all of them to the machines – Germans and Poles in common – Willi started as though he had been struck. He felt his hands commence to tremble, and he walked forward thinking: "But those SS men have whips."

The whistle screamed, saying: "Come in. Your machines are waiting."

2

On this first afternoon, although most of the Poles were assigned to jobs in the factory, only a few were sent into the forge room – and those at unskilled work. Superintendent Kohlberg had ordered it this way after consultation with Labour Front Leader Baumer. The machines in the forge room were among the most expensive in the factory. Kohlberg wanted to test all Poles earmarked for a vital department. Hence, although elsewhere in the factory the proportion was one SS man to ten prisoners, in the forge room there were five guards for thirty Poles – three on the floor with revolvers and whips, two on the overhead catwalk with carbines.

One of the prisoners was assigned to be Willi's helper. Willi had been hoping for this. In the walk from the commissary to the forge room he had conceived a plan, and when he saw Hartwig, the foreman, approaching with one of the prisoners, his heart began to pound with excitement. He wanted to convey something to at least one of these prisoners that he was sure any man would understand. It was simple. It was only to say "Brother!" – to say, "Look, man… I'm sorry for you. I understand what you're suffering. I sympathize." But until he could say this small thing to one of these Poles – so that the man might perhaps convey it to the others – Willi knew that he would not be able to rest. And if he had paused to ask himself why a small thing like this suddenly had become so important to him, he would have been baffled. He was merely aware of a burning need to separate himself from the rottenness that he felt about him – from the SS men on the catwalk, from Rufke and Hoiseler... and from all the others who had gazed with naked scorn upon these Poles.

The need was deeper and older than Willi knew. It was all of forty-two years old, and it was an encrusted yearning for absolution. For this was the obligation he had failed when he sat upon a park bench years before and heard two nursemaids talking... this was all of the shameful moments of his life compounded into one: when he had been silent as they wrested his son away from him... and silent when he listened to a child's pledge to die at eighteen... and silent when he heard that Karl had been killed. Now, suddenly, Willi's heart had begun to understand these things – not as politics, but as simple indecencies that had become one huge indecency, as the rottenness that was reaching out to embrace him. And now finally, with these Poles, his soul was groping towards an elemental gesture of protest.

For the first half-hour he watched his new helper. The prisoner's task was simple: it was to trundle a wheelbarrow across the forge room to a loading platform, to pile the barrow with steel castings, and then to push the load back to the steam hammer. There he dumped the castings on the floor by Willi's side. The prisoner was a young man, thick-set and muscular – although obviously undernourished and affected by a rasping cough. Willi watched him and presently began to turn around each time the man approached. He had planned a beginning to their relationship, and he was becoming impatient.

The Pole paid no attention. He kept his eyes submissively on his work. And finally, after a quick glance at the SS men on the catwalk, Willi turned from the hammer as the prisoner reached his side again. He put out his hand, touching the man's hairy forearm. "Pole," he said.

The prisoner paused. He looked up slowly. His broad, pasty-skinned face remained immobile, but there was a dull question in his eyes.

"Good!" Willi said. He patted the man's arm and pointed to the pile of castings. "*Very good.*" He articulated the words with heavy emphasis, feeling certain that thereby the Pole would understand him. And he smiled warmly, nodding his head and patting the man's arm again in demonstration of friendship.

The Pole understood. What had been an expressionless peasant face turned animal. The broad mouth parted, baring the teeth; the dull eyes answered Willi's smile with a blinding gleam of hatred. And as though he were a wolf seeking the soft spot in Willi's flesh, the Pole's glance descended to his throat. And so they stared at each other.

It ended there. A step sounded to one side. The prisoner turned away quickly. He dumped his load, wheeled the barrow and started off rapidly across the floor.

Elite Guard Latzelburger strode up to Willi with the anger of authority mottling his bulldog face. "What's going on here?" he demanded harshly. "You want me to report you?"

"I... had to tell him... where to put the castings," Willi stammered.

"Oh, you did? And do you speak Polish?"

"No. But I... showed him. It was only a little matter."

"Hereafter, if you need to speak to a prisoner, call me. I'll tell him what he needs to know, or I'll call the interpreter. Don't let me catch you speaking to one of them again." He strode off, snapping his whip angrily against his boot.

That was all. The afternoon passed. "Everything went as usual," was the report of Foreman Hartwig.

3

Some hours later Willi walked slowly down the road towards Berthe's farm. He walked under a brilliant, star-speckled sky with his head bowed and his heavy shoulders sagging. He was unshaven; the factory grime was still on his hands and face; he still wore his sweat-caked overalls and denim jacket. He was suffering under a sense of shame so acute that it made him feel physically ill. Before his eyes there was a single image: of the wolfish face of the Pole, of the blinding hatred in his glance.

Latzelburger had whipped one of the prisoners in the course of the afternoon. Willi had not known why, or even witnessed it, but he had viewed the Pole as they dragged him roughly outside, and he had seen the blood on his face, the pain-glazed eyes.

Later, when Hoiseler said to him "Did you hear what that Polack bastard did? He refused an order. Said it was too hard for him, or something like that", then Willi had a moment of rage such as he had never experienced before in his life – not in the trenches, not when Käthe had died, not even when Rudi had told him the story of the Frenchwoman. For an instant Hoiseler's face had been blotted out by a dizzy fury that blinded him...

But then his brain had whispered the old, familiar words, "*Be careful, be careful*", leaving him trembling, nauseous, his senses reeling.

Now he was coming to Berthe as a suppliant, to say: "Help me, Berthe. Life has run away from me. I can't bear another day in the factory. Either you'll get me transferred to the farm... or I don't know what I'll do. I can't live like this any longer."

The farmhouse was dark. He stepped past the creaking gate into the yard. He peered into the kitchen, and then into the bedroom. Berthe was not at home. He lit a lamp, leaving the windows unshaded. He didn't care that he might be punished for violating the blackout. If Berthe were off in the fields, he knew she would see it. Then he found a note marked "*Willi, darling.*" Berthe had gone to town. She asked him to wait for her. The note was signed "*Your wife.*"

Dejectedly Willi sat down. He held the note between his big hands. He stared at the signature, "*Your wife*". He yearned for those loving words to obliterate the image in his mind. Angrily, pathetically, he asked himself once again, as he had been doing all afternoon, "What's the matter with you, Willi? Why do you take the sins of others on your back? The Pole didn't understand – that's all. You'll speak to another Pole. You'll explain to him."

Slowly he got up. Blowing out the lamp, he went into the bedroom and lay down. He closed his eyes. His mind turned back to a sunny afternoon in a meadow when a child had cried, "Oh Daddy, Mommy, look – the fly-butter is flyning." And he asked himself with anguish and self-pity, "What has happened? Where is the goodness now? What sort of world is this?"

Willi awakened out of a confused dream to the sound of voices. He heard the throbbing motor of a truck on the road. The motor died. He lay quiet, groggy and disinterested. Then he heard Berthe's voice. It seemed to come from outside the bedroom. He sat up and peered out of the window. He saw her a distance away in the moonlight, walking rapidly across the field with a number of men. He guessed that they were going to the barn and wondered why. For a moment he debated whether to follow them, but then decided to remain where he was. It was Berthe he wanted to see – he had no stomach for strangers.

Wearily he stood up. He went into the kitchen and began to scrub the grime from his hands and face. He thrust his head under the tap and let the cold water pour down over his head. As he was drying himself, he heard Berthe's voice again. He crossed to a window. Berthe was striding a yard behind two men, who were in an obvious hurry. They were passing close by the house on their way to the gate. One of them was an SS man carrying a carbine.

A dull pain struck in Willi's stomach. There had been three men with Berthe on her way to the barn. He was sure of it. His mind stopped, refusing to conjecture further. He could only stare at the SS man with the carbine... and remember the Elite Guards in the forge room. He watched until they had passed the front door. Then he slipped outside.

The truck he had heard stood by the gate. Unlike most of the factory transport vehicles, the body was enclosed, as though it were a furniture van. He saw the SS man walk around to the rear of the van and test the bolt which secured its doors. He heard Berthe's animated "Goodnight, Erich" to the other man. "Thank you, Erich." The motor started with a roar. The two men went around to the far side of the cab. The door slammed; the truck moved off down the road towards the factory.

Willi remained where he was. The dull pain was knotting his stomach, and he could feel the sweat bursting out all over his body.

"Why, Willi," Berthe cried as she saw him, "have you been here all this time? Why didn't you let me know? That was Erich Rosenhart, the Peasant Leader. I wanted him to meet you." She embraced him lovingly, raising up on tiptoe to kiss his face. He saw that she was wearing her black dress, the one she reserved for important occasions.

"My goodness, Willi," she continued in an animated, almost strident tone, "look at you... you're still in your overalls. *Pfui*, you positively smell." She laughed at him affectionately. "I know: now that I've finally said I'll marry you, you no longer have to dress up for me, eh? Oh, you men!" She caught his arm. "Come in, dearest. You ate at the factory, I suppose? I'm starved. You saw my note? I had to go off to the village at five o'clock. Thank God Rosenhart brought me back by truck."

"Berthe," he asked dully as they entered the kitchen, "why did you go to the village?"

She bent over the lamp and struck a match. "Why?" She laughed, but her laughter was a bit shrill. "More excitement than I've had in years. Like a carnival. But let me get something on the table first. I'm so full of news I don't know where to begin."

Willi sat down, watching her as she bustled around the kitchen. He sat very still.

"Will you have a glass of milk, Willi? And there's a bit of pork left over. Will you finish it with me? It's the very last taste of pork I'll have to offer for God knows when."

He shook his head.

"Are you tired, darling? Was work hard today?"

"Yes," he said.

She paused to look at him sympathetically. "No wonder. Indoors all day, with all that noise and machinery. I don't know how you stand it at all." She sat down to her supper. Suddenly her expression became mischievous, her eyes sly. "But maybe now there's an end to it – what do you think of that, Willi?"

He looked at her questioningly, and her face turned radiant.

"Yes, my darling," she burst out, "tonight, right this minute perhaps, Erich is seeing the Labour Front Leader of your factory. He promised. So long as we're to be married, he's sure he can arrange it. Think of it: in only a few days you'll be transferred to the farm. I'm sure nothing will interfere. Well, darling, don't you have anything to say?"

"Berthe," he asked fearfully, "did you leave someone in the barn?"

Berthe's temper flared. For months they had been waiting for him to be transferred to the farm. Yet now that the moment had arrived, he passed off the news as though it were a weather report.

"Yes… there's someone in the barn," she replied sharply. "A Pole. He's to work for me. That's why I went to the village."

"Everyone… all the farmers have Poles now?" he asked stiffly.

She looked down at her plate. Flatly she replied: "All who could afford it. They're not cheap – seventeen marks I had to pay."

"To pay?" Willi whispered. It seemed to him that his heartbeat paused as he waited for her answer.

Berthe laughed harshly. "I can see you don't know our Farm Bureau. It's supposed to help the farmer, but it's a business, like everything else. My goodness, they must have made a fortune at the sale today. Of course, it all goes to the government."

"Berthe," Willi groaned, "Berthe."

"What is it?"

"How can you…" – his voice became a rasp – "how can you even *say* it? *You bought a man*, Berthe? You paid money for a man?"

"But how silly you are!" she replied roughly. "These are prisoners. I didn't buy a man in the way you mean it. I merely paid the government to have him work on my farm while the war lasts. Everybody does that." She tossed her head, and the tone of her voice altered, becoming shrill and gay. "Oh, I wish you could have gone to the village with me, Willi. I saw more old friends than I have since the war began. I wanted to show you off.

And such excitement there was! I came to town late, my bad luck, because those damn SS men who were to notify all the farmers came around to me the last one. All the strong ones were grabbed up by the time I came. That neighbour of mine, Winz! Four Poles, he hired – four, can you imagine? And a girl for his wife, to work around the house. My goodness, they won't have to do a stroke of work themselves. They'll live like kings."

"Where was the sale, Berthe?" Willi asked in a muted voice. "In the church?"

Her face turned scarlet, but she went right on with her chatter.

"No. Goodness – there wouldn't have been enough room in the church to hold all those people. It was in the square, where the soldiers' monument is. They had a platform. The Poles were brought up on the platform, so you could see them – then Erich auctioned them off. God knows what sort of a specimen I got. A lazy good-for-nothing, probably."

"But now you own him?" Willi whispered.

"No, I don't own him," Berthe replied, harshly again. "I only *hired* him, and I'll be out seventeen marks if he's no good. They're always so full of rules, those bureaus. We're to be held responsible if the Pole runs away. And the Bureau can rent him to us, but we can't rent him to anyone else – how do you like that? If he's no good, I'll be stuck with him." She shook her head and continued right on, without pausing. "However, at only seventeen marks I'll surely get some return. The Bureau swore he was a farmer. And they gave me a medical certificate to prove he's healthy. Anyway, mine speaks German, and that's a help." She burst out into shrill laughter. "I wish you could have seen Winz. It was comical. The last Pole he bought, Winz was looking him over, feeling his muscles and so on, and asking Rosenhart, 'Has he got any diseases? He's not flat-footed?', and Rosenhart was answering, 'He's healthy. He's strong as an ox – anyone can see it.' And suddenly Winz says, 'Open your mouth.' The Pole just stands there. 'Open your mouth,' the interpreter says in Polish. Still the man stands. Finally Erich says, 'Oh yes, it says here on the medical certificate that the Pole is a little deaf.' 'A little deaf?' Winz yells. 'I like that. Take him away. I wouldn't buy him in a million years. Even an ox can hear orders!' Can you imagine, Willi? Everybody was sick with laughing."

"Tell me, Berthe," he said, "did the Poles laugh?"

Berthe became quiet. Tight-lipped she asked, "Is something upsetting you, Willi?"

"Yes," he answered in a flat, hard tone. "I'm angry, Frau Lingg. I think the Farm Bureau cheated you. Don't you realize? When I killed your dog,

I paid you eighteen marks. And now you've paid seventeen marks for a man. Where's the comparison – to pay only one mark more for a dog than for a man? You've been cheated, Frau Lingg."

"What are you jabbering about?" she asked angrily. "What's this 'Frau Lingg' talk? You think it's funny? I don't think it's funny! What are you getting at?"

Berthe knew, of course. She was not stupid. And she was not without her own inward conflict over what she had done. Paying money for a man put up at auction – it seemed wrong to her, even if it was only hiring a war prisoner. She had felt instinctively that Willi would be angry. Elsie Guttmann had reacted to the sale in the same manner. She had told everyone that renting a man was a sin. She had called Rosenhart a scoundrel, yelling it in a voice so loud that her husband, out of fear that she would be arrested, had dragged her away by force. And there were others who had not bought, either. But it was all very well for Elsie Guttmann to be moral about it – she was in no danger of losing her farm. Berthe had her quotas to meet. Rosenhart had told everyone flatly: the harvest gangs would come first to those farms where the owners had hired Poles. The others would be regarded as not having done their duty by the State. So what else could she have done? No Pole – no harvest gangs. No harvest – her quotas would be unfulfilled. And then she'd lose her farm, hereditary peasant or not.

"Well, then, let's talk about it," she said with a sigh. "I know what you're thinking. We'll have it out right now... Only, be good enough to let me talk first, Willi."

Willi said nothing. He merely stared at Berthe – and sat motionless in his chair, one hand pressed to his breast. It seemed to him, as he looked at this woman he loved, that his veins had congealed – that his blood, to the last drop, had frozen to ice under the press of his despair.

Berthe flushed as she saw his face, but she kept her temper. "I'm a farmer, Willi. You're not. If I don't meet my quotas, they'll take my farm away. Do you want that?"

"I want... I want you to take back the Pole," Willi burst out hoarsely.

"Take him back?"

"Yes."

"Are you crazy, Willi? I already paid for him."

Willi said nothing. He chewed his lips and kept staring at her.

"But you don't understand," Berthe cried. "You must listen to me, Willi."

"Yes, I'm listening."

"Tomorrow morning they're sending a gang of prisoners to cut my hay." Her speech was hurried and her voice shaken – she was beginning to be frightened by Willi's manner. "*You* know what state my hay is in, Willi. Some of it's flowered already – it's dry and worthless. So they're going to try and save the rest by cutting it all in one morning. But do you know why they're helping me? Because I rented a Pole. 'No Poles, no labour help' – that's what Rosenhart said. 'You have to do your duty by the State if you expect help from the State.' Now, give me a straight answer, Willi: what should I do? Should I return the Pole and let my hay rot?"

"Yes," he whispered.

"What? So my cattle won't have anything to eat this winter? Is that all right with you?"

"Yes," he said. "Yes. Yes."

"Sure, how easy it is for you to talk," she replied bitterly. "It isn't *your* farm. You don't have your sweat and blood on every inch of it. What do you care?"

"I care!" Willi burst out in a strangled voice. "I care... I care..." He stopped, and when he spoke again, it was in a pleading whisper. "Berthe... darling... take the Pole back. Please, darling. It's wrong. You've bought a man like you'd buy a goat or a horse, Berthe."

"I haven't *bought* him," she interrupted. "I only rented him!"

"Berthe," he cried, "I beg you, darling, take him back. I'll work for you at night, on Sundays. When I'm transferred, I'll—"

"Oh, stop this nonsense!" she cried furiously. "I have to be practical. Even if you get transferred, do you think you're a farmer already? If Rudi was here it would be different – but he's not here. You and me alone – we can't save my hay now, or even harvest next month. So what should I do – lose my farm... starve... kill myself over a stinking Polack? So if the government rents me a Polish prisoner and says 'You'll pay *us* his wages, not him', what am I to do? Did *I* make him a prisoner? Am I to blame that he went to war with us? No, I'm not to blame! All I know is that now I can ask for labour help, I won't lose my farm."

Willi remained silent. A greyish pallor was spreading over his face. Berthe gazed at him boldly, feeling all of the anger that a stifled sense of guilt can provide.

"Hah!" she exclaimed. "I see you don't say so much now. In practical terms you know that I'm right. You know that I'm doing the only practical thing – that I can't do anything else."

Willi remained quiet, his hand still pressed to his breast. With a sense of terror and wonder he realized that he was sitting in a kitchen with a strange woman named Berthe Lingg. He observed that she was staring at him with fine, snapping black eyes, and that her round face was flushed. He knew that he had kissed this woman's lips, embraced her body, pressed his shut eyes to the warm, scented flesh of her breast. And he knew that until this evening he had not been able to look at her except with love, with an inward glow of gratitude and adoration... But now she was a stranger to him, and he saw it with terror. And he rose from his chair, silently, for there was nothing more he could say to this stranger. And then, without a backward glance, he started out of the room.

Berthe ran after him. She caught his arm as he reached the door.

"You listen to me!" she cried furiously. "Don't you walk away when I talk to you. This is your responsibility too! You think it isn't? We're to be married, remember. I'm carrying your child. We'll settle this right now. I'm tired of your goings-on."

Willi turned around. "Take your hand off me, Frau Lingg," he answered slowly.

She started back, terrified at what she saw in his face.

Willi went out. She heard his footsteps in the yard, and then the creaking of the gate.

"Oh my God," she muttered. The room began to turn around her in dizzy circles. "This is crazy!... Willi. *Willi.* You've got to listen, Willi – I love you..." She gasped, cried out in a muffled voice and fell sobbing to the floor.

4

Willi did not pause after leaving the farmhouse. Berthe's last, forlorn cry, which he heard as he walked out on the road, only strengthened his resolve.

Once, in ancient times, another man had walked as Willi walked now, implacably, with a blind need. To a lonely hilltop, to a consecrated altar, there had come the patriarch Abraham, bearing in his arms the body of his son that he might appease the wrath of Jehovah.* So now Willi left the road and strode towards the barn. In the barn was a man who had been purchased in a village square by one Berthe Lingg for seventeen marks, and Willi walked towards him, carrying in his heart a burnt offering.

There was a deed to be done. Every word that Berthe had uttered in her own defence had made this clearer to him. There was no room in his soul at this moment for sorrow over Berthe, for bitterness or rage. These emotions would come later. For the first time in his life, Willi was acting under the demand of an inner necessity that transcended what he was or what he wanted – the love of a woman, security, fear. For forty years he had been Willi Wegler, a man like millions of other Willis, who said, "I must look out for my family, for me and mine… I must avoid trouble." But now he was bigger than that Willi, more important: he was suddenly… anonymous. And this man had discarded the complex wisdom of the wise men whose cautions he had always heeded. His heart contained only a single precept now: that there was a deed to be done, and that it would not wait.

He found the barn doors bolted and locked. For a moment he considered throwing his weight at the doors and battering them down. The passion that governed him was not without cunning, however, and he decided against it. Berthe was his enemy now, and the farmhouse was only a hundred yards away. What had to be accomplished would not allow of bungling.

Quietly, hugging the walls in order to remain in shadow, he circled the barn. High up in one wall he saw the door through which hay was lifted to the loft, but when he searched the ground for a ladder, there was none to be found. Finally, on the moonstruck side of the barn, he found a slotted air vent a foot above his head. He scoured the surrounding earth for a rock or a box, but he saw nothing that would serve him. Crouching, clinging to the hollows as might a soldier crossing a battlefield, he worked his way back towards the farmhouse. As he passed the well, his eye caught the dull sheen of a bucket. He had no knife to sever the thick rope which held it, but he unwound the strands by patient twisting. Then, one by one, he ripped them apart with his hands.

He returned to the barn. He set the bucket down and stepped upon it carefully, seeking a secure balance. The air vent was in the wash of the moonlight. As he peered inside, he could see a silver filigree on the floor of the barn, but there was no sign of the prisoner. Cautiously, he looked back at the silent farmhouse. Then in a whisper he called, "Pole… Pole."

He could hear a scurrying within, as though from a rodent, but there was no other response. Lightly he tapped with his knuckles on the wooden slots of the vent. "Pole," he called more loudly, "Pole."

There was a groan from within, and then a strangled cough. Stephen Bironski, ex-pharmacist, ex-graduate of Cracow University, awakened from his troubled sleep on a maggoty straw pallet.

"Pole," Willi called again. "Pole?"

"Eh... what... who is it?" Bironski answered in Polish.

Willi groaned at the foreign words. Berthe had said that the prisoner spoke German. Was he to be defeated again by the barrier of language? "Pole, here, at the window," he whispered desperately, "at the window."

"Who is it?" came the reply in good German. "Where are you?"

Willi almost shouted in his hot excitement: "Up here. The little window in the wall – with slots in it. The one where the moonlight goes into the barn. Do you see it?"

"Yes, I see it," came the slow reply.

"Come over here. Can you stand on something? I want to talk to you."

There was no response this time, but Willi could hear the man moving about, then dragging something. Bironski's head appeared at the vent.

Like the others whom Willi had seen earlier, Bironski revealed the familiar stigmata of the prisoner: a shaven, scabrous skull, sunken cheeks, a pasty-white texture to his face. But this man was older than the one in the forge room.

"Pole, listen," he whispered excitedly. "Can you hear me?"

"Yes, sir."

"Don't call me 'sir'," Willi muttered. "I'm not your master. Call me anything else. My name's Willi. Call me that."

The Pole said nothing.

"What's your name?"

"Stephen Bironski – Pole, sir."

Willi bit his lip. "Bironski, listen to me." He stammered, fumbling for words. "I'm a German – but I don't hate you. I wouldn't lock you up in a barn or buy you for money like you were an animal. You're a man and I'm a man. I want to help you. Do you understand me, Bironski? I'm a German, but I want to help you. I have pity on you."

Silence... Then in a whisper, as though it were a slow, faint echo of his own voice, the word came back, "Help?"

"Yes. I want to help you escape," Willi cried with a wild exulting in his heart.

Again the moment of silence, and again the single echo, "Escape?"

"Don't you understand – to get away from here. I have it all figured out. I know—"

"Please," the Pole interrupted timidly, "I'm hungry. I've had nothing to eat all day. We had to march—"

"I'm sorry," Willi groaned. "I wish I could give you some food, but I have nothing… Wait! I have an idea. I'll get into the chicken house, I'll find you some eggs, maybe. But not now – later."

"Yes, eggs," Bironski replied, "eggs, if you please, sir. I'm sick. Eggs would be good for me. I need a doctor."

"Would you like to smoke?"

"Smoke?"

"I'll roll you a cigarette."

"No… no, sir. It's forbidden to smoke. But some eggs, sir…"

"I can't get them now. I'll have to wait till later. I might be seen."

"Yes, later, sir.… Please."

"But listen to me now, Bironski. Wouldn't you like to escape? Look, I have it all figured out. I'll get you some money, and different clothes. I'll give you my police card. And some food. Then when you're ready, I'll break open the doors. The lock isn't strong. It won't be hard. I can do it any night you say. And I can write a letter to your home, so they'll know you're coming."

The Pole was silent. He gazed fixedly at Willi through the slotted vent.

"Well? What do you say? You speak German. With my police card, you have a real chance."

"It's forbidden to escape," Bironski said dully.

"Of course it's forbidden. But they'll work you here like a dog till you die. With my police card you have a chance. What do you lose?"

"I'll only get caught," Bironski said dully. "They'll beat me." His eyes suddenly came alive, gleaming feverishly. "What are you doing this for? Why are you trying to get me into trouble? Sure – you'll bring me the eggs, and then they'll beat me for stealing. Go away. I haven't done anything to you…"

"No… Listen, I only want to help you. Why don't you trust me?" Willi groaned. "Don't you see this is dangerous for me too? Why don't you believe me?"

The prisoner's mouth opened. For a moment no sound came from the gaping mouth. Then, with a hoarse, venomous cry he answered: "Believe you? Believe a German? Believe a German?" He gasped, as though he were strangling. "Oh, what have I said? I didn't mean it. I believe you. I believe you, sir. Of course. Only, go away." He dropped out of sight in the darkness, but his voice came back in a forlorn, miserable plea: "Go away. Don't make trouble for me. Please, sir. I don't want the eggs."

Willi toppled off the bucket as though he had been struck. He fell to his knees, clapped his hands over his face and wept.

BOOK THREE

THE VISION OF JAKOB FRISCH

An August morning in the year 1942, from 6 a.m. until 11 a.m.

Chapter 13

Precisely at the dot of the hour the factory whistle screamed the birth of a new day. By Nature's clock it was still too early for the sun to be abroad, although its first rays were tinting the horizon. But it was more than time for men to be stirring. And for this reason the whistle screamed long and insistently to all for miles around, warning them that it was six o'clock, German war time – reminding them that their fatherland was embattled and they were needed at work.

In the factory bunk rooms men rolled on their cots. They sighed, forcing open heavy-lidded, pasty eyes. They waited for life to stream back to their torpid limbs and thought wistfully of other mornings – of the deep comfort of awakening to the smile of a warm-fleshed wife, of barking good-humouredly at a child, of the spicy odour of real coffee. Then they sat up with a groan and muttered curse, coughing and spitting the night's phlegm, already moving automatically to the rhythm of a day that would be as automatic as the last, as automatic as the next. A man's sleep was his private property – but little else in this new world. "This is war," they said, each with his own overtone. But all in common struggled into work clothes that were rancid-smelling from the sweat of past days and hurried to washrooms, to latrine, to commissary. This was war – the machines were waiting.

In the factory itself the night-shift men blinked and moved with new energy at the sound of the whistle. In a half-hour there would be grub, a cigarette, sleep. It would be inadequate grub, bad tobacco, an exhausted and fretful sleep. But this was war, and wars ended sometime. "Meanwhile," said the foremen and the Kohlbergs, said the political leaders and the Barons of Finance like von Bildering, "meanwhile get it out, watch the scrap, keep production going. Otherwise we'll lose, and then you'll remember these hard times as a picnic. We're all in this together, mates, for better or for worse. So keep things moving if you want to stay free, you workers. Keep things moving if you love your families, if you ever want to collect on your iron savings. Keep things moving, because there's a Soviet heel outside the door…"

On the surrounding farms the cows stamped in their stalls at the piercing scream of the whistle. They had been hearing it for seven months now, but it still unnerved them. Berthe Lingg, gripping the teats of a heavy-bagged animal, saw the stream of hot milk spurt and then stop. On other mornings she had laughed, but now she leant her head against the belly of the cow and thought, "I want to die." She stared at the foaming, half-filled pail and thought of Willi lying on his hospital cot. "But it's only a few days ago that Rudi came, that we were going to be married," she whispered half aloud. She saw a man's head upon a block, she saw an axe that rose and fell, and whispered, "Oh God, help me, what did I do?..." And then, because the whistle had stopped, she returned to her milking. There was a quota to be filled, and quotas are without compassion.

And in Wegler's bunkhouse, Fritz Keller, Party Cell Leader, buttoned his soiled jacket, hitched his trousers over his sagging belly and said wearily, "Well, lads, time for the home front to be doing its duty." This was a phrase of Keller's own contrivance, and once he had been proud of it. It seemed the proper way for a political leader to start his comrades on their day, and he invented all sorts of tonal variations by which to keep it cheerful. But this morning he might have been an embalmer saying, "Friends, the body is ready." A moment later he added in a mutter, "No – with my leaky heart I can't stand a night like last night. Goddamn Wegler, is all I say."

And young Pelz, his lips pressed tight together, glanced over at Wegler's empty cot and murmured, "I still can't believe it – Willi, a traitor!"

And old Rufke, combing his fine white head of hair, his clear eyes glittering, said joyously, "I'll remind you that we were ordered not to talk about this. However—"

"What's the difference?" Hoiseler interrupted. "*We* know. We just won't talk to others."

"However," old Rufke continued, "I'll tell you now that Wegler always smelt bad to me. Never could put my finger on anything, but he smelt bad."

"Gestapo Commissar Rufke," exclaimed Hoiseler. He broke wind. "Smell that, you smeller."

"Anyway," said Keller, starting for the door, "he'll get what he deserves, Wegler will. Let's go, lads. Time for the home front to be doing its duty."

So day came to the factory. The slowly brightening sky looked down upon this wood that disgorged tanks, gazed with serene indifference upon the camouflage nets and the false trees, upon the painted meadows, upon the berry bushes that had been contrived out of wire and cloth... and did not care. This sky had seen much violence, and would again. It did not care for men, for their good or for their evil.

2

6:05 a.m.

In the wing of the administration building now occupied by Gestapo Commissar Kehr, Baumer stood at the phone. He was listening to Doctor Zoder on the other end of the line, and his fingers drummed on the desk in a nervous tattoo. Behind the desk, sipping a lukewarm cup of barley coffee, sat the commissar. His handsome eyes were heavy-lidded and slightly bloodshot, but his porcine face remained calm, solid, unruffled – a proper attitude for a guardian of the State. He was studying a page in his black notebook.

The expression of quiet concentration that Kehr displayed was a hollow fraud – he might just as well have been reading a stock-exchange report. It was very discouraging. Petulantly he told himself that he understood no more about the Wegler affair now than he had five hours ago. As he was fond of saying to his colleagues, the business of arranging a series of clues into a pattern, of blending logic, philosophy and psychology to achieve truth – there was something artistic about that. It was orderly, it was neat, and it kept the world going around in its appointed course. But a police inspector justified his trust only when he was successful. No more than a pastor would enjoy seeing his flock take to drink and to riotous sin could Kehr now relish the spectacle of successful sabotage. This was not a matter of personal pride or of anxiety for his position. His record was too solid for failure in a single case to do him damage. If he was dismayed at the prospect of having to report failure, it was only because he maintained ideals about his profession. The physician of the State, as he was sometimes pleased to think of himself, could not permit a criminal cell in the social body. And for this reason, even though he felt baffled and excessively weary, he continued to pore over his notes, to analyse the mountain of dossiers on his desk... and to repeat to himself, each time his energy sagged: "Snap up, man – there's a clue somewhere. It's your moral duty to find it."

As Baumer clicked the phone, Kehr looked up with raised eyebrows. "Any news?" he asked hopefully.

The Labour Front Leader shook his head. His nervous fingers drummed on the desk. "Wegler is still unconscious."

"Are you sure your doctor is capable?"

Baumer nodded. His handsome, chiselled face was haggard, his blue eyes had a glassy sheen. "Yes, Zoder knows his business. He's going to try some sort of an injection later in the morning. But he doesn't promise anything. We're having bad luck, that's all." He grimaced wryly. "The fortunes of sabotage, one might say."

"It might make a difference if I could talk to Wegler. This way I'm handicapped," said Kehr, frowning.

"Alibis, alibis," Baumer thought with irritation. "If your head wasn't as fat as your behind, you would have turned up something already." Aloud he said: "Well, I'll leave you now. Before you do anything else I suggest you reach the men who know about Wegler. They have to be shut up."

Kehr nodded. "Any particular line you think I ought to follow?"

"Yes. What do you think of this? No lies, but a frank political explanation: that it will demoralize the workers if it becomes known that the recipient of a War Service Cross committed sabotage. Therefore you order them to keep it to themselves. If it leaks out about Wegler, we'll hold every one of them responsible."

Kehr stroked his plump chin. "All right, but..."

"But what?" Baumer gazed with an enigmatic smile at the uncomfortable face of the commissar. "Well? What were you going to say?"

"If you intend to hold Frau Lingg's Pole responsible for this, as you suggested to Herr Kohlberg..." Kehr paused again, eyebrows raised.

"I am!"

"In that case, wouldn't it be better to tell the men that I've uncovered something new – namely, that the Pole was Wegler's confederate? You understand? No use telling them that we're..." He coughed and fell silent once again.

"Hanging an innocent Pole?" supplied Baumer softly.

Kehr shrugged. "Well, yes."

Baumer laughed. "Of course. A creative idea. Congratulations."

"All right then?"

"Tell me something," said Baumer, "how do *you* feel about the Pole?" Kehr shrugged.

Smiling, Baumer said: "When we were at Kohlberg's, your face was like a pane of glass, my friend. You didn't like my idea one bit. You're a righteous middle-class gentleman, eh? Hanging an innocent man is not to your taste."

Stiffly Kehr replied, "I'm a detective, of course. Political decisions are really not in my line."

Baumer laughed. "That's not even a good evasion, Kehr. But I know what you're thinking: you wonder why we can't spread a story that will serve our needs, but ship the Pole to some other district instead of hanging him, eh?"

Kehr shrugged again.

"I'll tell you why." The smile faded from Baumer's face. He sat down on the edge of the desk and leant over towards Kehr. "Not for the reason you think," he said scornfully. "Don't you dare pass any moral judgements on *me*. I'm not Kohlberg. Oh... he's ready to hang the Pole too. But do you know why? Do you know what Kohlberg is?" His lip curled. "Kohlberg's a money man. He looks human – God knows he has a brain to think with like you and me... and a liver and lungs and even stomach trouble. But notice..." Smiling scornfully again, Baumer tapped the desk with his forefinger. "The whole mechanism exists only to serve the Kohlbergs... no, that's wrong... it's even more ridiculous than that: to serve the banking account that Kohlberg serves. A people, nations, principles – they're merely figures to his bookkeeper's heart. Show Kohlberg how he can make a profit from a Jew, he'll trade with a Jew. Show him how he can make a profit by Jew-baiting, he'll support the National Socialist Party. Show him that the Party is returning a loss, he'll ditch the Party and embrace a Jew. That's the anatomy of the Kohlbergs, my friend – and of their politics too. That's why he's willing to hang the Pole – the adding machine sees a profit in antagonism between Germans and Poles." Baumer suddenly struck the desk with the flat of his hand. "But it's not my make-up, Kehr – and don't forget it!"

Kehr smiled a bit, nodding politely. "All right," he thought to himself with amusement, "but why all this heat, Party Comrade Baumer? Who asked you for self-justification? What are you trying to prove – that you're an ethical man? And to whom are you trying to prove it?"

"I'll tell you something," said Baumer softly. "Perhaps it will explain the Pole to you, my friend."

"'My friend, my friend...'" thought Kehr satirically, "I'm not your friend. You'd hang me too if it suited your book. Kohlberg has an adding machine in his heart – but at least it's a clear proposition. What's in your heart, my idealistic cut-throat?"

"Years ago, when I first joined the Party, I was given an assignment," said Baumer softly. "There was a Communist leader in our town who was a needle in our side. The bastard had a tongue like a devil's whip: you listened to him and you came away feeling bruised all over. So the order came down: 'Finish him off – get rid of him.'" A rapt, hard look came over Baumer's face. "The job was given to two men – to an experienced Party comrade and to me. It was a test for me, you see... Well, don't think I didn't hesitate. To kill a man in cold blood – we're not brought up to think in terms like that. But then I sat down with myself. Either I believed my principles... or I was a stinking hypocrite. So I thought it out. And I began to see how simple it was when you didn't let a fog get in between your brain and the facts. What was so awful about cold-blooded murder? Why, every day on the streets I watched thousands of decent Germans rotting away from unemployment – I saw the cold-blooded murder of a nation at the hands of parasites. And I thought to myself, 'Why, you little bourgeois louse, don't these things matter to you?' And so I made up my mind. When the other lad said to me, 'You ask him for the cigarette, Baumer, and I'll put the knife in his back,' I answered, 'No, damn you – you give me the knife.'"

Baumer sighed and was still for a moment. Then he continued acidly: "That was a long time ago, Kehr. But I remember what I thought after I knifed him. That Red bastard was a big fellow, a blond Bavarian. I looked down at him and I thought, 'Why, you poor sucker, you might have been a decent German if somebody hadn't filled your head with so much crap. But you made yourself a Marxist bed, so now lie in it, goddamn you.'"

The Labour Front Leader smiled coldly. "Sure, that was cold-blooded murder, wasn't it, Kehr? And what's this war we're fighting? Aren't Germans being murdered every day? There's only one morality in this war: victory! Does victory require the importation of Russian labour? Good – then it's moral. Does victory require the maintenance of morale? Then it's moral to give Wegler a Service Cross – and immoral to admit he committed sabotage. Men are pawns, Kehr. You're a pawn and I'm a pawn and the Pole on Frau Lingg's farm is a pawn. And until I understood that I had no grasp on *real* morality... The nation is what must survive – that's morality. Nations don't exist for the profit of a few men like the Kohlbergs or von Bilderings, even if they think so. Nations exist for their racial destiny. And unless men serve that destiny, they're immoral... So that's why this Pole will be hanged, my friend." He stood up abruptly. "And I'll pass you the word when to have him arrested. I want the orders to come from you, not me. And I'll want him marched through the factory grounds handcuffed."

Kehr nodded.

"Let me know if you turn up anything," said Baumer shortly. "I have to arrange now for the trench-digging."

He went out.

"Well, now, and wasn't that a mighty speech?" Kehr thought. "Somewhat long-winded, yet such sensitive poetry. But can it be that your National

Socialist soul is uneasy, Party Comrade Baumer? Something troubles you down deep?" Softly he began to laugh out loud. "No, my fanatic, I detect the faint aroma of guilt. Too many words for a quiet conscience. In the interests of your new morality, you have abolished the Ten Commandments – but you sleep badly, like a married man in a whore's bed. Ha! Ha! You consider me a thick-headed detective – but I've seen your kind when they end up on the execution block. At the last moment you can see it in their eyes: the guilt, the soul craving its punishment. Continue, my fanatic. Wash your hands with words. The stain will remain." Kehr began to hum. He turned the pages of his black notebook. "Oh, the Eberts and the Stresemanns," he thought, "the Brünings* and the Hindenburgs – they're all gone. And after a bit, perhaps, the Baumers will go too. 'One time up – one time down,' as the proverb says. But the Kehrs – ah, now there's a tribe! No, the Kehrs will go right on, providing the State with its backbone."

He touched the buzzer on his desk. The door to the outer office was opened promptly by SS Leader Zimmel.

"Thunderbolt Zimmel. A little quick action, if you please. I want to see the following gentlemen within ten minutes: Fritz Keller, Hoiseler, Rufke, Pelz, Jakob Frisch, Weiner, Eggert. By about" – he consulted his watch – "eight o'clock, I will want the woman, Frau Lingg." He grinned oafishly. "See that she's wearing that sweater. I'll need something by that time to keep me awake. Well… On your way, Thunderbolt Zimmel. And don't lose your false teeth."

"Yes, sir," with a pleased grin. "*Heil Hitler.*"

Kehr grunted.

3

6:35 a.m.

For some five minutes the night-shift workers had been pouring out of the factory buildings. Invariably the men turned towards the commissary. The women, who were from the countryside, moved hastily towards the front gate, where trucks were waiting to take them to their homes.

Doctor Zoder stood near the door of one of the parts plants. Tall, a little stooped, frowning, he scanned the oil-streaked faces of the men as they came out. He was searching for Pastor Frisch. As the lines thinned and Frisch still did not appear, Zoder threw discretion to the winds. "Do you know Jakob Frisch?" he asked every other man.

"No... Is he a big man?... Can't say I do," were the disappointing replies.

Finally, almost the last man out, came Bednarick, the old foreman. Zoder hesitated slightly, then hailed him. "Hey, there, good morning."

"Herr doctor! Good morning, sir, *Heil Hitler*," replied Bednarick respectfully.

"*Heil Hitler*," Zoder echoed hastily. "I'm looking for you. How's that ringworm of yours? Thought you were going to come in and let me take a look at it?"

"It's been clearing up so fine I didn't want to bother. That salve you gave me—"

"Didn't want to bother! I know you Bavarians. You hate to see a doctor, even if it's free. Any itching?"

"No, sir. None at all."

"Any spots develop elsewhere on the chest?"

"No, sir."

"Good. You'll live. By the way – there's another patient I'm after. Works in your shop. He's trying to escape me, the coward. Due for a little surgery. Frisch, Jakob Frisch. I didn't see him come out."

Bednarick hesitated. "I think you'll find him in the administration building."

"What's he doing there? Transferred to bookkeeping?"

Bednarick glanced around cautiously and lowered his voice. "There's something up. An SS man took the pastor out at about two thirty this morning, brought him back at five, took him out again fifteen minutes ago."

"*Hm!*" said Zoder, trying to appear calm. "You think he's... *hm*?"

"I thought the worst the first time they came for him. But since then I heard from... well, I heard from someone that a lot of men have been taken up to the front office. There's some sort of investigation going on. Also, do you know what?"

"What?"

"The whole day shift is to be set digging air-raid trenches. How do you like that? Disrupting work and everything. They must expect a bombing. What do you think?"

Zoder shrugged.

"Man! It turns me to jelly inside," said Bednarick. "Were you in Düsseldorf?"

"No."

"It's murder. I saw the last war in the trenches. That was bad. But somehow just having to sit in one place and take a bombing—"

"Well... doesn't pay to worry in advance," interrupted Zoder, eager now to be off. "By the way – I wouldn't gossip about this if I were you." His tone was a bit severe.

"Certainly not, Herr Doctor. I'm... with you it's..."

"Of course, of course," said Zoder, clapping him on the back. "I don't want a good chap like you to get into trouble, that's all. You're safe with me."

"Thank you, doctor."

Zoder grinned idiotically and started off in a rush towards the administration building. He was greatly troubled by what Bednarick had said. If they were investigating Frisch, it wouldn't do for him to get mixed up in it. The pastor had a record, after all. Still... still, he thought, they were examining others too. If there were anything definite on Frisch, they would not have let him return to his shop. So long as he handled himself cautiously...

Zoder paused in his headlong walk. What in the world was he doing here anyway? he asked himself. It was absurd of him to run after Frisch. Why did he want to see him at all? He stood stupidly, his mind a sudden blank, his eyes vacuous. Then he began to laugh silently. "Zoder," he told himself, "you're played out. Your strings are out of tune – your sound box is cracked. Why don't you settle things the quick way, eh? A slight incision in the carotid? Or a bit of potassium to sweeten the barley coffee... Yes, yes – then you could settle down comfortably."

The thought brought a pleasant smile to his lips. He had taken to carrying a pellet of cyanide around in his watch pocket, and he found a great deal of satisfaction these days in contemplating suicide. He extracted particular pleasure from a fantasy in which he killed himself publicly – in the factory commissary, or at a political meeting, or in the town church. His amusement was derived from the thought of how his death would upset people. He would yell something like "I've poisoned the soup", or "The water supply system is infected", and topple over stiff as a board. They would scamper then, the mice! There would be such a terror-stricken mass vomiting as hadn't been seen since the Black Plague...

"Oh my God, stop running in circles like a chicken with its head off!" he told himself angrily. "You made a decision to see Frisch. Why? Because of that bastard Baumer, wasn't it? Baumer's coming at eight o'clock. You have to decide how to deal with him and Wegler. All right... see Frisch, then. Pull yourself together. What's the matter with you these days? You can't concentrate on a point for more than five minutes at a time."

As he came close to the administration building, the door in the far wing opened and a group of men came out. Frisch was among them. Zoder slowed his step, frowned and searched his wits for a method of getting Frisch away from the others. "*Heil Hitler*," he said as he approached them.

"*Heil Hitler…*" several answered.

"Up early, Herr Doctor," observed old Rufke.

"There's the man I'm looking for!" cried Zoder with a pretence of surprise. "Herr Frisch, why didn't you come in to see me yesterday, as I ordered you? You let that condition go, and it'll get chronic. You won't be able to work. It'll require surgery."

Quietly, looking at him closely, Frisch replied, "I'm sorry, doctor. Can I come in this morning?"

Zoder laughed. "I know you. If I let you out of my hands, another week will go by." He gestured to the others. "Go on to your breakfast, men. Don't wait for him. I'm not letting him get away from me now."

The others laughed and went off.

"Walk along with me," Zoder whispered. They started off side by side. "I have to see you right away," he explained urgently.

"Why?"

"Something important. I judge you know what it's about."

"What?" asked Frisch stiffly. He didn't trust Zoder.

"I have a patient…" Zoder's eyes flicked around. "Wegler."

"What about him?"

"He committed sabotage. Don't you know that yet?"

"What's it to me?"

Zoder became furious. "What's happened to you? Have you changed your opinions since I last saw you? What sort of a game are you playing?"

Frisch took a deep breath. "How about you? The last thing you said to me was 'Go to hell'."

"Oh," said Zoder, "that's it? You don't trust me. Listen, don't be a fool. I've come to you because I… Christ, I don't know why I've come. I need advice. At eight o'clock I've got to face Baumer. Wegler's in a sort of coma, y'see. Baumer wants me to bring him to consciousness."

"Can you do that?" asked Frisch quickly.

"There's a good chance of it."

"Well?"

"I don't know what to do, that's all." He bit his lip. "I know, you think I'm crazy. Maybe I am. But I have one pride left: my mind. I want to think clearly. I'm a man of science. Everything should be logical. That's why I come to you. You think I hold with you? I don't. I don't even like you. You stink with an attitude of superiority. I don't like Wegler any more than you, either. But I'm confused. I can't think this out for myself. It hurts my pride... Well... *hm?* What d'you say?"

They both fell silent as some workers, who were carrying shovels and pickaxes, passed nearby. Frisch's brain was racing. Indeed, he did consider Zoder to be a crackpot. For that reason alone he wouldn't trust him. The last time they had spoken together, over six months before, Zoder had told him his mad fantasy – that he was waiting for the day when a plague would wipe out all Germans. At the time Frisch had replied, "Very good, my friend – now that you tell me this so earnestly, I'll tell you something: either go back to the asylum where you belong... or drink some poison. You're no good to anyone."

"Go to hell!" had been Zoder's savage rejoinder. "I have a good mind to report you."

"Ah yes," Frisch had replied, "in memory of your daughter you will now join the Gestapo. Very good. A logical conclusion to your insanity."

Nothing had happened to him after that, so he had known that Zoder had kept quiet. And from that time on, for over six months, they had avoided each other. But now Frisch was chary of dealing with a man who, on one side of him at least, was definitely unbalanced. On the other hand, if Baumer...

"All right," he said quickly, "I'll come to your office. But not now. After breakfast."

"Pastor, there's no time," Zoder said urgently. "Baumer's coming at eight, I told you."

Frisch shook his head. "I must show up at breakfast as usual. The men in my bunk have all been examined by the Gestapo in the last few hours. Everyone is looking at everyone else with suspicion. If I don't turn up, there'll be questions."

"How long will it take you?"

"Fifteen, twenty minutes. I'll hurry. In case any questions come up, that old condition is bothering me again."

"I remember."

"I want to see Wegler. Would that be possible?"

"I don't know. It's dangerous."

"I didn't ask that."

"Why do you want to see him?"

"I'll tell you later."

"I'll see. I don't even know if he'll become conscious."

"Will he live?"

"His condition is not bad – but there's a persistence of unconsciousness. I suspect some cranial injury. There's no visible skull fracture."

"So long, doctor."

"You'll surely come?"

"Yes."

Zoder watched as Frisch turned towards the door of the commissary. Beyond the building a squad of workers with shovels were being lined up by SS men. An officer was giving them instructions. Zoder couldn't hear what was being said, but he knew what it must involve: they were preparing for the possibility of British planes. The mice were digging holes! He began to laugh to himself with pleasure. A phrase from the Bible popped into his head, as happened often to him these days. For thirty years he had not opened a Bible, but now he read in it secretly every night. There was a wrath in the Old Testament that pleased him. He wished he might tap the SS officer on the arm and spit it into his face:

And the Lord heard the voice of your words, and was wroth, and sware, saying,

Surely there shall not one of these men of this evil generation see that good land, which I sware to give unto your fathers...*

"No, it's not quite logical," Zoder thought to himself joyously, "but it fits, it fits. They'll see it, these wolves!"

His glee died. Where did Wegler fit? Wegler was somehow not a part of this logic. No, Wegler did not fit. "Oh, God damn you, Wegler," he thought. "Why don't you settle everything and kick the bucket? Your Prussian ancestors are waiting for you, you swine."

Abruptly, like a puppet who has been jerked by his master's stick, he swung around and hurried back towards the hospital.

4

6:40 a.m.

Nurse Wollweber looked up with her near-sighted squint as the door opened. She was bathing Wegler's face with a wet towel. "Do you want me, sir?" she asked.

"Yes. I want to look over the ward," said Zoder. "Come along. I may have to give you instructions."

"Now, doctor," she replied placidly, "why do you change the schedule? This isn't ward time: it's breakfast time. Ward time is seven thirty. It's been that way for months."

Zoder grinned and bowed. "Your Highness," he said with a mock stammer, "permit me – if you please, permit me to explain: at eight o'clock comes Party Section Leader Baumer. At seven o'clock comes a man with a serious rectal fissure, a sudden emergency. This is wartime. We must handle the unexpected. Our fatherland is in danger. *Heil Hitler*. Are you coming?"

"*Heil Hitler*. Yes, I'm coming. Of course, doctor. Excuse me."

"Take Wegler's pulse first."

"I just did, sir. Pulse 112; temperature 100.5; respiration 24."

"And what does your Aryan intuition say about that, Your Highness? Is peritonitis developing?"

"You're making fun of me, doctor. I only try to do my—"

"Leave a piece of damp gauze on his lips. No sign of consciousness, I suppose, or you would have told me?"

"Lies like a dead one, doctor."

"*Hm!* There must be a cerebral injury, eh? Or else he would be screaming for water by now."

"I suppose so, doctor. The beast! He doesn't deserve it. He deserves to die of thirst. He needs to suffer for what he's done."

"Quite so, quite so. An eye for an eye – like me."

"Like you, doctor?"

"Haven't you noticed?" He came quite close to her. "My backaches. Do you mean to say I've been successful in hiding them from you?"

"Your backaches – I didn't know…"

"Dear, dear… as though you hadn't been married. In my early days I was a gay dog, sister." He reached out and pinched her cheek. "Now, of course, I'm paying for it. I'm sure your two sons—"

"Go 'way," she said, slapping his hand. "What an idiot you are."

"Some night, Your Highness," he said, winking an eye at her, "some night, my beauty, I'm going to knock on your door. I'll steal into your Lutheran bed, me and my chancre…"* He started out of the room. "Come along, my dove."

Smiling and shaking her head, groaning a little from stiffness after her sleepless night, Sister Wollweber followed him out, water basin in hand.

And as she closed the door and saw Zoder's long, thin figure already half-way down the hall, she thought with pride: "A crazy one, yes – but what devotion to his patients. How proud one can be to serve the fatherland under a man like that!" Wheezing, she hurried after him.

With a groan of relief, Willi opened his eyes. Sister Wollweber had been in his room for almost ten minutes. The wet cloth had felt grateful to his burning forehead and throat, but it had required an almost superhuman effort for him to lie still. He had never before suffered physically like this. For the first few hours after he returned to consciousness the anaesthetic had continued to lull his senses. He had felt pain and thirst, but to a degree that could be borne. Somehow the 6 a.m. whistle, screaming from the powerhouse, had seemed to mark a dividing line. Now he knew for the first time in his life the rack of unending pain. And now, too, he recognized that his resolve to remain silent was rapidly crumbling. Of what use was it? he was beginning to ask. He had only to speak, and the doctor would give him some morphine. It would not affect the British planes if he slept. They would come or they would not come. During the night he had been able to occupy himself with one thought or another. But now his thirst had grown intolerable. A few minutes before, when the nurse had squeezed the moisture from a bit of gauze between his lips, he had almost bellowed out loud. To what end was all this suffering? his flesh asked. His flesh was not curious, his flesh had no pride or hate to sustain it. And under the hot flame that was consuming his body, his determination too was melting like wax in a candle.

Weakly, succumbing to his pain and self-pity, Willi began to cry. No tears came. There was no moisture in his body for tears. He raised his right arm by an effort; he pressed his fingers between his teeth, biting them. "Don't give up, Willi," his pride said. "Think of how it will be if the British planes come. You won't mind the thirst then."

"Water," his flesh replied. "Water."

Think of something. Hum a little song. Think of Käthe or of Berthe. You mustn't give in, Willi. Show a bit of courage on your last day, even if you never did before. If you were lying out on a battlefield now, there would be no possibility of a doctor's help. An ounce of guts, for Christ's sake. It's seven in the morning. The night has passed; this day will pass too. You only have to wait until midnight. That's five... seventeen hours. Either the planes will come then or you can rip the bandage. Don't be such a whining little coward, Willi."

This notion – that he had been a coward – had begun to gnaw at Willi's soul in the past hour. It was as though his mind were in the service of two people, not one – and the other was an enemy bent on torturing him. And these two people kept wrestling for his pride, for the few crumbs of self-respect that remained to him.

"You!" his enemy said. "When did you ever show a grain of courage about anything?"

"I was in the war," Willi answered.

"The war! What nonsense. You were scared throughout – like everyone else."

"I was decent, anyway. I lived decently. I never harmed anyone."

"Decent? When you sat on that park bench, were you decent? Did you warn the mother of that child?"

"A man can make mistakes. When I went to see the Pole, there was courage in that, wasn't there? I was ready to help him. If the Pole had been willing, I would have done exactly what I promised – brought him food and money, given him my own police papers, burst open the barn doors for him. It wasn't my fault that the Pole refused. And the signal I lit for the British planes – I suppose that was cowardly? That took courage, didn't it? I can take pride in that!"

"Well, well," his enemy answered with scorn, "you're actually fat with self-respect! Tell me, Willi Wegler, how do you regard your life? It's been well spent? You can look back at it without shame? You've acted intelligently, with a thought for your fellow man?"

"I'm only human," Willi muttered. "What do you want from me? I'm no angel. Who said I was? It's easy to look back now and say I should have acted differently…"

Willi groaned as he became aware that he was muttering aloud. It was terribly dangerous to do that. He had to keep watch on himself, or all would be lost. The nurse had said his fever was only a hundred. That wasn't sufficient to make him delirious. He had no excuse for being so weak.

"Ah, Willi, Willi," he murmured to himself, "have some pride on this last day. Fight it out. That Pole is in more misery than you are. Really, he is! Why are you crying? When Baumer gave you the War Cross – that was a time for tears, not now. You don't have to be ashamed now, do you? You've done something. You know that at least. God will know too. And if there is no God, men will know. Some men will know, somehow. It will be heard somewhere – it will surely be written somewhere. You believe that, don't you, Willi?"

* * *

Shame is a subtle thing. Two nights before Willi committed sabotage against his State, there was no thought of sabotage in his mind. When he went to Berthe Lingg's barn, it was not so much to help the Polish prisoner as to relieve himself of a moral burden. And if the Pole had accepted his offer of help, it is possible that Willi might have found his absolution in that single charitable act – and thereafter shut his eyes to the outside world. Or perhaps not. One cannot tell.

But the Pole rejected him. It was as though a suffering Catholic child had been rejected by his priest. And as Willi stumbled through the night walking blindly towards the barracks, he told himself over and over with rebellious pride that an injury had been done to him. He cried to the heavens that he had not been a beast like Rudi, that he had not purchased another human being for money, like Berthe. Wherein was he at fault? he asked himself. For the Pole to regard him as one with all the others – was it not unjust? The Pole was frightened… he didn't understand – and that was all.

None of this self-justification eased him. His pounding heart understood a truth that his mind could not yet face. Ironically, it was Julius Baumer who unlocked the riddle for him, who broke down the last dishonest defence that his brain had erected. And if it was already decreed that Willi Wegler was to stand in a hayfield the next night lighting a beacon to the enemies of his country, it was also written that Labour Front Leader Baumer was to supply him with the tinder.

Willi returned to his bunkhouse to lie sleepless and wide-eyed on his cot. When the whistle screamed and his comrades awakened, he closed his eyes for the first time. He couldn't bear to look at them. He hated them now – yet equally he was frightened by his own hatred. He had not taken leave of his senses. The desire that came to him as he heard their chatter – to leap up and bash their heads together – he knew it was crazy. He knew that his brain was beginning to whir with wild thoughts, like a machine that is going out of control. He didn't want that. It frightened him terribly.

Keller, like the proper Cell Leader he was, would not let Willi be. When he saw that time was passing and Willi still remained on his cot, he went over and shook him. "Hey, Willi," he called affectionately, "you still asleep? Time to get up!"

Without opening his eyes, Willi replied, "I'm awake."

"Just a bit played out, eh?" old Rufke observed gleefully, as he combed his fine white head of hair. "What's the matter with you, Keller? Don't you know when a man's been dreaming about his woman? Oh, you Willi, you can't get enough, can you? The weekend's too short for you."

"Come on, man," said Keller. "You'll miss breakfast."

"I don't want breakfast."

"You're not sick, are you?" Keller became anxious. The night before he had been summoned to the Labour Front Office by Baumer. In the presence of various assembled bigwigs he had been asked for a final political report on Wegler. He knew that it had been decided to award Willi a War Service Cross. "Man, if you're sick…"

Willi didn't answer.

"I'll get the doctor right away for you."

Willi opened his eyes, gazing up at Keller dully. "I'm not sick, Fritz. I'll be at work on time. I'm just not hungry this morning."

"All right, lad," Keller said affectionately. "See you later."

The others left, and Willi made a sudden decision. It had been his intention to feign illness for the day. He wanted time to be alone, to formulate a plan. He couldn't endure the thought of a future at the side of these Poles – these miserable creatures who hated him, and whom now he was beginning to hate in blind retaliation. He felt sure that with time to think he would contrive some clever plan whereby he would be transferred to another factory.

Keller's suggestion of a doctor brought him to his senses. The doctor would examine him and know right off that he was shamming. One such black mark on his record and his chance of being transferred would be lost. He would have to be practical about it, he realized. Somehow he would muster the strength to endure these Poles a few days longer.

With this resolve he forced his tired body up from the cot. He fumbled in his locker for his towel, for his sliver of ersatz soap and razor, and then trudged through the woods to the washroom. Preoccupied as he was, he paid no attention to what was occurring along the path. The woods were heavily strewn with rocks; half a dozen sweating SS men were hastily smearing each rock with green paint. If Willi had thought about it at all, he would have assumed that it was for purposes of camouflage. Labour of that sort was always going on around the factory, although it was not usually the work of SS men. It was when he entered the large washroom and observed that even the inside walls were being smeared with paint by a number of the lads in black uniform that he enquired about it. "What's up?" he asked. "More camouflage?"

"Mind your own goddamn business," one of the SS men replied furiously.

Astonished, Willi stammered. "I... only..."

"Keep your mouth shut if you don't want to get in trouble," the youth interrupted angrily. "I know these sly jokes. You workers aren't as funny as you think."

Willi shut up without more ado. Trouble? No, he didn't want trouble. He had never wanted that. He was even beginning to regret the madness that had prompted him to offer his police card to the Pole. That would have landed him in real trouble. So far as he was concerned, they could paint the whole factory green, and he wouldn't enquire about it any further.

He shaved, he held his head under the tap until the second whistle screamed its warning, and then he hurried to the forge room. And so, since he had missed the excited talk of the other workers at breakfast, he remained ignorant of the gossip that had electrified the factory: that during the night a number of subversive slogans had been painted on some rocks in the woods and on the walls of the wash house.

The forge room, he found, was not as usual this morning. The night-shift men, who invariably hurried out of the building, remained in orderly rows along the walk. But on the other hand, not only were the Polish prisoners marched out under guard, but none of the Poles on the day shift appeared at all. To climax this disorder, just as the day men took over the machines at the stroke of the half-hour, Hartwig shut down the main switch. Instantly the machines went dead, the clattering of the spot welders ceased, and only the fluorescent tubes continued to work as usual, shedding their bright blue light over a silent cavern.

A moment later the reason for all this was explained. Eyes lifted to the steel catwalk overhead as a door at one end, which led to an adjacent building, opened upon a quartet of SS men. Heels clicking on the iron grillwork, they walked smartly down to the centre of the building and stood at attention. After them came Superintendent Kohlberg, his dark, hairy face abstracted and solemn, and after Kohlberg came Baumer. The workers understood then, of course: it was to be a meeting.

With that understanding came tension. The tension was so tangible to Baumer, and so instantaneous, that he felt as though a solid wall had leapt up by magic to block him from contact with the workers below. How well he knew the signs – the slight, uneasy scrape of shoes, the stiffening bodies, the faces that gazed up like vacant clay masks! It seemed to him that if he reached out with his fist, he would strike not air, but a solid barricade of hostility. The notion brought a wry smile to his lips. He knew what was troubling these men. The day before, within an hour after the Poles had arrived on the factory grounds, he had begun to receive reports. "Four thousand Poles…" the workers were whispering to each other. "Hell, that means four thousand of *us* to the army." These were men of forty and forty-five and fifty. Party members or not, Baumer had expected this reaction. Most of them had fought through the last war – they preferred to win this one at home.

It was because Baumer was so sensitive to all of this that he had insisted at once upon the need for a series of meetings. As he emphasized to Kohlberg, it would be criminal to handle this army call in a routine fashion. The workers had guessed accurately: Baumer's secret orders, which he had had in his possession for two weeks, stated that five days after the arrival of the Poles a thousand German workers would have to be off to army barracks. Within the next four weeks, three thousand more would be requested. And God alone knew how many more after that.

To Baumer this was much more than a routine task of worker training and replacement. It was a political problem that required intelligence. Indeed, he felt that a moral obligation had been placed upon him: to see to it that the men who left *his* factory for the front would leave with enthusiasm. And so he had prepared a carefully thought-out plan for Kohlberg: some weeks back, he informed the superintendent, he had contacted the Munitions Ministry for permission to award a War Service Cross to one of his workers. He had received their consent, and had been waiting for the proper occasion. Now it had come. The first step would be to give the award. At that meeting nothing would be said about an army call. As a result, the workers would be relieved and pleased. The next day, however, there would be a second meeting, and at this one the army call would be announced. Thereupon Wegler, the simple worker who had received the decoration, would volunteer. "Do you understand?" he had asked Kohlberg. "Do you get it?"

"Certainly I get it," Kohlberg replied coldly. "For generations Germans have been called to the colours by classes. But now you're changing it. Of course I get it – splendid! You ought to advise the General Staff!"

"Nonsense," Baumer retorted. "Don't twist my words. Naturally we'll weigh their army class in sorting them out later. We have to examine health and skill too, don't we? All I'm saying is this: let's take this army call and change it from something dismal to a demonstration of patriotism. Once our man volunteers, others will follow. The main fact is that those who go will leave the factory with excitement, with a sense of victory. Don't you get it now, Edmund?"

"I get it, I get it," Kohlberg replied, and although it seemed utter nonsense to him and an absurd waste of working hours, he yielded as he always did to Baumer's Party position.

Now, the wry smile twisting his lips, Baumer gazed down at the workers of the forge room and considered how to begin. Since his meeting with Kohlberg, a new and ugly element had intruded into their community – this, too, would have to be discussed today: the subversive signs that had been painted in the woods and on the walls of the latrine. So many workers had seen them before they were reported, and so many more had heard of them, that this latest bit of underground activity couldn't be ignored.

Quietly Baumer gazed down upon his workers, and quietly the workers gazed up at the catwalk, at their Labour Front Leader with the little smile on his lips, at the two engineers who were connecting up the microphone apparatus that would carry the speech-making to every building in the factory. And as Baumer stepped up to the railing to adjust the height of the microphone, a sigh swept through the room like a rustle of wind. "Well, now, here it comes," was the thought that went through the minds of all of the healthy workers. "Here it comes – and that's that." And with hard, expressionless faces they waited meekly to hear their fate. "This is war," they thought. "We have no choice."

Baumer began quietly, in his usual, earnest tone. "Members of the German National Community... fellow workers in the great arms industry... today we meet for an unusual reason..."

Again a sigh swept through the building.

"The outside world is shaking in its boots at the spectacle of our victories. Consider: all Europe is ours. For a thousand miles deep we control the Russian colossus. Now, at the city of Stalin himself, we are driving home the last dagger that will free Europe of the Bolshevik menace. And England?" His tone became ironic. "The land of shopkeepers and imperialists? Why, England waits in fear and trembling for the day of our wrath – for the retribution our Führer has promised after the wanton bombing of our cities."

Baumer paused. His voice became very quiet, and his handsome face began to glow with pride. "I ask you: how has all this come about? Our enemies wring their hands and seek an explanation. But since they are stupid as well as corrupt, they will never find the answer. 'Tanks,' they say, 'planes, military strategy.' What fools. It is not metal or oil or gold that wins a war. Our enemies possess those things too. No, it is *men* that win wars, *men only*." His voice rang with pride. "And it is not any sort of men who win wars, but only those men who have a great purpose and who are ready to sacrifice for that purpose."

He paused as the ardent Party men started a round of applause. Then he said, very earnestly, "Today we honour this German spirit. You and I know of the brilliant deeds of our soldiers. We applaud them. But sometimes even we overlook the achievements of the home front. We think of our sacrifices, perhaps, of rationing, of long hours – we forget that these are not alone hardships, they are the glorious guarantee of victory. Without us, no German armies would be fighting a thousand miles deep in Russia. Without our unceasing flow of munitions, the German soldier would be fighting not before Stalingrad and Cairo – but before Dresden, Berlin and Stettin. But let me assure you: if ever we forget the home front, the Führer does not. And so, today, the Führer honours a representative of the men and women who are heroic warriors in the factories of the home front." His voice rang out. "Willi Wegler. Be so good as to leave your machine and come up here."

An expectant whispering rustled through the forge room. The workers who knew Willi turned to look at him – those who didn't gazed around with curiosity. Nothing happened. Willi stood before his steam hammer, motionless, stony as the monster he operated. The silence lengthened, became embarrassing.

"Wegler?" Baumer repeated into the microphone. He wondered if someone had blundered and the man were not present.

Still Willi remained transfixed. Baumer's words were ringing in his ears; his mind rocked with confusion, asking, "Me? It's me he means?"

Quickly Hartwig crossed the floor. "Wegler," he whispered anxiously, "didn't you hear? Go up."

There was general laughter as Willi bolted for the ladder that led to the catwalk. Baumer watched him come and felt both pleased and a little touched. Evidently the man was modest; he couldn't believe it when he was singled out to be honoured.

Smiling, the little group of officials made a path for Willi as he came hastily down the catwalk. He stopped before Baumer, towering over him. By contrast to the slim, handsome Labour Front Leader, Willi appeared the very model of a factory worker. In his grimy overalls, with his naked, heavy-muscled arms hanging loosely at his side, he seemed to Baumer to symbolize the life of the factory itself – the productive anonymity of men and machines. He felt delighted with the man they had chosen.

"Wegler," he said softly, earnestly – but not forgetting to talk into the area of the microphone – "it is my honour to pay the Führer's respects to you – and through you to every man and woman in this factory."

The claque of applause began on the floor, Hartwig leading it, and Baumer waited until quiet was restored.

"You have been singled out, Willi Wegler, as the exemplary type of worker in this great tank arsenal." Baumer turned his gaze from Willi to the men below. "Let me tell you a little about this man Wegler, who stands so modestly by my side. Wegler is a man of forty-two years of age. As a young man, he fought in the last war. He worked soberly and quietly for years, and raised a fine son. That son, still in his early twenties, died in Norway for Führer and fatherland. A few months later, Wegler's wife, his beloved helpmeet for twenty years, was killed in the bombing of Düsseldorf. I tell you this now because even those who know Wegler best have been ignorant of the trials of soul through which this man has passed. No, Wegler is not a complainer. He is not a whiner. If he feels bitterness, he knows at whom to direct it – at the enemies of our country. This is the conclusion Wegler came to. He decided it for himself, silently. No tears, no ranting – but silent determination."

Baumer paused for a half-instant. Wegler was staring at the iron grids, his face vacant. It made Baumer wonder a little. He would have expected some response to all of this sentiment.

"Fellow workers…" he continued more loudly, "this is what is meant by German national character. This isn't a political thing. Willi Wegler is not yet a member of the National Socialist Party. He has borne his trials so magnificently because his heart is a pure German heart and his blood is pure German blood – because above all else he loves his country." His voice waxed a trifle oratorical. "And so, today, we honour this man. We honour a man of forty-two who volunteered, without being asked, to work at one of the most difficult jobs in the factory: the steam hammer in this forge room. For seven months now, without missing a day or being a minute late, without uttering a single word of complaint, Willi Wegler has withstood the trials of a machine that has torn many younger men to pieces. And if today our tanks are ripping the Russian lines to pieces before Stalingrad, it is only because Willi Wegler – and you fifteen thousand workers in this factory – have done your duty so magnificently."

Baumer turned quickly. An SS man stepped forward, holding out a small flat box. "Willi Wegler, I have the honour, in the name of the Führer, to present you with the War Service Cross. It is a symbol of gratitude from the battle front to the home front. It is you who have made victory possible."

As Baumer pinned the Cross on Willi's breast, loud applause broke out from the factory floor. One of the engineers quickly reversed the sound system, and instantly the forge room rocked with the thunderous applause piped in from the other buildings.

Smiling, Baumer gazed up at Wegler. Behind his smile there was slight anxiety. He was beginning to be afraid that Wegler was a dolt. Even now he was standing without a sign of emotion on his face. It would be natural for a man in his position to grin, or to be on the point of tears if he were sentimental – or to express any of a dozen, varied emotions. But it was not normal for him to stand like a piece of statuary, or like a deaf-mute who didn't know what had taken place. Was he all muscle and no brain, this calm hero they had chosen? It would be dreadful if he were too stupid to speak to the workers the next day.

The applause ceased. Quite deliberately Baumer turned to Willi, fixed him with a stern glance and said quietly, "Well... do you have anything to say to us, Wegler?"

In the ensuing silence Willi stood opening and closing the box which had held the decoration. He was still too stunned to think.

"Well?" Baumer repeated with an uneasy laugh. He felt positively embarrassed. "Are you so overwhelmed by this honour that you're left speechless?"

With his eyes still fixed on the floor, Willi opened his mouth like a fish sucking for air, closed it, opened it again. "Please... I'd like to... please..."

"Yes?" Baumer said encouragingly. "Speak out."

"To go back to my machine... I'd like to... please."

There was an awkward moment of silence. Then Baumer, stirred to the core by what he understood to be the meaning of Wegler's reply, leapt at the microphone, gripping it with both hands. "Did you hear, everyone? 'Let me go back to my machine.' This hero of Labour has only one request: let me continue to build tanks – let me supply my blood brothers at the front!"

Baumer's voice rang out jubilantly: "There spoke the unity of the German people, my comrades! Some of us are Party members and some are not – but all of us are National Socialists. And if our enemies still don't understand this unity, we have ways of teaching it to them. They will learn it to their sorrow!"

Down below Hartwig started applause, but Baumer, impassioned now, couldn't pause for it. Wegler's patriotism had touched the very core of his doubts about the thorough loyalty of the average German worker. He felt intoxicated by this demonstration of patriotism.

"There is something else you must hear about this unity of ours, my comrades. When the war began, do you know what our enemies said? They said, 'The German workers hate the Party – they'll refuse to fight. The factories will be disrupted by sabotage.'

"And what did we say? We said the German workers had been won over by the National Socialist Party. We said that after 1933 a new German people was created, in which there were no classes, but only blood brothers." His voice rang out with jubilant pride. "Well? Who was right – the enemy or ourselves? Let me hear!"

There were instant cries from the floor: "We were! We!"

"And where have the desertions been?" Baumer continued. "In the Battle for Norway or France? Or maybe at Dunkirk?"

There were yelps of laughter from below.

"Or in our thousand-mile advance into Russia? Weren't many of our soldiers workers, and the sons of workers? Did they desert?"

"No! No!"

"*That* is the answer to our enemies," Baumer shouted. "It is also the answer to the miserable bedbugs who went around the factory grounds last night on their pitiful errand. Perhaps some of you don't know what I'm referring to? I'll tell you straight out: last night – because such bedbugs dare work only under the cloak of night – some subversive slogans were painted on one or two walls, and left like droppings on a rock or two in the woods. And a number of my Party comrades became excited. 'This is terrible,' they said. 'No,' I answered. 'It is not terrible. It only means that we still have a few bedbugs left in our German house. Very well… if we catch them… we'll step on them. If we don't catch them – because a bedbug is small and our house is big – then let them put their droppings on a wall once in a while. Little good it'll do them.'"

There was a burst of laughter and applause on the floor.

"Correct?" asked Baumer.

"Correct!" came the answer.

"And one more thing: are we enslaving others? Or are we liberating all nations from slavery to the Jews and the democrats – from their bondage to the Bolsheviks and the capitalists?"

"Hear, hear," someone called.

"You are Germans," cried Baumer passionately, "and you must understand: there will be a new and decent order in this world, and it is our destiny to achieve it. This war is a struggle between the new and the old – and either the old will perish or *we* will perish. And if we perish, then I warn you: it will not only be the National Socialist Party that goes down, but all of us – *you,* the whole people, the whole nation – because our enemies have sworn exactly that. But I tell you we will not perish. Never again a 1918! Once we see this war through to victory, we will enter upon a new and glorious life. Is that clear, my comrades?"

"Clear! Clear!" came the response from a dozen voices.

"What about these Polish prisoners, then? Do we have reason to pity them? Did we ask them to go to war with us? No! These miserable tools of the English have forfeited the right to rule as a nation. In the future all such people will be governed by those who have earned the right to govern. Is that clear too?"

"Clear! Clear!"

"So be it, then!" Baumer shouted passionately. "This is our answer to the bedbugs of the world!... That's all, my comrades. In the days to come, remember the fortitude and patriotism of Willi Wegler. Now... back to work. Foremen in all buildings – turn on the power. Our Führer, Hail to Victory – *Sieg Heil!*"

"*Heil!*" came the response from the floor in a full-throated, practised chorus.

"*Sieg...*"

"*Heil!*"

"*Sieg...*"

"*Heil!*"

Baumer lowered his hand. The ranks of the workers broke, the men moved back to their machines and the forge room leapt into workaday life. Baumer turned to Willi, his sweaty face glowing in satisfaction. "Come along with me, Wegler," he whispered. "I have a job for you to do..."

Only twenty-four hours had passed since that meeting in the forge room, but now Willi was lying on a hospital cot, consumed with thirst, tongue swollen, lips parched, belly and loins throbbing. And now he thought of the moment when Baumer had shouted into the microphone, "Willi Wegler... be so good as to leave your machine and come up here." And for a few moments he forgot his pain and thirst in the greater pain of that memory... in the galling wisdom that had come as lightning comes when the Cross had been pinned, gleaming, upon his breast. For in that moment he had to know the ugly truth at last: *that he too was guilty, and no less guilty than all the rest... that by his faithful work at the steam hammer he too had enslaved these Poles... that he too had carried a dead woman's sweater to Berthe Lingg along with Rudi... that he too had bought a Pole in the town square for seventeen marks – and that he had done these things by complicity, by his work and by his silence... and that he too was stained with guilt.*

And so now he wept with shame. He wept and he said to himself with hatred, "All those years when you carried your head so high, when you felt you were a decent man – you were not a decent man, but a blind man, becoming more blind with each year. All those years when you said to Richard and to Richard's wife, 'Your principles are not mine', you too had a principle. 'I am not my brother's keeper' – that was your principle. And so finally you ended up with a Service Cross on your breast – a slave master to slaves. And this can never be undone. The dead, who are dead at German hands, you helped kill. The cities that were bombed by German planes, you helped bomb. This is the way you ended your decent life, Willi Wegler, in this way only..."

He wept, and in his fever and anguish he spoke aloud again, praying: "Please, dear God, please, let the British planes come back. Let them bomb this factory. Let me live to see it! Let me have done this one thing in my life, I beg you. For in my heart I never wanted it to come to this."

Chapter 14

Captain Schnitter, leaning upon his cane and walking with the swinging hip movement peculiar to those who have an artificial leg, entered the Labour Front Office. "Good morning, Bright-Eyes," he said to the telephone girl. "Anything stirring this summer day?"

Frieda laughed without turning around, said "Yes, sir" into her mouthpiece and pulled a line from the board. Then she turned with a smile towards the grinning, rather handsome officer.

"Nothing at all, sir," she replied. "Quiet as a cemetery. Only, I've been working for sixteen hours steady, and if my relief girl doesn't come soon, I'll topple over."

"Poor Frieda," the captain said. "If you were my girl instead of Blumel's, I'd take care of you. When are you going to chuck him and take me on?"

"The minute your second child is born, sir. How's your wife, sir?"

"Fine. Fine. I want to see Party Comrade Baumer."

"Yes, sir." She plugged in a line. "Herr Kohlberg is with him now... Sir, Captain Schnitter would like to see you." She pulled out the line. "I hope your anti-aircraft battery is oiled up, sir."

"It is. Give me a smile, Frieda."

She obliged with a weary grimace.

"That's no way to smile. A summer morning, a pretty girl like you – why, even my wife wouldn't—" He turned urbanely as the door to the inner office opened. Baumer stepped out looking tired and very harassed. Swinging his hip, Schnitter crossed to meet him.

"What is it?" Baumer asked quietly. He had the tense, absorbed manner of a man who's trying to conserve his strength.

"The steam shovels have arrived for the machinery pits. We need men to go to work after them... follow up, I mean."

"I see." Baumer frowned. Then he called out, "Herr Kohlberg – if you please." A second later Kohlberg came out of Baumer's office. Under the dark shading of his bristly face, the superintendent's skin was grey. He looked like a man with a bad case of ulcers.

"Here's the situation," Baumer explained. "Captain Schnitter says the machinery has arrived."

"What machinery?" Kohlberg asked vaguely. His normally acute mind had been at loose ends all morning. The spectacle of men digging trenches on the factory grounds was disorganizing him.

Crossly Baumer replied, "We talked about it only half an hour ago. On the phone."

"I don't remember anything about machinery."

"Now, look here," said Baumer, controlling himself with difficulty, "you wanted some pits dug, so that in case of a raid we'd get some of your fancy machine tools out of the shops and into the pits!"

"Oh yes... Well?"

"I said I'd have to organize some steam shovels for a job like that."

"Yes, of course. Excuse me. Where's my mind this morning? The steam shovels have... That's wonderful."

"Two are at work already."

"Splendid. You're very efficient, Baumer."

"This is the problem," said Schnitter. "A big hole in the ground will protect your tools to a degree, but not enough. We need bags of earth, camouflage netting, chicken feathers, wire. For that more men are needed. It's no minor piece of construction to handle in a day."

"How about the night-shift men?" Baumer asked Kohlberg.

The superintendent shook his head violently. "If they have to spend the day digging, that means the factory will be shut down tonight as well. Don't you remember... Herr von Bildering is coming?"

"That's all right with me," retorted Baumer. "If you don't care about your machine tools, why should I?"

"Why can't you use the day men?"

"They're digging trenches for personnel protection."

"Have them work on the pits first."

"No!" Baumer replied flatly. "Personnel protection is my affair. Until those trenches are dug, not one of them will do anything else."

"Very well," said Kohlberg, giving in with a sigh. "Put the night-shift men on that, then. We'll just have to shut down the factory for twenty-four hours. Oh, it's all absurd. We won't get bombed. I'm sure it's all unnecessary – aren't you, captain?"

Captain Schnitter smiled with veiled disdain. "Frankly... no."

"Look here," said Kohlberg, "I don't mean we shouldn't take precautions. But the hurry everyone is in – the hysteria... Now, I've analysed it this way. Suppose the British did see the traitor's signal? They won't bomb without reconnaissance. They can't."

"Sir," Schnitter replied quietly, "suppose *you* were at the head of British Air Command. A report comes in of a signal at XZ location. What would you do?"

"Just what I said – order reconnaissance. The British aren't fools. How do they know, for instance, that the signal wasn't a trick – to lead them into an anti-aircraft trap? Furthermore, raids have to be planned."

"Correct," Schnitter answered. "However – the arrow pointed towards a wood, remember. Reconnaissance is one way of investigating – but it always warns the enemy. A second way could be the use of incendiaries in a quick raid. Understand me – I don't expect a raid in force without prior reconnaissance. But an experimental sortie by Mosquitoes* – that would be perfectly feasible. Everything depends on the mentality of British Air Command. If I may remind you of your Clausewitz: *The cardinal principle of war is surprise...* The British have read Clausewitz too."*

"Then you expect a raid tonight?" Kohlberg asked in a voice that could not conceal his anxiety.

Schnitter smiled disdainfully again. "All in all... no. I'm merely indicating the alternatives."

"Do we have anything more to discuss?" Baumer interrupted impatiently.

"I have nothing," replied Kohlberg. "By the way, you've arranged about the trucks?"

"Not yet."

"My goodness—"

"Please," Baumer interrupted, growing red in the face, "one thing at a time, please, please! Damn it, the pits aren't ready yet, are they? I'll take care of my end, I promise you. The pits will be deep – there'll be a wooden ramp so the trucks can drive down into them, and the trucks will be kept on a twenty-four-hour wait by every plant you say. All you have to do is to organize the men to load the tools. You do your end, I'll do mine. Don't badger me, damn it."

"All right, all right," Kohlberg whispered haughtily. "In front of the phone girl and everything! Do you have to lose your temper?" He turned on his heel and strode from the office.

Baumer grimaced with weariness and disgust. Quietly he said to Schnitter, "Look, I have something else to do. You stay with Frieda, will you? She'll know whom to call to get the night-shift men started and the materials you need."

The captain nodded.

"Did you hear that, Frieda?" asked Baumer.

"Yes sir. I'll know who to call."

"I'll be with Gestapo Commissar Kehr."

"Sir..." she asked hesitantly.

"Yes?"

"I hate to bother you at a time like this..."

"You never bother me, Frieda," he told her with a sigh. "You're one of the few people I can count on around here to be calm. Except the captain. Nothing ever bothers you, does it, Franz? What is it, Frieda?"

"Martha Guttmann should be here to take my place. She's late, and she's never late. I've been on so many hours without rest... it's not that I mind, sir... but when I get too tired, I begin to make mistakes. If I could only get a few hours' sleep..."

"Have you called Martha?"

"There's no phone at her farmhouse."

"Tell Zimmel to send a car for her."

"Thank you, sir," she smiled with gratitude.

"What a smile that girl has!" exclaimed Schnitter. "Hasn't she got a smile though, Julius? Isn't she pretty?"

Baumer grinned. "Prospect of a bombing makes you happy, eh, Franz? Something to do after seven months of quiet."

"I can't tell a lie," replied the captain. "I'm not altogether happy. The fact is I'm still shivering from the bombing I took at Smolensk. By the way... the morale of the workers doesn't seem very high to me. They're working at those trenches like gravediggers."

"I know," Baumer muttered, "I have reports already. I'm setting the meeting earlier – ten fifteen."

Schnitter nodded, and Baumer started out of the office. As he reached for the door, it opened upon Martha Guttmann.

"There you are," he exclaimed, "the one day you shouldn't have been late. Never mind. Get busy."

Martha put out her hand, touching his arm as he walked past her. "Please, sir," she said in a small, tight voice.

"Yes?" He looked at her closely. "What's the matter? You don't look well."

"No, sir," Martha replied tremulously. "I'm sorry I'm late. I came in to... ask if I could have the day off, sir."

"Look, child," he answered hoarsely, "if you're able to walk, you're able to work. We need you today. We may get a bombing. Frieda needs a few hours' sleep, and then both of you will have to stay at the switchboard."

"A bombing?" Martha echoed, wide-eyed.

"Yes. You see? Now—"

"But, sir. It's not that I'm ill. It's something special."

"Martha, I'm in a hurry."

"Please sir." She burst into tears. "My husband's been killed. I've just heard."

Baumer bit his lip. He hesitated, then put his arm around the sobbing girl and led her into his private office. He kicked the door shut, helped her into a chair and got her some water. She drank it, holding the glass with quivering hands.

"When did you hear?" he asked softly.

"Last night, sir. He was in Africa."

"Yes… Martha, look: it's not going to be easy for you, whatever you do. But I assure you – if you stiffen your backbone and keep on working, it'll help more than anything else."

"I know, sir. That's right, I know," she replied between sobs. "I want to keep on working. But just today, sir, it's so important to me – I want to go to church."

"To church?" Baumer repeated with astonishment.

"I know," she murmured forlornly, "I don't know why I want to. But I do."

"I didn't know you were a churchgoer. You're a Youth Leader, aren't you?"

She nodded tremulously. "I haven't been to church for five years. I don't know why I want to go, but I feel that today I must – somehow, I must. He's lying out there, unburied maybe. If prayer will do him any good—"

"It won't," Baumer said sharply. "You know it won't. You're being hysterical and silly. Go to church as much as you want. I don't give a damn. But today you stick on the job. Dammit, girl, we may get a bombing. We have to be organized for it."

"I don't care," she cried wildly. "Who cares if the factory is bombed? I have nothing to live for now. Oh my God, you don't know how I loved him!"

"Now, Martha – your husband died as a soldier. You're not being very brave."

"I don't want to be brave," the girl wept. "I only want my man back. God – why did there have to be war at all? What is it bringing us anyway?" Her face flamed. "Do I care if we take Egypt? What's Egypt to me? Let the big shots in Berlin—"

"Martha!" he interrupted sharply.

"It's true, it's true. All of Africa isn't worth my husband—"

Baumer seized her wrist. White-lipped, he ordered sharply, "Shut up! You talk like this where others hear you, and you'll be arrested."

"Oh!" she cried out. "You're hurting my wrist."

"Did you hear what I said? I want to hurt you. You have to be brought to your senses." He let go of her. "Do you think you're the only woman who's lost her husband? This is *war*! I don't know what was in your head until now, but there wasn't much. Is this how deep your convictions go? Do you think the Führer took us into war for nothing?"

"No – no," she gulped.

"Then get hold of yourself."

"If you'd only let me... today..."

"No," he replied sharply. "Today is the one day I insist on your working. You stay here now. I'm going out. When I come back, I'll expect you to be at work."

He left the office, shutting the door behind him. He crossed to the telephone board. "Let Martha alone for about ten minutes," he said to Frieda. "Then go in there and tell her to start work. Stay with her a bit to be sure she's in control of herself. Then you can rest for a few hours."

"Yes, sir."

"And if Martha says anything she shouldn't, report to me about it."

"What do you mean, sir?"

"You'll know what I mean."

Hard-faced, he started down the corridor. As he raised a cigarette to his lips, he saw that his hand was shaking. He squeezed his lips into a tight line. He felt furious with Martha. She had been his secretary for six months; he had found her devoted, self-sacrificing, with more political understanding than most girls of her age. This instant crumbling of character and purpose – it was unsettling. Somehow it was like the Wegler sabotage – only a little thing, but it pricked his confidence.

Angrily he banged into the ante-room of Kehr's office. He didn't even see the workers who were waiting there, or Berthe Lingg, who jumped up as he passed her. He thrust open the inner door and said in a loud, hoarse voice, "I want to talk to you!"

Quietly Kehr nodded and jerked his head at the man he was interrogating. As soon as the door had closed, Baumer said, "Well?"

Kehr shook his head. "A blank wall so far – except..." He didn't finish.

"Except what?"

"Unless you're willing to pay attention to my insanity theory – to discuss it calmly?"

Baumer took a deep breath. Then, low-voiced, he replied: "I knew it! All you're concerned about is a neat little theory that will pass in a report. Case closed. All's well on earth. A promotion for Kehr... Only, Wegler's organizational connections have not been uncovered. The Marxist slogans painted on walls you haven't traced down. The clogged drainpipes, the breakdown in the powerhouse, the fire in the canteen – all the little things in these last months that are as much the result of insanity as Wegler..." He sputtered, and then the rage burst out of him. "Oh, damn you, Kehr, you're an imbecile. Don't you understand yet that there's an underground cell here? Why didn't they send someone with political sense?"

"I'll ask you to keep your temper and to watch how you talk to me," retorted Kehr with stiff calm. "I've been here approximately six hours. In that time you expect me to solve matters of sabotage that are five months old?"

"I didn't say that!" Baumer shouted. "I'm trying to show you the *quality* of Wegler's act. How can you solve anything if you go at it with a ridiculous theory in your head? What has happened here is political, political..." – he banged the desk with his fist – "*political*. Do you even understand the word?"

Calmly Kehr replied, "You have only to reach for the telephone and call Headquarters. I'm sure they'll oblige you with another man. Until then, I'll conduct this case on the basis of my thirty years of police training. Now, unless you have something else to say to me, please leave me to work. I'm tired too."

Baumer hesitated. His mouth twitched. Then he said uncomfortably, "I've got a temper, I know. I always did have. I'm sure you're doing your best. Only, these days a man's best doesn't get anywhere." He paused, sighing. "It's like climbing a mountain in a dream... Damn it, you climb and climb... The devil! Please arrest the Pole on the woman's farm. Have him walked through the camp where the workers can see him. His guards are to pass the word along that he lit a fire to the British... I'm seeing Wegler in an hour. I'll let you know if I get anything out of him." He left abruptly.

Quietly Kehr sat back in his chair, closing his eyes. "That's all I need," he thought. "This case isn't difficult enough. I also need a son of a bitch with a brother-in-law on Himmler's staff, so he can say anything he wants to me and I can't talk back!" He rubbed his eyes with the back of his hands, then he chuckled. "Very well..." he thought philosophically. "We'll wait a few years, Party Comrade Baumer. We'll see then."

2

7 a.m.

Doctor Zoder sat humped over his office desk, leaning comfortably upon his elbows, his long hands cupping his face. He was wearing the full-length white robe in which he always inspected the ward. By his elbow a cup of muddy coffee, prepared for him by Sister Wollweber, was growing cold.

Outside all was strangely quiet. It was a workday, but over the distant clank of shovels he could hear bird cries, even the rustle of leaves in the morning wind. No tanks were clattering around the trial course; there was no pound from the forge room. A pleasant miracle.

Doctor Zoder's eyes were shut, but he was not asleep. He was daydreaming, his bitter lips relaxed in a tiny smile. This was not the summer of 1942. It was 1927. Time was something one could cozen, Zoder had found. "What?" one corner of his mind always asked. "1927? 1919? Nonsense, it's 1942."

"Never mind, don't spoil it, it's too delicious," the rest of him would reply.

So it was 1927, and Zoder was in his summer cottage by a lake in the Black Forest. In fact, it was morning and he was just awakening after a long sleep.

"My, what a nightmare you had," his wife was saying to him. "What ever were you dreaming about?"

His reply, of course, was gay. "Something silly. Imagine – I dreamt that the Hitler crowd got into the government and... *Hm*... I've forgotten it. But what an unpleasant dream."

"Well, get up, lazy, and have your breakfast. Ellie and I are starved."

Now Ellie came running into the bedroom. "Daddy, do you know what? Otto caught a turtle. A real snapping one. Come outside right away. You must see it."

So they were on the porch with the dog yelping ecstatically over the turtle, and the children screaming at the top of their voices.

"Where'd you catch him, Otto?"

"He was on our raft when I swam out this morning, sir." (Otto was always a polite boy. Whatever became of him? Dead now, probably. The Soviets didn't understand German manners.)

"Well, well. A turtle on a raft. Perhaps we can put that into our puppet show on Saturday."

A shriek from Ellie: "Daddy, can I buy him? Otto says I can have him if I pay."

"So you're a businessman at ten, Otto? How much?"

"Would one mark be too much, sir?"

"One mark for a brand-new snapping turtle? You're not sharp enough, Otto. I'll give you two."

A shriek of joy from Ellie. At eight she could never do anything quietly, he recalled. Between eight and eleven were her noisy years.

"And how will you keep the turtle, Ellie?"

"I'll build a pool for it with rocks. And I'll catch flies for it, and grasshoppers."

"Shall we make a turtle soup out of it when it's fat?"

An extra special shriek. "Daddy, you're a horror."

"Or shall we dissect it?"

"Daddy, you're a triple horror."

"Very well, if you're not scientific... Otto, I'm going in for breakfast. Remind me a little later – I owe you a mark."

"Er... ah..."

"Dear me, did I say *one* mark? Two, of course, two. Come on, Ellie. Otto will watch the turtle till we're finished."

So he would spin his fantasy, sometimes inventing one incident after another of a crowded, happy day – and all the while knowing that it was untrue. But today, as he followed his joyous, chirping daughter into the house, it was not his wife who sat at the table, but Pastor Frisch. And instantly the smile departed from his face – he rubbed his eyes, yawned... and realized that someone was knocking on the door of his office.

"Come in," he called hoarsely.

It was the pastor who entered. He came in diffidently, his near-sighted eyes searching the office with an inquisitive, distrustful glance.

Zoder jumped up. "Shut the door, pastor. Come in here." He walked hastily through an adjacent examination room and then into a cluttered office used for electrotherapy treatments. Frisch, following slowly, remained in the doorway of the dark room and shook his head as Zoder indicated a stool.

"It's a fine morning," he suggested quietly. "Why not walk outside? We can talk there." He waited, his head tilted a little, his right shoulder drooping.

"I can't leave for a walk," Zoder replied with irritation. "What's the matter with you? I told you – Baumer's due here by eight o'clock."

"It's only seven now." The pastor's tone remained quiet, but it was very stubborn.

"Suppose Wegler becomes conscious? Or needs some quick attention? What sort of a moment is this to go walking anyway?"

"Perhaps we'll be more comfortable in your other office then?"

"Why, are you…" Zoder stopped as comprehension came. "I see. You still don't trust me. You want to talk elsewhere because in here, with all this equipment, you think it would be easy to conceal a dictaphone?"

"Not at all," Frisch lied.

"Let me tell you something," the doctor said in an unfriendly, patronizing tone, "your safety is at my disposal anyway." In a waggish manner he shook a long, bony finger at Frisch. "Oh, you're a clever one, you are. Those subversive signs that had everyone so excited the other day… 'Germans – if you enslave others, you will yourselves be enslaved.' Ha! Ha! It used to be that when a pastor painted on rocks his sentiments had a more evangelical tone: 'Come Ye Suffering Ones to Jesus' – or something like that. But now you pulpiteers have become political. You preach like a Marxist these days, eh pastor?"

"Nonsense," the little man replied sharply. "What are you accusing me of? I'll leave right now. Do you think I had anything to do—"

Zoder interrupted with a burst of laughter. "I studied one of those signs before they were painted out, my friend. The SS man scratched his head and said, 'Someone stole some paint. But how? Any paint that's used for camouflage work around here is always locked away at night.' Ha! Ha! *I* could have told him." Zoder leant forward, a sly glint coming into his eyes. "How are your gums, my friend? Still bleeding? But weren't you afraid that Sister Wollweber would report to me? She did, you know. She said to me: 'Do you remember that Frisch fellow who used to come here for electrotherapy – the rectal case? He was back today complaining about a mouth infection. Asked if I had any potassium permanganate. So I gave him some crystals. Is that all right, doctor?'"

Frisch said nothing. He took off his eyeglasses and began to clean them.

Zoder smirked. "Very clever of you, pastor. You must have received an A in chemistry in your schooldays. A few crystals of potassium dissolved in water will make a quite satisfactory ersatz paint, eh? Accomplish a good deal on a rock or a washroom wall? Now listen, pastor: don't you think I could have reported that? Would the Gestapo need any more evidence with a man of your record?"

Softly, with sudden boldness, Frisch said, "Six months ago, when we first talked, I asked you to make use of your hospital privacy by listening to the British Short Wave… and to report about general factory matters. Are you willing to do that now?"

"No, damn you, no," Zoder replied unpleasantly. "Don't try to involve *me* in your crusade."

"I need some more potassium permanganate for my gums. Will you give me some, doctor?"

"Why are you goading me?" Zoder asked angrily. "I told you this morning: I don't hold with you or anything you're doing. Do you think I want to end up in a concentration camp for the sake of your nonsense? I may be crazy – but not enough to want that."

"Very well," Frisch replied, making a sudden decision. He sat down on a stool. "Why do you want to see me, then? I believe you. You could have reported about the potassium, and you didn't. What now?"

Zoder stood up. "First let me prepare things," he muttered. "That nurse of mine – I can't be sure she won't run in here. At a time like this I need an excuse for remaining away from Wegler. You're suffering that pain again in the region of the sacrum… understand?"

Frisch nodded.

Zoder set a sponge electrode on the treatment table. "Drop your trousers and sit down here. I'll put on a low current. We can't talk properly if you lie down, so if the nurse comes in, make believe you just sat up. Everything will appear normal. She's near-sighted anyway."

"Why a low current?" asked Frisch with rueful irony. "In the last few days my pains have come back again. Let's have a treatment while we're at it."

"Yes? Tension will do that, or… Of course, my dear man, you'll probably have a cancer of the bowel at forty-five."

"Thank you."

"Why be unpleasant to me? Thank your fellow Germans in the concentration camp."

Frisch sat down on the sponge electrode. He held its partner to his abdomen.

"Such interesting diseases have been developed in our concentration camps," said Zoder as he switched on the short-wave current. "The mystery of dinosaurian bones will pale before the task that confronts future anthropologists. 'Now let's see,' they'll cogitate. 'Evidently we have here a common grave of some twentieth-century Germans. But what a strange variety of injuries: broken kneecaps, crushed finger bones, pelvic fractures – quite remarkable. Could it be that the climate achieved a brittleness in the German skeleton? Or was it some calcium deficiency?'" Zoder cackled humourlessly. He pulled a stool over by the treatment table and sat down close to Frisch, peering up at him with anger. "You!" he said with scorn. "*You've* been through this, not me. Why do *you* want to preserve such monsters?"

Frisch shrugged. "I don't… Is that what you want to talk about?"

"No," Zoder muttered. He was silent for a moment. "Listen," he asked suddenly, "be honest with me. That time we quarrelled you said I was insane. Did you really think so?"

Quietly Frisch lied, "No, I was angry. Can I see Wegler?"

"Certainly not. It's too dangerous."

"I'll worry about that."

"Why do you want to see him?"

"A number of reasons."

"Impossible. My nurse is watching him like a bloodhound. You find me logical, don't you?"

"Yes. If you wanted to cooperate, we could work out a way for me to see him."

"I'm a tortured man, pastor. I'll be frank about it. I think of suicide often these days. What is there to live for? Do you have anything to live for, pastor?"

"Much."

"Oh yes!" Zoder chuckled without being amused. "The liberation of the German people, eh? And your cancer."

"What about Wegler? It might be useful if I could talk to him."

"All things must proceed by logic," muttered Zoder. "Look here: maybe I am a little erratic. I'm a man of science, I can observe things about myself. I don't forget that I was in an institution. The paralysis I developed in Poland – it was purely psycho-neurotic, I understand that."

"Wegler," repeated Frisch quietly. "Please… we have no time for pleasant conversation."

"I'm coming to that. This is part of it. You see, I understand myself. I know that queer thoughts come into my head sometimes. I don't sleep well. I'm nervous. But on the other hand, I retain my sense of logic. If you will be logical with me – will you now, *hm*?"

"Of course," said Frisch, not knowing what he was talking about.

"The Wegler matter is this: he either remains unconscious, or he's shamming. Before you came in, my nurse called me. She was passing his door and she swore to me she heard him talk. I went in to see him. I spoke to him, but he didn't answer. No… it's not what you think. He has temperature, but not enough for delirium. And I find no overt reason for his continued unconsciousness. But if there is a reason, I may bring him out of it by an injection of strychnine. However, that will give Baumer a chance to talk to him."

"Well?"

"The question is: should I do it?"

"Should you help Baumer?" asked Frisch with cold scorn. "Is that your big problem? Of course help Baumer! Guide yourself by what your dead daughter would have done. Naturally *she'd* approve of your helping the Baumers! Perhaps in his weakened state Wegler will even tell what he knows about me – because he does know something. That should please you, too. Baumer will increase your tobacco ration."

"Look," said Zoder hoarsely, "listen to me, please." His seamed, ugly face was suddenly miserable. "Why do you think I put Baumer off until morning? It was so I could talk to you. I know I'm not clear. I want to do the right thing. To help Baumer is not logical – but to help Wegler is not logical either. I must have a consistent principle. That's all I have left: my principle. You don't know what a volcano of distrust I carry inside of me, pastor."

"Towards whom?"

"Towards whom? Why, even for you," said Zoder with the rage bursting out of him. "For you because you're a German. For Wegler because he's a German. For myself because I'm a German. No... you won't catch me there," he added with cunning. "I'm too logical for that. I keep my mind on my human principle. You can't divert me."

Sadly Frisch thought: "It's come to this, then: to sit in a room with a madman and to argue the ethics of his insanity."

"Look here," said Zoder, "if you think I'm illogical, then prove it. I recognize what Wegler did. But do you think I didn't observe the Weglers in Poland? Wegler's a German. Who left the bodies of old men in the village streets? Who brained Jews with trench shovels for sport? 'Orders,' they would say, if they said anything, and shrug. No, you can't tell me about the Weglers. A decent man, when ordered to bayonet a child, will reply, 'Kill me, if you like, but this I won't do!' Or he'll shoot his officer and take the consequences. But what did the Weglers do in Poland? They shrugged and said, 'Orders.' Only, I never saw a German soldier ordered to rape a peasant girl. He did it happily, you may be sure, and even asked his friends to photograph the prank." Zoder's mouth twisted – his eyes, usually so lifeless, blazed with inexpressible fury. "And who are these

German monsters – these cannibals that walk like men and look like men but only know how to spray bullets from a gun? A few SS soldiers? Don't be naive! *The whole German army* – bone and flesh of the people. I saw them in action. And I saw their parents in the village square the other day. All over Germany housewives feel the muscles of Polish girls, and men examine the teeth of Russian, Slovak and God knows what other miserable human beings, and then buy them as work slaves. Is it to be believed? Yes, it's happening. Human flesh is being sold in our streets. Six million foreigners are already at work within our borders, Baumer told me. And trainloads more coming every day." Flecks of spittle appeared at the corner of Zoder's twisted mouth. "Damn them, I say!" he cried. "Damn them! Damn them!"

"Quiet!" Frisch interrupted. "You'll be heard."

"Damn them, damn them," Zoder whispered, "for now and unto eternity, damn them. This is a tainted people! This is a race dedicated to conquest. For seventy years we've been at it. All of us. Let them put you in the army and you'll shrug too – you'll say, 'I have to obey orders.'"

"And Wegler?" asked Frisch softly. "He's like the others? But you see, he's not like the others either. He set a signal light to the British. No, you haven't explained Wegler, my logical friend, or the anti-Nazi Germans who died before my eyes in the concentration camp. Furthermore, you *know* that you haven't."

Zoder remained silent, biting his lips.

"Listen to me," said the pastor. "We live in an evil time. Do I dispute that? I haven't been in Poland, but I can read our newspapers. 'Rotterdam will be free of Jews by the twelfth of July... SS troops have administered punishment to a village that concealed guerrillas.' I know what those things mean. I see the murder of the innocent between the lines. History won't be able to record the crimes of these awful years—"

"The crimes of Germans," Zoder interrupted.

"Yes, of Germans. But are you so new to this world that you think Evil has just been born? You've lived through this sickness, Zoder." Anger came into his voice. "Damn you... You've seen these scoundrels ride to power on the woes of our nation. You've seen our people gulled and silenced. There's no mystery to it. It's happened elsewhere. It may happen again. And now our people, deceived, brutalized, are visiting this plague upon the world. Yes, we're guilty of that! Must we do penance – strive for redemption? Must we purge our culture of its militarism, its race vanity? Yes – yes. And must we make the amends—"

"Amends?" Zoder interrupted, almost in a shout. "Can a single murdered innocent be restored to life? Can a hundred million hearts be eased by penance?"

"Quiet!" said Frisch. "You must—"

"What garbage!" Zoder interrupted again, but in a lowered tone. "Is this your morality, my man of God – this empty penance?"

"No," replied Frisch sadly. "You won't listen, and you don't understand."

"What don't I understand?"

"That Evil is not new in the world!" The pastor's voice became tremulous with emotion. "That Christians were burnt in Rome, and Rome was sacked by Goths… that Protestants in England killed Catholics, and Catholics in France butchered Protestants… *that Evil is not new*, my friend, and that no people has had a monopoly on good… and that Evil must be understood – it is not of the air or the wind: it has a source and a growth, a reason and a being, and it must be understood!"

Zoder's bitter mouth twisted. "Is this your logic? Society has advanced. I don't treat syphilis today with the incantations of a witch doctor. And no modern people can be absolved when it behaves like a cannibal tribe."

"Good!" said Frisch. "But what *conclusion* do you draw from all of this?"

"There must be *justice*!" Zoder whispered with his face close to the pastor's. "Mankind must be protected. This plague spot must be wiped out. That's why I live – to see justice done."

"Yes," said Frisch, "there must be justice. But still I ask: Baumer is coming at eight o'clock. Whom will you help – him or Wegler?"

"I don't know." Zoder groaned. He put a quivering hand over his eyes. "It's not logical. I should have let Wegler die and be done with it. I know – I know… Wegler is Baumer's enemy. So am I. That's why I'm confused. I wanted to talk to you…"

Frisch reached out suddenly, touching Zoder's shoulder. "Look at me," he said softly.

Zoder uncovered his eyes.

"You *know* that Wegler is not Baumer. He is a German, yes, but not Baumer."

Zoder nodded.

"Man – don't think I can't understand you."

The pastor's eyes, which had been so hostile before, were luminous and warm as he gazed at Zoder's sick face. "Be honest – the problem is not Wegler. You know that. You know that he must abominate these crimes as much as you. The problem is in your own soul. You cannot bear the inhumanity of our times, and in your fury you need to condemn – blindly and totally. But Wegler refutes you. And so you are left confused. No, the problem is not Wegler or even Germany: it is the spectacle of Man that confuses you."

Zoder turned his eyes away. "I am not confused," he muttered. "The principle is clear. I—"

"Listen to me," said Frisch softly. "Once I had a creed. It was from Micah: 'What doth the Lord require of thee, but to do justly, and to love mercy, and to walk humbly with thy God?'* I wore that on my heart. 'How wonderful,' I thought. 'This is the ethical path I will tread.' What nonsense! Did I understand morality? I did not. And do you know why? Because I understood nothing about Man and the necessities of his life. I was ignorant even of God, because I am convinced that one cannot understand God if one is blind to Man."

"I know Man," said Zoder. "He is vile. I have seen his footprint. It is bloody. There is a primeval slime in us. God help us, but we're rotten. Where in the animal world can you find the *conscienceless* cruelty of our German soldiery? Nowhere! An animal rends for food – but never wantonly. No, I don't believe your God or your conscience – or your Man."

Slowly Frisch said, "There was a time when I felt as you feel. But I am not so cowardly as you, Zoder – nor so illogical, either."

"What?" Zoder's lips trembled. "If you're going to call me insane again, I'll strike you. I swear I will. I don't like your face anyway. Do you know what sort of face you have? Like a bad drawing. No features, no character. Colourless. Why do I even listen to you?"

"You listen because you're a decent man," Frisch replied quietly. "But I tell you again, you're also a coward. If I ever considered you insane, I don't now, I assure you. I understand you better. I won't absolve you of moral responsibility. You're a guilty man, and you're a coward... and this logic you boast of... you keep it in your vest pocket for use as it pleases you." Frisch stopped talking. His face became wary. Outside men's voices could be heard. They approached closer.

"No, not there – over there," someone shouted harshly. "Not in a straight line, don't you understand? Zigzag – can't you understand?"

"They're digging air-raid trenches," said Zoder.

Frisch nodded and relaxed. "How much time have we?"

"It's seven twenty-five."

"Good." He coughed and his face twisted a little. "Zoder, be quiet. Listen to me – just for a few minutes."

The doctor shrugged. "I'm not your ally," he muttered, "nor you mine."

"When I was in the theological seminary," Frisch said hastily, "I had a purpose: to understand God. I thought I did. But there came a night when I understood nothing. You remember? It was when the Brown Shirts walked me to the railroad station. I ask you now, Zoder, what does a man feel when he has been beaten by God's creatures, humiliated, forced to behave like an animal before others... who stand by in silence? He feels despair. 'Why live?' I thought. 'For what? If this is what Man is, then he has no soul, he's a beast, and how can one live in his midst?'"

Outside the raucous voice shouted, "Unless your trench is as deep as a man's shoulder, it's no damn use to anybody. Get going there – put your back into it!"

"But then I went to a concentration camp," Frisch continued quietly. "There, for two years, I pondered the meaning of 'morality'. I talked of it with others. And slowly I perceived how irrelevant to living man had been the ethics of my seminary. 'Good and evil,' we used to say. 'Man must be virtuous.' What did we know of the source of good or evil? I tell you morality has nothing to do with the pulpit or the church. The church is only a meeting place where morality may be discussed, wisely or foolishly. Morality comes from the way people live, Zoder. Their virtue and their evil are like fruits growing in the soil of their existence. It is never the rich man who steals bread. He has no need. His morality is to steal empire, if he can. And what is the virtue of a father who looks upon his starving child? As a pastor I answer that it must be to steal. This is beyond censure, because it is inevitable. And what is the morality of a Russian whose home is invaded? It is to kill. And what is the morality that a pastor learns who has been in a concentration camp? I answer categorically, Zoder, without humility: it is to hate living Evil – it is to hate the men who use their power for Evil, and to hate the creeds that breed Evil." Frisch paused, his liquid, beseeching eyes fixed upon Zoder's face. "Oh, listen to me," he whispered passionately. "If you say 'Thou shalt not kill' and close your eyes to the 'Why?', then you too are not moral, but immoral. Men make wars, but why? It isn't the miserable German peasant dying in Russia for deluded patriotism who covets oil and grain. And even if he does, he has been twice deluded, because it wouldn't be to his profit if he lived, but to the profit of those who used him in the first place. Don't you see that, Zoder? Who taught our children the glories of war? Why? Who needed pawns? You're a scientist. When a man comes with a running sore, he's ugly, but you seek the germ. Have you no eyes for the germ cells here? *The manipulators*, Zoder! Who has been seeking empire – you, me, Wegler? Oh, God in heaven, see it! When children are hungry, their father steals! When a people like ours has been warped by hunger, then deceived, then puffed with vanity, they can be made rapacious. This is the living *method* of Evil, Zoder, and its sources can be touched – they are real, they have a history and an origin."

Through tight lips Zoder answered coldly, "Don't speak to me of what rulers have done to the German people. A people has the rulers it deserves. I know our empire-grabbers as well as you. But a man who kills an innocent child can't plead bad education. He knows what he does! He is corrupt and vile and beyond redemption. The morality of our German soul is to conquer the world. To use every fair land, every fair woman, every grape, every vine. This is our real morality."

"No," replied Frisch fiercely, "that is not the German soul! There is no fixed destiny to any people. Do you think I condone crimes? There are Germans who are beyond redemption, yes! Who should know that better than I? Who broke my body but Germans? But I ask you: are vile men new to this world? Have no other peoples seen it? And I ask you further: how has all of this come about? You're a scientist, you say. Will you show me this destiny in the German bloodstream? Is it some mystic infection?"

"What?"

"This national corruption... I insist that you show it to me in the bloodstream!"

"What are you talking about?" asked Zoder angrily. Suddenly he began to laugh. He clapped his hands together. "I used to have a dream," he replied irrelevantly, lost suddenly in his own train of thought. "In my dream I would have Hitler hauled into a courtroom. There, in test tubes, I would have samples of his blood, and of blood from a Frenchman, a Jew, a Chinese, a Negro. Then I would say, 'Now, you paperhanger bastard, put those blood samples under a microscope and tell me what difference there is amongst them.'" The savage gaiety vanished from his face as suddenly as it had appeared. "But there's no courtroom in Germany," he whimpered. "And there are no microscopes – not one!"

"Then how has all this come about?" Frisch asked softly. "Each generation is born naked and innocent. How do adults grow into barbarians?"

"Who knows?" Zoder muttered. "Let others answer if they care to. I only care to see justice done!"

"No," Frisch said with contempt, his soft eyes blazing, "you don't really care to see justice done. You're a cynic, and a cynic is always a coward. You've washed your hands of life. Do you think all Germans are guilty except yourself? You're guilty too. You listen to me, now: if Wegler is only shamming unconsciousness, then he has a reason. God's Grace upon him, and you must protect him. And if he is not shamming, you must equally protect him. I have come a long, bitter road, Zoder. Wegler has been my final prophet. Now I know what Man is, and what his morality is, and what Man's future can be. And now at last I believe I can understand God again. And as a moral man I'll guard Wegler with my life against your cynicism and your cowardice."

For a moment they were both silent, staring at each other. Then Frisch said, humbly, "You must listen to me, Zoder. I beg you. We have only a few minutes left. Give me a chance. My talk just now was boastful, I know. Wegler's in your keeping after all."

Zoder shrugged. "I promise nothing. If you have your conscience, I have mine. If you have your pastor's morality, I have my disgust."

"Very well. But listen! You said that the German army was made up of men like Wegler. But don't you see? Wegler is also a German who committed sabotage. And I know why. I know what was in his soul."

"How do you know?"

"I know because he came to me for help!"

"When?"

"Yesterday."

Zoder was silent for a moment, suspicious. Then he said, "Yes?"

"Yesterday afternoon, I was asleep in my bunk," said Frisch. "He came in and awakened me. He asked me to talk to him. We went into the woods. I knew he had been given a Service Cross. I didn't trust him. When I asked him why he wasn't at work, he had no explanation. Then he told me something that frightened me. He said, 'Last night I came home late, pastor... through the woods. I saw you. It was at a little distance, but I knew it was you.' Then he stopped. He hesitated. He gazed at me as though he were trying to see into my very soul. 'Why weren't you at work, pastor?' he asked me.

"I told him that I had been ill. That was the excuse I had prepared. My foreman let me off for half an hour. I had the crystals with me, and it was time enough to paint the signs."

Zoder nodded.

"Then Wegler said, 'Pastor – tell me the truth: was it you who wrote on those rocks?'

"What could I do? I didn't know Wegler. A silent man like so many here. All I knew about him was bad – his son in the SS... and now a Cross. So I denied it. I thought surely I was suspected, and that this was a clumsy trap."

Frisch paused, his eyes sad. "Then, when the Gestapo commissar called me in, I discovered why Wegler had come to me. He was a lonely, lost man, Zoder. We live in a jungle, where no man knows the mind or heart of another. He came to me in desperation, out of his moral anguish – but he was frightened of me, as I was of him. And then, when I turned my face away, he acted alone, a man trusting his own conscience."

"How do you know?" asked Zoder suspiciously.

"I know! Wegler was to be married to a farm woman. She told the commissar that Wegler felt guilty over a Pole she had bought. The commissar couldn't understand the meaning of it. He asked me, 'When does a man feel guilty?'

"'When he has sinned against God or against his fellow man,' I answered.

"'It doesn't make sense,' the commissar told me. 'How could Wegler feel guilty over a Pole when he had no contact with him?'

"But I understood. Can't you, Zoder? Wegler felt guilty as *you* feel guilty. He couldn't bear it that Germans were buying human beings like cattle. There's no other explanation! That's why he sabotaged! He wanted Germany defeated, as I want it defeated. Because only on the wreckage of this madhouse can something new be built." The pastor's eyes blazed. "But you're not Wegler's moral equal, Zoder, and you're not my moral equal. You've washed your hands of responsibility. And in giving up hope for Germany, you've given up hope for Man. You're blind – you crave solely to hate. And that's either cowardice or insanity. I leave you to choose."

"*What* can be born?" Zoder muttered angrily. "What can be born out of a people that are so tainted? One man has sabotaged. Another man writes upon a washroom wall. What does that weigh against this mass corruption?"

"Everything!" Frisch cried passionately. "Man is lower than the angels, yes. But as he can be led into evil, so he can be led into good. Man has stepped forward magnificently in history – alas, he has sometimes stepped back. *Don't you understand this?* I'm not talking any longer of our German people. I'm talking of Man. In the concentration camp I learnt how debased it is possible for men to become. But I learnt also how noble they are. And if some can be evil and others noble – then all can be noble. Do you think I'm without guilt? A thousand times no. Where was my moral rebellion when the first Jew was murdered?" Frisch suddenly struck his breast with his clenched fist. "I was silent, as you were silent, *as the whole world was silent*. There were no Jews in my flock, and I had never considered Jews my bond brothers in humanity. And why hadn't I? Because my kind, good mother had passed on to me a senseless, thoughtless prejudice that had been passed on to her by her mother... because even in my God-fearing seminary I found it. And not until a rope was put around my neck, and their senseless sign 'I Am a Slave of the Jews', did I understand that I had put that rope around my own neck – and that it had followed my silence as day follows night."

Frisch's slight body began to tremble. He held out his hand as though in supplication. "But this is Man, Zoder, and the manner of his bewilderment; this senseless suicide is the property of no one people when their woes betray them. I don't ask you to believe in the goodness of man as he is – but in his potentiality for goodness when his society no longer drives him to evil. Do you think even Wegler is not guilty? No, he's guilty too. He *earned* his War Service Cross. There's no comedy in this. There's only the bitter irony of Man. Do you think other nations, and other governments, have no share in the guilt for this German monster? Where were the saviours of Czechoslovakia? Where was the conscience of humanity at Spain, at Munich?"

Painfully Frisch pressed a hand to his forehead. "I tell you, it's hard for Man to be good, Zoder. Who is Man? A creature who has come up from barbarism. He has had to learn the use of fire, of the simplest tools. At every step he has inherited the savageries of his fathers. And only slowly does he learn the path of his own good, because he is what he is, and he has no supernatural wisdom. And often he follows false gods – for how can he help it? He is hemmed in by what he is, and by the life to which he is born. And always there are those who are anxious to corrupt him, who teach him to be submissive – *submissive,* so that when his false gods call he will obey, and then he will kill Jews, or make war for his manipulators, and he will say in his delusion, 'I achieve justice, I am protecting my home...'"

Frisch was weeping quietly. He took off his glasses. "Now I sit here blind," he said. "I am a sick man. My body has been ruined by other men. I don't know the future. I can't prescribe. This is the summer of 1942, and the world is at war. If Germany wins this war, you and I don't know what will become of Man for generations. If Germany loses, who can say what will be done to her by the victors? Perhaps they'll be wise in dealing with her ghastly crimes, or perhaps they too will be rendered senseless. But as surely as I sit here, blind and sick and ignorant, I have an unalterable

343

knowledge: I know that this evil time will pass. I know that the sun hangs black in the sky, that the bones of slaughtered men are like pebbles on the earth – but I know that all this violence will pass. And I know that Man will struggle forward to a golden destiny. In my blindness I see it. And if there were only one noble man in Germany and his name were Wegler, then I would say: *in his deed I see the moral future!* And this I believe. And if you don't help this man, Zoder, if you don't save him to the best of your ability from what may be done to him – then in my morality, as a pastor, I will seek you out and kill you. I swear it!"

He leant his head forward and wept.

Outside there was the steady thud of picks, of shovels digging the earth for shelter, of men's voices – uneasy, and tense, and low lest they disturb the sky.

Chapter 15

Now it had become easier for Willi to endure his pain and thirst. He recognized that it was so, and he laughed quietly to himself with the laughter that belongs to the dead or the very old, who do not care. For the first moments after the nurse had rushed into his room, and he had realized that she suspected him, he had felt only terror. But when Doctor Zoder had come to investigate, speaking to him, thumbing back his eyelids, his terror had given way to hatred. He remembered Zoder. After he had received the Service Cross, Baumer had taken him to his private office. This Doctor Zoder had been summoned.

"Listen, Zoder," Baumer had said in Willi's presence, "I want you to give this man a physical examination. It's something I should have thought of earlier. Obviously Wegler can't make a proper gesture in volunteering for the army if the army won't take him. Look him over, will you?"

And so Wegler had become acquainted with this Doctor Zoder.

"Do you cough?" Zoder had asked, without getting up from his chair.

"No, sir," he had replied.

"Sweat at night?"

"No."

"Haemorrhoids? That is, any bleeding when you move your bowels?"

"No, sir"

"Examination finished," Zoder had told Baumer with a laugh. "This is all the army will ask. It's no longer 1939. If a man can pass this, he can function on a firing squad."

Yes, Wegler knew this doctor. And the bursting hatred that gripped him now was a strength upon which to lean. All his life, it seemed to him, he had regarded men like Zoder as the wise men of the earth. A doctor had learning, the people said, and a doctor dealt in mercy. But in that one moment in Baumer's office he had understood them all: the doctors, the lawyers and the teachers... and the men of government, who were by nature wise and of goodwill and fitted to rule... and the generals he had always respected, and the laws he had always obeyed – and he had seen them in that moment as frauds. For he had lived under them and obeyed them and listened to their counsel – only to end up indecent and a bankrupt. Years before there had been a joke among workers like him. It was of the faithful employee who always came to work on time, who never joined a union, who never struck, who accepted his wage cuts – all in the hope that when he was sixty years of age he would receive a gold watch in tribute to his services. And then, in the forge room, Willi Wegler had been given his watch – the Service Cross of the slave masters. And in Baumer's office had seen himself finally – understood that he was even stupider, even more tragic, even more of a buffoon than the worker with the golden watch.

But now Zoder had restored his hatred. It lifted him beyond thirst, beyond the stabbing pain in his groin. His life had been stupid, yes. And he was to die for it. But at least he had flung the watch back into their faces. Let Zoder come again with his ugly mug. He would be silent. From the certainty of his grave, he would not speak. He had no thirst now. He had no pain. He had only a hatred.

2

8:00 a.m.

Baumer sat down on the chair before Zoder's desk. "*Heil Hitler*," he said hoarsely.

"Good morning," replied Zoder with a cackle of laughter. "Any old pots or pans? A watch that doesn't work, perhaps, or a set of teeth? We trade anything, sir. Highest prices in town."

"Is Wegler conscious?"

"As conscious as a doorpost. Want to try the strychnine?" He laughed.

"Yes."

Zoder jumped up and crossed behind Baumer to an open closet in which there was a sink, several shelves for drugs and instruments, a sterilizer.

Baumer asked, "Will you tell me why you laugh every other word you say, doctor?"

Zoder paused as he fished in the sterilizer with a pair of prongs. "I wouldn't know. Habit." He grinned at Baumer's back. "Of course, I find life incredibly amusing."

"Do you?"

Zoder set the hypodermic tube on a towel. "You're much too serious, Baumer. The trouble with you, if I may say, is that you're loaded down with ideals." He fitted the plunger into the tube, then inserted the long needle. "Ideals weigh a man down, make a humpback out of him." He cast a quick glance over his shoulder.

Baumer said wearily, "Who knows if I have ideals? Not I any more. I had a head full of ideals once. But now my head's full of problems. It's like starting off to see someone. You walk so long you're not sure if you've lost the way. So you just keep going. What else is there?"

"Correct," said Zoder gaily. "What's an ideal? An ideal is a chocolate candy with a problem inside." He came back into the room. The hypodermic, now filled, was balanced delicately in one hand, the plunger resting against the ball of his thumb. "You eat the candy, the taste is sweet, but what remains in the stomach is something indigestible. You ought to be a cynic like me, Baumer. Of course a cynic is a coward. He washes his hands of life. A mere spectator, you might say." With his free hand he held up a tiny vial, its top sawn off. "May I offer you the remaining drops of this strychnine? Its taste is bitter, but I can promise you an increased sensibility of touch, sight and hearing."

Baumer smiled wryly. "I wish there were something you *could* give me. I feel all washed up. My bones feel tired, I swear."

"The doctor prescribes a rest. The Riviera, plenty of wine, sunshine and French girls. Of course even that has a problem. You might return to me with a dose."

"I know what I want," said Baumer. "I'd like to stop thinking. I'd like to be a common soldier on the Eastern Front doing my duty. No worries – just to kill. Have you ever killed anyone, Zoder?"

"Not yet." The doctor grinned, his ugly face twisting into a gargoyle.

"It's a release to kill. I killed in the first years of the movement. It did things for me. There's a kind of wine in violence. A soldier knows he's doing his duty. He doesn't have to know about anything else. He can surrender to duty like a woman surrendering in the sexual act. Only, a man has to worry about being impotent. With the woman it makes no difference. She can perform if she's dead."

"I wouldn't know," said Zoder, grinning. "I'd like to try this hypodermic now."

"What do you expect from it?" asked Baumer, rising.

"Expect? Nothing. I merely hope. The action of strychnine varies with the individual and with the condition. I will hope for an excitation of both cardiac action and the respiratory system, resulting in consciousness. But only if he's still in shock. If it's a brain injury…" He gestured helplessly. "Well, shall we go?"

Baumer nodded. In silence they walked side by side down the long corridor. Outside of Wegler's door Zoder said, "No talking inside please. Once I inject, I want to be able to listen to his heartbeat."

"How long before he will become conscious?"

"Not long – *if* he becomes conscious. I promise nothing."

He opened the door. Sister Wollweber was seated by the bed, bathing Wegler's face with a wet towel. She jumped up instantly, dried her hands on her uniform (to Zoder's scientific discomfit) and rolled up the pyjama sleeve on Wegler's right arm. Then she produced a small bottle of alcohol and some cotton and swabbed the skin.

"That's a drip infusion of salt and glucose," Zoder whispered to Baumer as he pointed to the apparatus. "It's to maintain the level of the body fluid."

Baumer nodded with disinterest. He was gazing down on Wegler, at the flushed face, the swollen lips, the rise and fall of the huge chest. Seeing him again, this man who had stood by his side on the catwalk twenty-four hours before, Baumer was seized by an impotent fury. He felt like hammering Wegler with his fists. That the man had had the sheer gall to accept a Service Cross!... It was monstrous. How could one trust any worker when a man of his record revealed this implacable hatred for the National Socialists? Who knew how many of the others felt the same way? They worked and they kept their mouths shut, yes – but one never knew.

He watched Zoder bend over the muscular arm, squeeze for a vein and then slide the needle home. The doctor's thumb pressed down slowly on the plunger. When he had emptied the tube, he withdrew the needle delicately and stepped back. Sister Wollweber sat down by Wegler's side and pressed a piece of cotton to the puncture. Grinning and nodding at Baumer as though he were having the time of his life, Zoder took a stethoscope from his pocket. He pulled a chair over to the other side of the bed and sat down.

"Damn!" Baumer thought. "Let's have a bit of luck." He took his cigarette case out of his pocket and queried the doctor silently. Zoder shook his head with great vigour. Reluctantly, Baumer dropped the case back into his pocket. He stepped forward to the bed as Zoder applied the stethoscope to Wegler's chest. Alternately he glanced hopefully from Wegler's face to Zoder's. In the past several hours he had convinced himself that Wegler must be the brains of the opposition elements in the factory. If he could wring the truth from Wegler now, he would be able to sweep up the whole criminal scum at one stroke. If not – then who knew what might happen next? They would be obliged to patrol the countryside every night. What Wegler had done could be repeated.

A minute passed. Two. Three. Baumer's watch marked five minutes. Still Zoder listened, his mouth stretched in a saturnine grin – and Baumer felt as though he would jump out of his skin. Wegler *had* to be made to talk. So long as he remained silent…

Six minutes. Seven. Eight.

After exactly twelve minutes had elapsed, Zoder turned to Baumer with a cheerful grin. "Lucky at love, unlucky at sabotage," he said loudly. "It's no use, Baumer. There's a very slight increase of heart action. But the man just doesn't respond. Our strychnine is a failure. From now on we'll have to depend on Nature – and wait."

"Wait? No, I won't wait!" Baumer exploded. He plucked a small gold-plated knife from his vest pocket. "If your strychnine won't work, I know something that may!" He snapped open one of the small blades.

"Oh my God!" Sister Wollweber cried in horror, "Herr Baumer – what are you thinking about?"

"You! Out of here!" Baumer said to her.

"Just a second." Zoder rose, placing himself between Baumer and the bed. "In here, I give orders."

"*What?*"

Zoder's hands, hanging limp at his sides, began to shake. "In here I give orders," he said. "You won't bring that man to consciousness. You'll kill him. I'm responsible in here. I beg you, Baumer. A few hours more and he may be conscious."

"You said that to me last night," Baumer retorted furiously. "How do I know?"

"You don't. There's no certainty. But if you apply torture to him, you'll kill him. That's the only certainty."

"So I will! It's my business."

"Anything in the hospital is *my* business," Zoder cried almost incoherently. "I won't stand up before the Gestapo with ten doctors testifying against me. They'll say that the opportunity to examine a traitor was lost because I didn't apply the simplest medical knowledge. I can't stop you if you mean to carry through this idiocy. But not in here! You'll have to get the police. You'll have to take him out of here. It'll be on your head then, not mine."

"Oh, damn you!" Baumer exclaimed. "All right, all right." He shrugged with despair, giving up. "All right, then. Let me know if he comes around."

He left the room with his head bent and his shoulders sagging.

349

Horrified, Sister Wollweber whispered, "Doctor, did he actually mean to do that?"

Zoder didn't reply. His hands were still shaking; his face was drained of colour.

"How could he mean to do a thing like that?"

Slowly a wolfish grin appeared on Zoder's face. "Come, come," he said, "this man is a traitor. Do you mean to say you have pity for him?"

"No, of course not, no," the nurse replied with perturbation, "if a man is a traitor... But still, it isn't human..."

"There you are," said Zoder. "What sort of a German are you? Why, in our concentration camps, that's where traitors really get it: whips, cigarettes in their eyes, crushed testicles—"

"What are you talking about?" Sister Wollweber interrupted with a muffled scream. "You're a beast to say such things. Germans don't act like that."

Zoder grinned. "But why not? Aren't they dealing with traitors? You think I'm lying? Ask some of the SS lads."

The nurse stared at him, her plump, kindly face utterly bewildered.

"Well... you might take his temperature again, sister, and then go about your duties. There's no need to continue bothering about him. If he wakes up, we'll know it – he'll be yelling for water."

He grinned at her and went out. The smile left his face as soon as he was in the hall, and his body went limp. He made his way down the corridor as though there were shackles on his legs. He entered his office, crossed through the adjacent room and entered the electrotherapy room. Pastor Frisch was lying on the table. He sat up instantly. As Zoder remained silent, he swung down to the floor. "Well?" he asked.

Slowly, not gazing at him, Zoder replied, "It's all right." He sat down heavily. "I did it. I injected water. Baumer didn't know."

"Ah!" Frisch said. He gazed at Zoder with glowing eyes.

Suddenly Zoder began to weep. He sat straight up, biting his lips, the hot tears rolling down his face.

"I didn't help my daughter," he said in a voice tortured by grief. "I helped Wegler, but not my own daughter. I let her die miserably... miserably."

"There's no going back," Frisch whispered. "She's at rest now."

"Yes," said Zoder, choked by his tears, "but I didn't help her. And I am not at rest."

"No," Frisch said, "no, you are not at rest, I know." He bent down and kissed him. "I know you are not. I know."

3

As Berthe Lingg followed Zimmel into the office of Commissar Kehr, she threw back her shawl and composed her face into a fixed smile. Inwardly she was trembling with apprehension, and her knees seemed to be made of rubber. In the hours since her first interview she had been feverishly examining her position. Her great security, she knew, lay in the fact that it was she who had called the SS guards. But on the other hand, she had lied to Kehr about Willi's patriotism. Self-preservation had forced this upon her. Once she admitted that Willi had displayed antagonism to the government, the question would be asked of her, "And why didn't you report this information, Frau Lingg?" She had had no alternative but to lie and to conceal – and now she was frightened. Who knew what a detective might find out? Perhaps he had spoken to Willi in the mean time. If he had, and if he now knew enough from Willi, it would leave her in a dreadful position. They might punish her by taking her farm away, or God knows what. She knew that at all costs she must deny knowledge of Willi's traitorous ideas. This was her plan, and she would stick to it… But her heart began to pound as she saw the commissar look up from his papers and smile at her. "Oh damn these men with their smiles," she thought. "They smile one minute and trick you the next."

"Good morning, Frau Lingg," said Kehr, jumping up from his desk and coming around to greet her. He extended his hand as though to an old friend. At the same time he nodded to the grinning Zimmel to leave them alone.

"Good morning, Herr Commissar," Berthe murmured. "*Heil Hitler.*" She tried to make her smile as friendly as possible.

"I must say – after the succession of men I've been questioning, it's a pleasure to see a charming woman, Frau Lingg." He held her hand, even though she tried to withdraw it, and his moist thumb caressed her flesh ever so delicately. "But I'm afraid you've been crying, haven't you?"

"Oh… a little," Berthe replied hastily. She had been prepared for this question. A last glance in her mirror, as she followed Elite Guard Blumel to the squad car, had revealed her reddened, puffy eyelids. "I'm just nervous, Herr Commissar. A crazy business like this… anyone would be upset."

"Of course, of course," he replied kindly. He let go of her hand at last and set a chair for her close to his own. "I won't keep you long, Frau Lingg."

Berthe sat stiffly, her hands smoothing the shawl in her lap, while Kehr consulted his black notebook. She kept her eyes on a knothole in the wall above his shoulder. "So if he likes you, it won't hurt," she thought with satisfaction. She recalled his comment at their first interview: that he was a bachelor. She knew enough about men to be sure that when one of them hastened to announce that he was a bachelor, it was probably untrue. What Kehr had in mind was perfectly clear – she saw no reason to rebuff him now. But let the case be closed and she would send him packing with his bachelor talk. She was no barnyard mare to yield to every stallion who came along. Besides, the farther one remained from the police, the better – every farmer knew that.

"Now then, Frau Lingg," said Kehr, "this Pole of yours, Bironski… you said last night that Wegler didn't have relations with him?"

"No, sir."

"Why are you so sure?"

"I can prove it," she replied with confidence. "Willi lit the fire last night. It was only the night before that I brought the Pole home. Herr Rosenhart, the Peasant Leader, was with me. We locked the Pole in the barn together. And all the next day Willi was at the factory. So how could he have any doings with the Pole?"

"The Pole says Wegler spoke to him the first night."

"The Pole is a liar. Who believes a Pole? Willi didn't even see him. I know."

"Was Wegler with you all that night?"

"No, sir. He left… soon after I brought the Pole home."

Kehr regarded her quietly for a moment. Then he said, "What did Wegler feel about your buying the Pole?"

"Feel?" Her tone became a trifle shrill. "He… What should he feel?"

"You said he felt guilty over the Pole."

"Yes… but he said that *last* night only. Not the first night."

"I see." Kehr scratched his moustache and considered this for a moment. Berthe's replies satisfied his sense of logic, but not his sense of smell, as he always put it. He kept being troubled by the fact that her snapping black eyes were shifty as well as handsome. Yet he could find no basis for tangible suspicion. She was, after all, the saviour of the factory.

"So then, Frau Lingg, you are not aware that the same night you bought the Pole Wegler saw him and offered to help him escape?"

"No," she replied with astonishment. "It isn't possible. Who says so?"

"The Pole."

"*Ach*... do you believe what a Polack says? Anyway, he was locked in the barn, I told you."

"The Pole says that Wegler spoke to him through a little window... No..." He consulted his notebook. "An air vent in the wall. Is there an air vent through which they could have talked?"

"Why... why yes, sir."

Berthe remembered something suddenly and wondered how it would affect her position to reveal it.

"Yes?" asked Kehr, observing her hesitation.

"I remember... I didn't think of it before... yesterday morning I found my well bucket out by the barn. I thought maybe some kids cut the rope and threw it there just for mischief. But it's true: if Willi stood on the well bucket... He's a tall man... Yes, I think he could talk through the vent."

"See here," Kehr asked excitedly, "are you sure of that – about the bucket? Are you sure it wasn't standing by the barn before that night?"

"I'm sure!"

"It was *always* tied by a rope?"

"Yes, sir."

"And the rope was cut?"

"Yes, sir. The strands were all ripped. I remember, because I tied it on again."

Kehr sat back and closed his eyes. He felt like breaking out into triumphal song. His insanity theory was no longer a mere conjecture, by God. Let Baumer rave – now he had a basis for submitting it to Headquarters.

"Look here," he said, fixing his eyes on Berthe sternly, "this thing you tell me about the well bucket – it's more important than you realize. The Pole told me a story that I don't believe. He claims Wegler offered to help him escape – offered him money, clothes and even his own police papers. That's ridiculous from every point of view. Why shouldn't a Pole try to escape when he's offered such assistance? The answer is he had no such offer probably – he was merely trying to curry favour with me by making up a story. Or – looking at it from Wegler's point of view – why should a German want to help a Pole he doesn't know? Wegler felt sorry for him, the Pole says. Most unlikely! Who gives a strange man his own police papers? For what *sane* reason? You see, Frau Lingg – there's our answer. That's where your evidence comes in. What we can be sure of, now, is that Wegler probably did speak to the Pole. If he said what the Pole claims – which I can't believe – he was crazy. If he said anything else, he was just as crazy. Insanity is the only theory that links Wegler's patriotic record with this crazy business. Whatever Wegler's reason was for seeing the Pole, it couldn't have been a normal, sane reason... So now tell me: are you prepared to go into a courtroom and repeat this evidence about the well bucket? Because a court won't believe a Pole, but it will believe you."

"Yes, sir. It's the absolute truth," Berthe replied firmly.

Kehr began to laugh with satisfaction. His eyes sparkled as he thought of what he would presently say to Baumer. "Now listen – is there anything you can think of... anything... that makes you think Wegler was crazy?"

An angry flush spread over Berthe's face. "Yes," she burst out, feeling her own betrayal more keenly than anything else at the moment. "Why, he tried to kill me. He ran after me with a pitchfork – me, his betrothed. Why, he must have been crazy. Yes, that's it! Now I understand."

"What do you understand?"

"I understand now how a man I knew so well – yes, a man I loved, the criminal – how he came to do a thing like that. When a decent man suddenly becomes a traitor – what else is there to understand? He suddenly went crazy, that's all. Now it's all clear."

"And there was nothing – no sign at all beforehand that he was politically discontent?"

"No, sir," she lied. "He never gave one sign. Why – I would have reported him right away, of course."

Kehr laughed quietly. "Good, good," he said with satisfaction. "That fits in with his getting a Service Cross too. You've helped me a great deal, Frau Lingg. I'm extremely grateful."

"Is he... is he still unconscious?" Berthe asked nervously.

"Yes."

She relaxed with a slight sigh.

Kehr snapped his fingers. "I want to try something. Now listen: you're sure Wegler loved you, aren't you? There's no possibility that he was deceiving you all along in order to get the opportunity for sabotage?"

Berthe gasped – she felt as though Kehr had struck her with his fist. "Oh, no," she answered intensely, "it isn't possible. No, he was... truly he was a good man. No, it can only be that he went crazy."

"Well then," said Kehr, "you must do something for me, Frau Lingg. I want you to see Wegler."

The colour drained from Berthe's face. "See him?"

"Sometimes love can do what medicine cannot do. Wegler's unconscious. Who knows but that his insanity was only temporary? It might be that getting shot – the shock, you understand – has brought him back to his senses. It's worth your seeing him. If you speak to him and he hears your voice – who knows? It's worth trying."

"Oh, no, don't make me see him," she begged.

"I insist. Why shouldn't you?"

"I… to go there… Oh, I'm afraid," she cried, searching for some explanation.

"Afraid of what?"

"He might kill me."

"Nonsense. He's in bed… severely wounded."

"I don't care. You don't know what he's like. Strong as three men. Even if he's wounded, if he ever got his hands on me – maybe he's still crazy, how do you know?"

"Now, calm yourself," said Kehr gently. "You're being silly. I'll send a man with you. He'll stay just outside the door so Wegler won't see him, but you'll be perfectly safe. After all, it's a hundred to one Wegler won't even wake up. No, this one last thing you must do for me, Frau Lingg. From the hospital you can go right home. I'm sure it won't be necessary to bother you again. This case is coming to a close."

Berthe remained silent. She felt sick at the thought of seeing Willi again.

"You do this little favour for me and I'll do one for you, Frau Lingg." Smiling, he rose from his chair and leant against the desk close to her. "In fact, I've already done the favour out of consideration for you."

Berthe kept her eyes away from his.

Kehr's voice turned mellifluous. "This morning I had a visitor… Frau Anna Mahnke, the Community Welfare Leader."

Berthe stiffened.

"She came with some disturbing information about you…"

"I—"

"Now please," Kehr interrupted with a smile. "You just be quiet… Frau Mahnke's information was… Well, it was quite serious." He frowned. "I didn't know what to say at first."

Berthe sat white-lipped, her hands twisting her shawl.

"But then I thought: 'How can I let a charming simple woman like Frau Lingg get into trouble with the Party? Any disrespectful remarks she may have made about the Führer—'"

"I—" Berthe half-rose from her chair.

"Please!" said Kehr severely. "Anyway, I fixed it up for you, Frau Lingg. When Frau Mahnke left my office, it was with the promise that she wouldn't say a word to anyone. She'll keep her promise too, because she knows Frau

Lingg now has a friend high up in the Gestapo." Kehr smiled benevolently. "There," he said, placing his hand lightly on her shoulder, "that was a real favour I did you, wasn't it?"

"Yes," she whispered gratefully.

"I'm a kind man. My instinct is to protect a charming woman like you." He squeezed her shoulder gently.

"Thank you," she whispered, sitting rigid, staring past him at the knot-hole in the wall. "Who knows what gossip can do?"

"Yes," he replied. "Who knows?" Boldly, feeling mounting desire at this certain conquest, his hand stroked her hair in a delicate caress. "You're really a very charming woman, Frau Lingg. I have sympathy for all you've been through. Perhaps it would comfort you if I dropped in when this case was closed? Some evening soon, perhaps. We might have a cup of coffee together, and a chat."

"That would be... very pleasant," she replied.

"Fine," he said with delight, "splendid. You don't know how I'll be looking forward to it." Reluctantly he removed his hand from her hair. "Well... a few last items." His tone became brisk. "It's been decided that morale will suffer if the factory workers know Wegler committed sabotage. Therefore you're to tell no one. It will be given out that he's ill."

Berthe nodded.

"Also, you'll hear presently that the Pole on your farm – what's his name? Yes, Bironski – that it was he who did the sabotage. In fact, he's already been arrested."

"But... but he didn't do it."

Kehr was silent.

"But..."

"Perhaps you'd better forget questions, Frau Lingg. You understand? The Pole did the sabotage. If anybody asks you, that's all you say."

"And I'm to be without a Pole, I suppose?" she asked bitterly. "Seventeen marks I paid for him."

"I'm sure you'll get another," Kehr said. He scribbled on the pad again. "In fact, I'll talk to Baumer about it." He smiled. "You see how I care for your welfare, Frau Lingg?"

"Thank you."

"Well then, now we'll call Zimmel and you'll go over to the hospital."

Berthe stood up. Kehr looked her over with pleasure and triumph. "If Wegler should wake up, I'll come right over. If not, I'll be seeing you one of these nights soon, eh?"

She nodded, smiling back at him with sudden boldness. "It'll be a pleasure," she said – and added to herself, "You beast."

Kehr put his hand on her arm. "Let me help you to the door, Frau Lingg."

<h1 style="text-align:center">4</h1>

8:30 a.m.

Very rapidly now the face of the factory was being transformed. The hard-packed ground near the buildings and the softer, grassy turf in the wooded sections were being turned into one vast trench system. The men were digging under the prick of fear, and they used every odd tool that the factory or the surrounding countryside afforded. Under Captain Schnitter's orders, the thousands of workers had been divided into three gangs. Each gang worked for ten minutes at a back-breaking pace – then, at the sound of the foreman's whistle, they dropped their tools and climbed out of the trenches for a rest while a second gang took their place. There had been no need to explain matters. Once it became known that both shifts of the factory had been set to digging, it was clear to everyone that this was no mere precautionary measure. This was EMERGENCY, DANGER… It was Düsseldorf threatening, and the Cologne blitz… And most of them knew it in the prickling of their backs. The men who were digging worked ferociously, with open, panting mouths – they knew how much depended upon a deep entrenching. And the men who rested rolled cigarettes without end, oblivious to the tobacco hunger that would come with the morrow. They smoked and measured each other in tense glances; they shrilled dull jokes over which no one laughed; they whispered their open terror.

"Oh damn… damn… we've been snug as bugs here for seven months," Hoiseler said to Pastor Frisch as they lay on their stomachs resting. "You know what I'd do to Wegler if I could? I wouldn't hang him. That's too easy. I'd think up ways to make him suffer." His dark, sullen face twisted with malice.

Frisch winked over at Keller, who was lying on his side exhausted and panting, even though their gang had been almost ten minutes at rest. Work of this sort was hard on Keller, who had a heart murmur. "You know where I'd like to be now?" said Frisch. "In Greece. Wouldn't you, Fritz?"

Keller grinned at their stale joke and mopped his forehead.

"We're supposed to have these trenches shoulder-deep by nightfall, did you hear?" asked old Rufke. He had been excused from the digging because of his age, but he was helping fetch water. "Shoulder-deep by night must mean we get blitzed tonight."

"Shut up," said Hoiseler nervously. "It doesn't have to mean anything of the kind... Damn that Wegler! Lives with us for—"

"Quiet with that Wegler talk," Keller panted. "You heard the commissar."

"Nobody can hear us."

"Shut up anyway."

"The Pole is the responsible one," old Rufke said flatly. "He's in British Intelligence. He offered Wegler a lot of money – that's why Wegler did it."

Weiner, who had been lying on his back with his eyes shut, rolled over suddenly. "What's that?" he asked. "How do you know he offered Willi money?"

"By logic," Rufke replied. "What else is there to explain it? As soon as the commissar told us about the Pole, I guessed it."

Weiner grunted in obvious disgust and rolled over to his back again.

"Well now," Frisch thought, "this is the second time you've spoken in twenty-four hours, my grunting friend. The first time was when Rufke cast a slur on Catholics. You didn't like that. The second is now. That's a lot of talk from you. Bless my heart if I don't think you're a bit excited by this Wegler affair." He looked over towards Weiner's buddy, Eggert, who was sitting a bit apart from them sucking a cold pipe as he watched the workers in the trench. "And how about you, my second grunter? Anything stirring in you too, by chance?"

The whistle blew. The men in the trenches climbed out with the sweat glistening on their faces. The next gang leapt up. "Only ten more minutes' rest for us," said Keller. "This is hard on me. If Pelz can be excused because of his one arm—"

"Say," old Rufke interrupted, "what's that?"

"Where?"

He pointed. "Over there, through the trees."

Some twenty yards distant, walking at an angle to them, came a procession. First in line was an SS man with an automatic rifle at the ready, then came young Latzelburger holding on to a rope and pulling a manacled figure after him, and then another armed SS man. The prisoner was Stephen Bironski.

Rufke uttered a foul oath. "That's the Pole who was mixed up in the sabotage!" he cried. "I'll bet on it!" He ran towards the slowly moving squad. The others, who had leapt up at his words, followed with equal curiosity. By the time they reached the group, men were streaming up from all sides.

"What's doing?" a worker called to the SS men.

"Clear the way," Latzelburger replied. "Well, boys – do you want to know why you're digging air-raid trenches? This bastard is the reason. He set a fire in a hayfield – signalled to the British planes."

A despairing cry burst from Bironski's corded throat. "I didn't! So help me God, it's a mistake. There was another—"

Latzelburger turned around and struck him an open-handed clout on the face. The Pole staggered back – only to be struck heavily on the shoulder by the rifle stock of the SS man behind. He fell to his knees. He was already showing blood at one nostril and at the corner of his mouth. His right ear, swollen three times its normal size, looked like a flower bulb.

"Didn't I tell you to keep your mouth shut?" Latzelburger demanded furiously. He kicked him in the ribs. "Get up now, or I'll pull your damned head off." He jerked the rope as Bironski struggled to his feet.

"I'll kill you, you bastard," Hoiseler yelled suddenly. He ran at the prisoner with his fist clubbed.

"Keep off," Latzelburger ordered, jumping between them. "He's under arrest. He's to be tried."

"I'll kill him. I'll tear him to pieces," Hoiseler yelled.

"Don't worry, he'll get what's coming to him. Clear the way," Latzelburger shouted at the muttering workers. His bulldog jaw was thrust out, and obviously he was enjoying this exercise of authority.

Old Rufke swung his arm, a lump of sod in his fist. He struck the prisoner on the side of the face and burst out into a joyous hoot. "Did you see that?" he cried. "Did you see what I did?"

"Hey, cut that out!" Latzelburger yelled as he saw several men reach down for stones. "The next man who throws anything is under arrest… Get out of the way now."

Sick at heart, physically nauseated, Frisch stared at the departing procession… and stared at the workers who were watching, at the angry, swollen faces of the Hoiselers and the blank, stony faces of the Weiners… and then quickly turned on his heel and ran back to his trench. "Herr Bednarick…" he said, as he came up to his foreman.

"What's going on over there?" Bednarick interrupted curiously.

"It's a Pole. He sabotaged, they say. Lit a fire to the British."

"So that's why we're… Why, the swine," Bednarick exploded. "They ought to string him up for the crows."

"Sir," said Frisch, "I'd like a few minutes off. I have to go to the latrine."

"Now listen, pastor," the foreman replied gruffly, "what is this? I don't like this business of your always needing the latrine during working hours. That's an old dodge. Do you think I'm stupid?"

"Sir, believe me, it's not a dodge," Frisch replied humbly. "You know my condition. I just had another treatment this morning. You can ask Doctor Zoder. Whenever—"

"All right, all right, keep your bowels to yourself." Bednarick laughed. "But mind you... I'll be watching for you. Report right back."

"Yes, sir," said Frisch gratefully. "I have to go to my bunk for some medicine, and then—"

"I bet it's clap after all," said Bednarick jovially. "Oh you pastors! Be back here in fifteen minutes, now."

"It'll surely take me a little longer," said Frisch. What he had in mind would take half an hour.

"All right, all right."

Frisch ran off. Bednarick looked at his watch and then raised the whistle to his lips. He blew twice. "Get going," he bawled, "this is no picnic, damn it!"

The shift changed.

Chapter 16

Clicking his heels, SS Leader Zimmel said smartly, "*Heil Hitler!*"

"*Heil Hitler,*" responded Zoder.

Zimmel extended the written order from Gestapo Commissar Kehr, which had been countersigned by Baumer. Doctor Zoder glanced it over, muttered "Very well, but it's absurd" and then raised his eyes to Berthe. She looked away, biting her lip, and pulled the shawl closer around her.

"Come along," he said.

They followed him down the corridor. At Wegler's door Zimmel said respectfully, "She's to go in alone, doctor."

Zoder nodded. "You can talk to him all you want," he told Berthe, "but no shaking him or anything like that to wake him up." He opened the door very quietly. Berthe's face went white. She took a deep breath and stepped inside.

The shades in the room were drawn. Slowly she tiptoed closer to the bed. She saw the outline of Willi's figure under the covers – and then his face.

Willi's head was to one side, turned away from her. Yet even in profile she could see the death sickness upon him – the unnatural flush, the swollen lips, the cadaverous hollow between cheekbone and jaw. Her heart contracted with pain. In the walk from the administration building, as she listened to Zimmel's praise of her heroism, it had been easy to concentrate on Willi's perfidy rather than her own. But now, seeing his virile body so pitifully helpless, seeing again in her mind's eye the dreadful image of Willi's head on a block, of a bright axe swinging down, she wanted to cover her eyes and run from the room. Now she felt again the weight of her own guilt, and she sank down into the chair by his bed, bursting into bitter tears, forgetting that Zimmel was just outside the door and that he would observe her.

Willi knew instantly that it was Berthe. Hearing the door open, he had assumed it to be either the doctor or the nurse. He had prepared himself psychologically, as he did each time they came into the room, tensing his nerves for whatever was to happen. The realization that it was Berthe – he knew it from her tears – upset him terribly. He didn't want her to cry or to be unhappy. The hatred he had felt for her was small now. He longed to put out his hand and stroke her hair, to say "Berthe, girl, don't cry..." – to say "I'm so sorry you're having my child now, Berthe."

Berthe sank down on her knees by his bed. She whispered to him. Her tone was choked with guilt, piteous in its supplication: "Willi, Willi," she said. "Oh, Willi, my poor, sweet Willi."

Willi's fingers dug into the mattress. He felt her lips on his hand suddenly, the hand that was bound to the bed, and then he felt hot tears bathing his flesh. Without realizing it, he groaned, and his head turned towards her. He was wrenched with self-pity, with a sense of all he had lost in losing Berthe. Why had he done this mad thing? Like an idiot he had lopped off his life, taken their sweet, entwined future and wantonly destroyed it.

"Oh, my poor darling," Berthe whispered, "you're suffering, you're in pain!" She wept bitterly. "Oh, Willi, you can't hear me, but maybe God will hear me. I love you. I could die for what I did to you." She covered his hand with kisses. "If I could only undo it, Willi... If it could only be last night again..."

Through lids that were ever so slightly raised, Willi looked at her. He heard her say, "But why did you do it, Willi? What sense was there to it? You must have been out of your head."

He heard her say this, and at the same time he saw the sweater she was wearing – the sweater of the Frenchwoman that she had pretended to burn.

He closed his eyes. A sickness that was beyond bitterness flooded his veins. The love he had been feeling for her turned to raging scorn. He recalled what had happened between them the night before, and he thought savagely, "I should have killed you before you betrayed me – you're rotten like all the rest. Even your love is cheap."

Berthe's weeping ceased. She blew her nose and sat up on the chair again. "Oh, Willi, Willi," she murmured. Then she fell silent. She gazed at his sick face and thought again, "If I could only undo it... Why did it have to turn out this way? Dear God, why?"

On the night of their quarrel over the Polish prisoner, when Willi had left her so cruelly, without a word, Berthe had come to a painful decision – that Willi must yield to her over the Pole, or she would not marry him. With a heavy heart she had told herself that she knew men too well to be blinded by love. In thirty-six years she had seen a good deal in her small world. She had seen men with a taste for liquor who might be ashamed of their vice, but who drank anyway. And their wives might love them, comfort them or despise them – but still the man drank and the woman's life was a hell. It was the same with Willi, she concluded that night. A decent marriage would be impossible between them unless Willi could shake off the devils that plagued him. It was pure insanity for him to have quarrelled with her over the Pole. They might as well quarrel over the meat rations, or the wooden soles on her shoes. Life was always hard – it had been hard when she was a child, and it was even harder now. And life was always casting up unpleasant problems. But the only way in which she had ever found contentment was to shut her eyes to the bad and to open her heart to the good. And unless Willi too could learn this, she knew that their marriage would be a failure.

When the next evening came, Berthe waited in trembling anxiety for Willi to appear, hoping that she would hear his whistle at the usual time. After an hour of loneliness she had broken down and wept. Her heart urged her to seek him out at the factory, but her mind said, "No." Her mind warned that their quarrel was too big for that. "He'll come tomorrow night," she told herself.

She undressed and got into bed. But even though she was physically exhausted, she found it impossible to sleep. She tossed from side to side, and every few minutes she raised up on her elbow to peer at the old alarm clock on her bureau. Time and again her mind drifted into the same fantasy: of falling asleep and of being awakened by Willi's kiss; of opening her eyes to see him smiling, his anger forgotten; of having him pull her close to his hard, warm body and whisper, "I'm sorry – we'll never quarrel again."

And then, a little before ten o'clock, she heard the creaking of the front gate. Willi had come back – to beg forgiveness, she was sure. She leapt out of bed and put on her robe. Trembling with joy, she ran into the kitchen. Willi opened the front door before she could reach it, and for a silent moment they gazed at each other. The night was dark – Berthe could not see Willi's eyes or judge his mood. But the fact that he had come told her all she required. "Oh, Willi," she cried, and rushed to him, flinging her arms around him.

Willi embraced her without speaking. She pressed her body to his and reached up to cover his face with kisses. "Ah, sweetheart," she whispered, "I've been waiting for you to come. Please let's forget what happened last night. I love you, Willi. Dearest, I love you so much I can't stand it when we quarrel. It tears me to pieces."

In silence Willi stroked her hair. He stooped over to kiss her mouth gently. Then he said, "Will you make me some coffee, Berthe? I haven't eaten."

The mundane oddity of his request, at the very first moment of their reconciliation, disconcerted Berthe. Nevertheless, she said eagerly, "Of course, Willi." She pulled the curtains and lit the oil lamp. Willi sat down at the table, and she busied herself at the stove. Out of the corner of her eye she watched him closely. She still didn't know how to interpret his mood. He seemed at ease – he had embraced her and smiled at her. But his eyes were hot and nervous: they roamed the room in an abstracted manner. And even though it was only a little thing – she was distressed to see him in overalls.

Disturbed, with her long day of uncertainty weighing upon her, she could not wait to be tactful. She turned from the stove suddenly, fixing her eyes upon him. "Do you notice my fields?" she asked boldly. "My hay was cut this morning." Nervously she waited for his answer.

"Yes, I saw," he replied quietly.

Still uncertain, she continued, "It was cut by a gang of Polish prisoners."

"Yes?" Willi replied calmly. "Now your worries are over." There was no sarcasm in his tone.

"Oh, me... I never worry," she retorted with a flashing smile. Her voice changed, became affectionate. "You're the one who likes to worry." And then, because she didn't want him to feel that she was stony-hearted, she added: "I feel sorry for those prisoners. I could hardly stand to look at them, they looked so miserable. And do you know what they got for lunch?... Only a piece of bread and some watery soup. Men can't work on that, can they?"

Willi said nothing. His face was as calm as his manner, but his hot eyes gave the lie to both.

"But what's to do about it?" Berthe continued deliberately. "It's nothing we can help. Everybody has his own problems. My hay is practically worthless, for instance. Half of it has flowered already – it's like straw, not hay. And that Pole of mine... Hah – what a liar Rosenhart is! He swore the Pole was a farmer – but in five minutes I saw he's never worked on a farm in his life. We were stacking the hay this afternoon – I did in ten minutes what it took him an hour to do. Can you imagine?"

Still Willi said nothing.

"But why talk of things like this?" Berthe asked, with a feeling of triumph. She crossed to him suddenly, bending over to kiss his mouth. "We should be doing this, shouldn't we?" She stroked his face. "Darling," she whispered, "are you still a little angry with me, eh? Don't be angry any more."

Willi smiled gently. "I'm not angry any longer."

Trembling with happiness, she took his hard, big hand in both her own, kissing it, then she pressed it to her body. "Think of it," she whispered, "in here is our baby. In a little while he'll be kicking all day, trying to get out in a hurry." She laughed softly, feeling only slight contrition over her lie. "If he's a boy, he'll be like you, won't he, Willi? He'll kick my ribs to pieces, I bet."

With a slight sigh Willi said, "Yes."

"Darling?" She waited for him to look at her. "Would you like to be married now? I would. There's nothing to stop us any more. Let's get married right away."

Willi gazed at her quietly for a moment. Then he answered slowly, with a groan, "Yes, more than anything else, I'd like to be married to you, Berthe... and happy. But listen... I saw Baumer today."

"Oh?" she asked doubtfully, sensing trouble. "The Labour Front Leader?"

"I'm not to be transferred to the farm."

"You're not? Oh! God in heaven, why?" Then, trying to be courageous about it, she said, "Well... in a few months, we'll apply again. Meanwhile—"

"Berthe," he interrupted gently, "they've called me for the army."

Her face went sick. She stared at him, unable to speak. She wanted to say "Never mind, the war will end soon" – but she couldn't. "Oh," she finally muttered. "Oh." And then, in despair, "So I'm to lose you too!"

He remained silent.

"Who knows if you'll ever come back?" she burst out forlornly. "You may be away for years. You'll forget me. Or you'll be killed – that's what will happen to me: you'll be killed. I know it."

Willi shook his head, smiling in a curious manner that offended her.

"How can you be so easy about it?" she asked angrily. "You smile like you were talking about the weather. Don't *you* care, Willi?"

Slowly he said, "I'm not going to their army."

She gazed at him in confusion.

"I tell you, Berthe..." He stopped, drawing a deep breath. Of a sudden his hands began to tremble; he took them from the table, as though he wished to hide them from her, and gripped his knees.

"I tell you, my darling," he repeated again, "I'm not... It's not what you think." He stared at her with his hot eyes. "Since last night there's been many things... I mean, many things have happened."

"What has happened?" she asked.

He seemed not to have heard the question. "I'm sort of... like keeping control of myself, Berthe. I have something to do."

"What?" she asked in exasperation. "What do you have to do? And what sort of talk is it to say you won't go into the army? If you're called, you have to go."

He shook his head. "I..." He stopped. Now that he had to explain, he didn't know where to begin, or how. He had not come to Berthe because he believed she would understand the decision he had made, but out of loneliness. In the whole world there was no longer anyone to whom he felt kin – not one human being to whom he dared speak with a frank heart. And so he had come to her. Yet now that he faced her, what was there to say? It was not alone the War Service Cross he had received – he could tell her about that – or the final humiliation of Baumer's proposal to him: that on the morrow he must volunteer for the army, and by his lead act as pimp for the other workers. These things he could tell Berthe, perhaps – but how could he explain the forty years that had preceded them? It was not one thing any longer that he could not bear – it was a life, a world, a total shame. And now that he knew it, there were no words to say it: there was only a turmoil in his heart that could not be spoken.

"Willi, what do you have to do?" Berthe asked again. "What are you talking about?"

"I have to... do something," he whispered awkwardly. "A... deed." His calm was breaking now. His voice was beginning to tremble.

"What do you mean, a 'deed'?" The very unfamiliarity of the word irritated her.

"Your Pole – the Pole you bought..."

"What about him?" she asked sharply.

"He holds us... I mean..." he stammered, "we're guilty. Me too. We're responsible."

"You don't make sense, Willi," she cried in exasperation.

"You don't understand, Berthe?"

"No."

"It's like... I mean... what Rudi did, you see... I'm guilty too. It's like *I* brought you the sweater. I've been part of it. I make tanks. And you've been part of it too – with the farm. We're all guilty. All the killings, we're part of it."

"No, I don't understand," she replied hotly. "I think you're drunk. Hey – is that it? Have you been drinking, Willi?"

He shook his head.

"Then why don't you talk so I can understand what you mean? What's the matter with you anyway?"

"They gave me a War Service Cross today," he burst out suddenly. He struck his forehead with his clenched fist. "Oh my God, what sort of a man am I? Why didn't I understand before? When my Richard turned away from me, why didn't I see the rottenness? How can a man live his whole life and be such a fool? We're swine, Berthe! They've turned all of us into swine." His voice choked up for a moment. Then he burst out: "And now they want me to volunteer for their army. It's more war they want, and more killings, and more sweaters, and more people to sell in the village for seventeen marks." He smashed his big fists down on the table. "*I won't do it, I stop here! Right now, I stop! Somebody has to say no to them.*"

Bewildered, frightened, Berthe backed away from him.

"Berthe," he cried emotionally. "You…" He suddenly became very quiet again. "Don't you see… I have to do something? It's needed."

"What?" she asked tremulously.

"It's needed to say… to say no, Berthe. To… do a deed. To be against them."

"To be against the government?" she asked. "Is that what you're saying?"

He nodded. "Yes. To be against the rottenness."

Trembling she whispered, "My God, do you know what you're talking about? They'll kill you, Willi."

He said nothing.

"My God, what will you do?"

"Something."

"What? You don't even know. You're just talking wild."

"No," he replied very quietly, "I know. I didn't know before. But since I came here, you told me what to do. I know now. The right thing. I know it."

"I told you? What did I tell you?"

"Berthe," he asked wretchedly, "will you help me?" He knew she would not. "I don't want to be alone."

"What are you going to do?"

"Will you help me?" A shiver ran through his big frame. "Will you?"

"I…" She stopped, turning towards the door. The air-raid siren at the factory had burst into sudden, wailing life. It rose and fell, shattering the night quiet, warning the countryside to beware – that British planes would soon be flying overhead. Quickly Berthe glanced over at Willi. Then, making a sudden decision, she did something that was not at all necessary in view of her heavy blackout curtains: she reached for her oil lamp, turned down the wick and blew out the light.

"Willi darling," she said with the quiet of desperation, "you're upset, and so am I. What you ask me I can't decide yet. We have to talk about it a little more." She crossed to him. "It's good you came to talk to me. Now I know you really love me – when you come to talk to me about a thing like this." Her arms slipped about him, and she pressed her body close against his. "My sweetheart, I can see how upset you are. Believe me, I understand. And I'll help you. But I have to know you love me first." She bent down and kissed his mouth hard and long, her lips ardent against his. "Do you love me, Willi?"

He didn't reply at once, and then it was with a sigh. "Yes, I love you so much it's the hardest thing of all."

"Thank you for saying it, my darling. Now come – we'll talk. We'll decide what's right to do. Come into the bedroom, Willi. We'll hold each other and talk."

"Yes," he replied quietly. "But first I must go outside for a minute. You go in there and wait for me."

"You'll come, dearest?"

"Yes, I'll come."

She pressed his head against her breasts. "You and me," she whispered. "You and me." She released him and padded quickly across to the bedroom. Deliberating, feeling that he needed a moment in which to be alone, she shut her bedroom door.

Willi remained still for a moment. Then he rose quietly. He picked up the lamp on the table and crossed on tiptoe to the sink. He stooped beneath the sink for the gallon can in which Berthe kept her store of kerosene. Carefully he tipped it, listening for the slosh of its contents. It was half full. Carrying both the lamp and the can, he silently went outside.

Once in the yard he began to run. He had formulated his plan after Berthe told him about the hay. He had not known beforehand what he must do, or how – but she had instructed him. To use the hay cut by the Polish prisoners – this was the thing he must do. In the early days of the war he had read of German sympathizers in Poland who had fashioned arrows in their fields to direct the Luftwaffe bombers. The newspapers had boasted of it. Now he would do a deed in kind.

Running wildly, the sweat of tension and fear and hysteria bursting out hot from every pore in his body, Willi circled the house and ran into the hayfield that bordered the factory grounds. He knew that he had only a limited span of time in which to fashion his arrow. He did not reflect upon his lack of cautious preparation for what he was doing, or the possibility that the bombers might veer away from the district, as they sometimes did. He didn't even know whether he had sufficient kerosene – or whether the wind would be strong enough to keep his arrow flaming after the kerosene had been consumed. He didn't care. Once, many years before, he had sat upon a park bench, arguing himself into cautious impotence, while a nursemaid trundled an abused child away from the protection he owed to it. His heart had never forgotten the shame of that cowardice, however his mind might have blurred it. Now he had that shame to account for, and others. Now there were his lost Richard and his dead Käthe and Karl; there was the image of a Frenchwoman he had never seen, and the unforgiving hatred in the eyes of a Pole; and there was himself – his own shame that was greater than all the others, his need to feel cleansed. And sometimes it happens thus with a man or with many men – or even with a people: that out of the slow and beaten flesh a bitter fruit will spring... and when the time comes, there is no stopping it – and it comes not slowly but with violence, not with reason and yet with the logic of generations. And this was the moment for Willi Wegler, after forty-two years – this was the deed he knew he must do.

The field was not large, two hundred yards in length and a hundred in width. At one end there was the barbed-wire fence marking the factory, at the two opposite corners were the farmhouse and the barn. Scattered about the field were several dozen small haystacks – in one of them, waiting for his hand, there was a pitchfork.

Willi paused for an instant in the centre of the field, measuring the relationship of the stacks. Then he ran for the pitchfork. He attacked a stack with hysterical energy, tearing it apart, then he ran to a second and a third nearby. Quickly one side of an arrow began to take shape, the hay piled several feet high. He worked without sense of time, knowing only the urgency of haste: that it would be essential to set the fire when the first squadron of bombers approached.

After a little more than five minutes, when he had only half completed the second side of the arrow, he heard Berthe's stupefied cry: "Willi... Willi... what are you doing?" She ran up to him, her half-open robe flapping in the wind, her bare legs exposed.

Willi paid no attention to her. He was running between some of the more distant haystacks and the unfinished arrow, carrying a great bundle of hay between his arms at each trip.

"Willi… God in heaven, are you out of your head?" she shouted at him. With comic futility she ran after him, back and forth, trying to seize his arm. Then, as he stopped to sweep some hay into place, she caught up with him, gripping his overalls with both hands. "Willi… Willi," she cried, half laughing and half sobbing, "what on earth are you doing?"

"Let me be!" he shouted, and broke away from her.

"Willi… Willi… Willi…" she called after him fruitlessly.

From a distance there came the first throbbing beat of an enemy squadron. With that Berthe suddenly understood. She saw the shape of the piled hay – an arrow pointing towards the factory – and then she saw the can of kerosene. A dizzy, animal fear struck in the pit of her stomach.

"Aaah!" she cried. "The British planes! That's what you're doing!"

"Go into the house!" Willi shouted at her. He dropped an armful of hay to the ground. "Get away from here."

Berthe seized him, flinging both arms about him. "They'll bomb us!" she shrieked hysterically. "They'll bomb us!"

Willi tore her arms loose. But as he turned to run back for more hay, she caught hold of him again. He swung around. Without a word he shoved her backwards with all his strength, hurling her to the ground. Then he ran off.

The planes were closer now. The arrow was not quite finished, but Willi knew this was the last bundle of hay he dared carry. There was no telling how many squadrons might come over. If the first planes did not see his arrow, it might never be seen.

It was then that he heard Berthe. He could not see her as she ran towards the barbed-wire fence, for the moon was clouded over, but he heard her incoherent screams for help. For a moment he stood stupidly, transfixed with confusion and disbelief. Then he dropped his armful of hay and snatched up the pitchfork. He ran towards the screaming voice. He didn't know that she had tripped and fallen, and that she was crawling senselessly on hands and knees towards the wire, but he was guided by her cries.

Then he stopped. The first planes were approaching overhead. He dropped the pitchfork and ran back, cursing, to the arrow of hay. He picked up the can of kerosene, unscrewed the top and then walked, sweating, down the length of the arrow, letting its contents gurgle out. The can was almost empty before he reached the second side of the arrow, and he used the remainder more sparingly, in little pools. When the can was empty, he dropped it and ran to the head of the arrow. He dropped to his knees, pulling a box of matches from his pocket. With a hand that was beyond trembling or error he struck several matches at once. The kerosene caught instantly. In wild elation he ran three feet down and started another blaze. He leapt to the opposite side of the arrow, lighting the hay there. Then he leapt back again, running thus from side to side, working back towards the spread ends. The blood pounded in his head. He no longer heard Berthe's cries, or even the roar of the second squadron of planes, which was already passing overhead. Finally he ran back to the lamp. As he unscrewed the spigot, he heard something that his years in the trenches would never let him forget: the whine of a bullet and the sharp crack of a carbine. He swung around. Near the fence he saw a black uniformed figure and the gleam of a rifle barrel. He saw and understood, and with his limbs quivering in terror he ran towards a dead spot in the arrow where the hay had not yet caught fire. He threw the lamp down on the hay and fumbled for a match...

But then the world exploded.

"So now you cry," Willi thought with unforgiving bitterness as he lay on his cot and heard Berthe's muffled sobbing. "No... now I don't pity you your crying. I'm not much of a man, Berthe. It would be easy for me to forgive what you did to me. You were afraid of the English planes – I can understand that. But I don't forgive you the sweater. If I were God himself, I would never forgive you the sweater, Berthe." He lay in cold and implacable resolution, his heart dead to this woman he had loved so dearly, and if he could have spoken to her, he would have said merely, "Go away, Berthe – go back to your farm, to your bought Pole, to your sweater. You have it as you want it – what I have is better for me."

Berthe sat by the bed, dry-eyed now, her fingers fumbling with the shawl on her lap. She thought hopelessly, "What can I do now? I'll be alone, and now that swine from the police will be after me. Oh, God, how miserable life can be!" But then she thought: "Rosenhart always wanted me. He's not... But he's a kind man, anyway. And he'll be a protection. The Peasant Leader of the community... Not many farm women would pass up a match like that..."

Doctor Zoder tiptoed into the room. He bent over the cot, peering at Willi. Berthe sighed and shivered. She thought: "They'll make me leave now. They won't even let me speak to him. If he would awaken for only a moment... if I could only say one little word to him..."

Zoder put his hand on her arm. He gestured towards the door.

"Please," she whispered.

Zoder shook his head. "He won't wake up. It's no use."

She gazed down at Willi, and her mind whispered, "This is the last time you'll see him." Then, obedient to Zoder's hand, she turned towards the doorway. She had only reached the corridor when her knees buckled and she fell forward into Zimmel's arms.

2

8:55 a.m.

Pastor Frisch had learnt in the concentration camp that men have many sides to them – and so he was no longer surprised at anything even he himself might do. This was good, because it helped him now to understand his desire to laugh out loud. In actual fact, he was acutely frightened.

His fear came from what he was doing, and what he was about to do. With a pencil stub, he was printing on slips of paper. Later, when the meeting started, he intended to distribute his homemade leaflets in the empty barracks and in the woods. His laughter, which was pure hysteria, came from an irony: that to write a truth in the year of our Lord 1942 it was necessary for a man to hide in a latrine.

With his trousers down he was seated in the last cubicle of a long row of toilets. Since there was no door to shield him, it was necessary to fold and hide each slip of paper before he commenced to print another. And twice a minute he whispered to himself, "If you were less frightened, Jakob, your printing would be neater."

He used a tiny pencil stub, because he knew it would be essential to break it apart with his teeth and to flush it out of existence when he was finished. He wrote with the paper pressed against the sole of one of his shoes. If anyone entered, he was prepared to explain why he had removed a shoe. And if he were caught walking in and out of a bunkhouse, he had decided to explain that an SS guard, whose name he did not know, had ordered him to clear all men out of their bunks for the meeting. But in spite of these cautions, and in spite of his belief that the confusion in the factory would give him security, he began to cry softly by the time he had started on his fourth slip of paper.

"Willi Wegler... not Pole... lit fire to British," he printed. "Proof... Wegler is in hospital... shot. Hitler leads us to disaster. Follow Wegler. Sabotage!"

He paused, hastily concealing his pencil and paper as feet sounded at the other end of the latrine. He waited until he heard the man settle himself. Then he began again.

He printed his tiny leaflets, and he blinked his eyes against the salt tears of his fright, and he whispered to himself: "Against all their newspapers, their armies, their might, there will come a day when truth will be heard. It will grow through their stone... But, dear God, how alone I am... how deeply alone!"

Softly he folded a slip of paper, unfolded another.

3

10:15 a.m.

Conversation in the Party Office stopped for a moment as the whistle screamed from the powerhouse – a long, steady note that blotted out all other sound. Baumer looked at his watch, yawned, rubbed his face and exclaimed, "It'll take about ten minutes for the workers to assemble."

Sipping his coffee, Commissar Kehr said, "You were..." He stopped, raising his eyebrows.

"Oh yes. I was wondering if it would make a good impression for you to speak to the workers. You know... your investigations prove that the Pole, Bironski, did the sabotage. The man confessed, in fact."

"It's not a good idea, I assure you," Kehr objected. "A speech is not in my line. It'll sound much better coming from you."

"All right, I'll start with the sabotage, then. After that, I'll take up the recruiting."

"Has any anti-aircraft arrived?" asked Superintendent Kohlberg.

"Not yet. I'm expecting three batteries by noon. Four more by evening."

Kohlberg cracked his finger knuckles. "That doesn't sound like much."

Baumer smiled. "Between ourselves, it isn't. But we can expect fighter planes."

"Aaah – what the devil!" Kohlberg exclaimed hoarsely, as he had been doing all morning. "I'm sure the British know nothing about us."

"The way you keep repeating that," observed Baumer, "you must believe in the power of mind over matter." He laughed. "Well, shall we go?"

"Is it to be the forge room again?" asked Kohlberg as they stood up.

"No. I want photographs of the volunteers. The meeting will be out of doors, on the testing grounds. We'll go up to the roof of the final assembly. By the way, Edmund – some Poles have been transferred to your machinery pits. The pits are coming along fast."

"I know," said Kohlberg. "I've just been out there. You've handled this all very efficiently."

Baumer nodded. "If the English will cooperate, we'll all be happy. Commissar Kehr here – in spite of what I admit to be bad-tempered interference on my part – seems to have solved the Wegler affair very neatly. If your insanity evidence stands, Kehr, it frees everyone around here from severe criticism, especially me."

Kehr stroked his chin and tried to keep a grin of triumph off his face.

"And as for you, Edmund," Baumer continued almost gaily, "if you can persuade Herr von Bildering to stay over till tomorrow, perhaps he'll see a factory that's a credit to your administration – and a guarantee of continued dividends for the Reich's Steel Trust." He burst out laughing – laughing louder than the jest warranted.

"Let's hope so," Kohlberg muttered.

"We may even be cited as a model factory, who knows?" Baumer started out, but then paused at the door. "But on the other hand, it's also possible that we'll be severely bombed tonight." He went out, grinning.

In the outer office a number of SS men jumped up. Baumer nodded to them and crossed to the doorway. As he came abreast of the telephone board, he paused to glance closely at Martha Guttmann. Martha, conscious of his glance, continued to stare at the board in front of her until she felt his hand on her shoulder. Even then she tried to avoid his eyes.

"How are you feeling?"

"I'm all right, sir," she replied stiffly.

"Sure?"

"Yes, sir… only I…"

"What?"

"I wish I could take back what I said," she whispered hurriedly. "I'm so ashamed I could die. I don't know how I could… I was out of my head, sir."

"Never mind," Baumer interrupted with sympathy. "I don't expect you to go around singing when you hear that your husband's dead. I'm no fool. I have my feelings too."

"Thank you, sir," she replied with gratitude. Tears came into her red-rimmed eyes. "I'll do my best to take my husband's place."

Baumer patted her shoulder. "You know," he said in a low tone, "when you march down a road there's only one thing to do: keep marching. Those who turn back learn the road only goes one way. And that's quite an irony, isn't it?"

Smiling a little, he patted her shoulder again and walked out.

"But what a faker I am," he said to himself. "I don't really accept the insanity theory for one moment. Wegler's act was political. Only, I'm too tired to fight it any more."

Behind him, his entourage fell into step.

For a moment, as the whistle sounded from the powerhouse, Wegler had hoped that it was the signal for an air raid. But then, as he recognized the sound for what it was, disappointment left him doubly wretched.

There was not a great deal of courage left in his heart now, and Willi knew it. He had the sense that he was wearing down, cracking within, like a stone that is being pounded by sledgehammers and must soon shatter – all at once.

He wanted the game to be over. He was losing interest. He had conquered pain, thirst, tension, fear – and he was being conquered by them.

Twice already his fingers had groped over the bandage around his abdomen. He had heard Doctor Zoder refer to a rubber drain, and had probed for it. Touching it, he had felt a responsive pain deep inside his belly. He assumed that if he tore it loose, he would bleed to death. But each time he had said to himself, "Well, no… I'll wait a bit longer."

Now he was counting numbers. He counted up to a hundred – then he counted from a hundred back to one. He had been doing this ever since Berthe left the room.

Whenever he stopped counting, the same thought came into his head: "Oh, what a mess I've made of my life – what a fool I've been." And then, hastily, he would commence to count again, from one to a hundred, and from a hundred back to one.

He was hanging on, fighting for another hour, another fifteen minutes.

But he knew that he was becoming tired of counting too.

The whistle had been silent for a few minutes when Weiner, coming into his bunkhouse, saw young Pelz lying asleep. "Hey," he called as he crossed to his locker, "wake up, Pelz."

Pelz opened his eyes. "I know," he said, "you're the second friend to wake me up and tell me there's a meeting. Don't you think I heard the whistle?" He shook his empty sleeve. "What do I want to go to a recruiting meeting for?"

"You're sure it's a recruiting meeting?" Weiner took a pipe and an envelope of tobacco from his locker.

"I'll bet on it," the youth replied. "I have a nose for such things." He swung off the bed. "Oh hell – I'm awake now. I might as well go."

"We better hurry," said the older man. "We're late." He banged his locker shut, and they went out.

Pelz filled his lungs with air and burst out laughing. "This is the life, I say. No work and meals as usual. We ought to have an air-raid scare once a week."

Weiner grunted, maintaining his usual silence. The amount of conversation he had already allowed himself with Pelz was more than his usual day's quota.

"By the way," said Pelz gaily, "do you know I'm getting married?"

Weiner turned to look at him. "Congratulations," he muttered.

"By telephone," Pelz added. "This Sunday. What do you think of that? The girl's in East Prussia, and I'm here. Efficient, eh? Or does that offend you? Maybe, as a Catholic, you don't…"

Weiner shrugged. His square, liver-skinned face remained non-committal.

"By the way," said Pelz, "I was glad to see how you shut up Rufke last night. That old barber gets…" He broke off, pointing off at a right angle in the woods. "Say – there's Jakob, isn't it? Over there – going into the bunkhouse! I can tell that near-sighted walk of his."

Weiner looked, nodded. The bunkhouse was some sixty yards away.

"Let's get him," said the youth. "If the meeting's dull, we can always ask him to imitate Kohlberg shaving."

They walked along the path. "Good morning, Mamma Woodpecker," Pelz said as they heard a swift tapping high upon a tree trunk. "How's the grub collection this morning? Can you spot him, Weiner?"

The older man shook his head and kept walking. "We'll be late."

"Who cares?" said Pelz. "It's a lovely day in a quiet wood. Makes me feel like a farm lad again – off for a day's fishing." He paused, turned back a step and reached down to a bush. A slip of paper was speared upon the point of a twig.

"C'mon," said Weiner.

Pelz didn't answer. His eyes were glued to the paper. "Look!" he said sharply. "Read this."

Quietly, his face impassive, Weiner read it.

"What do you think of that, eh?" Pelz asked with anger. "The same business as the other night. A real nest of scum we must have in our factory."

Weiner, in his familiar, absurd gesture, pulled at the lobe of one ear, then the other. "Maybe – I think we'd better turn this right in to the SS office."

Pelz nodded. "'Hitler leads us to disaster,'" he read scornfully. "What a..." He stopped, frowning, and gazed towards the bunkhouse into which Frisch had disappeared. "Listen," he asked sombrely, "how long ago is it the whistle blew? About five or six minutes, right?"

Weiner nodded.

"Well then... this paper was just put here!"

"How do you know?" asked Weiner quickly.

"Because until just a minute or two ago this path must have been crowded with men headed from that bunkhouse to the meeting."

Weiner said nothing. He pulled at his ear.

"Listen," Pelz said in a strained voice, "what's Jakob doing in that bunkhouse anyway? It isn't *our* bunk. It isn't on the way to the meeting either."

Weiner shrugged. "He's got a reason, I suppose."

"Sure," said Pelz, "that's what I think too." Quickly he started for the barracks. "Only, I'm going to find out."

"Listen..." said Weiner. He shut up and followed.

Ten yards from the door Pelz stopped. He pointed as Weiner came up to him. "Number two," he said furiously. He kicked at the small stone which held a slip of paper on the path. He reached down. "The same muck!" he muttered. "Think of it: Pastor Frisch!" And then, with the hot blood rushing into his face: "Why, the son of a bitch! The stinking hypocrite! It's him who painted those signs. I bet he was in with the Pole too!"

"Don't go too fast," Weiner cautioned. "We don't know for sure he put these papers here."

"What do you mean?" Pelz retorted hotly. "What did he just go in there for? I tell you, we'll find one of these in every bunk. C'mon, we'll see!"

Weiner caught his shoulder. "Wait! He may still be inside. Maybe we can collar him. Go in slow. Stand quiet. We'll be able to see right through to the other end."

Pelz nodded. Tight-faced, he ran to the barracks door. "Shut the door after you," he whispered to Weiner. "Then he won't see the light."

They slipped inside quietly and quickly. Weiner closed the door behind them. They stood, blinking after the bright sunlight, staring down the long centre aisle. The place was divided into sections for eight men, but there were no doors between the sections, merely an open frame.

"See anything?" Weiner whispered.

Pelz shook his head. "He's slipped out the other end already."

Weiner pointed towards the next section. "Go slow," he whispered. "One at a time."

Quietly they moved from one section to the next, until they had reached the centre of the large barracks.

"He's not here," said Pelz in a normal voice. "Let's see if we can spot him outside."

Weiner tapped his shoulder. "Wait! Look over on that cot."

Pelz crossed to the cot. "What?" he asked. "I don't..." He gurgled unpleasantly. Weiner's thick forearm was around his neck, throttling him, pulling him backwards off his feet. With his other hand, powerfully, Weiner pressed the youth's head forward. Pelz's hand clawed at the rigid bar that was choking him. His feet kicked out spasmodically, futilely. Something snapped in his neck, but still he struggled. And then, abruptly, he hung limp.

Weiner let the crooked body drop to the floor. It fell face down, grotesque and ugly.

His lips moving in silent speech, his face grey, Weiner crossed himself once, twice.

Then, shoving his trembling hands into his pockets, he walked quietly outside.

4

10:30 a.m.

On the testing grounds, under the camouflage canopy that had been hiding tanks from the sky for seven months, the workers stood quietly, waiting for the meeting to begin. There was little conversation, and there was no laughter.

On the roof of the assembly plant Labour Front Leader Baumer yawned, glanced at his watch and said, "Looks as though we're all here." With an ironic smile he murmured to Kohlberg, "Do you suppose there'll come a time when we can declare a holiday on speeches? After the war, perhaps. We'll have a week of celebration, without speeches."

He stepped up to the microphone. "Problems and more problems," he thought as he looked down at the blotchy mass of white faces. "I used to think the struggle would ease. That was naive of me, I suppose. Only, how does one keep from getting tired?"

"Members of the German national community," he began – and then stopped. As though the sky had split in half, the air-raid siren had begun its rising, wailing scream.

Baumer remained still, one hand frozen to the microphone. Behind him the SS men, the plant foremen, stood transfixed. And in front of him there was not a ripple of movement in the solid mass of workers.

The undulating wail of the siren continued. Suddenly a bellow rose from the massed workers, an animal sound that surged up to meet the scream of the siren. The lines wavered and broke. Bellowing like cattle, the workers stampeded.

Baumer swung around. "Round up the Poles!" he shouted at Zimmel. "The Poles must be guarded!"

He ran for the ladder that led down from the roof to the floor of the final assembly.

The siren kept on.

In the hospital Willi Wegler was at sixty-three, counting towards a hundred. He heard the siren, listened to it and continued to count. He had reached sixty-seven before he understood what had happened.

His mouth opened. His chest began to heave. He commenced to laugh and to cry at the same time, and his fingers dug convulsively into the mattress. "Now let them come," his heart cried. "O dear God, now let them come. Don't let them go any place else. It must be *here*. Please, God, make it here!"

5

10:40 a.m.

Quietly, hands in his pockets, Weiner walked along the zigzag length of a trench, peering at the huddled figures of the workers. He stepped down. Eggert was sitting with a cold pipe in his mouth, gazing up at the sky. By his side there was an empty space which he had staked out with his cap. Weiner picked up the cap, hung it over Eggert's knee and sat down beside his friend.

All along one side of the narrow trench there were others sitting in tense silence. With pallid faces they gazed upward. One man only was not staring at the sky. He had bowed his head over his knees, and the muted sound of his sobbing could be heard.

Weiner tugged at an ear lobe. Then he leant over and put his mouth to his friend's ear. He whispered, a hand shielding his lips.

Eggert listened. He turned to look into Weiner's face.

"Ah!" he said. There was a bright gleam in his eyes. "Pastor Frisch, eh? We'll have to see him."

Then both sat back. Like the others, they stared up at the sky.

6

10:45 a.m.

In the Party Office Baumer sat quietly at the telephone, listening to Captain Schnitter at the other end. In the even, though slightly staccato, tones of a disciplined officer, Captain Schnitter was saying: "No, the direction of the sweep isn't established yet. A small force of Mosquitoes is headed this way, but it may still veer off. Fighters are trying to intercept. That's all!"

Baumer hung up the phone. Almost with disinterest he spoke to SS man Blumel, who stood in the open doorway of his office. "Warn Protection Services that planes are still headed this way."

Blumel ran across the outer office to relay the order to the girls at the switchboard. The message delivered, he rushed back to his post in the doorway. He stood at rigid attention, hoping that his face did not betray his fear: this was his first bombing.

Baumer sat very quietly, the fingers of one hand drumming a gentle tattoo on the desk. His relaxed posture, his quiet manner on the telephone, did not indicate real calm: they were the products of a nervous fatigue that was now beyond his control. At this moment of crisis he found that he was almost indifferent to events in the outside world, and he wondered about it. There was no sensible reason for him to remain sitting at his desk. Anyone else could relay Schnitter's bulletins as well as he. He knew too that he was needed at the Command Post of Air Raid Protection Services... and that he could be performing a more useful function if he circulated amongst the frightened men in the trenches. But he couldn't move. For the moment he didn't care what happened. He only wanted to sit very still and quiet, as might an old man at twilight, hesitating over the evening to come, yearning forlornly for the day for ever gone – and thinking nothing.

The buzzer sounded at his phone, which was in direct contact with the factory anti-aircraft defence. "Yes?" he asked. His fingers stopped their drumming.

"The English absolutely read Clausewitz," Schnitter's voice said with relish. "A second Mosquito squadron is coming in at a tangent. Air Command is certain this is the target. They're coming in low, so be prepared for delayed action explosive, incendiaries and fragmentation bombs. You have perhaps ten minutes. That's all."

"Blumel – attack coming in a few minutes," Baumer said quietly. "Protection Services to expect incendiaries, delayed action explosive and fragmentation bombs. No one is to leave his post. That's all."

Blumel ran to the switchboard.

"Now it's time to start moving," Baumer's brain advised him. But he continued to sit still, his fingers drumming. And then abruptly he was on his feet, eyes blazing, clenched hands thrust towards the sky.

"All right, come on then!" he shouted. "Today you bomb us – but tomorrow… tomorrow… tomorrow…"

He ran from the office.

7

11 a.m.

Now it was not necessary for Willi to count numbers or to fight his thirst, or even to probe his life. For now, fairly close outside, as though hammers were being pounded upon a tight drum, the anti-aircraft battery had begun to fire.

Now Willi's life was over, and he accepted it. He listened to the drumming of the guns, he felt the quivering of his bed, and thought, "I'll wait until the first bomb drops. Then I'll know."

But in fact he already knew. He knew that his signal had been seen… he knew that this small deed he had done would weigh, and would be weighed. And slowly his hand groped down to his bandage.

Outside, drowning out the anti-aircraft fire, came the roar of planes, low-flying, in swarm. From metal bellies that Willi could not see there was a quick vomiting of incendiaries and of white blossoming parachutes that bore demolition bombs.

The earth split! The hospital shook with earthquake! Outside was convulsion… shattered, flaming buildings – a wood, a factory, a land upheaved.

Willi's mind said one last word: "*Now!*" His heart answered with its quiet beat.

In his soul was a measureless peace.

Notes

p. 3, DOCTOR BERNARD ROBBINS: Doctor Bernard S. Robbins (1905–59) was professor of clinical psychiatry at the New York Medical College and a founder of the American Academy of Psychoanalysis. Albert Maltz and his first wife Margaret were close friends of Doctor Robbins and his wife Lee from the late 1930s. The Robbinses encouraged Maltz as a writer and were enthusiastic about his work. Maltz and Margaret were in psychotherapy for several periods during their marriage, and it is very likely that Bernard Robbins introduced them to psychoanalysis.

p. 5, *Many mistakes... "Where is the way out? Where is the road?"*: This epigraph is taken from Book One of *Dead Souls*, an 1842 novel by Nikolai Gogol (1809–52). The translation quoted by Maltz is by Constance Garnett.

p. 5, *Roaming in thought... become lost and dead*: The first two lines of the poem 'Roaming in Thought', from the cluster 'By the Roadside' in *Leaves of Grass* by Walt Whitman (1819–92). The beginning of the second line has been amended from "And the vast that is Evil" to match the 1891–92 edition of *Leaves of Grass*, which was recommended by the author.

p. 11, *Stirlings*: The Stirling was a British four-engined heavy bomber used during the Second World War.

p. 21, *Himmler's staff*: Heinrich Himmler (1900–45) was a leading member of the Nazi Party and the main architect of the Holocaust.

p. 22, *Noske wasn't the State, nor was Ebert or Rathenau*: Gustav Noske (1868–1946) was a German politician of the Social Democratic Party (SPD). Between 1919 and 1920 he served as Minister of Defence of the Weimar Republic. On 22nd July 1944, he was arrested by the Gestapo as one of the suspects of the 20th July plot to assassinate Adolf Hitler. Friedrich Ebert (1871–1925) was another SPD politician who served as the first president of Germany from 1919 until his death in office in 1925. Walther Rathenau (1867–1922) was one of the founders of the German Democratic Party (DDP) and served as foreign minister of Germany from February to June 1922.

p. 27, *At the gates of Stalingrad*: The Battle of Stalingrad, a disastrous loss for the German forces and their allies and a turning point in the Second World War, took place between 23rd August 1942 and 2nd February 1943. It resulted in the destruction of the German 6th Army and the withdrawal of considerable German forces from other areas of occupied Europe. This reference places the events of the first part of the novel in late August 1942.

p. 28, *Horst Wessel*: Horst Wessel (1907–30) was an Assault Leader (*Sturmführer*) of the *Sturmabteilung* (SA), the paramilitary wing of the Nazi Party. In January 1930 he was killed by two members of the German Communist Party (KPD). Although rumoured to have been a pimp, he was regarded as a hero and martyr by the Nazis.

p. 34, *the Reichstag fire*: An arson attack on the Reichstag in Berlin, home of the German parliament, on 27th February 1933, four weeks after Hitler had been sworn in as chancellor, which prompted the suspension of civil liberties in Germany and led to a fiercer persecution of the Communists, who were held responsible for the fire. The event is seen as a pivotal moment in the rise of the Nazis to power.

p. 36, *Confessionalist Church*: The *Bekennende Kirche*, more commonly known as the "Confessing Church", a movement within German Protestantism that rejected government efforts to unify all Protestant Churches in a single pro-Nazi German Evangelical Church.

p. 36, *Pastor Niemöller*: The German theologian and Lutheran pastor Martin Niemöller (1892–1984), the founder and leader of the Confessing Church.

p. 38, *read from the twenty-third psalm*: The following quotations are, respectively, from Psalms 23:1–3; 23:3–4; 23:5–6.

p. 39, *SA men*: See note to p. 28.

p. 39, *for the ruler is ordained by God*: See Romans 13:1: "For there is no power but of God: the powers that be are ordained of God."

p. 39, *Dr Ley, leader of the German Labour Front*: The German politician Robert Ley (1890–1945) was the leader of the German Labour Front from 1933 to 1945.

p. 40, *The Party claims... Protestant or Catholic*: Ley's words were reported in the article 'The Strange Case of Pastor Niemöller' by Paul Hutchinson in *The Atlantic* of October 1937.

p. 50, *Stresemann*: The German statesman Gustav Stresemann (1878–1929), who served as chancellor of Germany from August to November 1923 and as foreign minister from 1923 to 1929.

p. 65, *Kinder, Kirche, Küche*: "Children, church, kitchen" (German).

p. 71, *Mein Kampf*: Hitler's 1925 autobiographical manifesto. The German title literally means "My Struggle".

p. 87, *Stettin*: The German name of Szczecin, a city which was then under German rule, now in north-western Poland.

p. 97, *'Sieg Heil'*: "Hail victory!" (German), words that frequently accompanied the Nazi salute.

p. 98, *in a sweatbox*: That is, in solitary confinement.

p. 101, *Wellingtons*: The Vickers Wellington was a long-range medium bomber used by the British during the Second World War.

p. 106, *a Wotan fable come to reality*: Wotan is the name used for Odin, the god of war in Germanic and Norse mythology, by Richard Wagner (1813–83) in his opera cycle *The Ring of the Nibelung*.

p. 107, *the Versailles plunder*: A reference to the Treaty of Versailles (28th June 1919), signed after the end of the First World War, which ratified that Germany should disarm, make ample territorial concessions and pay reparation costs to the victors.

p. 108, *the fall of France*: Germany occupied France in June 1940.

p. 127, *old-line Prussian general like Hindenburg*: General Paul von Hindenburg (1847–1934), who led the Imperial German Army during the First World War and later became president of Germany from 1925 until his death.

p. 132, *Pan*: "Mr" (Polish).

p. 141, *Goebbels… you might say*: Joseph Goebbels (1897–1945), chief propagandist for the Nazi Party, had a club foot.

p. 154, *'Render unto Caesar the things that are Caesar's'*: See Matthew 22:21, Mark 12:17, Luke 20:25.

p. 156, *'Find the woman in the case!'*: An allusion to the famous French phrase "*cherchez la femme*" ("Look for the woman"), used to indicate that the cause of a crime or difficult situation must be a woman.

p. 156, *erratic*: Eccentric.

p. 175, *Chamberlain*: The Tory politician Neville Chamberlain (1869–1940), who served as prime minister of the United Kingdom between 1937 and 1940, pursuing a policy of appeasement and containment towards Nazi Germany.

p. 175, *a treaty*: The Munich Agreement of 30th September 1938 between Nazi Germany, Italy, France and the United Kingdom.

p. 175, *When the German armies quickly overran Poland*: Germany invaded Poland on 1st September 1939, an event that prompted military reaction by France and Britain, and marked the beginning of the Second World War.

p. 176, *After Poland came Norway*: German forces invaded Norway on 9th April 1940.

p. 186, *Emil Jannings playing Oom Paul Kruger, the Boer leader*: Emil Jannings (1884–1950) was an Oscar-winning Swiss-born German actor popular in Hollywood in the 1920s. Paul Kruger (1825–1904), the figurehead of the Boers in South Africa, who served as State President of the South African Republic from 1883 to 1900, was affectionately nicknamed "Oom Paul" (Afrikaans for "Uncle Paul").

p. 190, *May First*: The 1st of May, Labour Day, is a public holiday in Germany.

p. 197, *baggage*: "A worthless good-for nothing woman; a woman of disreputable or immoral life" (*OED*).

p. 210, *rigamarole*: A variant spelling of "rigmarole".

p. 231, *Messiah*: A 1741 oratorio by George Frideric Handel (1685–1759). The quotation that follows is from movement 23 (Part Two, Scene 1). The words are taken from Isaiah 53:3.

p. 253, *the New Order*: The New Order ("*Neuordnung*" in German) was the political and social system that the Nazis wanted to impose on the territories they occupied.

p. 290, *Once, in ancient times… the wrath of Jehovah*: See Genesis 22 for the story of Abraham and the Binding of Isaac.

p. 303, *the Brünings*: A reference to the German politician Heinrich Brüning (1885–1970), who served as the chancellor of Germany during the Weimar Republic from 1930 to 1932.

p. 308, *And the Lord… unto your fathers*: Deuteronomy 1:34–35.

p. 309, *chancre*: A painless ulcer that develops on the genitals in venereal disease.

p. 325, *Mosquitoes*: British twin-engined, multi-role combat aircrafts.

p. 325, *If I may remind you… Clausewitz too*: A reference to the Prussian general and military theorist Carl von Clausewitz (1780–1831). The quotation is from his work *On War* (Book Three, Chapter 9, 'The Surprise'), published posthumously in 1832.

p. 338, *'What doth the Lord… with thy God?'*: Micah 6:8.

CALDER PUBLICATIONS

EDGY TITLES FROM A LEGENDARY LIST

EVERGREENS SERIES

Beautifully produced classics, affordably priced

Alma Classics is committed to making available a wide range of
literature from around the globe. Most of the titles are enriched by an
extensive critical apparatus, notes and extra reading material, as well as
a selection of photographs. The texts are based on the most authoritative
editions and edited using a fresh, accessible editorial approach. With
an emphasis on production, editorial and typographical values, Alma
Classics aspires to revitalize the whole experience of reading classics.

For our complete list and latest offers

visit

almabooks.com/evergreens